" 'Why rea
The question sho
is such a slow pony that
—Ha

continued . . .

OMEGA

Winner of the John W. Campbell Award
A *Locus* Best Science Fiction Novel for 2003

"A satisfying answer to the mystery of the omegas that is appropriately cosmic without straining credulity."
—*The New York Times Book Review*

CHINDI

Selected by the *Washington Post Book World*, *Locus*, and
***Chronicle* as one of the Best Science Fiction Novels of 2002**

"Jack McDevitt is a master of describing otherworldly grandeur . . . [A] sweeping novel of suspense and spectacle."
—*The Denver Post*

PRAISE FOR
THE ALEX BENEDICT NOVELS

FIREBIRD

"McDevitt hit a grand slam with this one. It's got a huge payoff for sci-fi fans, and I'm still shaking my head and wondering how he pulled it off." —Wired.com

"A terrific read full of exciting scientific revelations, social intrigues, and fascinating looks into the past . . . I can guarantee you that once you finish *Firebird*, you will find yourself searching for the earlier books—all of which I highly recommend."
—*Underwords*

"A great entry . . . A fast-paced thriller." —*Midwest Book Review*

ECHO

"Twenty years from now, reviewers will be comparing other writers to McDevitt . . . Highly recommended." —*SFRevu*

"If you've been looking forward to another of McDevitt's captivating combinations of big ideas and life-threatening dangers, you'll find that *Echo* was worth the wait." —*The Jesup (GA) Press-Sentinel*

THE DEVIL'S EYE

"A fast-paced novel . . . A book that has more ghost hunters than an Indiana Jones adventure, with twists that reveal secret after secret."
—*The Florida Times-Union*

SEEKER

Winner of the Nebula Award
A *Kansas City Star* Noteworthy Book for 2005
A *Locus* Recommended Book for 2005

"[A] classy riff on the familiar lost-colony theme. The novel delivers everything it promises with a gigantic wallop."
—*Publishers Weekly* (starred review)

POLARIS

"An exemplary merger of mystery and science fiction . . . An intelligent, provocative entertainment by a man who brings energy, style, and a fresh perspective to everything he writes."
—*The Washington Post Book World*

PRAISE FOR

TIME TRAVELERS NEVER DIE

Hugo and Nebula Award Nominee

"An entertaining romp through past and future, ringing in new changes in the genre . . . A good, fast read that leaves you thinking."
—Joe Haldeman, Hugo Award–winning author of
Work Done for Hire

"[A] witty, charming, yearning novel that puts a new twist on time travel . . . A first-rate work by one of the true masters of the genre. Enjoy!"
—Robert J. Sawyer, Hugo Award–winning author of
Red Planet Blues

"Believable and realistic . . . A powerful story full of mystery, romance, and surprises."
—Ben Bova, Hugo Award–winning author of *Transhuman*

THE
|||HERCULES|||
TEXT

JACK McDEVITT

ACE BOOKS, NEW YORK

ACE

Published by the Berkley Publishing Group
An imprint of Penguin Random House LLC
375 Hudson Street, New York, New York 10014

THE HERCULES TEXT

An Ace Book / published by arrangement with Cryptic, Inc.

ISBN: 978-0-425-27601-3

PUBLISHING HISTORY
First Ace mass-market edition / November 1986
Second Ace mass-market edition / May 2015

PRINTED IN THE UNITED STATES OF AMERICA

10 9 8 7 6 5 4 3 2 1

Cover art by Tony Mauro.
Cover design by Rita Frangie.
Interior text design by Laura K. Corless.

Penguin
Random
House

For John and Elizabeth McDevitt
with love

ACKNOWLEDGMENTS

I'm indebted for the technical assistance of Bob Neustadt of the U.S. Customs Service and Mark Giampapa of the National Optical Astronomy Observatory. Miscarriages of their ideas should be laid at my door. Bill Steigerwold of the Goddard Space Flight Center helped me find my way around that venerable institution. And Bud Sparhawk provided an assist.

Thanks also to my editor, Diana Gill, and to copy editor Sara Schwager.

||| FOREWORD |||

When we first talked about reissuing *The Hercules Text*, I knew immediately that I'd have to update the original novel. Its computer technology was out-of-date. The Cold War, which fueled much of the narrative, was long over. Not only in the sense that the superpower confrontation has, if not ended, at least substantially cooled. But our national mind-set has also changed. Who today would believe that a major power might seriously consider launching a preemptive strike over a question of weapons development, a scenario that was front and center in the original *Hercules Text*? Somehow it seemed not entirely implausible in 1986.

It's possible that my original perspective was simply deranged. But it didn't feel that way then. I can still recall the nuclear-attack drills in high school, during which we descended, in an orderly manner, down to the basement cafeteria and sat under tables, which would presumably protect us when the bomb dropped. At home, left over from my father's days as a WWII air-raid warden, we had a bucket of sand for tossing on fires. For some reason we never threw it out. It served as a reminder that terrible things were possible.

In 1962, at the height of the Berlin Crisis, I was driving home on the Baltimore–Washington Parkway, headed for Philadelphia. At the time there was major construction going on, crews building overpasses and widening highways, but catastrophe seemed so imminent it was difficult not to wonder why we were bothering. The night was thick with the conviction that it was all going to get knocked down in the near future.

It didn't happen, of course, a reality for which we can be grateful to a series of U.S. presidents and Russian premiers who kept their heads. Had they not been there, today's world might have been little more than a pile of smoldering ash.

But the current reading public has a different perspective, and so it seemed prudent to go back and reframe *The Hercules Text* in the light of these happier times. I've done that, and the experience has left me, as the original effort did in 1986, with the suspicion that we do not really want to hear from the stars. No matter how hard we root for SETI. And no matter what the outsiders may have to say to us. No news is good news.

||| ONE |||

Harry Carmichael sneezed. His eyes were red, his nose was running, and his head ached. It was mid-September, and the air was full of pollen from ragweed, goosefoot, and thistle. He'd already taken his medication for the day, the latest anti-allergen. It seemed to accomplish little other than to make him drowsy.

Through the beveled stained-glass windows of the William Tell, he watched the Ramsay Comet. It was now little more than a bright smudge, wedged in the bare, hard branches of the elms lining the parking lot. Its cool, unfocused light was not unlike the cool glow of Julie's green eyes, which seemed preoccupied with the long, graceful stem of her wineglass. She'd abandoned all attempts to keep the conversation going and sat frozen in a desperate solitude. She felt sorry for Harry. He could see it in the set of her jaw, in her tendency to gaze *past* him, as though a third person hovered behind his right shoulder. Years from now, he suspected, he would look back on this evening, remember this moment, recall the eyes and the comet and the packed shelves of old textbooks that, in the gloomily illuminated interior, were intended to create atmosphere. He would remember his anger and the terrible sense of impending loss and the numbing conviction that he was helpless. That nothing he could do would change anything. But most of all, it would be her sympathy that would sear his soul.

Comets and bad luck: It was an appropriate sky. Ramsay would be back in twenty-two hundred years, but it was coming apart. The analysts were predicting that on its next visit, or the one after that, it would be only a shower of rock and ice. Like Harry.

"I'm sorry." She shrugged. "It's not anything you've done, Harry."

Of course not. What accusation could she bring against faithful old Harry, dull Harry, who'd taken his vows seriously, who could always be counted on to do the decent thing, and who'd been a reliable provider? Other than perhaps that he'd loved her too deeply.

He'd known it was coming. The change in her attitude had been gradual but constant. The things they'd once laughed over had become minor irritants, and the irritants scraped at their lives until she came to resent even his presence.

So it had come to this, two strangers carefully keeping a small round table between them while she used a shining knife and fork to slice methodically into beef that was cooked a little more than she would have preferred.

"I just need some time to myself, Harry. To think things over a bit. I'm tired of doing the same things, in the same way, every day." I'm tired of *you*, she was saying, finally, with the oblique words and the compassion that peeled away his protective anger like the skin on a baked potato. She put the glass down and looked at him, for the first time, it might have been, during the entire evening. And she smiled. It was the puckish, good-natured grin that she traditionally used when she'd run the car into a ditch or bounced a check. My God, he wondered, how could he ever manage without her?

"The show wasn't so good either, was it?" he asked drily. The William Tell was a dinner theater, and they'd just suffered through a dreary mystery-comedy. Although Harry could hardly be accused of having made an effort to follow the proceedings. Fearful of what was coming later, he'd spent the time trying to foresee and prepare for all eventualities, rehearsing responses, defenses, explanations. He'd have done better to watch the performance.

The final irony was that there were season tickets in his pocket.

"No," she said. "I didn't really care much for it." She didn't add anything that might have given him comfort, that she was distracted, that it was a difficult evening, that it was hard to keep her mind on anything so trivial while her marriage was disintegrating. Instead, she surprised him by reaching across the table to take his hand.

His love for her was unique, the only truly compelling passion he had ever known, the single element that fueled his days, that gave purpose to everything he did. The passing years had not dimmed it; had in fact seeded it with the shared experience of almost a decade, had so entwined their lives that no emotional separation would be possible, now or ever. Harry would not be able to leave her behind.

He took off his glasses, folded them deliberately, and pushed them down into their plastic case. His vision was poor without them. It was an act she could not misinterpret.

Bits and pieces of talk drifted from the next table, where two people, slightly drunk, whispered angrily at each other about money and relatives. Harry and Julie had never done anything like that. Relations between them had always been cordially correct. Even when, at last, the knife had come out.

A handsome young waiter, a college kid probably, hovered in the background, his red sash insolently snug round a trim waist. His name was Frank. It was odd that Harry, who usually forgot incidental names immediately, should remember that, as though the detail were important. Frank arrived every few minutes, refilling their coffee cups, asking whether he could get anything else for them. Near the end, he inquired whether the meal had been satisfactory.

It was hard now to remember when things had been different, before the laughter had ended and the silent invitations, which had once passed so easily between them, stopped. "I just don't think," she said abruptly, "we're a good match anymore. We always seem to be angry with each other. We don't talk—" She looked squarely at him now. Harry stared back at her with an expression that he hoped suggested his sense of dignified outrage. "Did you know that Tommy wrote an essay about you and that idiot comet last week? No?

"Harry," she continued, "I don't exactly know how to say this. But do you think, do you really believe, that if anything happened to Tommy, or to me, that it would have any real impact on you? That you'd even notice we were gone?" Her voice caught and she pushed the plate away and stared down into her lap. "Please pay the bill, and let's get out of here."

"It isn't true," he said, looking for Frank the waiter, not wanting to endure a scene in the restaurant. But Frank was preoccupied. Harry counted out some twenties, dropped them on the table, and stood up. Julie slowly pulled her jacket around her shoulders and, with Harry in her wake, strode between the tables and out the door.

Tommy's comet hung over the parking lot, splotchy in the September sky, its long tail splayed across a dozen constellations. Last time through, it might have been seen by Socrates. The data banks at Goddard were loaded with the details of its composition, the ratios of methane to cyanogen and mass to velocity, of orbital inclination and eccentricity. Nothing exciting that he had been able to see, but Harry was only a layman, not easily aroused by cold gas. Donner and the others, however, had greeted the incoming telemetry with near ecstasy.

There was a premature chill in the air, not immediately evident perhaps because no wind blew. She stood on the gravel, waiting for him to unlock the car. "Julie," he said, "ten years is a long time to just throw away."

She watched a van pull into the lot. "I know," she said.

————

Harry took Farragut Road home. Usually, he would have used Route 214, and they'd have stopped at Muncie's for a drink, or possibly even gone over to the Red Limit in Greenbelt. But not tonight. Painfully, groping for words that would not come, he guided the Chrysler down the two-lane blacktop, through forests of elm and littleleaf linden. The road curved and dipped past shadowy barns and ancient farmhouses. It was the kind of highway Harry liked. Julie preferred expressways, and maybe therein lay the difference between them.

A tractor-trailer moved up behind, watched its chance, and hammered by in a spasm of dust and leaves. When it had gone, its red lights faded to dim stars against dark forest, Harry hunched forward, almost resting his chin on the steering wheel. Moon and comet rode high over the trees to his left. They would set at about the same time. (Last night, at Goddard, the Ramsay team had celebrated, Donner buying, but Harry, his thoughts locked on Julie, had gone home early. She seemed not to have noticed.)

"What did Tommy say about the comet?" he asked.

"That you'd sent a rocket out there and were bringing a

piece of it back. He promised to take the piece in to show everybody." She smiled. He guessed it took an effort.

"It wasn't our responsibility," he said. "Houston ran the rendezvous program."

He felt the sudden stillness and sneezed into it. "Do you think," she asked, "he cares about the administrative details?"

The old Kindlebride farm lay cold and abandoned in the moonlight. Three or four pickups and a battered Ford were scattered across its overgrown front yard. "So where do we go from here?"

There was a long silence that neither of them knew quite how to handle. "Probably," she said, "it would be a good idea if I went to live with Ellen for a while."

"What about Tommy?"

She was looking in her bag for something. A Kleenex. She snapped the bag shut and dabbed at her eyes. "Do you think you could find time for him, Harry?"

The highway went into a long S-curve, bounced across two sets of railroad tracks, and dipped into a tangled forest. "What's that supposed to mean?" he asked.

She started to reply but her voice betrayed her, and she only shook her head and stared stonily through the windshield.

They passed through Hopkinsville, barely more than a few houses and a hardware store. "Is there somebody else?" he asked. "Someone I don't know about?"

Her eyelids squeezed shut. "There's nobody else. I just don't want to be married anymore." Her purse slid off her lap onto the floor, and when she retrieved it, Harry saw that her knuckles were white.

Bolingbrook Road was thick with leaves. He rolled over them with a vague sense of satisfaction. McGorman's garage, third in from the corner, was brightly lit, and the loud rasp of his power saw split the night air. It was a ritual for McGorman, the Saturday night woodworking. And for Harry it was an energetic island of familiarity in a world grown slippery.

He pulled into his driveway. Julie opened her door, climbed smoothly out, but hesitated. She was tall, a six-footer, maybe two inches more in heels. They made a hell of a couple, people had said. A mating of giants. But Harry was painfully aware of the contrast between his wife's well-oiled coordination and his own general clumsiness.

"Harry," she said, with a hint of steel in her voice, "I've never cheated on you."

"Good." He walked by her and rammed his key into the lock. "Glad to hear it."

The babysitter was Julie's cousin, Ellen Crossway. She was propped comfortably in front of a flickering TV, a novel open on her lap, a cup of coffee near her right hand. "How was the show?" she asked, with the same smile Julie had shown him at the William Tell.

"A disaster," said Harry. He didn't trust his voice sufficiently to elaborate.

Julie hung her cardigan in the closet. "They did all the obvious gags. And the mystery wasn't exactly a puzzle."

Harry liked Ellen. She might have been a second attempt to create a Julie: not quite so tall, not quite so lovely, not nearly so intense. The result was by no means unsatisfactory. Harry occasionally wondered how things might have gone had he met Ellen first; but he had no doubt that he would in time have betrayed her for her spectacular cousin.

"Well," she said, "it was a slow night on the tube, too." She laid aside the book. The strained silence was settling into the room. She looked from one to the other. "It's getting late," she said. "Gotta go, guys. Tommy's fine. We spent most of the evening with Sherlock Holmes." That was a reference to a role-playing game. Tommy enjoyed being Watson and loved prowling the tobacco shops and taverns of 1895 London in the company of the great detective.

Harry could see that Ellen knew about their problem. It figured that Julie would have confided in her. Had she known that her cousin intended to end it tonight?

Ellen kissed him and held him a degree tighter than usual. Then she was out the door, Julie strolling casually behind, and he heard them talking in hushed tones on the walkway. Harry shut off the television, went upstairs, and looked into his son's room.

Tommy was asleep, one arm thrown over the side of the

bed, the other lost beneath a swirl of pillows. As usual, he'd kicked off the spread, which Harry adjusted. A couple of *Peanuts* books lay on the floor. And his basketball uniform hung proudly on the closet door.

He looked like a normal kid. But the upper right-hand drawer of the bureau contained a syringe and a vial of insulin. Tommy was a diabetic.

The wind had picked up somewhat. It whispered through the trees and the curtains. Light notched by a venetian blind fell across the photo of the Arecibo dish his son had bought a few weeks before on a visit to Goddard. Harry stood a long time without moving.

He'd read extensively over the last year about juvenile-onset diabetes, which is the most virulent form of the disease. In an earlier age, Tommy would have faced a high probability of blindness, or an army of other debilities, and a drastically shortened life expectancy. Maybe not now. Research was moving ahead, and everyone was hopeful. The breakthrough could come at any time.

No one knew how it had happened. There was no history of the disease in either of their families. But there it was. Sometimes, the doctors had said, it just shows up.

Son of a bitch.

He would *not* give up the child.

But before he got to his bedroom, he knew he would have no choice.

It began to rain about 2:00 A.M. Lightning quivered outside the windows, and the wind beat against the side of the house. Harry lay on his back, staring straight up, listening to the rhythmic breathing of his wife. After a while, when he could stand it no more, he pulled on a robe and went downstairs and out onto the porch. Water rattled out of a partially blocked drainpipe. The sound had a frivolous quality, counterpointing the deep-throated storm. He sat down on one of the rockers and watched the big drops splash into the street. A brace had fallen off, or blown off, the corner streetlight. Now the lamp danced fitfully in gusts of wind and water.

Headlights turned off Maple and came slowly down the

street. It was Hal Esterhazy's Plymouth. It pulled into his driveway, paused while the garage door rolled open, and vanished inside. Lights blinked on in Hal's house.

Sue Esterhazy was Hal's third wife. There were two exes wandering around out there somewhere, and five or six kids. Hal had explained to Harry that he remained on good terms with his former wives and visited them when he could though he admitted it wasn't very often. He paid alimony and child support to both. Despite all that, he seemed perfectly content with his life. And he owned a new van and a vacation home in Vermont.

Harry wondered how he did it.

Inside, the telephone was ringing.

Julie picked it up in the bedroom before he got to it. She came to the head of the stairs and looked down. "It's Goddard," she said.

Harry nodded and put the handset to his ear. "Carmichael."

"Harry, this is Charlie. I hate to bother you at this hour, but the Hercules signal changed tonight. I just got off the line with Ed. He's pretty excited."

"So are you," said Harry. Charlie was the duty officer at the Research Projects Lab. "Why? What's going on?"

"You've been following the operation, right?"

"A little." Harry was assistant director for administration, a personnel specialist in a world of theoretical physicists, astronomers, and mathematicians. He tried hard to stay on top of Goddard's various initiatives in an effort to retain some credibility, but the effort was pointless. Cosmologists tended to sneer at particle physicists, and both groups found it hard to credit astronomers, perceived as restricted to confirming the notions of theorists. Harry's M.B.A. was, at best, an embarrassment.

His job was to ensure that NASA hired the right people, or contracted out to the right people, to see that everyone got paid, and to keep track of vacation time and insurance programs. He negotiated with unions, tried to prevent NASA's technically oriented managers from alienating too many subordinates, and, when necessary, lent a hand to the public-relations director. He'd stayed close to Donner and the comet but had paid little attention to any of Goddard's other activities over the past few weeks. "What sort of change?"

At the other end, Charlie was speaking to someone in the background. Then he got back on the line. "Harry, it stopped."

Julie had come halfway down the staircase, watching him curiously. He almost never got calls at night.

"I thought you'd want to know," Charlie said.

Harry's physics wasn't very good. Ed Gambini and his people had been observing an X-ray pulsar in the Hercules constellation since early spring. They thought the system consisted of a red giant and a neutron star. But the last few months had been a difficult period for them because most of Goddard's facilities had been directed toward the comet. "Charlie, that's not all that unusual, is it? I mean, the goddam thing rotates behind the big star every few days, right? Is that what happened?"

"It's not due to eclipse again until Tuesday, Harry. And even when it does, we don't really lose the signal. There's an envelope of some sort out there that reflects it, so the pulse just gets weaker. This is a complete shutdown. Ed insists something must be wrong with the equipment."

"And you can't find a problem?"

"The Net's fine. NASCOM has run every check it can think of. Harry, Ed's in New York and won't get back for a few hours. He doesn't want to fly into Reagan. We thought it might be simplest if we just sent the chopper."

"Do it. Who's in the operations center?"

"Majeski."

Harry squeezed the phone. "Okay," he said. And, as if it mattered: "I'm on my way."

"What is it?" asked Julie. Ordinarily, she would have been impatient with a late call from Goddard. But tonight, she only sounded subdued.

Harry explained about Hercules while he dressed. "It's an X-ray pulsar," he said. "Ed's been watching it on and off for several months." He grinned at his own joke. "Charlie says they aren't picking it up anymore."

"Why's that important?"

"Apparently because there's no easy explanation for it." He climbed the stairs, walked past her, and went into the bedroom.

She followed him in, shrugged off her nightshirt, and slipped into bed. "Maybe it's just some dust between here and the source."

He grabbed an armful of clothes. "Skynet isn't affected by dust. At least not the X-ray telescopes. No, whatever it is, it's enough to bring Gambini back from New York in the middle of the night."

She watched him dress. "You know," she said, striving for a casual tone but unable to keep the emotion entirely out of her voice, "this is what we've been talking about all evening. The Hercules Project is Gambini's responsibility. Why do *you* have to go running down there? I bet he doesn't head for your shop when some labor-relations crisis breaks out."

Harry sighed. He hadn't got where he was by staying home in bed when major events were happening. It was true he didn't have direct responsibility for Hercules, but one never knew where these things might lead, and a rising bureaucrat needed nothing so much as visibility. He resisted the impulse to suggest she was no longer entitled to an opinion anyway and simply told her he'd lock the door on the way out.

The X-ray pulsar in Hercules was somewhat unusual. It was believed to be a completely independent system, unattached to any other body of stars. More than a million and a half light-years from Goddard, it was adrift in the immense void between the galaxies.

It was also unusual in that neither of the components was a blue giant. Alpha Altheis, the visible star, was brick red, considerably cooler than Sol, but approximately eighty times larger. If it were placed at the center of our solar system, it would engulf Mercury.

The Alpha component was well along in its helium-burning cycle. Left to itself, it would continue to expand for no more than ten million years before erupting into a supernova.

But the star would not survive that long. The other object in the system, Beta Altheis, was a dead sun, a thing more massive than its huge companion, yet so crushed by its own weight that its diameter probably measured less than thirty kilometers, the distance between the Holland Tunnel and Long Island

Sound. Two minutes by jet, maybe a day on foot. But Beta was a malignancy in a tight orbit, barely fifteen million miles from the giant's edge, so close that it literally rolled through its companion's upper atmosphere, spinning violently, dragging an enormous wave of superheated gas, dragging perhaps the giant's vitals.

It was the engine that drove the pulsar. There was a constant flow of supercharged particles from Alpha to the companion, hurtling toward it at relativistic velocities.

But the collision points were not distributed randomly across Beta. Rather, they were concentrated at the magnetic poles, which were quite small, a kilometer or so in diameter and, like Earth's, not aligned with the axis. Consequently, they also were spinning, approximately thirty times per second. Incoming high-energy particles striking this impossibly dense and slippery surface tended to carom off as X-rays. The result was a lighthouse whose beams swept the nearby cosmos.

Harry wondered, as his Chrysler plowed through a sudden burst of rain, what kind of power would be required to shut down such an engine.

The guards waved him through the gatehouse. He made an immediate left and headed for Building 2, the Research Projects Laboratory. Eight or nine cars were parked under the security lights, unusual for this time of night. Harry pulled in alongside Cord Majeski's sleek gray Honda and hurried under dripping trees into the entrance at the rear of the long, utilitarian building.

The Hercules Project had originally been assigned a communication center with an adjoining operations area. But Gambini was politically astute, and his responsibilities and staff had kept growing. He'd acquired two workrooms, additional computer space, and four offices. The project itself had begun as a general-purpose investigation of several dozen pulsars. But it had quickly focused on the anomaly in the group, which was located five degrees northeast of the globular cluster NGC6341.

Harry strolled into the operations center. Several technicians sat in the green glow of monitors. Two or three, headphones pushed off their ears, drank Cokes and talked quietly. Cord Majeski leaned frowning against a worktable, scribbling on a clipboard. He was more linebacker than mathematician, all sinew and shoulder, with piercing blue eyes and a dark beard intended to add maturity to his distressingly boyish features. He was a grim and taciturn young man who nevertheless, to Harry's bewilderment, seemed inordinately successful with women. "Hello, Harry," he said. "What brings you in at this hour?"

"I hear the pulsar's doing strange things. What's going on?"

"Damned if I know."

"Maybe," said Harry, "it ran out of gas. That happens, doesn't it?"

"Sometimes. But not like this. If Beta were losing its power source, we'd have detected a gradual decline. This thing just stopped. I don't know what to think. Maybe Alpha went nova." He dropped the clipboard onto the table. "Harry," he said, "we need access to Optical. Can you pry Donner loose for a few hours? He's been looking at that goddam comet for three months."

"Submit the paper, Cord," said Harry.

Majeski tugged at his beard and favored Harry with a growl. "That takes time. We're supposed to be able to observe a target of opportunity."

"And you shall," said Harry. "Take a few minutes from your schedule and complete the form."

––––––––

Harry told him he'd be in his office if needed and went back out to the car.

He had no serious interest in pulsars. In fact, on this night, nothing short of a black hole bearing down on Maryland could have engaged his attention. But it was an opportunity to get away from the situation at home. To give it a rest and hope maybe it would all go away.

The rain slackened to a cold drizzle. He drove north on Road 3 and eased into the lot outside Building 18, the Business Operations Section. His office was on the second floor. It was a relatively spartan place, with battered chairs and bilious green walls and government wall hangings, mostly cheap art deco that GSA had picked up at a cut-rate price from one of its bargain-basement suppliers. Photos of Julie and Tommy stood atop his desk, between a Rolodex and a small, framed reproduction of a lobby card from *The Maltese Falcon*. Tommy was in a little-league uniform, *Pirates* scripted across his chest. Julie stood in profile, thoughtful against a gray New England sky. It was from their honeymoon.

He lit the desk lamp, turned off the overhead lights, and lowered himself onto a plastic sofa that was a little too short for him. Maybe it *was* time to quit. Find a deserted lighthouse somewhere along the coast of Maine. He'd seen one advertised in Providence once for a buck, but you had to move it. Maybe he could get a job in the local general store, change his name, and spend the rest of his life playing bridge.

His years with Julie were over. And in the terrible unfairness of things, he knew he'd lost not only his wife but Tommy as well. And a sizable portion of his income. He felt a sudden twinge of sympathy for Alpha, burdened with the neutron star it couldn't get rid of. He was forty-seven, his marriage was a wreck, and he suddenly realized he hated his job. People who didn't know what it was like envied him. He was, after all, part of the Great Adventure, directing the assault on the planets, working closely with all those big-shot physicists and astronomers. But the investigators, though few were as blunt, or as young, as Majeski, did not count him as one of them.

He was a compiler of schedules, the guy who answered questions about hospitalization and retirement benefits and other subjects so unutterably boring that Gambini and his associates could barely bring themselves to discuss them. He was, in the official terminology, a layman. Worse, he was a layman with a substantial amount of control over operational procedures at Goddard.

He drifted off to a fitful sleep. The wind died and the rain stopped. The only sound in the building was the occasional hum of the blowers in the basement.

When the phone rang, the office was full of daylight. Harry looked at his watch. It was just after eight. My God, had he slept that long?

"Harry." It was Charlie again. "The pulsar's kicked back in."

"Okay," said Harry. "Sounds like the equipment. Make sure you haven't overlooked anything. I'll get maintenance to run some checks later." This was a Sunday. He'd wait until tomorrow unless someone pressed him. "Ed get here yet?"

"We expect him anytime."

"Tell him where I am," said Harry. He hung up, convinced that the night's events would unquestionably be traced to a defective circuit board.

The Space Flight Center was peaceful Sunday mornings. And the truth was that, although he tried not to examine his motives too closely, he was always happy for sufficient reason to sleep in his office. It was odd. Despite his passion for Julie, there was something in the surrounding hills, in the mists that rose with the sun, in the solitude of this place that was usually so busy, that drew him. Even now. Maybe especially now.

MONITOR

AL KALA CLAIMS RESPONSIBILITY
FOR CRUISE SHIP ATTACK

RELIGIOUS LEADERS
JOIN HANDS FOR PEACE

. . .

SENATE SINKS
NEW DEFENSE BILL

(*Washington Post* News Service)—A coalition of
northern Democrats and farm belt Republicans
voted down an administration defense package,
handing the President another setback—

. . .

RUSSIA PROPOSES NEW MEASURES
AGAINST NUCLEAR BLACKMAIL

. . .

SOLAR SYSTEM AGE REVISED
TO 5 BILLION YEARS

SAMPLES RECOVERED FROM RAMSAY
COMET A BILLION YEARS TOO OLD

. . .

U.S. DISASTER AID
TO ARGENTINA GOES ASTRAY

FOOD, MEDICAL SUPPLIES SHOW UP
ON BLACK MARKET; MORE QUAKES
EXPECTED; TYPHUS RAGING

...

COCAINE HAUL IN DADE COUNTY BIGGEST EVER

...

DIVORCE RATE UP AGAIN

(*New York Times*)—Nearly three-quarters of all marriages now end in the courts, according to a recent study conducted by Princeton University—

...

PROUD PARENTHOOD SUES TO QUELL WEB PORNOGRAPHY, VIOLENCE

||| TWO |||

If Edward Gambini had been awake all night, it didn't show. He scurried around the operations center, driven by restless energy, a thin, birdlike man with a sparrow's quick eyes. He possessed a kind of avian dignity, a strong sense of his position in life, and the quality that politicians call charisma, and actors, presence. It was this characteristic, combined with a superb sense of timing in political matters, that had resulted in his appointment the previous February, over more seasoned candidates, to manage the pulsar project. Although Harry was considerably the taller of the two men, he always felt dwarfed in Gambini's presence.

Unlike most of his colleagues, who reluctantly recognized the advantage of befriending administrators, Gambini genuinely liked Harry Carmichael. When Carmichael occasionally lamented his career choice—he'd begun life as a physics major at Ohio State but quickly decided that quantum mechanics would be forever beyond his grasp—Gambini assured him he was better off. Although, of course, he never explained why, Harry understood his meaning: Only a mind of the first water, like Gambini's own, could prosper in that abstract discipline. Harry's dry sense of humor and cautious personality would never have emerged intact from detailed study of the Hilbert-Schmidt method or Bernoulli's Theorem.

Gambini cheerfully conceded that persons in Harry's line of work had a valid place in the world. Somebody has to write the checks, Harry, he had said. And he'd added that rational bureaucrats were hard to come by.

It was just after nine when Harry arrived at the lab, carrying a cinnamon roll for Gambini who, he knew, would not yet have eaten.

Cord Majeski sat in front of a monitor, his jaw pushed into one palm, while lines of numbers moved down the screen. His eyes did not move with them. The others, computer operators, systems analysts, communications technicians, seemed more absorbed in their jobs than usual. Even Angela Dellasandro, the project heartthrob, tall, lean, dark-eyed, stared intently at a console. Gambini picked out a spot well away from everybody and took a substantial bite out of the cinnamon roll. "Harry, can you get full optical for us tonight?"

Harry could. "I've already made arrangements. All I need is a written request from you or Cord."

"Good." Gambini rubbed his hands. "By the way, you might want to stick around for a while."

"Why?"

"Harry, that is a *very* strange object out there. In fact, I'm not sure it should exist at all." He leaned against a worktable piled high with printouts and Coke cans. Behind him, centered on a wall covered with photos of satellites, shuttles, and star clusters, was an Amtrak calendar depicting a switcher in a crowded freight yard. "In any case, it certainly shouldn't be where it is, way the hell out in the middle of nowhere."

"Why's that? Don't stars get ejected from galaxies?"

"It's not that it got booted from wherever it formed. It's that the binary didn't come unglued. Alpha and Beta are still orbiting one another. Whatever tossed them into the outer darkness should have ripped them apart in the process." He shook his head. "There's another mystery: It appears to have come from the general direction of the Virgo Cluster."

"And—?"

"The Virgo Cluster is sixty-five million light-years away from where Altheis is now. The system is moving away from it at about thirty-five kilometers per second. That's slow, but the point is that the vectors don't converge. That means it didn't originate in Virgo, but the stars aren't old enough to have got where they are from anywhere else. And I say that despite the fact that Alpha, the red giant, is *old*." Gambini leaned toward Harry, and his voice took on a conspiratorial tone. "There's something else you should know."

Harry waited, but Gambini only sat quietly for a few moments, then slid off the table. "My office," he said.

It was paneled in red cedar, decorated with awards the physicist had received over the years: the 2002 Nobel for his work in high-energy plasmas; the Man of the Year in 2003 from Georgetown; Beloit College's appreciation of his contributions to the development of the Faint Object Spectrograph; and a dozen or so others.

Before transferring to NASA from his former position with the Treasury Department, Harry had indulged in the bureaucratic tradition of hanging plaques and scrolls on his walls, but his stuff had looked pathetic by contrast. He'd owned the Treasury Department's Exceptional Achievement Award, a diploma from a three-day executive development program, a statement of appreciation from a D.C. high school for which he'd done an assembly on Careers in the Federal Government. So Harry's eyewash now rested in a box in his garage, and the wall behind his desk boasted a mountain landscape and nothing else.

Gambini's office was located behind a broad glass panel that overlooked the forward section of the L-shaped operating spaces. A thick, woven carpet covered the floor. Every flat surface was awash with paper and books, and several yards of printout had been draped over a chair back. Gambini snapped on a CD player set in a bookcase, and the room filled immediately with Bach.

He waved Harry to a seat but seemed unable to settle into one himself. "Beta," he said, crossing the room to close the door, "has been transmitting bursts of X-rays in an exceedingly regular pattern during the entire time we've been observing it. The details don't matter, but the intervals between peaks have been remarkably constant. At least, that was the situation until last night. I understand Charlie informed you that the signal stopped altogether somewhat after midnight."

"Yes. That's why I came in."

"It was down for precisely four hours, seventeen minutes, forty-three seconds."

"Is that significant?"

Gambini smiled. "Multiply it by sixteen, and you get Beta's orbital period." He watched Harry expectantly and was clearly disappointed at his lack of response. "Harry," he said, "that *can't* be a coincidence. The shutdown was designed to attract attention. *Designed*, Harry. And the duration of the shutdown was intended to demonstrate *intelligent* control." Gambini's eyes glittered, and his lips rolled back to reveal sharp white teeth. "Harry," he said, "it's the LGM signal. It's happened!"

Harry shifted his weight uncomfortably. LGM meant *Little Green Man*. It was shorthand for the long-sought transmission from another world. It was the signal for which the SETI people had been listening without success for more than sixty years. When Skynet had gone online two years earlier, its first task had been to survey extrasolar terrestrial planets in an effort to find one whose spectranalysis suggested a high oxygen content. Evidence of *life*. The results had been disappointing. "Ed," he said carefully, "I don't think we should jump to conclusions."

"Goddammit, Harry, I'm not jumping to conclusions!" He started to say something else, caught himself, and sat down. "There *is* no other explanation for what we've seen. Listen—" He grew suddenly calm. "I know what you're thinking. But it doesn't matter what *anybody* thinks. There's no question about it!" He looked defiantly at Harry, daring him to object.

"*That's* the evidence?" asked Harry. "That's all there is? Hell, maybe something got in the way."

"It would be a spectacular coincidence, Harry." Gambini smiled tolerantly. "But yes, there's more." His jaws worked, and an expression that was a mixture of smugness and impatience worked its way into his leathery features.

"What?"

"The consistency of the pattern is on the record. With minor variations, in intensity and pulse width and so on, the basic sequence of events never changed during the last few months. There were almost always fifty-six pulses in a series, and the series repeats every three and a half seconds. Slightly less, actually." He got up, came around the desk, and held out his arms toward the ceiling. "Son of a bitch, I can't believe it yet. Anyhow, after we recovered the signal this morning, we could still recognize the pattern. But there was an odd difference. Some of the pulses were missing, but only from alternate series. And always the same pulses. It was as if you took, say, Beethoven's Third Piano Concerto and played it straight through, then played it again, with some notes removed but substituting rests rather than shortening the composition. And you continued to do so, first complete, then truncated, with the truncated version always the same." He took a notepad out of the top drawer and wrote 56 at the top. "The number of pulses in the normal series," he said. "But in the abbreviated series, there are only forty-eight."

Harry shook his head. "I'm sorry, Ed. I'm lost."

"All right, forget all that. It's only a method for creating a recurring pattern. What's particularly interesting is the arrangement of the missing pulses." He printed the series: 3, 6, 11, 15, 19, 29, 34, 39, 56. His gray eyes rose to meet Harry's. "When it's finished, we get fifty-six pulses without the deletions, then the series runs again."

Harry nodded as if he understood. "Say it in English, Ed."

Gambini looked like a man who'd won a lottery. "It's a code," he said.

When Skynet had first gone operational, Gambini had talked as if he expected to solve the basic riddles of the universe. Life in other places, the creation event, the dark-matter issue, were all going to give way to modern technology. But it hadn't happened that way, of course. Those questions were as far from solution as ever. He had been particularly interested, for philosophical reasons, in the role of life in the cosmos. And Skynet had allowed them to examine directly, for the first time, terrestrial worlds circling distant stars. Gambini and Majeski, Wheeler at Princeton, Rimford at Cal Tech, and a thousand others had looked at the surveys and congratulated one another. Planets floated everywhere! Few suns seemed so poor, so sterile, as to be destitute of orbiting bodies. Even multiple star systems had somehow produced, and held on to, families of worlds. Often they fluttered in eccentric orbits, precluding the kind of stable environment believed necessary to support life, but they were there. Planetary-system-formation theory acquired renewed energy. And Gambini had offered Harry his opinion one Sunday afternoon this past April, the day after opening day, that he no longer had any doubts: The universe was rich with life.

That optimism had all changed in the long shadow thrown by the Faint Object Spectrograph. Light analysis showed that planets of terrestrial mass located within the biozone of a star—at a distance from their primary that would allow liquid water to exist—tended to be like Venus rather than Earth. The data had, in fact, revealed the nearby universe as an unremittingly hostile place, and the Saganesque vision of a Milky Way populated with hundreds of thousands of life-bearing worlds had given way to the dark suspicion that humans might be, after all, alone. Gambini's dream faded, and, ironically, it was his own work with the Faint Object Spectrograph that had driven it offstage.

It was a grim time, traumatic for the Agency and its investigators. If, after all, there was nothing out there but rock and gas, why were taxpayers being asked to pump money into long-range projects? So there had been talk of cutbacks, and in fact the cash flow to the Agency for special projects, like Skynet, had slowed considerably. During the next fiscal year, it was expected to go down again. Harry had no inclination to get anyone's hopes up, then take another beating. "I think we need better evidence," he said, as gently as he could.

"Do you?" Gambini's tongue flicked across his lips. "Harry, I don't think you've looked closely at the transmissions." He picked up the pad on which he'd scrawled the numbers and held it out. While Harry pretended to study them, he gazed down at his phone and punched in a code. "We'd better tell Quint," he said.

Harry frowned. "I wouldn't be in a hurry to get the director out here." Quinton Rosenbloom was NASA's operations chief, now also wearing the hat of director at Goddard. An automobile accident a few weeks before had left the position unexpectedly empty. The change in leadership at this time was unfortunate. The old director had known Gambini well and would have been tolerant of this latest aberration. But Rosenbloom was an old-line conservative, utterly dedicated to hardheaded good sense.

Harry continued to examine the numbers, but he still saw nothing out of the ordinary.

Gambini frowned at the handset. "I'm getting his answering machine," he said. Rosenbloom did not carry a cell phone on weekends, and he did not particularly like to be disturbed. Gambini's correct course would have been to leave some indication of the nature of the emergency with the recorder. That would have resulted in a response within a few hours.

But Harry liked to annoy Rosenbloom, and here he could do it indirectly. "Tell the machine he needs to call as soon as he gets in. Don't tell him why."

Gambini shrugged and complied.

"I assume there's some sort of sequence," Harry said.

The physicist nodded. "Of the most basic sort. At the start of the series, there are two pulses, marked off by the pulse that does not appear. Then two more, then four. An exponential group. Followed by the three that appear between sites eleven and fifteen, another three between fifteen and nineteen, and nine between nineteen and twenty-nine. Two-two-four. Three-three-nine. Four-four-sixteen. Could anything be clearer?"

———————

Quint Rosenbloom was overweight, rumpled, and short-tempered. He had a talent for alienating the help and operated on the management theory that his primary responsibility was to throw up roadblocks against every initiative he didn't think of personally. He needed his glasses adjusted and could have used a competent tailor. Nevertheless, he was a bureaucrat with some technical talent and could be counted on to maintain an efficient, if not very productive, organization. He'd come to NASA from COSMIC, the Computer Software Management and Information Center at the University of Georgia. His initial assignments had encompassed systems integration for the Ground Spaceflight Tracking and Data Network. But the application of bureaucratic pressure appealed to his mathematical instincts. He enjoyed wielding power.

He did not generally approve of theorists. They tended to get confused easily, and their hold on everyday reality, uncertain in the best of times, inevitably made them unreliable. He recognized their value, much, perhaps, as the theorists recognized the value of the signature on their paychecks. But he preferred to stay at least one level of management above them. Thus, Harry became the contact with the operational people.

Ed Gambini was a classic example of the type. Gambini was addicted to asking the sort of ultimate questions about which one could speculate endlessly with no fear of ever arriving at a solution. Rosenbloom did not see that as a problem in itself, of course, but it biased one's judgment sufficiently to render it, in his view, unreliable.

He had vigorously opposed Gambini's appointment, but his own superiors, whose scientific backgrounds were limited, were impressed by the physicist's Nobel Prize. Moreover, in an action that Rosenbloom could not bring himself to forgive, Gambini had gone over his head. "The little bastard knew I wouldn't have given him the job," he once told Harry. There'd been a food fight, and, in the end, Rosenbloom had been overruled.

If Rosenbloom doubted Gambini's results when he saw them that Sunday morning, it wasn't because he felt such a thing wasn't possible, but rather that it simply did not happen in well-run government agencies. He also sensed that, if events were permitted to take their course, he would shortly face one of those fortunately rare situations in which there would be considerable career risk, with little corresponding opportunity for advantage. If it were eventually proved inaccurate, Rosenbloom would be blamed for not having used more discretion. If it was correct, on the other hand, Gambini would get all the credit.

The director's irritation was obvious from the moment he arrived at the operations center. "I guess he doesn't like coming in on a Sunday," Gambini remarked, while both men watched him stride stiffly through the whitewashed door. But Harry suspected it went deeper than that. Rosenbloom just flat out didn't like waves, and a Sunday call always suggested problems with which he'd as soon not deal.

It was warm. He had slung a worn green blazer over one shoulder, and his knit shirt was stuffed into his pants. Someone at home had reached him at the golf course, and after a short conversation with Gambini, he'd come directly in. "I don't have an explanation for your dots and dashes, Ed," he said. "But I'm sure someone else will. What's Majeski's opinion?"

"He can't offer any alternative."

"—To little green men. How about you, Harry?"

"It's not his field," observed Gambini.

"I thought I asked *him*."

"I have no idea," said Harry, his own temper rising.

Rosenbloom exhaled and stared for a long moment at the ceiling. "The Agency," he said reasonably, "has a few problems just now. The rest of the moon operation's going to hell. The administration is unhappy with our foot-dragging over the military's pet projects. The Bible thumpers are still after us. And I don't need to remind you that there's a presidential election next year."

That had been another embarrassment for the Agency. The year before, a NASA investigator had shown pictures of a quasar to the media and jokingly remarked it might be the Big Bang. That got translated quickly to claims NASA had seen the creation event, and there'd been outrage from the religious right. "We spend a lot of money, and the taxpayers are asking why. It wouldn't take much for Hurley to just cut off the flow. To take us by our collective throats and hang us out to dry. If we start talking about little green men, and we're wrong, we're going to hand him the rope." He was sitting on a reversed wooden chair, which he now tilted forward. "Maybe," he added, "even if we're right."

"We don't have to make any statement at all," objected Gambini. "Just release the transmissions. They'll speak for themselves."

"They sure as hell will." Rosenbloom was the only person in the organization who would have taken that tone to Ed Gambini. There was much about the director's methods for handling subordinates that reminded Harry of a tractor-trailer with a loose housing. "Ed, people are already jittery. We had that terrorist scare in Chicago last week, the economy's a mess, Pakistan and India are threatening each other again. The President is not going to want to hear about Martians."

Harry's eyes were beginning to water. Pollen was getting down into his throat, and he sneezed. He felt slightly feverish and began to wish he could take the day off and go to bed.

"Why not?" asked Gambini. "What has an LGM signal got to do with Pakistan?"

Rosenbloom took a deep breath, and his expression suggested he was addressing a child. "It upsets the status quo. With an election coming up, the last thing the White House wants is another bump in the road."

"Quinton." Gambini twisted the name slightly, drawing out the second consonant. But he kept a straight face. "Whoever is on the other end of that transmission is far away. *Far* away. There were cavemen here when that signal left Altheis."

"It is my earnest desire," Rosenbloom continued, as if no one else had spoken, "that this entire issue just go away."

"That's not going to happen."

"Then let someone *else* find the LGMs. If they're really there, surely that won't be so difficult."

"Quint." Gambini's tone hardened. "You can't just ignore a discovery like this and hope someone else finds it. That's crazy."

Rosenbloom nodded. "I suppose you're right." His chair creaked as he adjusted his position. "Harry, you didn't answer my question. Would *you* be willing to stand up there and tell three hundred million Americans that you've been talking to Martians?"

Harry gazed back into those intense eyes. He didn't like to be perceived as opposing Gambini on Gambini's grounds. Still, it was hard to believe the entire thing wouldn't turn out to be a defective flywheel somewhere. "It's like UFOs," he said, trying to be diplomatically noncommittal, but realizing too late he was saying the wrong thing. "You can't really take them seriously until somebody parks one in your front yard."

Rosenbloom's features reflected a sense of serenity. "Carmichael," he said reasonably, "has been here longer than any of us. He has an instinct for survival that I admire—" He smiled reassuringly at Harry. I am not exaggerating, he seemed to be suggesting. *This is really the way I feel.* Harry was embarrassed. "And," he continued, "he has the best interests of the Agency at heart. Ed, I suggest you listen to him."

Gambini, stationed behind his cluttered desk, ignored Harry. "What admin thinks is irrelevant. The fact is that nothing in nature creates exponential sequences."

Rosenbloom lowered his head into his hands and pressed his fingertips against his temples. "You're wrong, Ed," he said in a tone that suggested he was being patient. "You spend too much time in observatories. But Harry understands the realities here. Don't you, Harry?"

Harry squirmed. "I think Ed has a point."

Rosenbloom charged through the remark. "How badly do

you want to see Skynet finished? How important are the Mare Ingenii telescopes?"

Gambini's cheeks were reddening. He was visibly angry, but he said nothing.

"Okay." Rosenbloom held his hands out to indicate he was speaking pure truth, down off the mountain. "You push this business with the pulsar, create another stir, and I guarantee you it'll be the end. The Senate would love to be able to kill off the whole batch of appropriations. Keep in mind, all you've got is a goddam series of beeps. They might be decisive for you, but to the Congress, they're just beeps."

"Quint, what we have is hard evidence of intelligent control of a pulsar."

"All right, I'll buy that. You've got *evidence*." He got ponderously to his feet and pushed his hands into his jacket pockets. "And that's it. Evidence is a long way from proof. Harry's right: If you're going to talk about little green men, you better be prepared to march them into a press conference. This stuff is *your* specialty, not mine. But I looked up pulsars before I came down here this morning. If I understand my sources, they're what's left after a supernova blows a star apart. Isn't that correct?"

Gambini nodded. "More or less."

"Just so you can reassure me," he continued, "what's your answer going to be when someone asks how an alien world could have survived the explosion?"

"There's no way we could know that," objected Gambini.

"Well, you'll want to have a plausible story ready for Cass Woodbury. She's a cobra, Ed. She'll probably also want to know how anyone could control the kind of energy a pulsar puts out." He drew a piece of paper from his pocket, unfolded it with deliberate ease, and adjusted his glasses. "It says here that the power generated by your basic X-ray pulsar could go to around ten thousand times the luminosity of the sun. Could that be right? How could anyone control *that*? *How*, Ed? How could it be done?"

Gambini sighed. "We may be talking about a technology a million years beyond ours," he said. "Who knows what they might be capable of?"

"Yeah, well, you'll have to excuse my skepticism, but that's a poor answer. We'd better be ready with something a little more convincing."

Harry sneezed his way into the conversation. "Look," he said, wiping his nose, "I probably shouldn't be part of this at all. But I can tell you how I'd use the pulsar if I wanted to signal with it."

Rosenbloom rubbed his flat nose with fat short fingers. "How?" he asked.

"I wouldn't try to do *anything* with the pulsar itself." Harry got up, crossed the room, and looked down, not at the director, but at Gambini. "I'd set up a blinker. Just put something in front of it."

A beatific smile lit up Rosenbloom's languid features. "Good, Harry," he said. "It must come as something of a surprise to some of us that there's imagination outside the operations group." He turned back toward Gambini. "Okay, Ed, I'm willing to concede the possibility. It *might* be artificial, or it might be something else entirely. I suggest we keep our minds open. And our mouths shut. At least until we know what we're dealing with. In the meantime, any public statements will come from my office."

"Which means there'll be none."

"For the moment, yes. There'll be none. And if the signal changes again, you notify *me* first. Clear?"

Gambini nodded.

Rosenbloom looked at his watch. "It's what, about ten and a half hours now since it started. I take it you're assuming this is an acquisition signal of some sort."

"Yes," said Gambini. "They'd want to attract our attention first. Somewhere down the line, when they think we've had enough time, they should switch to a textual transmission."

"If they do, what are the chances we'll be able to read it?"

"Hard to say. Surely they'll understand their audience will need some help. Presumably, they'll supply that."

"That sounds like a lot of presuming." The director's eyes fell on Harry. "Harry, you get in touch with everybody who was in here last night. Tell them not a word of this to anyone. Any of this gets out, I'll have somebody's head. Ed, if there are any special people you want to bring in, clear it with my office first."

Gambini frowned. "Quint, aren't we losing sight of our charter here a little? Goddard isn't a defense installation."

"It also isn't an installation that's going to have people laughing at it for the next twenty years because you can't wait a few days—"

"I have no problem with keeping it away from the media," Gambini said, his temper visibly rising. "But a lot of people have worked on different aspects of this problem for a long time. They deserve to know what happened last night."

"Not yet." Rosenbloom appeared maddeningly unconcerned. "I'll tell you when."

———————

The director's aura lingered oppressively in the office. Gambini's exaltation was gone, and even Harry, who had long since learned the advantage of maintaining a clinical attitude in these squabbles, felt unnerved.

"Damn fool," Gambini said. "He means well, he wants to protect the Agency, but he's a walking grenade." He flipped through the Rolodex, found a number, and punched it into his phone. "Last night, Harry," he said quietly, "you and I lived through the most significant moment in the history of the world. I suggest you record everything you can remember. You'll be able to write a book on the subject soon, and people will read it a thousand years from now." He leaned into the phone. "Is Father Wheeler there? This is Ed Gambini at Goddard."

Harry shook his head. He hated turf wars; they caused ill will, rancor, and inefficiency, and he habitually regarded people who engaged in them with contempt. Although he'd caught himself indulging on occasion. But this one was particularly irritating.

The walls in Gambini's office were lined with books, not the reassuring personnel manuals and federal regulations in black binders that filled Harry's shelves, but arcane volumes with abstruse titles: Kip Thorne's *Black Holes and Time Warps*, Stephen Hawking's *The Grand Design*, Baines Rimford's *Molecular Foundations of Temporal Asymmetry*, Gunter Epstein's *The Quantum Core*. Other volumes lay open on tables, and well-thumbed copies of *Physics Today*, *Physics Review*, *Cosmology*, and other magazines were scattered about.

The casual disarray upset Harry's sense of propriety. The first requisite of a government office is order. He was surprised that Rosenbloom had not commented, had not even seemed to notice. Probably it suggested that there was not, after all, so wide a difference between Gambini and the director.

"I'd appreciate it if you could reach him and ask him to call me right away," Gambini was saying into the phone. "It's important." He broke the connection. "Wheeler's in D.C., Harry, lecturing at Georgetown. With luck, we can have him here this afternoon."

Harry made a face.

"What? What is it, Harry?"

"You're playing games with your career. I thought Rosenbloom made himself reasonably clear. He wants approval before anyone is called in."

"He can't do anything to me," said Gambini. "I could walk out of here tomorrow and call a press conference, and he knows it. And he can't touch you, either. Hell, nobody else knows how to run the place. Anyway, if it'll make you feel better, I'll see that his office gets informed. But if we have to wait for Quinton's okay, we might as well close up shop."

Harry didn't like the hostility. "He'll have no objection to your bringing Pete Wheeler in." Wheeler was a Norbertine cosmologist who shared Gambini's intense interest in the possibilities of extraterrestrial life. He'd written extensively on the subject and predicted long before Skynet that living worlds would be exceedingly rare. He also had a direct connection with Rosenbloom, who had been his partner in a number of area bridge tournaments. "Who else do you want?"

"Let's go outside," suggested Gambini. Reluctantly, because the pollen would be worse, Harry acquiesced. "When things begin to happen, we're going to need Baines Rimford. And I'd like to have Leslie Davies on hand. Eventually, if a textual message *does* come through, we should also get Cyrus Hakluyt. If you could get the paperwork started, I'd appreciate it."

Rimford was probably the world's best-known cosmologist. He'd become a public figure in recent years, appearing on television specials and writing books on the architecture of the universe that were always described as "lucid accounts for the general reader," but which Harry could never understand. In the early years of the twenty-first century, Gambini maintained, Rimford's only peer was Barbara Hasting. His name was attached to assorted topological theorems and temporal deviations and cosmological models. Yet he, too, like so many physicists, found time to play bridge. He was a ranking expert. And he had something of a reputation as an amateur actor. Harry had once watched him perform, with remarkable energy, as Liza Doolittle's father.

But who were Davies and Hakluyt?

They came out through the front doors into a bright, sunlit afternoon, cool with the smell of mid-September. Gambini's enthusiasm was returning. "Cyrus is a microbiologist from Johns Hopkins. He's a Renaissance man, of sorts, whose specialties include evolutionary mechanics, genetics, several branches of morphology, and assorted other subdisciplines. He also writes essays."

"What sort of essays?" asked Harry, assuming that Gambini meant technical papers.

"They're more or less philosophical commentaries on natural history. He's been published by both the *Atlantic* and *Harper's*, and a volume of his collected work came out last year. I think it was called *The Reluctant Brontosaur*. There's a copy of it down in my office somewhere. It got a favorable review in the *Times*."

"And Davies?"

"A theoretical psychologist. A *working* theoretical psychologist. Maybe she can do something for Rosenbloom."

"Ed—?"

"Okay. Look, if we find ourselves listening to an intelligence of some sort, you're going to need a good psychologist."

"Why?"

"Who else is more likely to be able to reconstruct the psyche on the other end?"

It was going to be a lovely day. And Harry, noting the solid reality of a passing pickup, of the homely personnel offices across Road 3, of lumber and sheeting stacked against one wall of the building from which they'd just come, the residue of a remodeling project ordered by the director, then abandoned, wondered whether Rosenbloom wasn't right about Gambini. "Why Wheeler and Rimford?" he asked. "What has cosmology to do with SETI?"

"Just between us, Harry, we already have all the astronomers and mathematicians we need. Wheeler's in because he's an old friend and deserves to be here. Rimford has been part of every major discovery in his field for thirty years, so we can't slight him. Besides, he's the best mathematician on the planet. If contact goes any farther, Harry, if we actually get a follow-up transmission, the astronomers are going to be close to useless. We'll need Baines and Pete to read it. And we'll need Hakluyt and Davies to understand it."

———

At around seven, Harry drove home. When he got there, Julie's car was gone. The air was filled with the smell of burning leaves, and the temperature was dropping rapidly. The trees already stood stiff and stark in the gathering dusk. The yard needed raking, and the neighborhood kids had knocked his wooden gate flat again. The damned thing had never worked right since the day he'd brought it home and mangled the assembly. Now you had to be careful how you opened it, or it came off its hinges. He'd repaired it a couple of times, but it never took.

The house was empty. He found a note propped up on a loaf of bread:

Harry,

We're at Ellen's. There's lunch meat in the fridge.

Momentarily, his heart froze. But she wouldn't have done that, left so soon, with no warning. Still, it brought everything back with painful clarity.

He cracked a beer and carried it into the living room. Several rolls of Julie's blueprints—she was a part-time architectural assistant for a small firm in D.C.—were tucked behind the dictionary stand. Their presence was reassuring. When the time came for her to leave, they would most certainly go with her.

A dozen of Tommy's plastic dragonmen were gathered into a shoe-box fort on the footrest. They were absurd creatures with long snouts and alligator tails and clearly inadequate batwings. Yet they were nevertheless comforting, old friends from a better time, like the antique secretarial cabinet he and Julie had bought in the first year of their marriage and the birch paneling they'd struggled to put up three or four summers back.

The beer was cold. And good.

He shook off his shoes, turned on the TV, but reduced the sound to a murmur.

The room was pleasantly cool. He finished the beer, closed his eyes, and sank into the sofa. The house was always quiet when Tommy was out of it.

———

The telephone was ringing.

It was dark, and someone had placed a quilt over him. He groped uncertainly for the instrument, found it, and lifted it to his ear. "Hello?"

"Harry, did you get Optical for us?" It was Gambini. "Control isn't aware of any change."

"Wait a minute, Ed." The television was off, but he could hear someone moving around upstairs. He tried to look at his watch, but he couldn't find his glasses. "What time is it?"

"Almost eleven."

"Okay. I notified Donner that he was being preempted, and I sent a memo over to Control. I'll call them to make sure they haven't forgotten. You're scheduled to pick up the system at midnight. But they tell me Champollion won't line up until after two."

"Are you coming in?"

"Is anything going to happen?"

"Hard to say. This'll be our first look with the whole system. Up until now, it's been mostly radio and X-ray. The only optical images were taken with the orbiting units." Harry heard Julie moving around upstairs. "But no, we'll probably just collect some technical information. Nothing likely to be worth your making a special trip. Unless, of course," he added mischievously, "the bastards are sending a visual signal as well."

"Is that possible?"

Gambini thought a moment. "I'm not sure what's possible, but that wouldn't be the way to go."

Harry stayed on the line, talking about nothing in particular, waiting perhaps for Julie to appear. A bedroom door opened and closed, and he heard her on the stairs, saw her pause near the window at the bottom, silhouetted against the soft glow of the starlight in the garden. "Hello," she said, not really *saying* it but making the impression with her lips.

Harry nodded. "Ed," he said, "I'll be over in about an hour." And the pleasure he got from the act, from letting Julie know he was walking off again, surprised him. He hung up and asked if she was all right, not wanting the remark to sound flat but unable to inject warmth into it. "I'm sorry I missed Tommy," he added.

"We got home about an hour ago," she said. "He's in bed. Is something happening?"

"Hercules again."

She looked disappointed. Had she expected that he would put up more of a fight to keep her? His responses to her now were ruled by his pride and also by a sense that any direct effort to hang onto her would be rebuffed, would only earn her contempt and reduce any remaining possibility that he might still save his marriage. "I've got to get a shower and some fresh clothes," he said. "Things are pretty busy. I'll probably sleep at the office again tonight."

"Harry." She turned on a small table lamp. "You don't have to do that."

"It has nothing to do with us." Harry said it as gently as he could. But it was difficult to control his voice. Everything came out either gruff or strained.

He detected a fleeting uncertainty in her features. "I talked with Ellen," she said. "She can make room for us, for Tommy and me, for a while."

"Okay. Do what you think best."

He showered quickly and drove back to Greenbelt. It was a long ride.

The Rev. Peter E. Wheeler, O. Praem., lifted his rum and Coke. "Gentlemen," he said, "I give you that excellent scientific organization, the federal government, which has, I believe, provided us with an historic moment." Gambini and Harry joined the toast. Majeski also raised his glass, but he was clearly more interested in surveying the women among the clientele, many of whom were young and possessed of striking geometries. It was midnight at the Red Limit.

Overhead, in high orbit, an array of mirrors, filters, imagers, and lenses rotated toward Hercules.

Sandwiches arrived: a steak for Gambini, roast beef for Harry and Majeski. Wheeler contented himself by picking at a dish of peanuts. "Pete, you sure you don't want something to eat?" asked the project manager. "It might be a long night."

Wheeler shook his head. His penetrating dark eyes, receding black hair, sharp features, and prominent incisors combined to create a resemblance with Jason Homandi, who had made his fortune portraying Dracula. It was a resemblance to which he was sensitive, as Harry had learned in an unfortunate moment years before when he'd thoughtlessly mentioned it and watched Pete grow uncomfortable.

"You need some dinner," Harry told him. "It could be a long night."

"I ate before I came over," he said, with the smile of the celebrated vampire. "Nothing worse than a fat priest." Wheeler was relatively young, barely forty, although the last time he'd been at Greenbelt, he had solemnly informed Harry he was over the hill. That was, of course, dogma: If a cosmologist hasn't made a major contribution by the time he hits thirty, it's not supposed to happen.

Wheeler sipped his drink. "You're not," he asked, "expecting a textual signal in the X-ray ranges, are you?"

"No," said Majeski. He was gazing past the priest at a pair of young women seated near the bar. "They wouldn't be able to get enough definition into the transmission to make it practical. Too much quantum noise, for one thing. We're assuming they'll switch to a wide-band signal of some sort. Something they'd figure we couldn't miss."

"But we're taking no chances," added Gambini. "Everything we have is locked on them now. Including the all-channel. If they transmit anywhere at all in the EM range, we should pick it up."

"Good," said Wheeler.

"Let's hope," added Majeski, "they're on the same sort of temporal dynamic we are. It would be nice to find, during our lifetimes, what they have to say for themselves." One of the two women in his line of sight looked his way. He excused himself, took his drink, left the roast beef, and sauntered over to her table.

"Pity you can't deal with your aliens in so direct a manner," Wheeler said.

Gambini shook his head. "I wonder how the twentieth century would have gone if we'd had a lascivious Einstein."

The priest considered it. "Possibly there'd be no atom bomb," he said.

"We'd be better off," said Harry.

"Actually," Wheeler said, "it wouldn't have made a difference, I don't think. Albert wasn't indispensable. The timing would have been different, but it still would have happened."

They fell into good-natured banter. When the laughter subsided momentarily, several minutes later, Harry asked why Optical had suddenly become so important.

Gambini explained between mouthfuls of steak. "We don't know what to expect," he said. "It's logical to assume there'll be a second phase to the transmission, since the acquisition signal does nothing more than alert us to their presence. A civilization able to manhandle that pulsar should be capable of damned near anything. And by the way, Harry, there's good reason to suspect that they *are* able to manipulate the pulsar, whether they use a screen or not. Anyhow, we'd like to try to get a look at their neighborhood."

Wheeler finished his drink. "Ed, I take it we're sitting on this little bombshell."

"Rosenbloom wants to wait awhile before we announce anything."

"Exactly the right course," Wheeler said, looking hard at Gambini, who did not respond.

Later, while the project manager was in the washroom, Harry asked the priest what he thought about the Hercules signal. "What do *you* think? Is it artificial? Is there somebody actually out there?"

Wheeler tried to attract the attention of their waiter. "It's hard to argue the evidence, Harry. I don't know what's behind it any more than anyone else does. But we're talking about something we all want very much to find. And that automatically makes these kinds of conclusions suspect. Let's wait awhile and see what happens."

Harry pushed the food around on his plate. "What *could* cause a signal of that type? Naturally, I mean."

The waiter arrived, and Wheeler asked him to bring a fresh pot of coffee. "I haven't the slightest idea. But I can tell you what it isn't."

Harry leaned forward expectantly.

"It isn't," Wheeler said, "what Ed thinks it is."

"How do you know that?"

"Harry, do you know what a pulsar is?"

"It's a collapsed star that blinks."

The priest's eyes seemed to be looking into the distance. "It's the corpse of a supernova. A *supernova*, Harry. Ed himself tells me they're estimating it happened less than six million years ago." He caught up a few peanuts, dropped one, and swallowed the others. "A blast of that magnitude would either incinerate or scatter any planetary group that existed anywhere in the neighborhood. If anybody's out there with a radio transmitter, he doesn't have a world to sit on."

"Rosenbloom raised that point," said Harry.

"It's a valid objection."

———

Two twenty-four-meter telescopes are mounted atop the west wall of the Champollion Crater, on the far side of the moon, at thirty-seven degrees north latitude. Two more are under construction near the Mare Ingenii in the southern hemisphere. The Champollion reflectors are the heart of Skynet. Functioning in tandem with an Earth-orbiting array of eight 2.4-meter Hubbell Alphas, they are fully capable of reaching to the edge of the observable universe.

The system, which was barely two years old, had been completed only after a long struggle over financing. There'd been internal bickering, delays, cost overruns, and, in the end, political problems. The dustup over the creation event had, incredibly, damaged efforts to fund the second pair of telescopes. The discovery that most planetary systems out to more than a hundred light-years were as desolate and devoid of life as the moon had guaranteed that the imagination of the taxpayer, and consequently the interest of the politician, would not be engaged.

Skynet also included a system of radio and X-ray telescopes and, for enhancement, an extensive bank of state-of-the-art computers. When operating as a fully coordinated optical unit, when, in other words, all ten reflectors were locked onto the same target, the system could, in Baines Rimford's memorable phrase, spot a squirrel in a tree in Andromeda. During Skynet's early months of operation, Harry had stood under the monitors with Gambini and Majeski and Wheeler, silently absorbing the blue-white curve of majestic Rigel, the vast trailing filaments of the Whirlpool Galaxy, and the fog-shrouded surface of the terrestrial world Alpha Eridani III. They'd been rousing days, filled with promise and excitement. The investigators, the news media, and the general public had all got caught up in a frenzy of expectation. Harry had been forced to put on four extra people in the public-relations office to answer telephones and quash rumors. He, like everyone else, had been carried along by the surging tide.

But the big news never came. The long, bleak winter was filled with the increasingly familiar carbon-dioxide-and-methane readouts. The atmospheres of several dozen worlds, located well within the biozones of their suns, had shown no evidence of living systems. In April, with the coming of spring, Harry had been forced to impose a temporary termination of Ed's consultancy and send him on a vacation.

Linda Barrister, who supervised space-center communications, was talking softly to NASCOM when Harry followed Gambini and the others into the operations center. She smiled prettily, spoke again into the phone, and looked up at the project manager. "They're still a few minutes from calibration, Doctor."

Gambini nodded and strode over to the bank of monitors

that had been tied into Optical. But he got bored quickly and began to wander through the spaces, holding brief, whispered conversations with the technicians.

Majeski went back into the conference room, which had been converted into extra workspace.

Wheeler eased comfortably into a chair.

"You don't expect much out of this, do you, Pete?" asked Harry.

"Out of Optical? No, not really. But who knows? Listen, last year I'd have argued that no binary system could exist where this one is. There are a few questions to be answered here."

Two technical assistants, both bearded, fortyish, and overweight, pulled their earphones down on their necks and bent forward over their consoles.

Somewhere, probably in one of the workrooms, a radio was playing the jumbled cacophony that passed for music these days. Harry leaned against a supply cabinet. Directly overhead, an auxiliary monitor was flashing sequences of numbers more quickly than the eye could follow. "It's the satellite," Linda explained. "TDRSS." The Tracking and Data Relay Satellite System. "It's tracking the X-ray pulse from Hercules." She touched a slim finger to her right earphone. "Champollion's locked in," she said.

Gambini, who was trying to maintain his customary dignity, trembled with excitement. Despite the air-conditioning, damp crescents stained his shirt. He moved closer to Linda's monitor.

"We're getting input from the system," she said.

The lights dimmed.

Majeski came back into the room.

Wheeler pulled off his plaid sweater and tossed it into a supply cabinet.

"Recording," said one of the bearded technicians.

The monitor blinked on, darkened, and a starfield appeared. A red point of light began to grow in intensity until it outshone the other stars. Someone exhaled, and there was a general rustling throughout the several rooms of the operations center.

"Alpha Altheis," Pete whispered. "That's it."

Harry listened to himself breathe.

"The others are mostly foreground stars," Wheeler said. "Probably a couple of galaxies in there, too."

"Mag is two-point-oh," said Linda. That was a magnification of two hundred thousand times actual apparent size.

"Take it in," said Gambini.

The peripheral objects rotated forward off the screen. The red star continued to brighten.

"Looks ordinary enough," said Harry.

Wheeler pulled over a chair and sat down. "You wouldn't want to live there," he said.

Harry did not take his eyes from the monitor. "Why not?"

"If there *were* a world, there'd be no stars in its sky. The moon would be red. Its sun is being eaten by an invisible *thing.*"

"Three-oh," said Linda.

"A culture that developed under these conditions—"

"—Would," observed Majeski, "sure as hell be God-fearing."

Alpha Altheis grew brighter. Its disk became discernible. Then someone across the room grunted. "What the hell's *that*?" Gambini, trying to get closer, stumbled over something in the semidarkness, crashed heavily, but popped back up without missing a beat.

A yellow pinprick had appeared to one side of the giant star.

"Spectro," snapped Gambini.

Linda checked her instruments. "Three-six," she said.

Wheeler was out of his chair. He laid a hand on Harry's shoulder. "There's a third star in the system."

"Class G," said an analyst. "No readings yet on mass. Absolute magnitude six-point-three."

"Not very bright," said Gambini. "No wonder we missed it."

Harry grinned at Wheeler. "There goes your supernova problem," he said. "Now we know where the planets are."

"No, I don't think so. If that class G *is* part of the system, which out there it damned well would have to be, the explosion would have taken out *its* worlds, too. Still—" Wheeler looked perplexed. He turned back to Gambini. "Ed?"

"I see it, Pete," said the project manager. "It doesn't make much sense, does it?"

Harry could make out nothing but the two stars, a bright sharp ruby and a yellow point of light. "What is it?" he asked. "What's wrong?"

"There should be a shell of gas around the system," said Wheeler. "Some remnant of the supernova. Ed, what do you think?"

Gambini's brow had furrowed. "That there's been no supernova here."

Wheeler's voice was barely audible. "That's not possible, Ed."

"I know," Gambini said.

MONITOR

. . . The sites at Champollion and Marii Ingenii
for the fixed, 24-meter telescopes were chosen
to provide an optimum number of objects both
within and outside the Milky Way that could
be simultaneously targeted by both units. This capability will permit a degree of image enhancement
approximately 30 percent beyond that of either unit
acting alone. The advantage declines somewhat
when the fixed telescopes are employed as part of
the overall system of fixed and orbiting units. But
even under these circumstances, the improvement
would be considerable.

A fully operational Skynet will constitute a stride of
incalculable value, of far more benefit to the species
than any other project now technologically within
reach. Even a mission to Alpha Centauri would pale
in contrast.

In light of the funds that have already been
expended on Skynet and the relatively modest sum
that would be required to complete the system, we
urge—

—From NASA's Annual Report to the President

. . .

Let us look at the facts.

We know that, beyond this Earth, the universe is
unremittingly hostile, a place of extremes, a place
that is mostly a void, a place with a lot of rocks and
gas and not much else. It is the sort of place that
some Northerners might want to visit, but it holds
little interest for Tennesseans.

We know also that even NASA can no longer provide a shadow of any tangible benefit to be derived from examining boulders so far away that light reflected from them cannot reach us during a man's lifetime.

We also face the stark fact that the government would like to spend an additional $600 million to complete the telescopes based at Mare Ingenii. Their argument for doing so seems to be that, having already wasted so much on the project, it would be unconscionable not to waste some more.

The time has come to call a halt.

—Editorial, *Memphis Herald* (September 15)

. . .

. . . The reality of it all may be that our concepts have so thoroughly outstripped our technology that the latter can no longer keep up. Case in point: Skynet.

Theoretically, it should be possible to use the techniques I have described in this paper to create a magnetic lens whose diameter would be equal to the Earth's orbit. This lens could be manipulated to create a focal point in the same manner that a glass lens does. One hesitates to speculate on the sort of magnification such an achievement would permit. And while we cannot yet construct such a device, we know how it can be done, and there is no reason why it should not work.

—Baines Rimford, *Science* (September 18)

||| THREE |||

Baines Rimford stood on a wooded hill out near the edge of the Milky Way, looking toward galactic center. He could sense the majestic rotation of the great wheel and the balance of gravity and angular momentum that held it together. Relatively few stars, gliding along their lonely courses, were visible over the lights of Pasadena.

The sun completes an orbit around the center of the galaxy every 225 million years. During this latest swing, pterodactyls had flown and vanished, the ice had advanced and retreated, and, near the end of the long circuit, man had appeared. Against that sort of measure, what was his own life span? It had occurred to Rimford, at about the time he approached fifty, that the chief drawback in contemplating the enormous gulfs of time and space that constitute the bricks and mortar of the cosmologist is that one acquires a dismaying perception of the handful of years allotted to a human being.

To what microscopic extent had the sun depleted its store of hydrogen since he'd sat reading about Achilles and Prometheus on the front porch of his grandfather's row home in South Philadelphia? How much deeper was the Grand Canyon?

He was suddenly aware of his heartbeat: tiny engine of mortality whispering in his chest. It was one with the spinning galaxies and the quantum dance, as he was one with anything that had ever raised its eyes to the stars.

It was in good condition, his heart, as far as he knew. As much as could be expected for a mechanism designed to self-destruct after a few dozen winters.

Somewhere below, lost in the lights of Lake Avenue, a dog barked. It was a cool evening. The air conditioners were off, and people had their windows open. Fragments of the Dodgers game drifted up to him. Pasadena was, if more prosaic, at least more comprehensible than the universe. One knew why traffic lights worked and where it had all come from. And taken from the perspective of Altadena and Lake, the Big Bang seemed a rather unlikely way to try to account for it all.

Curious. In the days when he had been constructing the cosmic model that bore his name, many of his creative insights had come while he stood atop a hill like this one on the edge of Phoenix. But what he remembered most clearly from those solitary excursions was not the concepts, not the sense of galaxies rushing outward before the push of expanding space, but rather the dogs. While he juggled matter and energy, the night had seemed full of barking canines.

It was getting late. The comet and the moon were both low in the west. Rimford wasn't much interested in comets, and he couldn't understand people who were. There was, he felt, little to be learned from them that we didn't already know. There was only the trivia of their composition, and perhaps the opportunity to add to or subtract from the Earth's age a few more million years.

He started slowly down the hill, enjoying the cool night air and the solitude. Near a cluster of palms, about a hundred yards from the crest, there was a spot from which he could see his house. Like a child, he always stopped to savor its warm light and familiar lines. All in all, he had little of which to complain. His bachelor existence got lonely at times. He would have liked to have had a family, but somehow he never got around to it. Otherwise, life was good. Except that it was desperately short.

There was a story in Herodotus of a Greek philosopher who'd visited an Asian kingdom, where the ruler inquired of him who was happiest among men? The philosopher understood that the king himself wished to be thought of as occupying that enviable position. But the visitor responded in an unexpected manner. "Perhaps," he replied, "it might be a farmer of my acquaintance, who lived near Athens. He had fine children, a wife who loved him, and he died on the field of battle defending his country." Rimford didn't expect to see any armed combat, but he had nevertheless waged the good fight, not for a particular flag but for humanity. And if he lacked a family to grieve for him when the time came, he had nonetheless good reason to believe many would mourn his passing.

In the dark, his lips curved into a smile. He was feeling satisfied with himself. The probability was that the Rimford universe would one day join Euclidean geometry and Newtonian physics as systems with much to recommend them but which didn't quite get things right. It didn't matter. When the great strides of the late twentieth and early twenty-first century were being appraised, they would know that Rimford had been there. And if he and Hawking and Penrose had got some of it wrong, they would be seen to have got much of it right.

He was content.

His colleagues expected him to retire shortly. And possibly he would. He had sensed the decline of his conceptual abilities recently. Equations that had once erupted into his consciousness now floated intangibly out on the perimeter. His creative work was over, and it was time to step aside.

Agnes, the divorced sister who lived with him, was on the phone when he walked in. "He's here now," she said into the instrument. She held it out to him with a wink. "Ed Gambini," she said. "I think he needs help."

———

Leslie Davies drove in Monday evening from Philadelphia, spent the night with friends in Glen Burnie, and proceeded next morning down the Baltimore–Washington Parkway to Goddard.

The Space Flight Center is nestled among the close-cropped hills and somber middle-class homes of Greenbelt, Maryland. The complex consists of a thick cluster of office buildings, laboratories, and support structures, spread across a rolling tract of almost twelve hundred acres. There are a few dish antennas mounted on concrete aprons and on rooftops, a water tower, and a visitors' center. The overall impression is less of a high-tech space-age facility than of a small military base.

She identified herself at the front gate. They gave her a temporary plate, logged her in, and provided directions to the Research Projects Laboratory.

Leslie had no idea why she'd been asked to come to

Goddard. Gambini had been secretive over the phone, assuring her only that she wouldn't regret taking the time. Nonetheless, she suspected they were having some serious personnel problems. Early in her career, she'd specialized in working with people in the technological professions, and particularly in the space sciences. They tended to score quite high in stress-analysis surveys. Worse, there was evidence in a wide variety of studies that the types of personalities drawn into these occupations tended to be initially unstable.

But even if people were coming apart here, why they should choose to come to *her* was a mystery. God knows, there were plenty of shrinks in D.C., and undoubtedly a few with the right qualifications.

Whatever it was, though, she was glad for the change of pace. She'd been doing cross-discipline research on the consciousness problem for a Penn study group, and having a difficult time. Moreover, her practice, which was limited to two mornings a week, wasn't going well. She'd begun to suspect that she wasn't really helping her patients, and she was too good a psychologist to hide that fact from herself.

A well-tailored young woman met her at the entrance to the lab and inquired whether she'd had any trouble finding the space center. She got a visitor's badge and was led down one floor. "They're expecting you," her guide said. Leslie repressed an urge to ask who was expecting her and why. They turned left into a short corridor. Raised voices spilled out of an open door ahead. One of them she recognized as belonging to Ed Gambini.

He and two men she did not know sat around a conference table poking fingers at one another. Her entrance did nothing to quell the action. The young woman who'd accompanied her signaled that Gambini would be with her presently and withdrew. Leslie stood just inside the door, trying to make out the direction of things. She caught references to red giants, vectors, radial-velocity curves, and sling effects. The youngest of the three was doing most of the talking. He was bearded, blown-dry handsome, energetic. He spoke with the cool confidence of a man who has never known disappointment. He was holding forth on something called Fisher's z-distribution when he took her in at a glance and casually dismissed her.

Leslie bristled but observed that he generated a similar effect on others. Ed Gambini sat with his back toward her, bent forward in a posture that could only be described as hostile. He pressed his fingertips together in an unconscious steeple, demonstrating clearly that the speaker was a subordinate. And probably also indicating a repressed desire to inflict damage.

The man opposite Gambini was lean, with black hair, angular features, and quick, perceptive eyes. He, too, was showing signs of impatience. A visitor's badge was pinned haphazardly to the pocket of a plaid shirt.

Gambini had somehow become aware of her presence. He swiveled around, rose, and shook her hand. "Leslie," he said. "Good to see you again. Have you had breakfast yet?"

She nodded. Once, years before, during more enlightened times, she and Gambini had sat on a commission to advise the NSF on funding for a series of science projects. She remembered him from those days as a man with a wide range of interests, unusual in the narrow disciplines of the scientific community. It had made him an ideal choice for the commission.

What she recalled most vividly, though, was an evening after they'd listened to a presentation for approval of a grant to expand the SETI program. It had been a night full of numbers. An astronomer whose name she couldn't recall had delivered an impassioned plea, illustrated with flip charts, slides, and massive collections of statistics purporting to imply the existence of thousands, and possibly millions, of advanced civilizations in this galaxy alone. It was a subject in which Gambini was intensely interested, and yet he'd voted against the proposal. When Leslie had asked why, he'd replied that he could not take mythical projections seriously. "All the numbers are predicated on the terrestrial experience," he'd complained. "As far as we know, Jehovah assembled us bag and baggage. No, if they're serious about the money, they'll have to give us a rational reason why they should have it." And later, while they'd sat in a small restaurant on Massachusetts Avenue, he'd added that, next time, if they asked him, he'd be glad to do the presentation for them.

"Yes," she replied, "I've eaten."

"This is Pete Wheeler." He indicated the man in the plaid shirt. Wheeler stood, and she offered her hand.

"And the young lion here is Cord Majeski."

Majeski nodded, anxious to get back to the discussion.

"I assume," Gambini said, "you'd like to know what this is about."

———

Julie packed Monday evening. Harry hauled the bags downstairs and left them by the front door.

In the mornings, he was usually gone before Tommy got up. But he delayed his departure next day, and ate breakfast with his son while doors opened and closed upstairs, while Julie gathered up whatever else she planned to take. Tommy was pleased to see him, and said so. But the boy, who knew only that at the end of the school day, he and his mother would be going to visit her cousin for a while, slid rapidly into the sports section. When it was time to leave for school, she appeared, watched Tommy pull on his jacket, and handed him his U.S. Marines lunch pail.

"Tommy," she said, "don't forget not to get on the bus this afternoon. I'll pick you up right after school."

"How about Daddy?" He looked around at Harry. "Are you coming to Ellen's, too?"

Julie paled. "He's going to stay here," she said, as though he'd threatened to follow her.

They'd agreed on this approach last night. But somehow it sounded different now. "Tom," Harry broke in, determined to get it over, "we aren't going to be living together as a family anymore."

"Damned fool," snapped Julie.

Harry glanced at her. His usually placid demeanor vanished. "Which of us were you referring to?" he asked coldly.

Tommy's eyes grew very round. He was nine years old, had brown hair, freckles, and a taste for dinosaurs and baseball. He looked from Harry to his mother, and his cheeks reddened. "No!" he said.

Julie knelt beside him. "It'll be all right."

"No, it won't." Tears forced their way to the surface. "You know it won't."

Harry felt proud of the boy. Tommy hurled the plastic lunch box across the kitchen. It bounced off a counter, popped open,

and the sandwich and diet Coke and nonfat cake spilled out.
"No!" he screamed, coming to Harry and burying his face in
his arms. "Daddy, you're not leaving us."

Harry held the child tightly. "It isn't exactly my choice,
Tom," he said.

"Good," hissed Julie. "Blame it on me."

"Who the hell do you want me to blame?" Harry's voice
was thick with rage.

Her eyes flickered angrily. But she looked toward Tommy
and shook away whatever she'd planned to say.

The boy was sobbing uncontrollably. "So much for school,"
she said finally. "Harry, I think things would be easier if you
went to work."

"By all means," he rasped. "Let's not have any difficulties
about this."

She tried to disengage Tommy, assuring him that he would
still see his father frequently. But the child would not let go.
She looked up at Harry, pleading silently for him to leave.

Harry glared at her, said good-bye to his son, an act that
provoked a fresh scream, and walked out.

———————

It was somewhat after nine thirty when he arrived in the Hercules conference room and met Leslie Davies. She was slender
and efficient, with a classically chiseled jaw, brooding eyes,
and wearing a gray business suit.

Wheeler and Majeski were also present.

"Leslie thinks," said Gambini after the introductions were
complete, "that the aliens would operate along logical parameters similar to our own."

"It never occurred to me," said Harry, "that there'd be any
doubt. What other logical parameters are there?"

"There *are* other possibilities," said the psychologist.
"Logic depends heavily on things like the range and quality of
perceptions, the core value system, communications methods,
and so on. But"—she looked at Gambini—"we need to wait a
little. We don't have much to speculate with so far."

"Maybe wait a lot," offered Harry. "Cord mentioned that
the Altheans might be on a different time scale from ours." He
grinned. "I don't even know what that means."

"Perceptions," said Gambini. "Subjective time. A minute for them might seem considerably longer to us. Or shorter. It's a phenomenon *we* experience. For example, time flies if—"

"—We're having fun," Leslie finished. "But I don't think that's likely to become a relevant issue." Though she was a diminutive woman, she commanded attention. Her sea-green eyes seemed extraordinarily reflective of both mood and color. They were set wide apart and enhanced to a degree by curving lips and, when she chose to show them, strong white teeth. There was, Harry concluded, something of the shark about her. Her reddish brown hair was cut short, and her manner of speaking was pointed. No small talk or loose gabble here. She appeared to be, on the whole, an economical woman disinclined to waste either movement or words. "Their temporal sense can't be too much different from ours," she continued. "I doubt we'll have to wait the ten thousand years or so that some of you were concerned about for additional events—"

"How do we know that?" asked Harry.

"It's obvious," she said. "The signal itself demonstrates a capability to modulate extraordinary amounts of power in fractions of a second. There's other evidence as well. For example, that they switched off and on in a single morning. If nothing else, I'd say because water runs at the same rate everywhere in the universe."

"That's not quite so," said Gambini. "It depends on the gravity quotient. But I take your point."

Harry didn't.

"Living things have to be in sync with water," Gambini explained. "To get a drink, to avoid getting drowned by the incoming tide, to be able to get clear of the water hole before a predator grabs you. Right, Leslie?"

She nodded. "I think we're safe in concluding that, if there is to be a text transmission, we'll have it within a reasonably short time."

"I have a question for you, Leslie." Harry was thinking about Pete Wheeler's proposition. "Would we be different in any substantive way if our skies were blank? If we had no stars, I mean. And a badly distorted sun?"

Her eyes settled on him. They had lit up at the question. "This project is going to produce a lot of speculation. Some of it will remain extremely hypothetical, and that's an example. The reason is that we're finely attuned to our environment. Circadian rhythms, menstrual cycles, all sorts of physiological characteristics are tied in to the seasons, the rising and setting of the sun, lunar cycles, solar cycles, you name it. Furthermore, the visible tableau in the skies has always affected the way we think about ourselves although, since everyone sees more or less the same astronomical show, we can't be sure about the details. We ally ourselves with sun gods and think of death as a retreat into the underworld. Into the darkness.

"Look at the difference between Norse and classical mythology. In the Mediterranean, where the sun's warm and people can go for a dip whenever the mood hits them, the gods were, on the whole, a playful lot, mostly concerned with war-gaming and seductions. But Odin lived in a place like Montana, where people went to work when it was dark and came home when it was dark. The result: not only a far more conservative pantheon in northern Europe but one that is ultimately doomed. In the end, they face Ragnarok, the ultimate dissolution. Germany, where the winters are also bleak, had a similar fatalistic system."

Her brow creased. "I'd never thought of it before in quite these terms, but I can't help wondering if the Germans would have marched in 1914 and again in 1939 had they possessed some Mediterranean beaches."

Wheeler looked up. "The Arabs," he said, "have Mediterranean beaches. And they've certainly shown no reluctance to spill blood."

"Their lands are hot, Pete," she replied. "And I think there's a special situation in the Middle East, too. Related to religion. Well, no matter. The thesis probably wouldn't hold up under close examination. To answer Harry's question in a word: Yes, certainly your aliens would be influenced by their peculiar environment, and I'd be willing to hazard a guess that the influence would not, from our point of view, tend toward a positive direction. But I don't think I'd care to go further than that.

"Incidentally, does anyone care to theorize why they're transmitting in the first place? Whoever sent the signal is a million years dead."

"If their life spans are anything like ours," said Gambini.

"That's probably a safe assumption. But yes, why would they do it? Presumably, it required an engineering feat of considerable magnitude, and there was no chance of a reply, and certainly no assurance of success. One wonders why they'd bother."

"Speaking of assumptions," said Majeski, "aren't we assuming organic life-forms? We could be listening to a computer of some sort. Something for which the passage of time means very little."

"I don't deal in computers," she said, smiling sweetly.

Gambini nodded. "Nevertheless," he said, "it's a possibility we have to consider. But let's get back to the question of motive."

"They're throwing a bottle into the ocean," said Harry. "The same way we did with the plaques we put on the early Pioneers and Voyagers."

"I agree," said Leslie. "In fact, unless we're dealing with something that is, in some way, not really subject to time, a computer, a race of immortals, whatever, I can imagine no other motive. They wanted us to know they were there. Out between the galaxies, they would have been isolated beyond our imagination, with no hope of intercourse of any kind outside their own world. So they assembled a vast engineering project. And sent us a letter. What activity could be more uniquely human?"

In the long silence that followed, Pete Wheeler picked up the coffeepot and refilled the cups. "We don't have the letter yet," he said. "Cord, you dated Gamma. What sort of result did you get?"

"I don't know," said Majeski. He was wearing a strange expression.

"You don't know? Was the lithium exhausted?"

"No, that wasn't the problem."

"What's Gamma?" asked Harry.

"The class G sun in the system," said Majeski.

"Let me bring Harry up to date," said Gambini. He opened a manila envelope lying on the table in front of him. "A class 'G' star," he explained to Harry and Leslie, "uses up its supply of lithium as it gets older. So we can get a fairly decent idea of its age by looking at how much lithium remains." He extracted from the envelope several pages of trace paper with color bars and passed them around to Wheeler. "This is Gamma's spectrogram. We've run it several times, and it keeps coming up the same way."

Wheeler was visibly surprised by what he saw. He leaned forward and straightened a crease in the sheets. "How long have you known about this?" he asked.

"We got the readouts yesterday," said Gambini. "Then we checked the equipment and ran it again. We've relayed the test data to Kitt Peak." He held out his hands helplessly. "They came up with the same result."

"What is it?" asked Leslie.

"One of the problems we've had all along," said Gambini, "is to find a source for the Althean system. Where did it come from? The component stars had to coalesce before being expelled from their parent galaxy. Altheis could not have formed by itself, in the void. And here we were, looking at three stars, which appear to have been out there for a longer time than they've been burning. So it was very difficult to account for their presence at all."

"And now," said Leslie, "you feel you have a solution?"

Wheeler was still staring at the spectrogram.

Gambini nodded. "We have an intriguing possibility."

Harry cleared his throat. "I'm sorry, Ed, but your explanation went right by me. What are we talking about?"

"This is an extremely atypical spectrogram for a class G," said Wheeler. "There are no metallic lines, not even H and K lines. No calcium, no iron, no titanium. No metals of any kind. Gamma appears to be pure helium and hydrogen. Which is why you couldn't date it, Cord. No lithium, either."

Majeski scratched the back of his neck.

Harry broke the silence: "I still don't think I know what it means."

Gambini tapped a pen restlessly on the tabletop. "All G's are Population I stars. They're metal-rich. Even Population II stars, which are not, have some metals boiling in the pot somewhere. But *this* one"—he held up a second set of spectrograms—"has none."

All the color was gone from Wheeler's cheeks. "So what does that tell us?" Harry demanded.

The priest turned puzzled eyes toward him. "There's no

such thing as a metal-free star," he said. "*It's not a natural star.* Ed, what about Alpha?"

"Same thing. Somehow, the original spectrogram was made and filed, and apparently no one ever looked at it. We got it out after *this* turned up. Neither one of those stars seems to have any metal at all."

MONITOR

CUBA DEMANDS
RETURN OF GUANTANAMO

CLAIMS STORAGE OF NUKES
VIOLATES LEASE

. . .

GUERRILLAS INCREASE PRESSURE
ON THAIS

BANGKOK ACCUSES HANOI
OF ARMING INSURGENTS

. . .

FRENCH DEMAND NEW SAFETY RULES
FOR OIL TANKERS

DEPLAINE: "LE HAVRE SPILL IS ENOUGH"

. . .

TERM-LIMITS CAMPAIGN
GAINING GROUND

SUPPORTERS LEAD IN EARLY POLLING
ACROSS COUNTRY

. . .

CRUISE TERRORISTS INDICTED

PROSECUTORS SEEK DEATH PENALTY

. . .

AL KALA WARNS OF FURTHER ATTACKS

CLAIMS RESPONSIBILITY FOR BAGHDAD BOMBING

. . .

DOCTORS IN MEDICARE SCAM

PHYSICIANS IN SEATTLE, SPOKANE CAUGHT IN FBI STING

. . .

TULSA BRIDGE COLLAPSES DURING RUSH HOUR

HUNDREDS FEARED DEAD

PASSED INSPECTION LAST MONTH

. . .

GUNMAN KILLS SIX IN LIBRARY

GOES HOME FOR GUN AFTER 30C FINE

BLAMES SPREE ON FULL MOON

. . .

RIOTS IN BRAZZAVILLE

. . .

NRC RECOMMENDS
BEEFING UP SECURITY

(*Minneapolis Tribune*)—In the wake of the near seizure of the Plainfield nuclear power plant by a lone gunman last week, the Nuclear Regulatory Commission has issued a new set of guidelines . . .

. . .

KANSAS COED WINS MISS AMERICA

AVIATION MAJOR HOPES
TO BE COMMERCIAL PILOT

||| FOUR |||

Rimford was scheduled to come into Reagan on an afternoon flight.

Ed Gambini insisted on driving out to pick him up. Harry, who'd briefly met the celebrated cosmologist on several occasions but who'd never really had an opportunity to talk with him, went along. Despite his excitement, Gambini seemed reluctant to discuss the Althean transmission. Harry wondered whether he wasn't psyching himself to play the hard-nosed skeptic for his incoming guest. They engaged, instead, in some desultory conversation about the weather, their mutual dislike for Quint Rosenbloom, and the probability that the Redskins would finally give up the fight and change the name of the franchise. The Lobbyists, maybe, would be a good choice. But on the whole, the two men rode south on the parkway locked in their own thoughts.

Harry was trying to come to grips with the fact that Julie was gone, and beside that hard piece of reality, the eccentric behavior of a trio of stars unimaginably far away seemed of little consequence. But it was a pleasant sort of early-autumn afternoon when he could bring himself to look at it and absorb its texture, filled with lovely young women in short-sleeved jackets, and hordes of kids in their big-shouldered armor on high-school fields. It was the sort of afternoon to be out with a woman, strolling through tree-lined parks.

"Tell me about Gamma," he said. "Is it really possible that someone *engineered* it?"

The sun was bright on the surface of the Anacostia. They threaded their way between clean white government buildings, riding with the windows open. For a time, Harry thought Gambini had not heard. The physicist guided the midnight blue government car onto the Southeast Freeway. To their right, and ahead, the Capitol dome glittered. "Harry," he said, over the rush of wind, "there's damned little that's impossible if you have the resources and the time to figure out the technology. I don't think you can travel faster than light, and I'm damned sure you can't go back in time. At least not on the macroscopic level. And you can't add to the sum total of energy in the universe. But a little architecture with a star? Why not?

"The real question isn't whether it *can* be done but whether we're looking at a bona fide example of that kind of achievement. Stars always show metal lines in their spectrograms. *Always.* Maybe a lot, maybe a little, but a star without metal just doesn't happen in nature. Not anymore."

"They did at one time?"

"At the very beginning of star formation, Harry. More billions of years ago than you'd care to count. But it doesn't happen now, and any of the very old ones still around would have cooked up some metals a long time back." He looked bewildered. "Gamma's a Population I star, which is to say it's second-generation. All class G's are. They're made up of the remnants of Population II stars, which manufactured the metal that we find in the universe today. Even the iron that helps keep *you* running."

"I was cooked in a star?"

"That's an accurate way to put it if you're talking about building materials. When Population II stars explode, we get the makings of stars like the sun." He hesitated. "I can't imagine any natural process that would produce a Population I star without metal lines."

A battered green pickup roared past, doing about seventy-five.

"So Pete was right that somebody removed the metals. But why would they do that?"

"That's the wrong question. Harry, Pete didn't say somebody removed the metals. What he said was, Gamma's not a natural star. Listen, nobody's going to go to the trouble of draining metal from a star. There'd be no point. I mean, my God, it doesn't improve the star. It's not as if it would work better. And surely they weren't mining." His face twisted slightly, as though the sun were in his eyes, but it was off behind his shoulder. Harry decided that a decision was being made as to whether he could be trusted. "I'm not entirely sure how this will sound, and I wouldn't want to be quoted, but I'll tell you what I believe, the only thing I can think of that *does* make sense.

"Gamma is probably not a natural sun. I think it was built. *Assembled.*"

"My God," gasped Harry.

"The metal serves no purpose, so they left it out."

"Ed, how the hell could anybody make a sun?"

"There's no physical law that precludes it. Obviously, or nature wouldn't be able to do it. All that's required is energy, and a lot of gas. Out where they are, there's a hell of a lot of free hydrogen and helium. All they'd have to do is get it together somewhere, and gravity would take care of the rest."

They crossed South Capitol Street. A long freight train was moving east, boxes and hoppers mostly, with a few loads of lumber. "And that," he continued, "raises another interesting possibility.

"X-ray pulsars are notoriously short-lived. They're the mayflies of the cosmos. They blink on, last maybe thirty thousand years or so, and blink off. The odds against finding one in an independent system, one not attached to a galaxy or to any other kind of star cluster, are extremely long." His voice had dropped almost to a conspiratorial whisper.

Harry watched the car's shadow racing along the guardrail. "You're suggesting," he said, "that they built the pulsar, too."

"Yes." Gambini's face was radiant. "That's exactly what I'm suggesting."

———

The flight was almost an hour late. Normally, the delay would have irritated Ed Gambini, but on that morning, no mundane frustration could reach him. He was meeting a giant, and because of the nature of the discovery at Goddard, Gambini realized that he, too, was on the threshold of joining the immortals. Even Harry felt the wash of exhilaration.

He understood the importance of the meeting with Rimford. The California cosmologist might well see other possibilities, suggest alternative explanations. If, however, he could not, Gambini's hand, and probably his confidence, would be immeasurably strengthened.

They waited at the cocktail lounge in the main terminal. Gambini sat toying with a drink, totally absorbed in his thoughts. Harry recalled the obsession of a year earlier, when Skynet was working its way through the long series of unpromising extra-solar terrestrial worlds. He wondered whether Gambini might not be another Percival Lowell, seeing canals that were visible to no one else.

When Rimford's flight was called, they strolled over to the gate. A long line of passengers filed out and dispersed into the waiting crowd. A few stragglers came down the ramp, and Harry had begun to wonder if they'd met the wrong plane when the man came out of the tunnel.

His appearance was quite ordinary. His hair was whiter than it looked on TV, and he dressed like a mildly prosperous Midwestern businessman. Harry almost expected him to produce a card. But, like Leslie, he had penetrating eyes. Rimford appraised Harry during the introduction, and Harry felt that his soul lay open to the older man.

His handshake was warm. "Nice of you to invite me, Ed," he said, wrapping an arm around Gambini's shoulders. "If you've really got something, I wouldn't want to miss it."

They walked down to the baggage pickup, while Gambini outlined the evidence to date.

Rimford listened, nodding occasionally, commenting that this or that was *good*. When the project manager finished, Rimford's eyes had become luminous. He turned to Harry and remarked that it was an outstanding time to be alive. "If you two are right about this," he said, graciously including Harry in the equation, "nothing is ever again going to be the same." Despite the expressed sentiments, however, he looked perplexed.

"What's wrong?" asked Gambini, whose nerves remained close to the surface.

"I was just thinking how unfortunate it is. They're so very far away. I think we all assumed that, when contact came, *if* it came, the signals would originate within a fifteen- or twenty-light-year bubble. At most. That there'd be at least a possibility for a two-way conversation." He threw his bags into the trunk and climbed into the front seat beside Gambini. "Ah, well," he said, "we should be grateful for whatever we can get. But what we have here sounds more like an archaeological find. And an old one, at that."

Harry rode in back.

The visitor had a lot of questions. He asked about the orbital periods of the Althean system's components, the characteristics of the pulsar, and the quality and nature of the incoming signal. Harry couldn't follow much of it, but his interest soared when they addressed the physical peculiarities of Alpha and Gamma. Gambini very carefully did not advance his hypothesis, but Rimford blinked when the project manager showed him the spectrogram. "You have any explanation for this?" he asked.

"No," said Gambini.

"None at all. Not even a speculation?"

"No."

From that moment, he did not appear to be listening to Gambini's comments. For the most part, he sat staring pensively through the windshield, his eyes hooded.

By the time they reached Kenilworth Avenue, everyone had lapsed into silence.

———————

Harry had never before paid much attention to the men and women who habitually ate alone at the Red Limit, Carioca's, or the William Tell. But now, installed in a dimly lit booth trying to read the *Post*, he was painfully aware of the blank expressions and drawn countenances that marked so many of them. Solitude is seldom voluntary, at least among the young. Yet here they were, the same people night after night, well-heeled derelicts, alone with their flickering candles and pressed linen napkins.

Harry was glad to see Pete Wheeler come in. He'd decided to eat at the Red Limit on the probability that somebody from the office, or from operations, would appear. He'd avoided coming right out and asking someone to join him for dinner since that would have entailed explanations, and he did not want to admit to anybody just yet that he'd lost his wife. He'd been giving serious thought to how he would break the news to his coworkers. He and Julie had agreed the marriage had ceased functioning and had decided it would be best for all concerned to terminate it. That would be the approach to take. After all, there was some truth to it. Somewhere.

Wheeler saw him right away and came over. "Well," he said, "I think we've impressed the Great Man."

"He came in impressed," said Harry.

"Ed's making plans to take him out to his condo for the weekend. I'm not sure he isn't more excited at having Rimford call him by his first name than by all the rest of this business." He smiled. "You ever been there, Harry?"

"Once." Gambini had a place overlooking the Atlantic near Snow Hill, Maryland. He retired to it most weekends, and even occasionally for extended periods when the mood struck him, and he felt his physical presence at Goddard was not necessary. The condo was tied in with the space center's communications and computer network though his external access to some of the more sensitive systems was necessarily restricted. "Anything new with Hercules?"

"No," said Wheeler. "The signal just keeps repeating."

"What's so funny?"

"I'm not sure. Leslie, probably. Ed's notion that we can bring in a psychologist to put the Altheans on a couch." He shook his head. "He always derided the attempts of Drake and Sagan and the SETI people to create a statistical basis for estimating the possibilities of civilizations in the galaxy, on the grounds that we were limited to a single sample. He's not very consistent."

They ordered drinks and steaks, and Harry settled back comfortably. "Are they really out there, Pete? Aliens, I mean. You looked convinced the other day."

"By the spectrograms? Actually, Harry, if it had been anybody but Ed, I think I'd have been persuaded right from the beginning. The evidence is hard to argue against. It's the concept that's difficult to buy. Especially when you consider that Ed wanted so badly to find something like this. That alone makes everything suspicious. He undermines his own credibility."

"Are you implying that some of this might be fraudulent?"

"No, no. Nothing like that. More the sheer lack of objectivity. The sense that some of Ed's enthusiasm might have rubbed off on the rest of us. And I know that doesn't make a lot of sense. But I hate jumping to conclusions. Even when—"

"—When—?"

"—There don't seem to be any alternative explanations."

The drinks arrived, rum and Coke for Wheeler, scotch and water for Harry. When the server withdrew, Harry picked up his glass, tasted it, and put it down. "Which means," he said, "you think we *do* have some sort of civilization in the Althean system."

"Call it an intelligence. Yes, there must be something there. And I suspect Rimford is telling that to Ed right about now. We're all headed for the history books, Harry."

"All of us?" Harry laughed. "Who was Columbus's first mate?" Nevertheless a sense of elation surged through him. It was nice to be part of a major discovery. Even if his role was limited to standing on the sidelines and cheering. Some of it must have shown because the people at the next table were watching him curiously. He didn't care, though. And that, too, was odd: Harry was always very concerned about how he was perceived by others.

Wheeler ignored his drink. "I can't help thinking," he said, "that we're bound to get some surprises out of this. Ed thinks he has everything under control, but there are too many unknowns here."

"How do you mean?"

"We keep assuming they're like us. For example, everybody's waiting for the follow-up message. But the Altheans have announced their presence. They may not see any reason to go further. After all, what have *they* got to gain?"

"I never thought about that," said Harry.

Pete's eyes were bright with mischief. "It could happen. It's really a pretty funny picture, in which our people get old waiting for the rest of a transmission that's already complete. Can you imagine what that would do to Ed and Majeski?"

"You're vindictive, Pete," Harry said in a light tone though he was nevertheless uncomfortable at Wheeler's amusement. "It would kill Ed."

"I suspect so. And I think that says a great deal about what Ed's done to himself." He tasted the drink and signaled his approval. "A number of things could happen. We tend to assume that any transmission will contain a lot of technological material."

"Why do you say that?"

"All the enthusiasm about communication from a civilization that can make stars and punch buttons on pulsars. It's not just a matter of getting a big hello out of the dark. These people all think we're going to learn stuff. Learn a lot. It's implicit in the way they address the subject.

"The Altheans may tell us how they did it. The pulsar and Gamma. Think what kind of boost that sort of knowledge would give us. I was listening to a conversation between Ed and Rimford this afternoon. They're talking in terms of GUTs."

"GUTs?"

"Grand Unified Theories. But this is a species that has had a technology of a very high order for a long time. They may take it pretty much for granted that everybody already knows the technical stuff. They may think it's too trivial to bother with. Or dangerous to another civilization."

"Dangerous? How could that be?"

He shrugged. "Maybe they've included instructions on how to build a pocket nuke on the cheap? Or how to make a lightbender."

"Slow down, Pete. What's a lightbender?"

"A way to make yourself invisible. Imagine what life would be like here if everyone could put on a jacket and become invisible."

"Well, I think this is getting a little far out."

"Sure it is. But the whole thing is far out. In any case, if we *do* get a textual transmission, a second message, I'd be surprised if they don't send us something entirely different from what we expect. Something they're proud of but which might not amuse Ed."

"For example?"

Wheeler's dark eyes glittered in the candlelight. More than the others, for whom cosmology and astronomy were primarily mathematical disciplines, he had the appearance of a man who understood what a light-year really was. "How about a novel?" he suggested. "A clash on a cosmic stage between creatures of advanced philosophies and alien emotions. Perhaps they would judge it to be their ultimate achievement and wish to share it with the universe at large. As we might wish to share *Hamlet*. But, of course, to us, even after translation, it might be incomprehensible."

Harry grinned. "I don't think NASA would be pleased."

"Maybe they'll send us a symphony."

Harry emptied his glass. "As long as it doesn't sound like 'Chopsticks.' But you don't really believe anything like that's going to happen?"

The steaks arrived. The server laid out the meals while Wheeler considered Harry's question. "Anything's possible in this kind of situation," he said at last. "We've no experience. And the senders can expect nothing in return save the satisfaction of having put out a signal that they probably believe no one will ever receive. You mentioned the plaques on the Pioneers and Voyagers. We didn't have room to say much on those, but even if we had, I'm sure it would never have occurred to anyone to put in the instructions for, say, splitting the atom, in case some fossil-powered civilization happened on it. No. We've already received the only significant message that will be coming. *We're here.* If there's more, I hope we have the sense to recognize it for what it is, extract whatever profit is to be had, and show whatever caution the occasion calls for."

The steaks were good, and the plates were heaped with wedge fries and toasted rolls. "There's too much," Harry said over his coffee.

"Are you working late tonight?" asked Wheeler, probably wondering why Harry wasn't eating at home.

"No." The word trailed off uncomfortably. Harry had known the priest longer than he'd known Gambini, but the relationship had always been at long range. Now he looked across the table, tempted again to take advantage of the opening and say something about Julie. Talk about it and get it out in the open. But how many pathetic stories had Wheeler been forced to listen to over the years simply because he wore a collar? "I gave the cook the night off," he said.

But Wheeler must have read the truth in his tone. He gazed carefully at Harry. Harry moved his dinner around. "You can do me a favor," the cosmologist said, finally. "I'm going out to Carthage for the evening. I'll be back tomorrow about noon."

He wrote down a number and passed it across the table. "Call me if anything changes. Okay?"

"Sure."

They got the check, split it, and walked outside. "How's Julie?" Wheeler asked casually.

Harry was surprised. "I didn't think you'd ever met her."

"She was at one of the director's brunches a couple of years ago." Wheeler looked toward the west and checked his watch. The moon had begun to settle toward the horizon. "The comet's gone."

Harry grunted something.

"She's a hard woman to forget," Wheeler added.

"Thanks," mumbled Harry. They crunched across the gravel toward Wheeler's car, a late-model beige Ford. "We're having a little trouble right now."

"I'm sorry to hear it."

Harry shrugged.

Wheeler looked around. "Where's your car?"

"It's at the front gate. I walked over."

"Come on," he said. "I'll take you back."

They pulled out of the parking area, crossed Greenbelt Road, and swung onto the lot at the main entrance. Wheeler glided to a stop beside Harry's Chrysler. "You got a few minutes to listen?" Harry asked.

"If you want to talk," said Wheeler.

He described the increasing tensions over the past months, Julie's conviction that he spent so much time at work that there was little left for the family, his own growing resentment that she seemed to refuse to understand his own professional commitments. He talked about the dinner with Julie on the night of the discovery, with its melancholy result and her subsequent departure. He concealed, or attempted to conceal, his indignation. When he'd finished, he folded his arms defensively. "You must have a lot of experience with this sort of thing, Pete. What's the chance it'll blow over?"

"I'm not sure how experienced I am," said Wheeler. "As a rule, Norbertines don't do much parish work, which is, of course, where you run into domestic problems. I haven't done *any*. But I can recommend a good counselor, if you like. You're not a Catholic, are you, Harry?"

"No."

"Doesn't matter. I can do that, or I can tell you what the consensus is on this sort of problem, how it happens, and the course of action that's usually prescribed."

"Go ahead," said Harry.

"From what you've told me, there's no second man, there's no strain over money, no heavy drinking, and no one's being assaulted. Usually, when there's no obvious cause for a breakup in a marriage that's been going reasonably well for a number of years, what's happened is that the two people have stopped sharing a single life. Each has slipped into an orbit of his or her own, and the two probably don't converge much, except at meals and bedtime. The people involved may not even be aware of it, but the marriage becomes boring, for one or both.

"You're near the top of your profession, Harry. How many nights a week do you work?"

"Two or three," said Harry, uncomfortable at the turn things had taken. "Sometimes more."

"How about weekends?"

"About one a month."

"Only one?"

"Well, actually I work part of every weekend." Harry squirmed. "But my job demands it. It's not a nine-to-five kind of thing."

"I see," said Wheeler. "When you're not here, they have to close the space center."

That hit a nerve. Harry glared silently at the priest.

"Sorry," said Wheeler. "Learn to delegate. Give some of your help a chance. They'll do fine."

"Pete, a lot of this stuff, I just have to be here—"

"You know, Harry, I still occasionally do some of the sacred functions."

Harry blinked at him. "I don't follow."

"People get seriously ill, they take to their deathbeds, they send for me."

"Okay."

"Last face some of them see is mine."

"Okay."

"Not one of them has ever told me he has to hang on

because they can't get along without him down at the office."
A brisk wind moved through the trees along the edge of the
lot. "Chances are," he continued, "when you *are* home, you
don't have much time for her, either."

Harry was beginning to feel picked on. "No," he said. "I
don't think that's true. We go out fairly regularly, to movies
and the theater and to local clubs."

"You'd know better than I."

"This kind of thing happen often? I mean, between people
who've been married awhile? I thought once you got past the
first couple of years, you were reasonably safe."

"It happens all the time."

"What can I do?" asked Harry. "I don't think she's going to
be open to small talk right now."

Wheeler nodded. "Harry, marriages are hard to salvage
once they go bad. I'm sorry to tell you that. I only met your
wife once, but she struck me as a woman who doesn't act hast-
ily. If that's true, it might be hard to win her back. But I think
you can make the effort.

"I'd try to get her away from all the old associations, take
her somewhere for a couple of days just to talk things over.
Make it as nonthreatening as you can, but get her to a location
where neither of you has been before. And then talk with her.
Not about the marriage or your job or your other problems.
Just try to take it from the start. You and she."

"It would never work," said Harry quietly. "Not now."

"That's certainly true if you've decided it's true. Still, you've
nothing to lose. I can even offer you the ideal location."

"The Norbertines are in the motel business?"

"As it happens," said Wheeler, "we have a novitiate near
Basil Point on Chesapeake Bay. It was donated to us a few
years ago, but the truth is that it's of no practical use. It's too
big. The property's in a magnificent location, with a lovely
view of the bay. I usually make it a point to go out there when
I'm in the Washington area. There are only about half a dozen
of our people there now. One of them, by the way, is Rene
Sunderland, who's probably the best bridge player in the state.

"It has a couple of big houses that we've turned into an abbey
and a seminary. But the seminary only has two students."

"Doesn't sound like much of a future," said Harry.

"That's a subject for another time." Wheeler turned on the car's heater. Harry suddenly became aware that the temperature had dropped, and his feet were cold.

"Back in the nineties," Wheeler continued, "the owners added a lodge. We keep it available for visiting dignitaries, but we just don't see many of those. The only ones we ever get are the abbot and the director of the National Confraternity of Christian Doctrine, both of whom like to play bridge with Rene. That means they stay in the main building. Consequently, the lodge has been unused for about four years. I'm sure I could have it made available for a good cause."

Harry thought it over. Maybe that was what he should have tried Saturday night instead of the goddam poverty-stricken play in Bellwether. But now it was a bit late. "Thanks, Pete," he said. "I'll keep it in mind."

Usually, Wheeler enjoyed the two-hour ride to Carthage. But that evening, he crossed a barren landscape of skeletal trees and long brown grass and flat hills. There was decay in the motionless air, as though *this* Route 50 had detoured through time and curved back now through a Virginia grown old.

The highway weaved and dipped through bleak furrowed pastures, past abandoned tractors and combines. Shadowy farmhouses stood apart from the road. Occasional junk cars, their engines and carburetors spread on wooden boards or hung from trees, were sunk hubcap deep in dust and dried mud alongside ramshackle barns.

Out near Middleburg, he turned on a talk show. He paid no attention to it, but the sound of voices was soothing.

At first he thought it was Harry's problem that was bothering him. But there was something else, something deeper, connected not with one more marriage gone to ruin but with the thing in Hercules. The constellation was invisible at the moment, hidden by a few drifting clouds. Ahead, toward Carthage, the sky was heavy and without stars. Occasional lightning glimmered on the horizon.

It was a familiar, if ominous, cloudscape. In recent years, Wheeler had come to love the familiar and the nearby, to cherish things that one could touch, or know directly, stone and sand and rain and trees. Polished mahogany and chilled glass-ware. The hand of a child. The long barrel of a telescope.

But as human vision penetrated ever farther into the night, the things of Earth receded. Every step forward always implied something lost. You get Galileo, and humans get shoved out of the center of things. You get TV, you lose back-porch conversations. He wondered what they'd lose when the Hercules event had ended. And it occurred to him that every-one might be better off if the gathering storm could drown any future signal.

Just past Interstate 81, the windshield began to pick up spray.

It was almost eleven o'clock when he arrived, under a steady drizzle, in Carthage. Saint Catherine's tower, with its big gray cross, rose out of the center of the commercial dis-trict. He swung behind the church and eased onto the small parking lot used by the priests and staff. A cruising police car paused, watched him get out, and continued on.

The rectory was a two-story, flat, brick building. A light burned at the rear, over a door slick with rain. As he approached, the door opened, more lights came on, and Jack Peoples appeared. Jack waved, extended a hand for his bag, and pulled him inside.

He never seemed to change much. He'd added a few pounds since the last time Wheeler had seen him. But his hair was still black, and he still radiated energy, still projected enthusiasm when inspired by the right cause. There had been few enough of those in recent years, given the continuing backward drift of the Church toward the nineteenth century.

Had things gone differently for Peoples, Wheeler supposed, had he not been born into an old-line Catholic family that had traditionally sent most of its sons into the priesthood—though from his generation, only Jack had received the call—he might have been a moderately successful accountant or computer technician. He had talent in those directions. He was also a man who inspired confidence. "Good to see you, Pete," he said, glancing up past the bell tower at the murky sky. "Looks like heavy weather."

Jack had been one of those young priests who'd jumped on the Vatican II bandwagon, who'd worn themselves out offering relevance to sex-ridden adolescents and guitar Masses to weary parents. He'd been one of the first to tear out the kneeling benches, but the Community of God had never really arrived. The Almighty remained at His customary distance, and in the end, the parishioners who were to find joy and peace in one another went back to worrying about careers and mortgages in lives more hermetically sealed than ever, leaving Jack Peoples, and others like him, buried in the wreckage.

They'd met twenty years before in a speech seminar and traded visits back and forth ever since. The older priest was a fountain of Church lore and gossip, wryly dispensed with a wit that would have got him in trouble with the cardinal, had some of the stories got back.

Tonight, Wheeler's visit had a formal purpose: to celebrate with Jack his simultaneous elevation to monsignor and appointment as pastor of St. Catherine's. The appointment had been effective the previous Sunday. It was long overdue: Jack had been the only priest there for three years.

Wheeler declared his pleasure at the changes in Jack's status, fully aware that the older man, still a rebel, would shrug it off as of no serious consequence. Nevertheless, he could see that Jack was pleased.

He took his bag up to his room—the same one was always prepared for him when he came to St. Catherine's—showered, and returned downstairs to the pastor's office.

Jack put down a book and broke out some apple brandy. "How's the program going at Georgetown?" he asked.

The rain had picked up and was rattling against the windows. "I got a break," Wheeler said. He sat down on a worn-out leather couch. "I don't know whether I told you or not, but the course is a survey of Baines Rimford's work. And Rimford just turned up in town. I think I can get him to come out to the university for an evening."

They whiled much of the night away discussing church politics. Jack, who had left the Norbertines early in his career to become a diocesan priest, tended to attach considerable importance to the ecclesiastical decision-making process, as though it had a serious effect on world affairs. For Wheeler, whose perspectives had been altered by his visits to the cosmic gulfs, the Church's power structure had acquired a ghostly ambience.

Abruptly, somewhere around 2:00 A.M., when the cheese and the dip were exhausted and a second bottle stood empty on an end table, Wheeler realized that he wanted to talk about Hercules. There'd been a lull in the conversation, and Jack had gone out through glass doors to put some coffee on. Like the adjoining church, the rectory had been built near the end of the nineteenth century. Its delicately carved balusters, hanging lights, and glass-enclosed bookshelves were meticulously maintained. Numerous volumes of standard theological works were packed into the wall behind the pastor's desk, along with books on church finance, several collections of sermons, and a handful of Dickens novels that someone had donated and Jack kept prominently on display. "For my retirement," he'd told Wheeler.

Wheeler followed him into the kitchen. He was filling a plate with Danish pastries. "Jack," he said, "something's been happening at Goddard. Actually, it's the reason Rimford's in D.C."

He outlined the events of the past week. Jack often served as a sounding board against whom Wheeler bounced various speculations. It was a role he'd come to relish, and with it the implied compliment to a parish priest who was thoroughly grounded in Thomas Aquinas and little else. This time, however, the usual array of obscure concepts was missing. Jack listened, nodded occasionally, and chewed on his lower lip.

"What do *you* think it is?" he asked when Wheeler had finished.

"I think we've heard from another species."

Jack smiled. "They're not going to like it at the Vatican," he said. "It doesn't really violate anything, but it's doctrinally uncomfortable." He filled two cups and passed one to Wheeler. "You say the transmission was sent a million years ago?"

"Yep."

"That's a long time, Pete. They're dead and gone by now. Probably the entire civilization, if that's really what it was."

In the silence that followed, the electric clock atop the refrigerator got very loud. "When are they going to announce it? Was it on the news tonight?"

Wheeler sipped his coffee. "They're holding on as long as they can. No one wants to take a chance on having the organization look silly. So there'll be nothing official until there's no question what the signal means."

"*Is* there a question?"

"Not in my opinion." They wandered back toward Jack's office.

"I wonder," said the pastor, "if it'll have much effect outside." He was referring to the world beyond the church doors. "It's hard to know how people will react to something like that."

Wheeler resumed his seat on the sofa. "I doubt it'll change anything. The faith survived finding out that the Earth moved, and later that we were clearly not at the center of things. It'll survive this."

Jack was leaning back on the edge of his desk. "What about you?"

Wheeler sat thoughtfully staring at the theology books. "To me," he said, "it's just one more tear in the fabric. For whom did Jesus die?"

Jack drew himself up until he was sitting on the desk. This was the kind of conversation he loved although he would never have allowed any but a handful of his colleagues to engage him in such a debate, which might conceivably weaken a lesser faith than his. "For the children of Adam," he said quietly. "Other groups will have to make their own arrangements."

"But Adam never existed. We both know that."

He shrugged. "I was speaking metaphorically, and we both know *that*. Jesus's death was a demonstration of love. For *us*. That's not to say God doesn't love all His creatures, but here at least He appeared in human form. And He died in that form. It's hard to miss the point."

"Jack, to be honest with you, I find this business uncomfortable. I was convinced, I've always believed, that we were alone. There are probably *billions* of terrestrial worlds out there. Once admit a second creation, and where do you stop? Surely, among all those stars, there'll be a third. And a millionth. Where does it end?"

"I don't think any of that matters. God is infinite. We've always said that, haven't we? Maybe we're about to find out what the word really means."

"Maybe," said Wheeler. "But we're also conditioned to think of the crucifixion as the central event of history. The supreme sacrifice, offered by God Himself, out of love for the creature made in His image."

"And—?"

"How can we take seriously the agony of a God who repeats His passion? Who dies again and again, in endless variations, on countless worlds, across a universe that may itself be infinite?"

———

Shortly before dawn, after an exhausted Jack Peoples had gone to bed, Wheeler roamed through the rectory, examining stained-glass windows, thumbing through books, and for a while standing just outside the front door. The wet street glistened in the reflection from an all-night drugstore.

The church was built in a style that Wheeler thought of as Ohio Gothic: squat, urban, rectangular, gray stone, with a blockish tower. Its windows were populated by lambs and doves and kneeling angels. The rectory stood at right angles to the larger structure. Between the two buildings lay a fenced-off grass plot, containing the tomb of Father Whitcomb, the parish's first pastor. A rough-hewn stone cross stood guard, with his dates.

The clouds were clearing, and a handful of stars floated over the church tower. The sky to the east beyond the warehouses had begun to lighten.

Why is creation so large? Skynet looks out across fifteen billion light-years, to the Red Limit, the edge of the observable universe. But it is an "edge" only in the sense that there had not been time for light coming from even more remote places to reach terrestrial telescopes. There's every reason to believe that an observer placed at the Red Limit, the cosmological Red Limit, not the bar, would see in all directions much the same sort of sky that bends over Virginia. In a sense, Wheeler thought, St. Catherine's itself, at this moment, is at the edge of someone's observable universe.

If there was any truth at all to the old conviction that the universe had been designed for man, why was so much of its expanse beyond any hope of human perception? *Forever?*

Or so far it could never affect him in any way?

Wheeler turned back inside, locked the door, and wandered through the connecting corridor into the church and through the sacristy. He emerged near the pulpit.

The glow of the sanctuary lamp fell across long rows of pews. Security lights in the rear illuminated holy-water fonts and the stations of the cross. He could still see the worn places in the marble floor where worshippers stopped regularly to burn candles in the alcoves of St. Anthony and Our Lady of Victory. The old marble altar, which had served in the days of the Tridentine Mass, had long since been removed and replaced with the modern butcher block that clashed with the decor and architecture in all but the relatively new churches.

He came outside the altar rail, genuflected, and sat down in the front pew.

The air was heavy, filled with the sickly-sweet smell of melted wax. High behind the altar, in a circular stained-glass window, Jesus sat serenely by a running brook.

He was remote now, a painted figure, a friend from childhood. As a boy, Wheeler had occasionally, in the exuberant presumption of youth, asked for a sign, not to confirm his faith, which in those days needed no confirmation, but as a mark of special favor. A bond between friends. But Jesus had remained silent then, as now. Who, or what, had walked along the Jordan with the Twelve? Too many times, Wheeler thought, I've looked through the telescopes. And I've seen only rock and the light-years.

Ah, Lord, if I doubt You, it is perhaps because You hide Yourself so well.

————

At about the same time, in the operations center, Linda Barrister was filling in the lines of a *New York Times* crossword puzzle. She was good at them, and they helped keep her reasonably alert when her body ached for sleep. She was trying to recall the name of a Russian river with seven letters when she was suddenly aware that something had changed. She checked her watch. It was precisely 4:30 A.M.

The auxiliary overhead monitor carrying the TDRSS relay from Hercules X-3 was silent. The signal had stopped.

MONITOR

MICHAEL PAPPADOPOULIS ADDRESSES THE NATIONAL PRESS CLUB, OCTOBER 1

WHERE IS EVERYONE? Recently, Edward Gambini of NASA spoke to the annual Astronomical Symposium at the University of Minnesota, supposedly on the subject of the interior mechanics of class K stars. During his remarks he addressed himself to the question of stable biozones, the probable time periods necessary for the development of a living planet, and finally—or inevitably if we can accept his logic—the appearance of technological civilization.

I'm somewhat puzzled as to the connection between science fiction and the mechanics of class K stars. It seems these days that no matter where Dr. Gambini goes, nor what his proposed subject matter, he eventually finds himself talking about extraterrestrials. Little green men. And presumably little green women. (Laughter)

Two weeks prior to the Minnesota exercise, he was in New York to speak at a meeting of Scientists Concerned About the Disposal of Nuclear Weapons, presumably to discuss a strategy for ridding the world of these cumbersome hazards. What the Concerned Scientists actually got, however, was a plea that we restrain our destructive instincts so that we can ultimately join the "galactic club" we will one day discover.

I can think of more pressing reasons to maintain strict controls over the various national stockpiles of nuclear weapons.

The fact is that anyone who invites Edward Gambini to speak on anything can expect to hear about aliens. And SETI.

If all this strikes us as a little bit odd, it becomes almost grotesque when we realize that Skynet, to which Dr. Gambini has access, has looked quite closely at local planetary systems and found nothing that supports the idea that anything might be alive out there.

Many people have argued compellingly that this result implies that we are indeed alone in the universe. It is a position with which any reasonable person would be hard-pressed to argue.

There is an even more telling point to be made. Surely, if civilizations were to develop with any sort of regularity, which in the statistically immense soup dish of the universe they would have to if they were to develop at all, the Milky Way would, after these last several billion years, be overrun with them. There would be tourists and exporters and missionaries everywhere.

Even one civilization, using relatively unsophisticated vehicles for interstellar travel, the sort of vehicle that we ourselves should be able to build in another century or so, would by now have filled every habitable world in the Milky Way and points west. So if they're there, as Enrico Fermi asked in the last century, why haven't we seen them?

Where is everybody?

||| FIVE |||

Harry had never known a colder October in Washington. The sky turned white, and drizzly knife-edged winds sliced through the bone. Temperatures dropped below freezing on the first of the month and stayed there. He was, of course, delighted. The assorted pollen that sometimes hung on until nearly Christmas was damped down, and he could count on seven months before the cottonwood and poplar would unleash his allergies again. In late summer and autumn, Harry loved terrible weather.

That was also the month Harry conceded his son. He could see no way to provide a home for the boy without Julie. And the fact humiliated him because he knew that Tommy expected his father to put up more of a fight.

He was playing in a bantam basketball league with other third and fourth graders. Julie went to all the games, and Harry had always gone when he could, which was fairly often. For the most part, the boy played well, and Harry was proud, not only of his individual skills but of his relationship with the others on the team.

But after the separation, Julie became uncomfortable in Harry's company, and she suggested they work out a schedule to divide the responsibilities. He reluctantly agreed.

At home, the gas heater didn't sound very good. It banged and hammered and threw loose parts around. He called the service contractor, who cleaned it, charged eighty-five dollars, and went away. After that, the thing stopped working altogether. Harry had to buy a new one.

The Hercules group remained silent, and hope faded that the transmission would be followed swiftly by a second signal. Toward the end of the month, Wheeler's suspicion that the aliens might indeed have nothing more to say began to gain respectability. But silence, Gambini argued, was not the natural state of a pulsar.

So they continued to watch.

The second Thursday of November was a bleak, wintry day that clawed the last of the leaves out of the elms behind the Business Operations Section. Rosenbloom showed up unannounced at the space center and summoned Harry and Gambini to the director's suite. "I think both your careers," he said without preamble, "are about to take off. The President has been informed about Hercules, and he'll be making a statement tomorrow afternoon from the White House. He'd like both of you to be there. Three o'clock."

"Why *me*?" asked Harry.

Rosenbloom looked at him suspiciously. "I was wondering about that myself, Harry. He asked for you specifically. By name."

"That amazes me. The President knows *me*?"

The director glowered at him. "Apparently," he said.

And Harry realized what it was: the Clinton Effect. All the presidents succeeding Bill Clinton had picked up his technique of presenting persons who had been on the scene when things happened. Preferably these were heroes of a sort, but most important, they were ordinary Americans who had been on the scene when good things happened. No VIPs. So the President had done his homework and come up with Harry. Harry had done nothing heroic, but he was superbly ordinary.

Since Rosenbloom spent so little time at Goddard, the director's suite smelled of furniture polish. He lowered himself into a chair beneath a charcoal of Stonehenge. "Ed," he said, "you'll probably be asked to say a few words. The reporters will damned well want to talk to you in any case. You might think about what you're going to say. I suggest you try to come up with some immediate benefits we've gotten out of the Hercules contact or out of the technology we've used. Probably there'll be some peripherals into laser surgery or fiber optics or something. You know, the same way we handled the space program. Look into it." He shook his head as if he were sending the uninformed into battle. "Under no circumstances do we want to speculate about another signal. I would like to take the tack that the intercept suggests engineering on a large scale far away. *Very* far away. You cannot overemphasize the distance. We should leave the impression that the incident is over, and we now know we're not alone. And let it go at that. We do not know anything else. Whatsoever."

"What's the President going to say?" asked Gambini. His mouth was set in an angry line.

"*What hath God wrought?* Same old thing. Even as we speak, I understand he has his people hunting for appropriate biblical remarks."

Gambini laced his fingers across his stomach. "It should be an uplifting show. But if it's all the same to you, Quint, you and Harry go. I think I'll pass on this one."

"You don't have that option," said Rosenbloom stiffly.

The two glared at each other. "I'm not exactly proud of the fact," said Gambini, "that we kept this quiet for, what is it now, two months? Some people out there are going to be very unhappy with us, including some prospective future employers, and granters of prizes, and I'd just as soon not be too visible."

Rosenbloom waved his hand as if he were flicking away an insect. "I understand your feelings, Ed. Nevertheless, it's a command performance." He turned to Harry. "I don't think they'll want you to do anything more than take a bow. But you'll have reporters to deal with, too."

"I'm an administrative type. They won't expect technical stuff from me."

"Media types can't read. They'll know you're with the Agency, and that's all they'll be aware of. Same guidelines as Ed's, okay? No speculation. No crazy predictions. By the way. I'd just as soon we not bring up this artificial-sun business. It sounds kind of goofy. Let's go for lots of talk about the vast distance between them and us. Right? If Julius Caesar had sent off an Apollo flight, it wouldn't be there yet. *That* sort of thing. No chance of the aliens dropping by. And maybe you could come up with one of those scale illustrations where Earth is an orange, and the aliens are over in Europe somewhere. Or on the moon. Yeah: The moon's better. Okay?"

"Somebody," said Harry, "is going to wonder why we waited so long to make this public. What's our answer?"

"Tell them the truth. We literally did not believe our instruments. We had to wait for confirmation. We wanted to be sure before we said anything. Nobody can object to that."

"If you think so," said Gambini, "*you* stand out there."

"I'll be available to the media, Ed. Have no fear."

After they'd left the director's office, Gambini grumbled about his proposed role in the press conference. "Play it for all it's worth," advised Harry. "You might take some heat, but you'll get some long-range benefits as well. After tomorrow, the whole country will know who you are."

———————

To Harry's surprise, no one, not even Ed Gambini, seemed more caught up in the Hercules Project than Leslie Davies. After the initial series of conferences, she'd returned to her Philadelphia office, but she came back to Goddard every few days to spend time with the investigators, to be on the spot, Harry thought, when history was made. "It has to happen," she told Harry expectantly. "Ed's right. If something weren't on its way, the pulsar would be back to normal."

She invited him to dinner, and Harry gratefully accepted. The only other staff members who lived bachelor lives, and who were consequently available as dinner companions, were Wheeler and Gambini. But the priest was back at Princeton, and Gambini showed little inclination for company.

At Harry's suggestion, they skipped the Red Limit and drove instead to the Coachman in College Park, which offered a more exotic atmosphere. "Leslie," he said after they were settled at a table, "I don't really understand why you're so interested in all this. I wouldn't think a psychologist would care much one way or the other."

"Why not?" she asked, startled.

"It's not your field."

She smiled. It was a deep-water response, reserved, non-committal, amused. "Whose field is it? Harry, anybody who wouldn't be absorbed by the Hercules contact is dead. Or should be."

"Yeah," Harry said. "I guess it was kind of a dumb thing to say."

"Anyway," she continued, "I wonder whether any of these people have the potential for professional profit I do. For Ed and Pete, the project is only of philosophical interest. I shouldn't say 'only,' I suppose, because that's where the primary payoff will be."

The server showed up, took their orders, crab cakes for Harry, the catch of the day for Leslie. And some white wine.

"But I may be the only person here," she continued, "with a serious professional stake. Listen, if there *are* Altheans, they can be of only academic interest to an astronomer or a mathematician. Their specialties have no direct connection to the existence, or nonexistence, of thinking beings. That's *my* province, Harry. If there *is* a second transmission, if we get anything at all that we can translate, I'll get the first glimpse into a nonhuman psyche. Do you have any idea what that means?"

"No," said Harry. "I haven't a clue."

"Maybe more important than learning about Altheans, we might get a handle on qualities that are characteristic of intelligent creatures as opposed to those that are culturally induced. For example, will the Altheans turn out to be, or to have been, a hunting species? Will they have a code of ethics? Are they subject to mental illness? To irrational behavior on a wide scale?"

"Such as?"

"War. Crime. Do they subscribe to group mythologies that induce antisocial behavior?"

"Religion," said Harry. "And politics."

"Call it tribalism. And do they indulge in individual acts of cruelty? Are they a race of benevolent beings? Or do they fall somewhere between?

"Have they an aesthetic concept? Do they like music, or is that purely a human aberration? Do they keep lethal weapons in their homes? Do they organize themselves into large social groups?" She canted her head and looked at him from beneath lowered lids. "Well, I guess we've already answered that last one. Without political organization, you wouldn't get large-scale engineering projects. And we know they've a taste to be heard by someone else."

The wine arrived. Harry tasted it, nodded his approval, and

the server filled their glasses. "You think we'll get all those questions answered?" he asked when they were alone again.

She shrugged. "Probably not. If they do nothing more than say hello, we'll be left to wonder about them, and they'll become an intriguing mystery, never to be solved. In the end, we may not learn a lot about the Altheans, but we stand to learn a lot about ourselves."

Harry had gotten into the noxious habit of comparing every woman who in any way stirred his interest with Julie. Although Leslie was not unattractive, she lacked the native sensuality of his wife. It was not, he realized, simply a matter of matching an ordinary human being against Julie's classic features. There was also the fact that Leslie was more accessible. Friendlier. And oddly, that, too, counted against her. What sort of comment was *that* on the perversity of human nature? "Did you know," he asked, "that the White House is going to make an announcement tomorrow?"

"Ed told me. I'm going to plant myself in a bar in Arlington and take notes on the customers' reactions." She smiled at him again. It was an innocent gesture, carrying no agenda save to signal that she was enjoying herself. It had been a long time since he'd seen a similar display from Julie.

"Leslie, if they were going to send another signal, why would they wait so long?"

She shrugged. "I can think of *some* reasons. Maybe it's just a matter of getting the equipment ready. Or getting the message ready. Maybe they're a lot like us, and there's a committee arguing about propriety and content. Maybe we're only listening to a computer, and something's burned out. I'll tell you one thing: If we don't get another transmission, you're going to have a real problem with Ed." She was obviously enjoying the wine, but her face grew serious. "How well do you know him?" she asked.

"Ed? I've worked with him off and on for a long time."

"He lives in heart-attack country. Doesn't he do anything other than sit in front of computers?"

"He looks through telescopes."

"That's it?"

"Pretty much. Years ago, when I first met him, he used to

go to Canada on hunting trips. But he got bored with them. Or got feeling sorry for the deer, or something. I don't remember. Anyhow, it's pretty hard to imagine him in a bowling alley or on a golf course."

"He needs something." Her eyes grew distant. "He's so obsessed with trying to analyze the architecture of the cosmos that he never sees a sunrise. Baines isn't like that. Nor Pete. I wish he'd learn something from them."

———

Neither Harry nor Gambini had previously been to the White House in an official capacity. In fact, Gambini freely admitted that, despite having lived a substantial portion of his adult life in Washington, he'd never before been inside the building. They entered, as instructed, through a connecting tunnel from the Treasury Department and were escorted to a first-floor office, where they found Rosenbloom and a self-important, energetic man whom Harry recognized as Abraham Chilton, the administration's press secretary.

Chilton had been a highly popular conservative radio and TV commentator before joining the White House staff. He had a voice like a whip crack and a debater's skill that served him well in his daily jousts with the press. He looked point-edly at his watch as Gambini and Harry entered. "I'd appreci-ate it," he said, "if you gentlemen could contrive in future to arrive on time."

"We were told three o'clock," objected Gambini.

"The press conference starts at three. You didn't want to walk in there cold, did you? *We* start, or try to, at two." Rosen-bloom looked uncomfortable. "Which of you is Gambini?"

The physicist nodded frostily.

"The President will ask you to say a few words." He reached into a briefcase and withdrew a single sheet of paper. "We'd like your remarks to be along these lines. Try to sound spontane-ous." He threw Harry off stride with a sudden laconic grin that suggested no one should take any of this too seriously. But as quickly as Harry defined the sense of the gesture, it was gone.

"The three of you will be seated in the front row when the President enters. He'll make a statement. Then he'll introduce each of you and invite *you* to the lectern." He indicated Gambini.

"Dr. Gambini, when you're cued to speak, do so, be brief, and turn it back to the President. But stay up there in case he needs you. Don't forget to stay with the script. After that, the President will take questions. We'll close it out after thirty minutes. When Eddie Young asks his question, that'll be it. Young's a little guy with blond hair, except that most of it is gone now. He's from NPR. He'll be sitting right behind Dr. Rosenbloom. After the President leaves, you gentlemen will find yourselves subject to a barrage of questions. We'd debated getting you out of here quickly to prevent that, but there's no point. They'll catch up with you wherever you go, so we might as well get it over with. Anything unclear so far?"

"I won't be saying anything?" asked Harry.

"No. Just stand when he mentions your name and smile at the cameras." He scrunched up his features as if he were trying to decide whether he'd forgotten anything, and apparently decided not. "Okay. We don't have much time left. Let's go over what the reporters are likely to ask."

———

John W. Hurley strode smiling through the curtains and took his place behind the lectern that bore the presidential seal. A flip chart was set to his immediate right; the NASA Administrator, Ames Atkin, sat to his left. Hurley was of less than average height, the shortest president in modern memory, and consequently a running target for "short" jokes. Cartoonists loved to portray him talking things over with Washington, Lincoln, or Wilson. But he responded in good humor, laughed at the jokes himself, and even told a few. His lack of stature, usually a fatal handicap to serious political ambitions, became a symbol of the man in the street. Hurley was the president everyone identified with.

Approximately two hundred people were packed into the small auditorium. Television dollies rolled up and down the central aisle as the President graciously acknowledged the applause, looked squarely down at Harry in the front row, and smiled. "Ladies and gentlemen," he said, "I know you've all seen the numbers on the economy that came out today, and you expect me to do a little crowing this afternoon. Truth is, I don't intend to mention the subject." Laughter rippled through the room. The fact was that, while the President's point of view generally tended to be well to the right of most of the members of the press corps, he was nevertheless popular with them.

He looked out at his audience with sudden gravity. They grew quiet. "I have an announcement of some importance," he said. Pens came out, all other movement stopped. "On Sunday morning, September 17, shortly before dawn, the United States intercepted a signal that appears to have had an extraterrestrial origin." Harry was struck by the absolute stillness in the crowded room. In back, somebody muffled a cough. "Our scientists tell us the transmission originated from a small group of stars outside our own galaxy. These stars are located in the constellation Hercules and are, I am informed, extremely far from Earth. Far too distant to permit any possibility of a two-way conversation. Mr. Atkin tells me"—nod to Atkin—"that the signals started on their way toward us one and a half million years ago."

Chairs scraped, but still, except for some startled exclamations, the press corps held its collective breath.

"There was no message. The transmission was simply a mathematical progression that apparently leaves itself open to no other interpretation than the one I have given you. I should take a moment, by the way, to point out that this achievement would not have been possible without Skynet.

"We are continuing to monitor the star group, but it has been silent now for several weeks, and we don't expect to hear any more." He paused, and when he spoke again, his voice was thick with emotion. "We know nothing, really, about those who have announced their presence to us. We cannot hope ever to talk with them. I am given to understand that their star group is receding from us at a rate of approximately eighty miles per second. It is reaching us only now because of the great distances involved.

"It's unfortunate that these . . . beings . . . did not see fit to tell us something about themselves. But they *have* told us something about the universe in which we live. We now know we are not alone."

Still no one moved. One of the TV technicians, riding on the back of a dolly, briefly lost his balance. "Two of the men

responsible for the discovery are here," the President continued. "I'd like them to join me now to help answer any technical
questions you may have: Ames Atkin, the Administrator of
NASA, and Dr. Ed Gambini, who leads the research team at
the Goddard Space Flight Center." Someone began to clap, and
that broke the spell. The room erupted into thunderous
applause. Harry, who'd expected to be recognized with the others, was both relieved and disappointed at being overlooked.

Atkin got up. He was a majestic presence, gray, deliberate,
intellectual. He gazed out at the audience and smoothly tossed
back the first page of the flip chart. He delivered a quick
course in pulsars, using a series of illustrations assembled that
afternoon under Majeski's direction. He described the Althean
system, discussed the distances involved, and invoked a touch
of poetry to compare the incident to ships passing in the night.

The President thanked him and turned it over to Gambini,
who looked surprisingly nervous. The project manager briefly
recounted his reaction the first evening, his initial disbelief,
then the awareness that he was being overtaken by history.
The line was right out of his instructions, and he sounded
wooden while delivering it. He stayed within the parameters
set for him by the White House, but he was clearly angered. It
had been, he said, a near-religious experience, realizing there
was someone out there. "The mind that sent the Hercules
transmission," he said, "recognized that no habitable world
could exist within less than a million light-years. And so it
needed a transmitter of incredible power. It used a star." And
here was the only place at which he wandered from the script:
"Anyone wishing to say hello across such an immense distance, down the span of one and a half million years, sounds
to me to be very much like ourselves. I can understand that
imperative, as I suspect everyone in this room can. Whatever
is out there, whatever its technology might be, it has some
characteristics that *we* can recognize. And we are fortunate to
have made its acquaintance."

When he had finished, they took questions. A political col-
umnist for the *Washington Post*, referring to Beta, asked how
an object only a few kilometers in diameter could have such a
destructive effect on a star so much larger than the sun. Gambini tried to describe Beta's density, and the President,

demonstrating his touch for the picturesque, suggested that the newsmen think of it as an iron sun. "Yes," observed Gambini appreciatively. "Though iron would never do that thing justice. A matchbox full of the stuff would weigh more than North America."

That remark drew skeptical questions. Surely Dr. Gambini was exaggerating.

A reporter from the *Wall Street Journal* was recognized: "If the signal took one and a half million years to get here, they must all be dead. Anybody want to comment on that?"

Atkin gave it as his opinion that the Altheans, by this time, were undoubtedly gone.

Someone wondered whether it was possible that any of the aliens, in the distant past, might have visited Earth?

"No," said Gambini, who could not conceal the fact that he found the question entertaining. "I think we can say with confidence that they've never been much closer than they are now."

"Then there's no military threat?" That came from the *Chicago Tribune*'s representative.

The President laughed and reassured the world.

"Do we have any idea what they look like?"

"Do they have a name?"

"Where are they going now?" That last was from an ABC correspondent, a young black woman with a dazzling smile. "And isn't Alpha a prime candidate to explode?"

Gambini was impressed. "They're headed toward the globular cluster NGC6341, but it won't be there when they arrive." To answer the second part of the question, he began a discussion of H-R diagrams and stellar evolution which the President broke into, gently, explaining that Gambini might want to go into detail for those who were interested after the general meeting broke up.

Hurley took his last question from Ed Young of NPR: "Sir, do you see any effect on international tensions as a result of this incident?"

He sidestepped adroitly. "Ed," he observed, "there's been a notion around for some years now that technological civilizations self-destruct, that we can expect to blow ourselves up at some point in the near future, and that nothing can prevent it.

At least we are reassured that that need not happen. Dr. Atkin informs me that a civilization would have to be quite old to manipulate stellar bodies in the manner that has happened here. So with that encouragement, the Hercules transmission should prove beneficial to all the nations of the Earth." He turned, waved at his audience, wished them good day, shook a few hands, and was gone.

———————

Harry unlocked the front door, dropped his briefcase on the floor, threw his coat over the back of the sofa, and turned on a lamp. He sank into an upholstered chair and reached for the TV remote. The house was filled with noises, an upstairs clock, the refrigerator, the quiet murmur of power in the walls. A plastic paperweight, inscribed "SUPERMAN works here," which Tommy had given him at Christmas, rested atop his desk.

His impression that Gambini had performed well at the press conference was borne out by the coverage. The physicist, once over his initial nervousness, had displayed dedication and competence. He was a gray figure, perhaps, beside the President's colorful showman and the aristocratic Administrator, but he rose almost to eloquence on several occasions. And anyone who knew the project manager would not have missed the wistfulness with which he responded to questions about the fifty days of silence.

The media reports themselves were restrained, considering the enormity of the story. Holden Bennett, on CBS, began with the simple statement, "We are no longer alone." Virtually the entire thirty-minute newscast was devoted to the press conference, with an announcement of a one-hour special at nine. There were clips of the space center and the Research Projects Laboratory.

The networks also ran shots of slowed traffic on Greenbelt Road as people who'd heard the news earlier in the day scrambled to get a look at the site of the discovery. In fact, with the trees bare, the lab itself was visible from the highway.

Man-in-the-street interviews revealed mixed interest. Some people were excited, but many felt that the country was spending too much money on projects of no conceivable benefit to anybody at a time when the taxpayers were being asked to shoulder a crushing burden. A few people wondered whether, despite the assurances of politicians, an invasion might be a real threat. Others tried to connect Hercules with Roswell.

Reports from Paris, London, Brussels, and other capitals indicated that European reaction was unruffled. Beijing denounced the United States for withholding the information so long, arguing that the event was of supreme importance to all nations. The Chinese premier went on TV to wonder what else the American government knew that it was keeping to itself.

CNN was interviewing a pair of Middle Eastern foreign ministers when the phone rang. "Mr. Carmichael?" The voice was resonant and full and vaguely familiar.

"Speaking."

"Eddie Simpson. We'd like to have you on tomorrow's show—"

Harry listened politely, then explained that he was far too busy now, thanks anyway. A second invitation came six minutes later, after which the phone rang continually. At about eight thirty, a local TV news team arrived, headed by Addison McCutcheon, an energetic Baltimore anchorman. Harry, too tired to argue about it anymore, refused to let them in but allowed them to interview him on his front steps.

"There's nothing more to say," he protested. "You know as much as we do now. Anyway, I'm not an investigator. All I do is make out the paychecks."

"What about the charge," asked McCutcheon pointedly, "leveled this evening by Pappadopoulis, that the government kept this quiet hoping to gain military advantage from it?"

Harry hadn't heard that one before. "Who's Pappadopoulis?"

McCutcheon took on a condescending tone. "He won the Pulitzer a few years ago for a book on Bertrand Russell. He's also the chairman of the philosophy department at Cambridge, and he had some very unkind things to say about you earlier this evening."

"About *me*?"

"Well, not you, per se. But about the manner in which Goddard caved in to the politicians. Would you care to comment?"

Harry was uncomfortably aware of the cameras and lights. He heard a door open across the street and got the impression that a crowd was gathering at the foot of his driveway. "No," he said. "Pappadopoulis is entitled to his opinion, whatever it might be. But we never got to a point where we were talking about military considerations." Then, mumbling apologies, he pushed his way inside and closed the door.

The phone was ringing again.

It was Phil Cavanaugh, an astronomer who had worked occasionally on contract at Goddard. He was outraged. "I can understand that you might not have wanted to put out any interpretations, Harry," he said, his voice trembling, "but withholding the fact of the transmission was unconscionable. I know it wouldn't have been your decision, but I wish somebody there—you, Gambini, somebody—had had the guts to tell Hurley what NASA's responsibilities are!"

Later, Gambini phoned. "I'm in a motel," he said. "And judging from how hard it's been to get through to you, I guess you've been having the same sort of problem I have. I think I've been excoriated by every major scientific figure in the country. Even the philosophers and theologians are after me." His snarl dissolved briefly into a chuckle. "I've been referring them all to Rosenbloom.

"Listen, Harry, I wanted to let you know where I am in case anything important comes up—"

———

At a quarter to nine, Julie phoned. "Harry, I've seen the news." Her voice was tentative, and he understood that this was a difficult call for her to make. "I'm happy for you," she said. "Congratulations."

"Thanks." Harry tried not to sound hostile.

"They'll be giving you Quint's job."

"Maybe." The house was in darkness. But Harry could see more lights in the driveway. "Tommy wants to talk to you," she said.

"Put him on." Somebody knocked at the door.

"Dad." The boy's voice quavered with excitement. "I saw you on television."

Harry laughed, and the boy giggled, and Harry felt the strain of it through the phone. They talked about the Altheans and Tommy's basketball team while the knocking got louder. "We've got a game tomorrow morning," he said.

When she got back on, Julie was subdued. "Things must be very exciting at work."

"Yes." Harry couldn't get the stiffness out of his tone, and he wanted nothing so much as to sound natural. "I've never seen anything like it."

"Well," she said, after another long hesitation, "I just wanted to say hello."

"Okay." The knocking had become insistent.

"It sounds as if you have visitors."

"It's been bad all night. TV crews and reporters. I've had a small crowd in front of the house most of the evening. Ed's having trouble, too. He's off hiding in a motel somewhere."

"You should do the same, Harry."

He paused, caught his breath, and felt his pulse begin to quicken. "I don't like motels." He squeezed the words out. "Listen, I have to go. I have to do something about those people outside."

"Why don't you lock up and get out? Seriously, Harry."

He caught an invitation in the words, but he no longer trusted his judgment where she was concerned. "Julie," he said, "I think a celebration's in order. And I need to talk to somebody. How about joining me for a drink? Strictly—" He couldn't find the word he wanted.

"Harry, I'd like to, I really would—" She sounded doubtful, and he realized she wanted to be asked again. But he, by God, didn't want to be seen as if he were pleading.

"No strings," he said finally. He was having trouble breathing. "A lot's been happening—"

She laughed, the deep burgundy sound that he knew so well from better days. "Okay," she said. "One-night stand. Where will we go?"

Where indeed? She was probably talking about a restaurant, but he was more hopeful. Still, a hotel would never do. Too structured. He needed romance, not seduction. "Leave that to me," he said. "I'll pick you up in an hour."

He had trouble getting through to Wheeler, who was apparently also being deluged with phone calls that evening. In the end, he had to call a mutual friend and send him over to the priest's apartment. When the Norbertine called back, Harry explained what he wanted. "Try to stay off the phone," Wheeler said. "I'll set it up and get back to you. It should only take a few minutes. I'll ring once and call again."

Harry used the time to shower and change. The phone rang several times. But Harry let it go until he heard Wheeler's signal. "It's okay," the priest said. "There are two drainpipes behind the lodge. They'll leave the keys in the one on the south side. You'll need your own towels and stuff. They'll put breakfast in the refrigerator."

"Pete, I owe you."

"Sure. Good luck."

Harry made it a point to be a few minutes late. Ellen opened the door and asked how he was doing and said how glad she was to see him. Her voice and demeanor suggested she, too, had high hopes for the evening.

Julie entered from the back of the house, in white and green. She was wearing heels, reminding him of her occasional joke that she'd married Harry principally because there was no one else with whom she could dress properly.

In that moment, crowded with hesitation and regret, she was incredibly lovely. Her lips compressed briefly with confusion, then she broke into a wide smile. "Hello, Harry," she said.

On the highway, they talked freely. It was as if they were old friends again, facing a common problem. The aura of tension and anger that had infected the weeks since her departure had dissipated. Though Harry knew it would return when the interlude ended.

"Living with Ellen's not bad," she said. "But I'd prefer to be on my own."

"I sleep most nights at the office," Harry admitted.

"Some things never change."

Harry bristled. "I didn't sleep over that often."

"Okay," she said. "Let's not get into it tonight."

They traveled the expressway east toward Annapolis. Harry turned south on Route 2 and asked if she'd like to eat at the Anchorage. They'd been there before, but it had been a long time ago. "Yes," she said. "That sounds good."

It was a quiet atmospheric place, near Waynesville. Harry pulled in a few minutes later, and they crunched across the pebbled parking lot, went inside, and were seated at a table in back.

The drinks warmed them. "You should be well on your way now, Harry," she said. "You were right there with Hurley."

"I don't think the President's sure who I am. They were supposed to introduce me along with the Administrator and Ed. But I guess something happened. Either Hurley forgot my name, or he decided three's too many. Hard to say. But it can't hurt, I suppose. The only thing I worry about now is the possibility that someone'll come up with an alternative explanation for the signal. If that happens, then I get to be one of the people who made the President look dumb."

"He'll look fine no matter what happens," she said. "He was very careful to point out that he was just relaying information you guys had passed on."

The Anchorage was a fortunate choice. Besides being located on the road to Basil Point, it turned out to have a moody piano player and bayberry candles in smoky globes.

———

Ed Gambini had checked in at the Hyattsville Inn under an assumed name. He hated motels because they rarely provided reading lamps, never gave you enough pillows, and always looked so distraught when you asked for more. So he lay in bed propped up as best he could manage, with the top pillow folded over, watching the specials on the news conference. All the major networks had run them, and he'd switched back and forth. On the whole, the coverage was intelligent. They'd got the facts right and asked generally sensible questions. And they'd seen through the administration's effort to pretend that the incident was over. And he himself looked pretty good.

Later, he watched an argument—he hesitated to call it a

debate—between "Backwoods" Bobby Freeman, television preacher and founder of the American Christian Alliance, and Senator Dorothy Pemmer, Democrat of Pennsylvania, on the Alliance's efforts to block the recent trend toward group marriage.

"How can you possibly defend," Freeman persisted, "legalizing an activity so clearly destructive of the family?"

The phone rang, and Gambini turned down the sound. It was Majeski. "Ed," he said, "Mel's on the line. Is it okay to give him your number?"

It was the call that Gambini feared. "Yes," he said without hesitation, and hung up.

Mel Jablonski was an astronomer from UNH. More than that, he was a lifelong friend. Gambini had met him at the University of California, when they'd both been undergraduates. Eventually, he'd served as Mel's best man, and Mel had helped Gambini get his appointment with NASA. They'd come a long way since then, but they'd kept in touch. "Ed?" The familiar voice sounded tired and far away.

"How are you, Mel?"

"Not bad. You're a hard man to get through to."

"I suppose. It's been a long day."

"Yes," Jablonski said. "I'd think so."

Gambini searched for something to say.

"Did you really hear that signal back in September?" Mel asked.

"Yes. We did."

"Ed," he said, sadly, "you are a son of a bitch."

A couple of other old friends found him, and told him they were with him if he needed help. But both also made it clear they thought he'd blundered. Those sentiments hurt even more than Jablonski's remark.

At about the time Harry and Julie were turning off the expressway onto Route 2, Gambini wandered down to the bar. It was filled to capacity, and it was loud. He took a manhattan out onto one of several adjoining terraces.

The evening was warm, the first decent weather Washington had had in a month. A clear sky curved over the nation's capital. Hercules was on the horizon east of Vega, his war club held aloft in its traditional threatening mode.

The home of life.

In the west, he could see summer lightning.

A middle-aged couple had followed him out. Silhouetted against the lights of the city, they were discussing in ponderous detail a recalcitrant teenaged son.

Gambini wondered whether there would indeed be a second signal. In the privacy of his own mind, it was a possibility that seemed very real. But even if no further communication came, the essential question was answered: We were not alone! Now we knew the miracle had happened elsewhere. Which suggested it was not a miracle but rather an ordinary consequence of sunlight and water. The details of that other event and those other beings, their history, their technology, their view of the cosmos, were of enormous interest. But for all that, they were only details and incidental to the central fact of their existence.

Gambini raised his glass in the general direction of the constellation.

————

The critical moment, for Harry, came when he edged off the Anchorage parking lot and signaled his intentions for the evening by turning south onto Route 2. Julie stiffened slightly but said nothing. He risked a glance at her. She was looking straight ahead. Her hands were folded on her lap, and her face showed no emotion. If he knew her at all, she had a toothbrush in her handbag but was nevertheless only now making up her mind.

They talked about the Altheans, whether there was any reasonable likelihood that some remnant of them had survived, about what kinds of changes evolution would produce in a species over a million years. And they discussed Julie's newest assignment, assisting in the design of a circular steel-and-glass annex of the Corn Exchange; and how their lives had changed. The latter was a subject both had tried to avoid, but it was there, and maybe it needed talking out. Harry was surprised to learn that his wife was also not very happy, that she was lonely, and that she was not optimistic about her future. Nevertheless, through it all, she gave him no reason to suspect that she regretted having left him. "It'll work out," she told him. "It'll work out for both of us." And then she corrected herself. "All three of us."

Storm clouds were piling up in the west.

Harry almost missed his turn. There was little to mark the road that Wheeler had directed him to watch for. It plunged left at a sharp angle into the trees. He passed an ancient, crumbling stone house and began a long, winding climb uphill.

"Harry," Julie said, "where are we going?" Her voice had the whispery quality of a shallow stream.

This is where I take all my women now, he thought. And he came close to saying it, but thought it best not to push too hard. "The property up here belongs to Pete Wheeler's order. It has," he said lamely, "a magnificent view of the Chesapeake." They came to a pair of gates in a rock wall, on which hung a metal sign announcing that they had arrived at Saint Norbert's Priory. Inside the wall, the road turned to gravel, and the trees fell away. They emerged beneath a pair of manor houses set on the lip of the rise that extended back down to Route 2.

The buildings were similar in mood, possessing an idyllic geometry of stone and stained glass, cupola and portico. One had a widow's walk. Behind them, far down, the waters of the bay were almost lost in the dark.

Julie studied the complex of buildings. "We're not going in there?" she asked. "Harry, for God's sake, this is a monastery." She barely suppressed a giggle.

"Not in there," he said. The road arced out to an overlook and dipped back into a screen of elms. Just inside the trees, there were lights. "That's where we're going." Beyond the parking area, the land dipped sharply, and his headlights swept over the tops of the trees. He shut them off.

She didn't move, and he felt the silence filling the car. "Wheeler!" she breathed. "Isn't he a Norbertine?"

"I think so," Harry said innocently.

"He helped you set this up, didn't he?"

Harry sighed.

"Sex in the seminary. I guess nothing's sacred." She turned serious: "Harry, I'm touched that you've gone to so much trouble, that you'd even *want* me now, after what's happened. I'll stay here with you tonight, and maybe we can make it like it used to be. But only for an evening. Okay? You have to understand, nothing has changed."

For a glorious, defiant moment, Harry considered laughing at her, packing her back down the road, and taking her home. But he only nodded passively and led her into a firelit front room. Someone had left two wineglasses and a couple of bottles of Bordeaux on a coffee table.

"Very nice," she said, standing on a thick hearth rug, "considering you pulled it off with so little warning." Wheeler had been better than his word: bacon, eggs, potatoes, and orange juice were in the refrigerator; beds were made up; more wine was in the pantry, and some scotch; and, despite Pete's admonition, there were plenty of towels.

They reminisced a bit, reflected how sorry they both were that things had come to their present pass, but that it was best to confront the problem, and to move on.

Tentatively, somewhere in all that, Harry kissed her. He had never loved her more.

She tasted good, and her breath was warm against his throat. Nevertheless, there was something mechanical in her response. "Seems like a long time," said Harry.

Gently, Julie disentangled herself. "It's warm in here. Let's go look at the bay."

On the Chesapeake side of the ridge, away from the manor houses, the slope was rocky and steep and generally devoid of trees. They followed a footpath along the rim. Eventually it turned into a flagstone walk which forked, one side toward the manor houses, the other continuing along the crest until it became a wooden stairway by which one could descend to a pier a hundred feet below.

They paused at the intersection of footpath and gravel walk. The lights of the manor houses were bright in the dark waters of the bay. "Wheeler's a genius," she said, as they stood looking down. "He's in the wrong business." A brightly lit freighter was passing slowly south toward the Atlantic, and its wake widened and broke in long, luminous waves. There were no stars, though Harry was not aware of that until he heard thunder and saw the sky brighten momentarily.

They took the left fork and descended the stairway. The long, jagged ridge appeared to be the result of an ancient cataclysm. Harry stayed in front, pushing branches out of the way, testing each stair before putting full weight on it. They reached bottom and stepped off onto a beach.

The pier was short, extending only about fifteen feet into the bay. At its base, hidden against the cliff, Harry noticed a small green boathouse with white doors. It had a fresh coat of paint and a TV antenna attached to the roof.

Julie strolled over toward it and peered through the windows. "Looks as if the fathers have a sailboat," she said.

It was hard to make out in the dark, but Harry could see the bow and mast.

There was a smell of ozone in the air. Out over the bay, a curtain of rain was approaching. "We should start back," he said.

"In a minute." She'd turned away from the boathouse and was admiring the far shore, enjoying the spectacle of distant lights. A bell buoy gonged. "How lovely," she said.

Harry watched the rain come.

She saw the oncoming storm but seemed too caught up in the moment. "Harry," she said, "where is it? The source of the signal?"

"You mean Hercules?"

"Yes."

"If the sky were clear, it would be in that direction." He pointed toward the horizon. "There are four stars that form a kind of box. That's Hercules' head. The pulsar is on the right side of the box, about halfway between the upper and lower stars."

He felt the first few raindrops.

She reached for his hand. "Harry," she said, "I'm proud of you."

Lightning flickered overhead, and the storm burst over them. Sheets of rain clattered against the cliff. "Time to run," he said. "We're going to get drenched."

She smiled at him. "I guess so."

He started toward the stairway.

"I might not have thought this out too well," she said breathlessly, as they broke into a trot. "These are the only clothes I have." They'd gone only a few steps when Julie stopped and, overcome by sudden uncontrollable laughter, pulled off her shoes.

"The boathouse," said Harry, leading the way.

The rain hammered into the beach, and its roar blended with the sullen moan of the tide. The lights of the novitiate, high above, disappeared. A large padlock secured the boat doors, but they found a side entrance and burst inside.

"I think," she said breathlessly, pulling her soaked dress away from her skin, "that we could use some heat."

Harry looked hopefully around for a space heater. "Only if you're willing to burn the boat," he said. It was maybe a sixteen-footer. Two masts. He found a battery-powered lamp on a shelf and blankets in the boat's cabin.

"Nice," she said.

She disappeared behind the boat and came back moments later carrying her clothes and wearing one of the blankets.

"My fault," she said. "But it's turned out pretty nice."

The rain beat savagely on the roof. Harry pushed the door shut, cutting off the draft. "It can't keep up long like this," he said. "When it lets up, we'll make a run for the lodge."

She shook her head. "I think I like it here," she said.

He frowned, not able to see more than her silhouette in the dark. But there was something strange in her voice. Then he felt her hands on his arms, pulling him forward, unbuttoning his shirt.

"My God," he said mockingly, "we're not where we're supposed to be. Somebody could walk in at any time."

A burst of lightning crackled immediately overhead. "In this?" she laughed. "Unlikely."

———

The incoming shift was expected to be no less than fifteen minutes early. Linda Barrister was usually reliable, but she'd had a big night with an old flame in town, had gone to dinner and a movie, and the time had gotten away from her. The other member of her shift, Eliot Parker, was at his station when she arrived, bleary-eyed and apologetic, more than an hour late. Parker was the youngest of the communications specialists. He wasn't much more than a kid, really, tall, freckled, exceedingly serious about his job, inclined to excesses of enthusiasm. On this night, he surprised her.

"Linda," he said, with an amused casualness she found hard to credit later, "it's back."

"What's back?" she asked, misled by his tone.

"The signal."

She looked at him, then glanced at the overhead monitor. Parker flipped a switch, and they got sound, a staccato buzzing like an angry bee. "My God," she said. "You're right. How long ago?"

"While you were taking off your coat." He looked down at his console. "But it's not the pulsar."

MONITOR

ATTACK DOG FIRMS INDICTED

RECENT CHILD DEATHS
CAST PALL OVER INDUSTRY

DEMAND CONTINUES HIGH

. . .

GALVESTON REFINERY FIRE SPREADS

THOUSANDS EVACUATED

SMOKE CASTS THICK PALL OVER CITY

DAMAGE IN MILLIONS;
HURLEY DECLARES EMERGENCY

. . .

MOONLIGHT RAPIST SHOT IN L.A.

"PICKED ON WRONG WOMAN"

IDENTIFIED AS ORANGE COUNTY
INSURANCE SALESMAN

FATHER OF THREE SHOT DEAD

. . .

BOMB EXPLODES
IN LEBANESE BUS TERMINAL

FOUR DEAD;
ISLAMIC TERRORISTS BLAMED

. . .

TWO MORE INDICTED
IN PENTAGON SPY CASE

FIRST TEST OF
PEACETIME DEATH PENALTY EXPECTED

. . .

HOUSING STARTS UP AGAIN

DOW BREAKS THROUGH 30,000 BARRIER

RETAILERS, TECHNOLOGY STOCKS
LEAD SURGE

. . .

GM UNVEILS SPECTER

FIRST FULLY AUTOMATED CAR
NOW AVAILABLE

. . .

TRENTON PLUMBER WINS
$200 MILLION IN LOTTERY

"WILL KEEP WORKING," HE SAYS

. . .

"LOVE IN THE STARS"
HITS TOP OF CHARTS IN FIRST WEEK

. . .

HURLEY REFUSES TO DEAL WITH
TERRORISTS IN NUCLEAR PLANT

DENIES PLAN TO KEEP CRISIS SECRET

WILL NOT EVACUATE SOUTH JERSEY

BUT PEOPLE ARE LEAVING ANYWAY

. . .

EAGLES WIN AGAIN; STILL UNBEATEN

||| SIX |||

At approximately 7:00 A.M., Harry delivered his wife to her cousin's split-level, three-quarters of a mile from home, and accepted a brief kiss from her. It was perhaps the bitterest moment of his life.

When he arrived late at his office, the phones were busy with reaction to the press conference. E-mail was pouring in. Four interns had arrived to help out. Calls were coming from people from whom he hadn't heard in years. Old friends, colleagues with whom he'd worked in Treasury before coming over to NASA, and even a brother-in-law who had apparently not yet heard about his domestic troubles got through to congratulate him. His mood soared, for the first time in months. He was beaming when he got to Ed Gambini's recorded message.

"Please call," it said. "Something's happened."

Harry didn't bother with the phone.

The operations center was bedlam. Extra technicians and investigators were gathered around monitors, laughing and pushing one another. Majeski waved a scroll of printout paper in his direction and shouted something Harry couldn't hear over the noise. As best Harry could recall, it was the only time Gambini's assistant had actually looked pleased to see him.

Leslie was in the conference room, bent over a computer. When she straightened, he caught an expression of such pure, uninhibited joy that she might have been approaching orgasm. (Julie would never have given such a display outside a bedroom.)

"What's going on?" Angela Dellasandro pointed at the TDRSS monitor. Assorted keyboard characters were flashing across the screen in rapid succession. "About one this morning," she said, her voice pitched high with excitement. "It's been coming in ever since."

"Since 1:09, to be exact." Gambini pounded Harry on the shoulder. "The little bastards came through, Harry!" His face glowed. "We lost the acquisition signal September 20 at 4:30 A.M. We get the second signal November 11, at 1:09 A.M. Figure in the change to standard time, and they're still operating on multiples of Gamma's orbital period. Eighteen and an eighth this time."

"The pulsar's back?"

"No, not the pulsar. Something else: We're getting a radio wave. It's spread pretty much across the lower bands, but it seems to be centered at sixteen sixty-two megahertz. The first hydroxyl line. Harry, it's an ideal frequency for long-range communication. But their transmitter—My God, our most conservative estimate is that they're putting out a signal at one and a half million megawatts. It's hard to conceive of a controlled radio pulse with that kind of power."

"Why would they abandon the pulsar?"

"For better definition. They assume they've got our attention, so they've switched to a more sophisticated system."

Their eyes locked. "Son of a bitch!" said Harry. "It's really happening."

Gambini seized his arm. "Yes," he said. "It really is."

Angela bounded into his arms, pulled his head down, and kissed him. "Welcome to the party," she said.

She was warm and enthusiastic, and she pressed the kiss a little too long. Harry disengaged himself reluctantly and patted her paternally on the shoulder. "Ed, can we read any of it?"

"It's too soon. But they know what we need to begin translating."

"They're using a binary system," said Angela.

"There're a couple of mathematicians we need to bring in, Harry, and it probably wouldn't hurt to get Hakluyt down here as well."

"We'd better notify Rosenbloom."

"It's already done." Gambini smirked. "I'll be interested in hearing what he has to say now."

"Not one word." Rosenbloom glowered behind his desktop. He looked like a man who had just stumbled into a war zone. "Not one goddam word until I tell you!"

"We can't hide this." Gambini's voice trembled with helpless indignation. "There are too many people who deserve to know."

"And too many who *already* know," added Harry. "It'll leak out no matter what we do. Anyhow, what's the problem? Where's the risk in releasing this? I mean, this is the scientific story of the age—"

"*That's* the problem," Rosenbloom said. "Something like this has to come from upstairs, not from us." He waved them to seats. "It probably won't take long, but until we get clearance, I don't want any of this to get out. Do you understand?"

"Quint." Gambini was visibly struggling to keep his voice level. "If we sit on this, if we hold this back, my career, Wheeler's career, the careers of all our people, will be finished. Listen: We aren't government employees. We're here on contract. If we participate in keeping this quiet, we have no cover. We can expect to become persona non grata. Everywhere."

"Careers?" Rosenbloom got out of his chair. "You're talking to me about careers? There are bigger stakes here than where you'll be working ten years from now. Look, Ed, how can we announce the second transmission unless we're prepared to release the transmission itself? And we can't do that."

"Why not?" demanded Gambini.

"Because I don't have the authority. Not for something like this. Look, we aren't talking more than a day or so. I just need to get clearance. Be reasonable."

"So we're stuck in the bureaucracy."

"That's not what I said."

"What *did* you say?"

"That I don't have the authority. Why is that so hard to understand?"

"You have the authority if you just assume it."

"It's potentially dangerous. We don't know what might be in there."

"For example—?"

"Maybe the makings for some home-brew plague. Or weather control. Or God knows what."

"That's ridiculous."

"Is it? When we know that, I suspect they'll let us release the goddam thing. But not till then. You'll be interested in knowing, by the way, that the Russians have launched a crash program to put up a Skynet of their own."

"That's another joke," said Gambini. "Skynet was supposed to be for everybody's use."

"And it is. Except for certain sensitive projects." Rosenbloom pushed the discussion away with a wave of his hands. "Look, none of this is my call, okay? And I'm tired arguing about it. The question we have to decide is what to recommend upstairs. We seem to have three choices. We can suggest they release the thing and damn the consequences; or we ride things out, say nothing, and deny all rumors; or we can admit what we've got but withhold the transmission. What are your thoughts?"

Gambini rose out of his chair. "That's easy," he said. "Release it."

"It's too late to keep it quiet," said Harry. "The story went out this morning. Don't you think these people have friends in the outside world?"

Rosenbloom shrugged. "It was an unfounded rumor. A misunderstanding. We misinterpreted some data. It's not a problem. Not at this stage." He looked at Gambini. "The White House will not release this to the general public, and if we recommend they do, they'll conclude we're not too politically astute and write off everything else we say."

"Maybe we need to back away from it," Harry said. "How about if we just shut Skynet down? Stop listening? Wouldn't that simplify things?"

He caught a withering stare from Gambini, but Rosenbloom looked receptive. "I've thought that right from the start," he said.

"Why am I not surprised?" Gambini wore an expression of utter contempt. "Look, I don't deny there's a risk. But it's minor, especially compared with what we have to gain. Has it occurred to you that there's also a risk in allowing the rest of the planet to suspect we have exclusive access to an extraterrestrial transmission? God knows what kind of meetings have been going on around the world since the press conference yesterday."

"I think," said the director, trying to lower the intensity of the discussion, "there's already been some consideration given to that. You may've noticed we've begun beefing up security. The White House will be sending some people over. I hear, by the way, that Maloney's pushing to get the entire Hercules operation moved out of here and sent to Fort Meade."

"Who's Maloney?" asked Gambini.

"White House special assistant," said Harry. "Specializes in security issues."

Gambini looked pained. "That makes no sense," he said. "Fort Meade isn't set up for this kind of operation."

"Why not?" Rosenbloom took a deep breath. "What are we doing here that can't be routed over there?"

"There'd probably be trouble with clearances," said Harry. "They don't let anybody in over there without fairly extensive investigation. It'd take time."

"Some of our people might not even pass," grumbled Gambini.

"I don't think you need worry about that, Ed," Rosenbloom said. "If this operation goes to Fort Meade, I doubt anyone except you and Baines and possibly Wheeler would be invited anyhow. Why should they? They have their own mathematicians and codebreakers. In fact, they'll probably feel they could do the job better than we can."

"Quint," said Gambini, "has anyone argued this thing with the President? Pointed out to him the advantages of going public? I don't suppose *you'd* be willing to take a stand?"

"What advantages?" asked Rosenbloom. "And no, it's not in the Agency's interests to push this. If he releases what he's got, and it blows up, which it very easily could, there'll be some bodies. I don't want ours among them."

"We've already got some bodies," said Gambini. "Do you have any idea what my standing is right now back home?" That would be Stanford, where Gambini was a full professor.

"Come on, Ed." Rosenbloom had come around to the front of his desk. A vein in his neck that usually began to swell under stress was showing itself. "We're doing what's right for us, and for the President. Try not to make waves. I know how you feel, but the hard truth is that Hurley wants it kept quiet, and he's right. Maybe, after it's all over, we can get you an award of some kind."

Gambini looked pensive. "You talked to Hurley this morning?"

"Yes."

"Suppose I refused to agree to any of this? Suppose I just walked out and told the world what I know?"

"I'm not sure," Rosenbloom said patiently, "just what your status would be. You'd undoubtedly be open to prosecution if you went to the media. Although we both know the Agency would be reluctant to prosecute you. I mean, how would it look?

"Think about it, Ed. An action like that wouldn't really change anything, except to put *you* on the outside. You'd only learn what was made available to the rest of the public. Is that what you want?"

Gambini got slowly to his feet, his mouth a thin line, his cheeks flushed.

"Quint," said Harry, "you are a bastard."

The director swiveled in Harry's direction, a look of genuine hurt on his porkchop features. Then he turned back to the project manager. "Now let's get together. Harry's probably right: We can't keep it quiet, so we recommend that the White House admit we have a transmission, classify it, and state that we've been unable to translate it. And we also recommend that it not be released until we know what it contains. For public safety."

Gambini stared at him.

Rosenbloom smiled. "And you, Harry? Are you also in agreement?"

"I don't disapprove of waiting to clear this with higher authority," said Harry. "But I don't think much of the way you treat your people."

Rosenbloom stared back at him. "Okay," he said at length. "I appreciate your honesty." There was another long pause. "Ed, you kept everyone on board this morning?"

"Yes," he said. "No one's gone home. But there're telephones in the building."

"Let's go talk to them. We'll do what we can."

———————

At 8:00 P.M., the transmission was still coming in.

Harry smuggled a case of French champagne into the Hercules spaces. It was a violation, of course, but the occasion demanded something appropriate. They drank out of paper cups and coffee mugs. Rimford, who'd been called back from the West Coast, had grasped the event without being told details and arrived with several more bottles. They went through it all, and when still another supply mysteriously appeared, Gambini stepped in. "That's enough," he said. "The rest'll be at the Red Limit this evening should anyone wish to claim it."

Harry found a hard copy of the first twelve pages of the transmission tacked to a bulletin board. The characters were binary. "How can you begin to make sense out of it?" he asked Majeski, who was watching him with curiosity.

"First," he said, leaning casually against a wall with his arms folded like a young Caesar, "we ask ourselves how *we'd* have encoded the message."

"And how would we?"

"We'd start by giving them a set of instructions. For example, they'd need to know the number of bits in a byte. We use eight." He looked at Harry uncertainly. "A byte," he explained, "is a character. A letter or number usually, although it doesn't have to be. And it's a result of the arrangement of the individual bits. As I said, we use eight. The Altheans use sixteen."

"How can you tell?"

Majeski brought up a sequence on one of the monitors. "This is the beginning of their transmission." It started with sixteen zeroes, then sixteen ones. And it went on like that for several thousand characters.

"That seems simple enough," said Harry.

"That part of it is."

"What would we do next?"

"What we would want to do, but can't as yet, would be to

create a self-initiating program. We'd have to assume certain things about the architecture of their computer, but there's reason to believe that the digital approach we use in our computers is the most efficient. If not, it would still be the most basic type, the type a technological civilization would be most likely to possess, or at least to know about. And we would want a program that would run in a fairly unsophisticated model, with limited memory.

"Ideally, the only action needed to get the thing up and running should be for the people on the other end, the whozits, to plug it into a computer and run a search program. In other words, any attempt to analyze the transmission, to look for patterns, triggers the program."

"Nice idea," said Harry. "I assume the Altheans didn't do that?"

Majeski shook his head glumly. "Not as far as we can tell. We've been running it through the most advanced systems we have. And I don't understand why we haven't had *some* kind of result. I really don't. It's the logical way to proceed." He bit his lower lip. "It makes me wonder whether a self-initiating program is really possible."

Harry went back to his office during the late afternoon. He was still feeling immensely pleased, and he found a fresh pile of messages stacked up. Edna had marked some for his attention. He read through and started returning calls. One had come from Hausner Diehl, the English Department chairman at Yale, whom he had met once at a graduation ceremony.

Diehl answered the phone himself. "I wonder if you can explain something to me," he said in a syrupy voice. "I don't want you to take this personally, but why was it necessary to withhold information on the Hercules discovery for eight weeks?"

Harry sighed.

After Diehl had lodged his complaint and added a warning that a formal protest was likely from Yale, he asked a disquieting question. "A lot of us here," he said, "are not convinced that the whole truth is out yet. Is there anything you're holding back? Anything we haven't been told?"

"No," said Harry. "There's nothing else."

And then came another tough question: "There has been no second signal?"

Harry hesitated. His face warmed. "We described everything we had."

His job did not usually require him to lie. It was not a tactic he was good at, and he was moderately surprised to get away with his reply, which was technically true. But he felt the weight of the deception nonetheless.

It was not a night to eat alone. He called Leslie.

"Yes," she said. "I'd love to."

———————

Harry would have preferred to get away from Goddard altogether for a few hours. Diehl's questions had been typical of those he'd been fielding all day. When this was over, he doubted anyone would believe him ever again. So he wanted nothing more than to put distance between himself and his office. But Leslie preferred to stay close, and so he conceded the point.

"Something could happen at any time," she explained. "This is not a night to go for a ride in the country." They went to the Red Limit.

A small candle burned cheerily inside a smoked globe while the server brought menus and introduced himself. When he was gone, Harry leaned across the table so he could keep his voice down. "You're not suggesting," he said, "that they might be able to start reading it tonight?"

"No," she said, "of course not. But Ed's worried."

"Why?"

"I think because they expected an immediate breakthrough after they saw the initial setup. When I left, he was saying they'd solve it quickly, or not for years."

"Is it possible," asked Harry, "that it might never be translated?"

"Now there," she said, raising her eyes from the menu, "is a dark thought."

They ordered the catch of the day and a carafe of white wine. Leslie by candlelight was even more attractive than he'd expected. "Harry," she asked quietly, after the meal had come, "are things not good at home?"

He hadn't expected the question. "You've been talking to Pete," he said.

"No. It's easy enough to see. You wear a ring, but you never go home for dinner." She shrugged. "And here you are with me."

"Yeah." He continued eating, drank some wine, patted his lips with a napkin, and said simply, "It's kaput."

"I'm sorry."

He shrugged.

"I didn't mean to pry."

Her lips caught the light. She wore a sheer white blouse with the top two buttons open. As surreptitiously as he could manage, he followed the creamy arc of her left breast down into the lapels. "I don't mind," he said.

She smiled, reached across the table, and touched his forearm.

"It blew up the night they picked up the signal." He shook his head. "No, I guess it happened long before that. But that was the night the news got delivered."

"Any children?"

"One. A boy."

"That makes it even more difficult."

Harry became aware of voices around them, of the tinkle of glass and plates, of soft music spilling out of the speakers. "Hell with it," he said. The fish came, and they avoided the subject while they ate. He drained the carafe and was about to order more when he saw her looking at him.

"You disapprove?"

"I only disapprove when I'm getting paid, Harry. Then I disapprove of everything." Her eyes registered regret. "I don't know why that should be. Maybe because the end is always bad."

Harry grinned. "You're a hell of a psychologist," he said. "Is that what you tell everyone?"

"No. I tell patients what they pay me to hear, what's good for them over the short run because that's all there is, really. To you, I can speak my mind."

"Speak your mind."

"You're an interesting male, Harry. In some difficult areas, you're highly adaptive. You've managed, for example, to fit in remarkably well with some of the foremost scientific minds of the age. And with some major-league horses' asses, if you'll excuse the language."

Harry frowned, inviting her to elaborate.

"People like Gambini and Quint Rosenbloom," she said. "Those two could hardly be less alike. Yet they both believe the human race isn't worth very much, and they both respect you. Cord Majeski talks only to mathematicians, cosmologists, and virgins. Baines talks only to God. Yet they all accept you. That's no small accomplishment."

"Thanks," said Harry. "I'll take the cash and run." He broke a roll in half, buttered it, and tasted it. "You don't like Cord?"

"Did I say that?"

"I think you did."

"I guess people like Majeski tend to bring my emotions close to the surface, one way or another. But that's irrelevant to the point under discussion."

"And what's that?"

"Harry, I hate seeing you like this."

"Like what?"

She toyed momentarily with her glass. "Any stranger off the street would know that you aren't behaving in character. Not for the last couple of months, anyhow. While I've been here."

"How would *you* know what my normal behavior is?"

"You smile easily, Harry. But I've yet to see you do it without downcast eyes. Hell, you're doing it now." An edge had crept into her voice.

"I'm sorry it's so obvious. This has been a strange time. Up and down between the transmission and Julie. What do you prescribe?"

She leaned forward. The blouse fell open a bit more. "I don't know. Is it possible to repair the damage?"

Yes, he wanted to scream at her. She's not really gone. It just needs a little time. "No," he said.

"You're sure?"

"I'm sure."

"If that's so, then you need to come to grips with that first. It'll take time."

He nodded.

"I'm talking too much," she said. "It must be the wine."

"You must have seen lots of these cases. Do people ever get back together?"

"I'm sorry to say this, but I don't think it happens in any substantive way. Even when there's a reconciliation, people discover that the spouse they remembered is changed. In a sense, *gone*. It's almost as if they've been replaced by someone else." Her eyes found his. They were bright. "Whatever people might have had, even when it was pretty good, it gets irrevocably fractured when somebody walks out. It's never the same again. A reconciliation is at best a holding action."

"You sound like Pete Wheeler."

"I'm sorry, Harry. But if he said that, he was right. Your wife's name was Julie?"

"Yes."

"Well, Julie's a damned fool. She won't replace you very easily. She may or may not be smart enough to realize that quickly. When she does, there's a fair possibility she'll be back. If that's what you want, and you play your cards right, your chances are pretty good. But you'll be trapped in a bad situation." She pushed what was left of her dinner away. "Enough for me," she said.

Harry was silent.

"Is that what you want?" she asked.

"I don't know. I know I'd like to have her back."

"I'd like to be twenty-two again." She watched him carefully. "I'm sorry, Harry. I don't mean to be cruel. But we're talking about the same sort of thing."

Majeski was annoyed.

He sat in Gambini's office with his head thrown back, his eyes closed, his cheeks puffed out, and his arms hanging at the sides of the chair. The project manager, perched on the edge of his desk, was explaining something. The mathematician nodded and nodded again. But his eyes rarely opened.

Harry watched curiously through the window until Gambini saw him standing there and waved him inside.

"Got a question for you," he said, as Harry closed the door. Majeski looked around to see who'd come in.

"Go ahead."

"What would happen if we sent a copy of the transmission over to NSA and they were able to make some sense out of it?"

"They've got a custom-made super Cray," Majeski interjected. "It might be enough to get us into the instructions. That'd be all we'd need. Just enough to get started."

Harry thought it over. He didn't know his NSA counterpart. They were a community unto themselves, competent, elitist, secretive, scared to death to talk to anyone who might deduce something from their tone of voice. "I don't think NSA has any interest in this project, and I suspect they're busy enough over there that they'd prefer not to get involved anyhow. But—" He glanced at Gambini. "You heard what Rosenbloom said today. The White House would like to get Hercules out of Goddard and into Fort Meade. If we go to NSA for help, we'd be putting ammunition into their hands. Do that, and we could probably kiss the program good-bye."

"My point exactly," said Gambini.

"So we work on the project at Fort Meade," said Majeski. "What's the difference?"

"The difference," said Harry, "is that *you* won't be working on it, Cord. The project goes over there, it becomes *theirs*. You work for NASA, not NSA. They'd use you only if they decided you were irreplaceable. Are you?"

"What you're saying is that the computers to solve the transmission may be available, but we can't use them without losing control of the project. That's ridiculous."

Harry shrugged. "Welcome to government work." He gazed at Gambini. "Is the transmission still coming in?"

"Yes, it is," said Gambini. "They must be sending us the *Encyclopedia*." He looked grateful for the change of subject. "This is what we're talking about," he said, showing Harry a disk. "We think this is the instruction manual. How to use the system."

"Why?"

"It's at the beginning of the transmission, and it's clearly separated from the rest of the text. It's an explanation."

"But," said Majeski, "we have to get a sufficiently powerful computer."

"And our equipment isn't good enough?" asked Harry. "I thought the theory was that the program should work in something basic."

"Who knows," said Gambini, "what's basic to the Altheans?

I'm not sure how to handle this, Harry. I hate to waste time with peripheral approaches when it's probably just a matter of finding the right computer, or the right software. If our assumptions are wrong, and we have to solve this thing by some sort of statistical analysis, you and I probably won't live long enough to see the result."

Harry turned the disk over in his hand. "Maybe," he said, "you're going at this the wrong way. You've been using the IBMs?"

"Of course."

"The biggest we have. And now we want to go bigger yet. But Majeski's logic suggests smaller. Less complex." Harry's eyes fell on Gambini's notebook computer. "I don't know much about these things," he continued, "except that the more powerful ones are also more complicated. More places to store information. More instructions required to make it work. Am I right?"

Majeski nodded. "Yes."

Gambini plainly thought Harry was wasting his time.

"Try the smaller unit," urged Harry. "Give it a chance. What can you lose?"

"It could be," said Majeski. "A program not designed to address all the memory in the IBM might run."

Gambini shook his head, looking from one to the other. "You mean a smaller computer can do things a bigger one can't?"

Majeski nodded.

Gambini opened the notebook, turned it on, and took the disk from Harry. The screen lit up. Majeski produced a search program and inserted it into one of the drives.

A window blinked on: INADEQUATE MEMORY FOR THIS PROGRAM.

Majeski shook his head. "Wait a second."

He went outside, and they saw him talking to one of the technicians. When he came back, he was frowning. "We don't have a search program that requires less memory," he said. "We need to use one of the desktops."

"So we're back to the bigger units," said Harry. "Round and round."

"We could rewrite one of the programs," said Gambini. "But it would take a while."

"Hold it." Majeski left the office again, opened a filing cabinet in the workroom, and came back with a disk. "*Star Trek*," he said. "This has been around here for years. It doesn't need much memory, and it includes a sequence that allows the *Enterprise* to analyze Klingon tactical positions." He grinned. "What the hell."

He loaded the game, indicated his choice for a mission, and, when the right moment came, activated the search instructions. Then he turned to Harry. "Go ahead," he said. "It's your idea."

The screen carried a simulation of the *Enterprise* view screen. It showed a handful of stars, several dozen planets, and a curious disturbance on the port side that might have been something with a cloaking device. Two status boards occupied the lower portion of the screen: ship's systems on the left, combat search and analysis on the right. It carried the legend NO CONTACTS.

Harry inserted the Hercules disk into a second drive and keyed it in. The starfield rotated slowly, and the *Enterprise* began to move.

Red lamps over both drives blinked on.

"It's reading," said Gambini.

The starship was accelerating. The disturbance that might have been a cloaked vessel suddenly dropped off the screen. The stars rolled past the *Enterprise*, much as they had on the old TV program, until they thinned out. Then they, too, were gone.

"This doesn't happen in the game," observed Majeski.

NO CONTACTS blinked off. The search and analysis board was blank.

And a cube appeared.

"Not part of the game!" Majeski dropped his elbows on the desk, laid his chin on his arms, and moved close to the screen.

The cube rotated at a forty-five-degree angle, stopped, and reversed itself.

Gambini watched hopefully. When he spoke, his voice was tense. "Maybe," he said. "Maybe."

It was a perfectly ordinary cube. And it was going to look goddam silly in the official releases. The Altheans might be good engineers, but they clearly needed some work in public relations. "Why?" asked Harry. "Why the hell do they send us a block?"

"It's not just a block," said Rimford. "They've said hello to us in the simplest way possible. When we discussed the problems related to communication between cultures that had previously been totally isolated, we thought purely in terms of passing instructions. But they've gone a step further: They must have thought we'd like some tangible encouragement, so they gave us a picture.

"And they've also set some parameters for the architecture of the computer they expect us to use to get at the balance of the transmission."

Majeski and his technicians had finished making adjustments to the IBM. The mathematician replaced a panel and signaled to Gambini, who loaded one of the standard search programs and then inserted the transmission disk.

They'd tied in several monitors, so everyone could see. The working spaces were jammed: Representatives from the off-duty shifts had arrived, and a party atmosphere prevailed.

Gambini waved everyone to silence. "I think we're ready," he said. He put the computer into its scan mode, and the laughter subsided. All eyes turned to the screens.

Red lamps blinked on.

"It's working," said Angela.

A door closed somewhere in the building, and Harry heard a boiler ignite.

The screens remained blank. The lamps went off.

And a black point appeared. It was barely discernible. While Harry was trying to decide whether it was really there, it expanded and developed a bulge. A line grew out of the bulge and crossed the width of the screen. Then it turned down at a right angle and described a loop. From the base of the loop, a second line appeared, drew itself out parallel to the first, and, at its opposite end, formed a second, connecting circle.

It was a cylinder.

Somebody cheered. Harry heard a pop and a fizz.

Rimford stood before a monitor, his face illuminated. "So much," he said, "for Brockmann's Thesis."

"Not yet," said Gambini. "It's too early to tell."

A twelve-character byte appeared beneath the cylinder. Rimford's breathing had become audible. Leslie joined him. "That'll be its name," he said. "The symbol for cylinder. We're getting some vocabulary."

"What's Brockmann's Thesis?" asked Harry.

Leslie glanced at Baines, and he nodded. "Harvey Brockmann," she said, "is a Hamburg psychologist who maintains that cultures completely alien to one another probably would not be able to communicate except on a superficial level. That would happen, he says, because physiology, environment, social conditions, and history are essential to the way in which we interpret data and, consequently, communicate and understand ideas. No parallel experience, no talk." Her demeanor grew thoughtful. "Ed will tell you that he may yet turn out to be right since we're still at an extremely early stage. But I think we've already seen features of Althean approaches to problem-solving that are very much like our own. We may get another demonstration of that before we're through here this evening."

That caught Rimford's interest. "In what way, Leslie?"

"Think about us," she said. "If we were encoding pictures for another species, what image would we absolutely not fail to send?"

"Our own," said Harry.

"Bingo. Harry, you'd make a hell of a psychologist. Now I tell you what I think we're going to learn. The capability to create a technological civilization imposes essentially similar disciplines of logic and perception that outweigh, and probably *heavily* outweigh, the factors proposed by Brockmann."

"We'll see," said Gambini. "I hope you're right."

Harry watched the cylinder vanish.

The point appeared again. This time they got a sphere. Again with a byte.

Then a pyramid.

And a trochoid.

"Does Rosenbloom know about this yet?" asked Harry.

"I'm not sure we're exactly ready for a visit by the director," suggested Gambini. "We can call him later, after we know what we have. That's the way he likes to do things, right? Meantime, we'll want to get these drunks out of here." He raised his voice, and several of the "drunks" applauded.

After a while, the cylinder reappeared, but at right angles to the original figure. A new byte became visible. "It'll be similar to the first one," said Majeski, "and that portion can probably be understood to imply the object itself. The variation between the two should equate to a difference in angle, or some such thing."

Harry didn't understand, but he let it go.

They got a third cylinder.

Geometrical figures continued well into the evening. Harry got bored, eventually, and excused himself to call Rosenbloom. It was after midnight by then.

The director was pleased neither with the late hour of the call nor the content of the message. "Cylinders," he said grumpily. "Okay, Harry. This is *not* what we needed. But keep an eye on things down there and let me know if anything changes."

Harry found a dark office and dozed for about an hour. When he returned to the operations center, he still felt washed-out. He found Gambini, described the director's response, and was about to say good night when he noticed that the physicist hadn't really heard anything he'd said. And in fact, the mood of the whole place had changed in a not-too-subtle way. "What happened?" he asked.

Various geometrical figures were still displayed on the battery of screens. Harry realized that the program was complete, that they'd gone through the instruction manual, and that the investigators were now beginning a more detailed examination. Gambini commandeered a unit. "There's something you should see." He keyed in a command and stepped back to allow Harry an unobstructed view.

Leslie appeared at his side. "Hi," she said. "Looks like serious doings tonight. You're partially responsible, Harry." She beamed at him. "Congratulations."

A sphere took shape and began to rotate. Well off its surface, four points appeared, expanded, and threw out parallel curved lines, which quickly circled the sphere. The image acquired shading and angle, giving it depth.

"My God," said Harry. "It's Saturn."

"Hardly," responded Gambini. "But I wonder if their home world has rings."

The figure vanished.

Again he saw the familiar black point. This time it lengthened gradually into a tetrahedron-like figure. It was spidery, and its limbs moved in a fashion that Harry found disconcerting.

"We think it's an Althean," said Gambini.

The following afternoon, Gambini retired to his quarters in the VIP section in the northwestern corner of the Goddard facility. He wasn't sure he'd be able to sleep, but the computers were doing the work now, and he wanted to be reasonably alert later.

He fell into bed with considerable satisfaction and sank toward oblivion with the happy thought that he had achieved his life's ambition. Had in fact far outstripped any ambition he'd ever seriously considered.

When the phone rang several hours later, he was slow to figure out where he was. He burrowed deeper into the pillows, listened to the insistent jangling, reached for the instrument, and knocked it over.

The voice at the other end belonged to Charlie Hoffer. "It's finished," he said.

"The signal?"

"Yes. The pulsar's back."

"Gambini looked at his watch. "Nine fifty-three."

"One full orbit," said Hoffer.

"They're consistent. What's the length?"

"We haven't done the calculation."

"Okay," Gambini said. "Thanks. Let me know if anything changes, Charlie."

He punched the numbers into a calculator. It came out to approximately 46.6 million characters.

Partial transcript of interview with Baines Rimford, appearing originally in Deep Space, *October issue:*

Q. Professor Rimford, you've been quoted as saying that there are a few questions you would especially like to put to God. I wonder if you could tell us what some of those questions are?

A. For a start, it would be nice to have a workable GUT.

Q. You mean a Grand Unified Theory, tying all of the physical laws together.

A. *(Chuckles.)* We'd settle for knowing how the strong and weak nuclear forces, electromagnetism, and gravity, interact. There's some reason to suspect they were once, briefly, a single force.

Q. When would that have been?

A. During the first nanoseconds of the Big Bang. If there was a Big Bang.

Q. Is there any doubt?

A. Well, there are still a few who will quibble. But no, I don't think there's much question that it happened. The real question today, I suppose, is whether the event was unique.

Q. You mean there might have been more than one big bang?

A. Well, not here, of course. But what you're really asking is whether the universe is unique. Whether it's the only one.

Q. Is it? Unique?

A. I don't know. Nobody knows. Probably, nobody ever will know.

Q. What else would you want explained?

A. I'd like to know why anything exists at all. Why isn't there *nothing*? I'd like to know why we have order. It amazes me that the universe consists of anything other than cold sludge sliding through the dark.

Q. I don't think I understand.

A. Let's go back to the Big Bang.

Q. If there was one.

A. The Big Bang seems to have contained precisely the amount of energy needed to provide a long-lived universe. Had it been infinitesimally weaker, things would have fallen back into a crunch very quickly. And I mean weaker on the order of an extremely small fraction of one percent. On the other hand, had it been even a little stronger, the galaxies could not have formed.

Or let's look at the strong force that binds the nucleus together. Again, there is no reason we can see why it should be precisely what it is. Yet, if it were stronger, even slightly stronger, we'd have neither hydrogen nor water. If it were weaker, we'd have no yellow suns. There are, in fact, damned near an infinity of such coincidences. They have to do with atomic weights and freezing points and quanta and virtually every sort of physical law you can think of. Change any one of a substantial number of constants, throw an extra proton, say, into the helium atom, and you stand an excellent chance of destabilizing the universe. We seem to live in a place that has been carefully designed, against literally cosmic odds, as a home for intelligent life. I'd like very much to know why that should be.

—Reprinted in *Systemic Epistemology XIV*

||| SEVEN |||

Edna closed the door behind the stocky, white-haired man. He was well pressed, in an expensive charcoal suit with a mismatched green tie and black shoes polished in a military manner. But this was no military visitor. His sharp gray eyes glanced casually around the office, as if Harry weren't in it, appraising its contents with idle disdain. At last, his gaze more or less bounced off Harry, returned, and came to rest. "Mr. Carmichael?"

Harry stood up and came around the desk. He wasn't looking forward to this one. "Yes," he said, extending his hand. "Good morning, Professor."

The visitor ignored it.

This was Michael Pappadopoulis, chairman of the Cambridge philosophy department, emeritus member of the Royal Society, senior fellow of the Philosophical Union, author of half a dozen seminal works including the classic *Divinity and Destiny*. Harry detected in his posture a faint drumroll.

He glanced over Harry, as if he were a not-especially-interesting specimen. "Good morning to you, sir," he said.

"Please have a seat, Professor. What can I do for you?"

Pappadopoulis remained standing. "You can assure me that someone here is aware of the significance of the Hercules transmission."

"You need not be concerned," said Harry amiably. "We know what it means."

"I'm happy to hear it. Unfortunately, your actions don't bear that out. NASA received the Hercules signal in the early morning of September 17 and chose, for whatever reason, to conceal its existence until Friday, November 10. Does that not seem a bit irresponsible to you, Mr. Carmichael?"

Harry squirmed. "I think," he said, "that making a premature statement before we were sure of our facts might have been irresponsible. We used our best judgment."

"I'm sure you did. And it's that judgment that is in question." Pappadopoulis was a heavy man, a proper container for the somber approach to neo-Kantian materialism that had made his reputation first in the academic community, then in the world at large. His face was set in an attitude of dispassionate annoyance, his tone was stiff and formal. His manner, Harry thought, suggested the contents of an old metaphysics tome, dry, dusty, intimidating simply by its presence. "I'm sadly aware," he continued, "that the same sort of procedure is likely to be taken again should further transmissions be received." He paused and reacted to something in Harry's face. "*Has* something else happened? Are we still concealing information?"

"We've released everything we had," Harry said.

"Please don't try to get by with evasions, Mr. Carmichael." He leaned across the desk, reflecting bored irritation and mild distaste. He was an easy man to dislike. Underneath the bravado, Harry suspected, and despite his reputation and accomplishments, the man had an ego problem. He was afraid people might not hold the appropriately high opinion of him, which was his due. "Is something happening now," he asked, "that the world should be aware of?"

When it happens, I'll let you know. "No." Damn Rosenbloom. And the President.

"I see. Why do I not believe you, Mr. Carmichael?" He appropriated a chair and lowered himself into it. "To your credit, you are a poor liar." He was breathing heavily, as if he'd walked a long distance, and he paused momentarily to gather himself. "Secrecy is a compulsive reflex in this country, as in mine. It strangles thought, delays scientific progress, and destroys integrity." He leaned forward. "Utterly *demolishes* it." His eyes slid shut, while he contemplated the wilful arrogance of the world around him. "I'd assumed that the only reason the information was released at all was that the transmission had apparently ended, and there has been nothing more. Is that in fact so?"

"None of this is getting us anywhere, Professor. I'll note your protest and see that my superiors are made aware of it."

"I'm sure you will. I take it, then, that there *has* been a subsequent transmission? Has it been a textual transmission? Have you made any progress in translating it?"

"If there are any additional transmissions," Harry said, "we will make the information public."

"Spoken like a true flunky." Pappadopoulis gazed at a portrait of Robert H. Goddard atop a bookcase. "He'd be embarrassed by all this, you know."

Harry stood up. "Good of you to come by, Professor."

Pappadopoulis nodded and lowered his eyes. *You are not worth my time, Carmichael.* As a good bureaucrat, Harry thrived on accommodation and compromise. He had little stomach for confrontation that could in no way be productive.

"What has happened has happened," Pappadopoulis observed. "My concern now is with the future. I had intended to ask what your position would be if more were forthcoming from the Hercules site. *Your* position, Mr. Carmichael. Not the government's. I'm saddened to realize that I have *this* kind of answer."

Harry moved a few steps in the direction of the door, inviting him to leave.

Pappadopoulis remained in his chair. "Even a civil servant should have a conscience. The people for whom you work, Mr. Carmichael, are interested only in whatever political advantage they can extract from all this. May I suggest that your greater duty is to all of us, and not to your callous employer. Stand up to the bastards!" His voice rose. "You owe it to everyone who's tried to understand the nature of the world in which we live. And you owe it to yourself."

"Professor, I really have no—"

Pappadopoulis pushed ahead: "Years from now, when you and I have long since passed from the scene, you could well be remembered for your courage and contribution. Sit silent, appease your pathetic masters, and I can assure you that you will richly deserve the oblivion you get." He reached into a vest pocket. "My card, Mr. Carmichael. Don't hesitate to call if I can be of service." He rose and turned toward the door.

"And please be assured that, if need be, I would be happy to stand by your side."

———————

The total transmission was in now, and the technicians ran off several copies. Each copy consisted of a set of six disks, labeled and wrapped in a plastic sealer.

Baines signed out a set and spent more than an hour in his office simply paging through the introductory manual, gazing at the geometric designs, trying to absorb the reality that these figures had actually been assembled by brains that were not human. The knowledge literally lifted him onto a new emotional plain.

Now, of course, he'd be working round the clock. And he'd need a copy of the complete transmission back in his quarters. Much more convenient that way. He looked around and found some blank disks.

He went back to his office, duplicated the set, returned the originals, and left with the copies. An hour later, he was in his villa, seated in front of a notebook computer, ready to take his first serious plunge into the arcane world of extraterrestrial communications.

Outside, a steady wind sucked at the trees.

———————

Harry strode into Gambini's office, described his conversation with Pappadopoulis, listened to a couple of similar stories from the project manager, and exchanged sympathies. "Somebody's got to talk to the President," Gambini said, pouring a cup of coffee for Harry. "He's only getting one side, the security consideration. He's up there, listening to people like Maloney, and a lot of conservative political advisors, who can only think about what might go wrong. They're so goddam shortsighted. Harry, I do not want to become part of a political exercise."

"It's a function of the job," Harry said. He'd been with government a long time and understood that projects with a downside were never, if it could be avoided, exposed to daylight until they'd been successfully completed.

"Dammit, Harry, I've waited all my life for something like this, never dared let myself hope it might actually happen, and the sons of bitches are getting in the way. Listen, Hurley has a chance to do some real good here. We won't get world peace out of this, but he has an opportunity to knock down some fences.

"We've never acted as a species. There was a chance at the end of the Second World War, and another at the end of the Cold War. But this, Harry, this: What more natural way to draw everybody together than the sure and certain knowledge, as Pete likes to say, that there's someone else out there?

"What really frustrates me is that Rosenbloom is perfectly content with the way things are going."

"But we *don't* know what might be in the transmission, Ed. I think there's a legitimate argument to be made."

"You're right. It *could* blow up, and people could get burned. But the odds are against anything like that happening. What the hell, Harry, it was a downhill slide during most of the last century anyhow, and I can't see that things are getting better in *this* one. Maybe we need a good gamble, one that we take together, to change the flow. We've got a mystery, and we'll do a lot better involving everyone than trying to solve it without telling anybody what's going on." His eyes narrowed. "I think we need to do an end run."

"No," said Harry. "*You* do an end run if you want. Leave me out of it. I don't want to wind up in Colorado with Fish and Wildlife."

Gambini straightened his tie and stared hard at Harry. "Okay. I can't really blame you. But you understand we're becoming historical characters, Harry. What's been happening here during the last few weeks, and what's going to happen as we get deeper into this thing, is going to be dissected and written about for a long time to come. I want to be sure that, when they start doing the summing-up, I don't show up on the wrong side."

"Funny. That's what Pappadopoulis said to me."

"It'll happen, Harry. This is too big for it not to."

"Why do you need *me*?" asked Harry.

"Because I can't just walk in the door over at the White House. But *you* can get me in."

"How?"

"They're having the annual National Science Foundation banquet over there Thursday. The President will be passing out awards to some high-school kids. It's a big media event, and it would be the ideal opportunity to get to him. But I have to get in first. NASA would have access to some tickets if we asked." Gambini leaned forward. "How about it, Harry?"

"You don't really care if they put me out in the mountains, do you?" Harry wished it would all just go away. Like his marriage. If Gambini went to the President, and it got back to Rosenbloom, Harry would be in the glue. On the other hand, what was the worst they could do to him? He was civil service, so he couldn't be fired. But they could put him in an office in a corner of one of the agencies downtown and sentence him to doing crossword puzzles.

He liked Goddard, but he felt inferior to the men and women who looked into deep space while he arranged their group insurance. Maybe he'd begun to imbibe their scarcely concealed contempt for his profession. "I'll see what I can do," he said.

"Invite Baines, too," said Gambini. "The President likes Baines."

———

"I can't help but wonder," John Hurley said in his rich baritone, surveying the two dozen young people seated at the two front tables, "whether we don't have another Francis Crick with us in the room today? Or a Jonas Salk? Or a Baines Rimford?" There was a brief stir, and a smattering of applause grew until it swept the room. Rimford rose with appropriate modesty and acknowledged the salute.

The President returned his attention to the high-school kids. "Perhaps, in a sense," he said, "it's sufficient for us to reflect on what has brought us together today and on what you now are. I'm sure Professor Rimford would agree that the future will take care of itself. So let's set that aside for now and enjoy the moment we have. You can take pride in what you have accomplished. It's what brought you here. But I suspect, for most of you, it is only the beginning."

Harry watched with interest. Hurley never used notes,

always seemed to speak spontaneously, and it was said of him that he could hold an audience spellbound while reading a telephone book. Some who'd been around Washington for a while thought he was the best orator since Kennedy. Maybe the best ever. But Harry never really thought of the President as an orator, and therein lay his peculiar genius. When one heard Hurley, it was never with the sense of listening to a declamation. Rather, one sat across from him in an easy chair, or in a dimly lit corner of a bar, and engaged in a conversation. Somehow he managed the illusion that the conversation was two-way, back and forth. And it didn't seem to matter who you were. Dockworker and economist: Hurley spoke to them all in their own language, and frequently did it at the same time. The gift of tongues, Tom Brokaw had called it.

Rimford appeared to be enjoying himself immensely. They'd arrived early, and he'd wandered among the young prizewinners, asking questions, listening to their answers, and shaking their hands.

The lateness of the request had prevented their getting choice locations. Rimford, of course, was awarded a seat at the President's table. Harry was in the back of the room, and Gambini sat to one side gloomily wedged between two garrulous representatives of the Indianapolis school district, which had a pair of recipients that year. When one of them invited him to change seats, he found himself beside a young woman from JPL who, discovering his identity, proceeded to object at length to his handling of the Hercules operation and persisted in glowering at him through the rest of the banquet.

"Professor Rimford," continued Hurley, "I wonder if we can impose on you to make the awards?"

"I'd be honored, Mr. President," Baines said, rising and ascending to the lectern while the audience applauded again. One of those tableaux that the media love followed: the President playing the role of flunky, calling out the names of the award winners, handing their certificates to Rimford, and standing modestly aside while the cosmologist made the presentations. It was, thought Harry, a brilliant performance. No wonder so many loved him despite the fact that he'd been able to deliver on so few of his promises.

When it was over, the President thanked Rimford, congratulated the students again, added a few closing remarks, and started for the door. Gambini, surprised by the suddenness of the retreat, jumped to his feet and hurried in his wake. But he had no Secret Service escort, and the media closed around him before he'd gone more than a few steps. Harry watched with growing dismay; Hurley was striding toward an exit while Gambini tried to break free.

The President paused to speak with Cass Woodbury of CBS. A couple of other reporters crowded in. Out on the floor, klieg lights blazed, and people laughed. Spectators, trying to get a closer look at Hurley, pushed against Harry's chair, and someone at his table knocked over a glass. Gambini was no longer visible.

———————

Hurley was still speaking with Woodbury, glancing at his watch, leaning toward the exit. Chilton, the White House press secretary, held the door that the President would pass through.

Harry got up slowly, more or less hoping that Hurley would leave so he would not have to get involved. But Woodbury continued to press him. Harry pushed forward and got between him and the exit. Hurley was trying to end the conversation with the journalist. "That's really all I have, Cass," he said. "New Jersey hasn't asked for federal help. But we'll be there if we're needed." He turned away, smiled into a TV camera, waved to someone down on the floor, and signaled to his people to get him out.

Harry was almost at his shoulder now. One of the agents had begun to eye him.

Another reporter tried to get in a question. Something about the Middle East, and another agent moved to cut her off as Hurley turned away and tried to get through the door. In that moment, Harry crossed his vision. "Mr. President," he said, knowing he was making a mistake.

Hurley needed only a moment to place the speaker. "Harry," he said, "I didn't know you were here today."

"Dr. Gambini is also here, sir. We'd like to have a word with you if it's possible. It's important."

The good humor that had marked the President's bearing throughout the presentation did not exactly drain away. But

Harry saw lines appear around his mouth, and the dark eyes
behind his bifocals grew wary. "Ten minutes," he said. "In my
quarters."

Dostoevsky, Tolstoy, Dickens, and Melville lined the walls of
the sitting room. The books were leather-bound, and one,
Anna Karenina, lay open on a coffee table. "These are worn,"
Harry told Gambini, examining the volumes. "You don't suppose Hurley, of all people, reads Russian novels?"

"If he does, I think he's smart to keep it quiet." Gambini was
sitting with his eyes closed, hands pushed into his pockets,

Sunlight streamed into the room. The NSF group was visible through arched windows, spread out across the White
House lawn below, officials, parents, teachers, and kids, taking pictures, comparing awards, and generally having a good
time.

They heard voices in the corridor outside; then the door
opened, and Hurley entered. "Hello, Ed," he said, extending
his hand. "Good to see you." He turned to Harry. "I wanted to
thank you for suggesting Baines. He was magnificent out there
today."

The President, thought Harry, had a taste for hyperbole.

Hurley took a chair and solicited comments on the prize-
winning projects. Gambini pronounced himself duly
impressed though Harry could see he was too preoccupied
with his own concerns to have paid much attention. "I'm glad
you came by," the President said. "I've been meaning to call
you. Ed, Hercules has interesting possibilities. I'm intrigued
by what you and your people are doing over there. But you
know how I get my information? You talk to Rosenbloom,
Rosenbloom talks to a couple of other people until it gets to
the top of NASA, then it comes over here to Schneider." That
was Fred Schneider, Hurley's ambitious science advisor. "By
the time it gets to me, I don't know how many distortions it's
picked up, what's being shaded, or what's been left out altogether." He pulled a memo pad across the table, wrote a number on it, tore it off, and gave it to Gambini. "That's how you
can reach me whenever you need to. If I'm not immediately
available, I'll get back to you. In any case, call every morning

at, um, eight fifteen. I want to be kept informed about what's going on out there. You understand?"

"Yes, Mr. President," said Gambini.

"I especially want to know about any breakthroughs in reading the stuff. I want to know what kind of material we're getting. And I'll be interested in hearing your views on the implications of any of this."

Somehow, Harry wound up with the phone number.

It was a bit warm in the room. "You *are* still making progress?" he continued. "Good. In that case, why don't you tell me what you have for me?"

"Mr. President," Gambini began hesitantly, "we're not being as efficient as we might be."

"Oh? And why not?"

"For one thing, our staff is too limited. We haven't been able to get the people we need."

"Security problems?" asked Hurley. "I'll look into it and try to streamline things a bit. Meantime, Ed, you have to realize the sensitivity of this operation. As a matter of fact, I issued an order this morning assigning code-word classification to the Hercules Text. You'll be getting some assistance with your security measures this afternoon."

Gambini looked pained. "That's exactly the problem, Mr. President. We can't get things done when we can't communicate with the experts in various disciplines. Security clearances take time, and we don't always know in advance who we're going to need. If we have to wait six months to get someone in here, we might as well not bother."

Hurley's jaw tightened a notch. "I'll see what I can do. Is that all?"

"Mr. President," said Harry, breaking a promise to himself to keep quiet, "there's a strong feeling among the investigators, and in the scientific and academic communities, that we've no right to keep a discovery of this magnitude to ourselves."

"And how do *you* feel, Harry?"

Harry looked into the President's penetrating gray eyes. "I think they're right," he said.

"The academic and scientific communities," Hurley replied with the slightest flicker of annoyance, "don't have to deal with the Chinese. Or the Arabs. Or a couple dozen desperate countries that would like nothing better than to develop a cheap new superweapon to lob over the back fence at someone they don't like. If *physicists* make a mistake, people don't die. My situation's a little different, and it requires caution." His eyes slid shut. "Who knows what might be in that transmission?"

"I think," said Gambini, putting everything he had into one roll, "we're being a little paranoid."

"Do you really? That's an easy assertion for you to make, Ed. If you're wrong"—he shrugged—"what the hell!" He closed the blinds and shut the sunlight out of the room. "Don't you think I know how this makes us look? The press thinks I'm a fascist, and the American Philosophical Society wrings its hands in anguish. But where the hell will the American Philosophical Society be if we set in motion a chain of events that leads to a catastrophe?" He sighed, and it signaled weariness, indecision, frustration. It was an expression unlike any Harry had seen him use in public. "You can't have the extra people until we're sure we can trust them. If that means an extra few days, or an extra few years, so be it. We keep the transmissions to ourselves. I'll give you this much: You can announce that there's been a second signal, and you can release the pictures, the triangles and whatnot. But the other stuff, what we haven't been able to read yet, until we can tell what it is, it stays under wraps."

An hour later, Majeski greeted them with the latest news. "We've found the Pythagorean Theorem."

MONITOR

ASU BLASTS HURLEY

SCIENCE GROUP
DEMANDS ASSURANCES ON HERCULES

. . .

MOVE TO LEGALIZE
GAINS STRENGTH IN CONGRESS

COCAINE, OTHER DRUGS,
TO BE DISPENSED THROUGH CLINICS

AMA ANNOUNCES
SUPPORT FOR MEASURE

. . .

DEADLOCK IN GENEVA

CHINA HINTS WALKOUT

. . .

OLYMPIAN HOPEFUL HAS LEUKEMIA

TRACK STAR BRAD CONROY
COLLAPSES DURING SPRINT

. . .

KIDS DERAIL FREIGHT TRAIN

IRON BAR UPENDS DIESEL; TWO HURT

. . .

CURE FOR DIABETES MAY BE CLOSE

. . .

DRIVE TO LIMIT PUBLIC ACCESS
AT PETRIFIED FOREST

PERMITS ONLY ANSWER TO VANDALISM,
SAYS MURRAY

BUT CRITICS WONDER
WHAT WILL GO NEXT

. . .

MILBOURN SEES NO DANGER
FROM INFLATION

MARKETS RALLY

. . .

HOW TO LIVE TO BE A HUNDRED

"PA" DECKER, ON HIS BIRTHDAY,
RECOMMENDS SENSE OF HUMOR

BUT IT'S GETTING HARDER, HE SAYS

. . .

TERRORISTS STILL HOLD
TWO HOSTAGES AT LAKEHURST

NUCLEAR CLOUD
COULD DRIFT OVER PHILADELPHIA

GOVERNOR RULES OUT USE OF FORCE

"WE CAN NEGOTIATE
WITH THESE PEOPLE"

. . .

AL KALA LEADER KILLED

ABDUL HADDI TAKEN OUT
DURING BOMBING STRIKE

. . .

PENTAGON DENIES CHARGES
OF OVERPAYMENT

THOUSAND-DOLLAR SCREWDRIVERS

TWO CHARGED AT UBS

||| EIGHT |||

Harry set up the press conference for 10:00 A.M. next day. He brought in an artist to produce some graphics of the Althean star system and spent a sizable chunk of the preceding evening helping a reluctant Ted Parkinson get ready to deliver a prepared statement, field questions, and release the introductory section of the transmission. Parkinson, who was Goddard's director of public relations, was unhappy. Like many of the others connected with the project, he felt his integrity had been damaged by the handling of Hercules. He was growling freely about management and implying without directly saying so that he wasn't excluding Harry from that despicable class.

Parkinson's platform skills and excellent working relationship with the press were an essential asset at the moment. He commented by way of tossing another dart Harry's way that he hoped it was a relationship that would survive the day. Although he made no direct threat to resign, the suggestion was clearly there.

In the morning, Rosenbloom was visibly upset.

"President's orders," Harry explained somewhat awkwardly, without getting into details.

The director huffed. "Where was *I* while all this was going on?"

"Don't know, sir. I left a message on your machine."

Rosenbloom's eyes narrowed. He scribbled a note to himself, then the mood seemed to pass. "It's a blunder, Harry," he said. "But the damned fool will do what he wants, and nobody can tell him different." He glared at the ceiling. "All right, go with it. But have Ted keep it as short as he can."

The pressroom, located at the visitor center, would not be adequate. Harry commandeered every loose chair he could find and grabbed the biggest available space, which was in Building 4. They changed the drapes and hung pictures of whirlpool galaxies, antenna arrays, and rocket launches. Most of the rear wall was already covered by the Fourth Uhuru Catalog Map, which displayed prominent X-ray features throughout the galaxy. Parkinson had several models of boosters and satellites brought over from the visitor center.

When they were finished, Harry pronounced himself satisfied. "We'll try to keep this room available," he told Parkinson, as the TV trucks began to arrive. "We're going to need it again."

He retreated to his office and absorbed himself with maintenance reports. A few minutes before ten, he turned on the television. Two NBC newsmen were speculating about the Goddard conference, and, not entirely to Harry's surprise, they guessed that a second signal had come in.

CNN ran aerial views of the facility and sketched a brief history of the space center, ending with clips from the presidential press conference of the preceding week. Then, precisely at ten, the cameras cut inside, and Parkinson entered the meeting hall.

The young public-relations director projected exactly the sort of image Harry wanted: a youthful, energetic appeal, laced with good humor and a sense of dedication. He did not intend Parkinson to produce the kind of media performance so common in the upper tiers of government, reading a self-serving statement and ducking for cover.

A computer stood beside the lectern.

Parkinson gazed out across his audience, and the journalists grew quiet. "Good morning, ladies and gentlemen," he began. "At 1:09 A.M. last Saturday, Skynet detected a second signal from the Hercules group."

He went on to describe the characteristics of the transmission, then he delivered the bombshell: "I can also tell you that we've been able to read certain small—" It was as far as he got. Pandemonium broke out. Some shouted for clarification. Did he mean we could understand what the aliens were saying? What *were* they saying? Would transcripts be made available?

Parkinson held out his hands and waited for the noise to subside.

"If you'll bear with me, ladies and gentlemen," he said, switching to a more deliberate pace to draw out the suspense. "We're able to read certain small portions of the transmission. What we have so far is only a beginning: a few mathematical images and some well-known theorems."

"*What* theorems?" called a woman from the *Washington Post*.

"Common ones. The square of the hypotenuse is equal to the squares of the other two sides. Like that.

"The material is contained in the first segment, or data set, of the transmission. The transmission itself now appears to be complete. It has been divided by the Altheans into four hundred seventeen data sets. This one"—he held up a disk—"appears to be designed primarily as a greeting and instruction manual. Let me take a moment here to say that, despite our progress, we are a long way from actually being able to read the text."

Someone wanted to know whether the Altheans had transmitted the signal deliberately to Earth. *Do they know we're here?*

"I'd appreciate it," said Parkinson, "if you'd hold the questions until I've finished. But I'll answer *that* one. No, they certainly do not know we're here. Keep in mind, the signals were sent a long time ago. From very far away."

That got a laugh.

He described the method that had been used to enter the binary code. "We had an assist," he said, "from the *Enterprise*." That got another laugh and broke the tension. Harry'd had reservations about telling that part of the story, but Parkinson insisted that it was exactly the sort of colorful ingenuity that made good copy and won friends. In the tradition of the space center, however, no individual credit was given, and Harry lost his chance for immortality.

"Now," Parkinson continued, "I'd like to show you the first pictures ever received from another world."

They'd made a video. It was about two minutes long, a montage of the cubes and cylinders contained in the instruction manual. While the images ran, Cass Woodbury in a whispery voice-over commented on the contrast between the "mundane figures and their transcendent significance."

The Saturn representation appeared. The audience buzzed

with surprise. Harry thought that, at that moment, an emotional link was forged between the human race and the entities at the other end of the transmission.

Now a vaguely spidery figure was taking shape on-screen.

"What's *that*?" asked a silver-haired woman from the *Philadelphia Inquirer*. Her tone suggested she thought someone was playing a joke.

"We don't know," said Parkinson. "It could be anything, I suppose. A tree. A wiring diagram. I suspect, before we're finished, we'll find a great deal we can't explain."

It was a good response. Nevertheless, an uneasy sensation crept over Harry. He'd debated leaving that one out and now wished he had.

————

They got a lot of coverage.

"There has been a second signal," said Holden Bennett, on CBS. His magisterial demeanor, concerned, somber, soothing, was in full flow. If anything explained his dominance of television news, it was his ability to couple a sense of crisis with the impression that he himself could see beyond its numbing daily impact into the green uplands.

NASA's recently adopted logo, a stylized representation of the original Hubbell, with its energy panels spread like butterfly wings, replaced him on the screen. "In a dramatic press conference minutes ago at the Goddard Space Center in Greenbelt, Maryland," he continued, in his exquisite diction, "officials announced that another transmission has been received from the Altheis star system in the Hercules constellation. This time, however, there is an important difference."

The logo faded to an aerial shot of the complex. "The first signal was nothing more than a repeating sequence, which, according to NASA spokesman Ted Parkinson, served only to alert us to the presence of a civilization in the stars. But now, this far-off civilization has actually sent us a message. And NASA analysts have already made a start at reading the text." The space center gave way to a brilliant, majestically rotating galaxy. "What's really out there? Cass Woodbury has been following the day's history-making events at Goddard. Cass—?"

And so it went.

In all, the coverage was restrained and almost understated. The network displayed the cubes and triangles, while a mathematical expert tried to guess what it might all mean. They showed the ringed sphere, and another expert, an astronomer, made the blindingly obvious comment that it was no doubt meant to represent a planet. But the final design was the real story, and the network allowed the image to take shape in precisely the manner it had occurred on the Goddard monitor.

The effect was chilling, in a way that Harry could not have foreseen. The object was somehow more clearly defined. More ominous. Sitting alone in his office, he found it strangely affecting, more so than he had at the lab. Here, it seemed to stir some primal emotion deep in his soul.

Elsewhere, an Arab terrorist group had bombed a Parisian hotel, and another drug scandal was erupting in pro football.

Addison McCutcheon closed off his ABC newscast with a scathing commentary: "At the conclusion of the press conference today, the government distributed copies of a part of the transmission they call 'Data Set One.' There are one hundred and seven other data sets, of which no mention was made save that they exist. When he was asked about these, Parkinson stated that they would be released as they were translated. The translation of *that* particular piece of double-talk is that the administration intends to withhold this historic story until it decides what the rest of us can know about it.

"Hangar 51 lives."

Ten minutes later, Gambini was on the phone. "You know what's going on over here?"

"Where?" he asked. "Are you at the lab?"

"Yes. You might want to take a look."

A man and a woman, two people he'd never seen before, were posted inside the main entrance. Plastic IDs, with *SECURITY* in large black letters, were clipped to their lapels. They'd erected a screening device, not unlike the metal detectors used in airports, and as Harry watched, two departing interns were required to pass through.

Signs were prominently posted: *COMPUTER DISKS MAY*

NOT LEAVE THE BUILDING. And: *WARNING: ATTEMPTS TO REMOVE DISKS PUNISHABLE BY FEDERAL LAW.*

"Who are you?" Harry asked the woman, who seemed to be in charge.

The woman frowned, as if he had said something untoward, and glanced down at her badge. "Agent Hart," she said. "Presidential Special Security Task Force. May I help you?" She was in her forties, tall, dark, a woman who might once have been attractive but whose assets had been overtaken less by time than by inflexibility.

"What are you doing here?" he demanded.

She fixed him with a cool stare. Then: "May I ask who *you* are?"

"Harry Carmichael," he said, trying not to sputter. "I'm—"

"I know your function, Mr. Carmichael." She reached behind her, picked up a plastic badge marked *TEMP*, and held it out for him. "We've established a presence at the main-gate security office. They'll have your permanent ID, which you'll be required to wear at all times."

"By whose direction?"

"I suggest you ask your questions there, Mr. Carmichael. They'll be better able to provide answers."

Katherine Hasson, a secretary, came out of one of the ground-floor offices. She nodded to Harry, walked through the screening device, and left the building. Gambini now appeared on the second-floor landing atop the stairway. He waved to Harry and shrugged.

"What is this thing?" Harry asked.

"It scrambles computer disks," said Agent Hart. "You can bring them in, but you can't take them out."

"You can't do that," said Harry.

She shrugged. "You'll have to talk to the people in charge, Mr. Carmichael."

Harry almost retorted *I'm in charge*. He thought better of it, saw that Gambini had disappeared, and brought out his cell phone.

———

Ten minutes later, he was in Rosenbloom's office.

"Harry," the director said, "I was about to call you to clue you in on what was happening." Pat Maloney was seated on a divan, and an African-American in a crisp gray suit took up the better part of a sofa. "You know Pat," he said.

Maloney nodded. He was a thin, nervous man with a neatly trimmed mustache, a three-piece suit, and a permanent cringe. He'd begun life as a real-estate agent, an occupation at which he'd apparently been successful, had got himself elected to the Jersey City Water and Sewage Board, and had moved on up to his present exalted position as White House special assistant for security.

Harry shook his hand. It was damp.

Rosenbloom turned to the African-American. "Dave Schenken," he said. "One of Pat's people."

Schenken appraised Harry. He was tall, beefy, clean-shaven, with hard eyes.

"Dave'll be spending the rest of the afternoon with you," said the director. "He needs to get an overview of the security system here, and he'll want to make some suggestions."

"Actually," said Schenken offhandedly, "we've already had a pretty good look at your security arrangements." His voice was dry, like paper that had been too long in the sun. "I wouldn't want to offend you, Carmichael, but I'm surprised nobody's walked off with one of your telescopes."

"We don't have any telescopes," Harry replied, and turned toward Maloney. "Look, maybe we should start by realizing this isn't a defense installation. We don't keep secrets here."

Maloney shook his head, signaling that Harry was dead wrong. "In fact, Dr. Carmichael," he said, "you will have to start keeping secrets, or we'll move the Hercules Project someplace where they can."

"I'm not a doctor," said Harry.

"Now, for the record," he continued, ignoring Harry's comment, "all the materials related to Hercules are classified. Dave will give you the details. Incidentally, the lower level of the Research Projects Laboratory is being converted now so you can continue to operate in there."

"Converted?"

"We've restricted access," said Schenken. "And we'll be making some structural changes to the building."

Maloney leaned back against the edge of the director's

heavy desk. "In addition," he said, "we're running security checks on the employees. At the President's direction, we've issued temporary clearances to the U.S. citizens. It may be—"

"Wait a minute," said Harry. "Not everybody here is U.S. We have some Canadians, Brits, a couple of Germans. A Russian."

"Not anymore."

Harry's pulse began to throb. He glanced at Rosenbloom, who was signaling him not to cause trouble.

"Sorry," Maloney continued. "I know that might be inconvenient, but you'll have to replace anybody who's not U.S."

"We can't do that—" said Harry.

"Out of my hands, Dr. Carmichael." He showed Harry his palms. "I'm only following procedure."

Schenken produced a bound volume, which he passed to Rosenbloom. "We'd like you to read this," he said. "Everybody involved with Hercules will get one. It's a description of the procedures for handling classified information. It lays out the responsibilities of management and the individual employee, and specifies penalties for failure to comply."

"We *have* a security force," protested Harry.

Maloney studied the desktop. "It's not adequate." He turned to Rosenbloom. "Dave will be running security operations here from now on."

"I understand," said Rosenbloom.

"Good." Maloney's gaze swung to Harry. "Try to understand, Doctor. The nature of the operation is different now. We are no longer talking about issuing parking tickets or ejecting a drunk from the visitor center. You now possess vital information that has to be safeguarded against determined efforts by foreign intelligence forces. Think what you like, but try to realize that this is not a game."

He nodded to Schenken, who visibly assumed command. "The situation is fluid," Maloney continued, "and as things now stand, Goddard has severe security problems. I would be less than honest with you if I didn't tell you up front that I intend to recommend the operation here be terminated and moved."

"Moved?" said Rosenbloom, finally reacting. "To where?"

"Probably Fort Meade. Meantime, we're going to tighten things as best we can."

"Can they do this?" Harry demanded of Rosenbloom.

"They can do what they have to," said the director. And to Schenken: "Let me know what you need."

Maloney nodded and glanced at Harry. "So we understand each other, Carmichael: I don't like this any more than you do. I understand the special problems you have, and we'll try not to create any more trouble than we have to. But we *will* maintain control over access to the project, and I will expect your complete cooperation."

————

Harry and Pete Wheeler had dinner that evening at Rimford's villa in the VIP section behind the geochemistry lab. While they grilled steaks and baked potatoes, they drank cold beer and talked about the security crackdown. Rimford did not share the anger of the other two. "It's inevitable," he said. "Who knows what we have here? You really want to take a chance that some of these nutcase dictators will learn how to build a better H-bomb?"

Harry had already called in the non-U.S. citizens to tell them their services had been discontinued, effective immediately. Several were NASA employees who would be transferred to other jobs. Three were consultants who would simply be paid off and turned loose. "Don't worry about it," Wheeler told him. "They understand how it is."

By the time the steaks were done, the conversation had turned back to the one topic that dominated everything. "Actually, we're not doing badly," said Rimford, answering a question regarding progress with the translation. "We can read the numbers now, and we've assigned working symbols to some of the bytes that seem to occur in patterns.

"Some of the symbols are directive. That is, we're pretty sure they perform the functions that correlatives or conjunctions would in a grammatical system. Others have a substantive reference, and we're beginning to get some of those. For example, we've isolated terms meaning *magnetism*, *system*, *gravity*, *termination*, and a few more. Other terms *should* translate because they're embedded in familiar equations or formulas, but they don't."

"Concepts," offered Harry, "for which we have no equivalent."

Wheeler grinned. "Maybe." It was getting dark, so they carried everything onto a screened porch, where they ate by the light of a table lamp. "How much in advance of us would they have to be to be able to do the things we know they can do? Are we likely to have anything at all in common?"

"We already know," said Harry, "that we have a common base in math and geometry."

"Of course," snapped Wheeler impatiently. "How could there be any other condition? No, I'm thinking about their philosophy, their ethical standards. I was interested in your story about Hurley's fears regarding the contents of the transmission." He looked at Rimford. "Maybe you're right about the security people." He refilled his mug and drank with a purpose. "But I think he's worried for the wrong reason. I'm not nearly so afraid of the technology we may find as I am of the possibilities for poison of other kinds."

"Cultural values—"

"Yes. And the assumption we may make that because they're older than we are, which they certainly would have to be, that they have the edge on truth."

Rimford gazed out the window at the dying light. "You know," he said, "before the Hercules signal, I'd concluded we were alone. The Fermi paradox made sense to me. A living galaxy, at the very least, should have filled the sky with transmissions. If there were other civilizations, surely there would have been evidence of their existence."

Wheeler held up the last piece of his steak, examined it in the lamplight, and finished it.

"I was driving through Roanoke one night," continued Rimford, "and it occurred to me why there might be no evidence." He was working on a baked potato while he talked. "Is there a correlation between intelligence and compassion?"

"Yes," said Harry.

"No," said Wheeler. "Or if there is, it's a negative one."

"Well, I don't guess we have a consensus." Rimford opened his arms to the skies. "I'm inclined to agree with Pete."

"What's your point?" asked Harry.

"Any society smart enough to survive its early technological period should conclude that even the *knowledge* of its existence could have deleterious effects on an emerging culture. I mean, *we've* figured that out. It even shows up as *Star Trek*'s prime directive. Who's to say what such knowledge might do, for example, to the religious foundations of a society?"

"That's an old idea," said Wheeler. "But you're suggesting we might be listening to a culture that is actively malevolent. That takes satisfaction in disrupting societies it hasn't encountered. And will never know."

"It might be perceived as a religious obligation," said Rimford, slyly.

Wheeler nodded, refusing to take the bait. "Wouldn't surprise me."

"There's a better explanation," said Harry. "The old cliché: Never ascribe to malevolence what can safely be attributed to stupidity."

"Morons with the technology of their bright ancestors," said Rimford. "Now *that's* an interesting thought." He refilled their glasses, and they gazed out at the surrounding woods. "There *is* something we need to consider, though. We know the Hercules transmitter is a product of extreme sophistication. What happens if we get a million years' worth of technology overnight?" His face was hidden in shadow. "Pete was talking about the philosophical problems that might arise. Here's a variant: Toward the end of the nineteenth century, some physicists announced that nothing remained to be learned in their discipline. From that point, it would all be simply a matter of measuring and cataloging. It's an interesting notion, and it's been showing its head again recently. The end of science. Break through to the Theory of Everything, and after that, it's over. What *would* happen to us, to all of us, if that indeed were to happen? If these people just flat out told us how everything worked? Left nothing for us to do?"

Harry had found a canvas chair, and he relaxed in it, setting his beer down on a side table. "It wouldn't affect most people at all, Baines. Most of us just want to pay the mortgage and watch TV. It's only a handful of troublemakers who'd worry because we no longer needed supercolliders."

Rimford made a sound deep in his throat and glanced at his

watch. "We may be about to discover the true nature of *time*. Except that *we* won't discover it. The Altheans will explain it to us." He shook his head. "I think the bastards, if they've really done that, are mean-spirited. And it's hard to believe they didn't know what they were doing."

"Maybe," said Wheeler, "this would be a good night to find something else to think about. How about putting a bridge game together?"

"Thanks," said Rimford, "but I've agreed to do an interview tonight. NBC is getting several people together to talk about the transmission. They've set up a studio in D.C."

"Be careful what you say," observed Wheeler. "How about you, Harry?"

Harry didn't much like Friday nights anymore. The prospect of getting through one painlessly was appealing. "Can we get two more?"

"I know where we can fill out a table," Wheeler said. "There are always a couple of guys at the priory ready for a game."

The Reverend Rene Sunderland, O. Praem., playing against three no-trump, startled Harry early in the evening by discarding a good ace of clubs on the opening lead. Moments later, when he got in with the diamond king, Sunderland trapped Harry's queen and ten of clubs against his partner's king and jack, using them as entries to set up his partner's long club suit. Down three. Harry looked to see if there was a mirror behind him.

It was only the beginning.

"They cheated," Harry complained later to Pete during a break for coffee and Danish. "There was no way he could have known. They're signaling each other. He's made half a dozen plays where it just wasn't possible to figure out the lay of the cards."

Wheeler and Harry trailed by more than seven thousand points by then. "If this were a Dominican house," Wheeler replied, "you might have a case. Listen, Harry: Rene is *very* good. And it doesn't matter who his partner is. I've sat opposite him, and he does the same kind of thing. He always plays as though he sees through the backs of everybody's cards."

"How do you explain it? What does *he* say?"

Wheeler smiled. "He claims it's a result of his devotion to the Virgin."

The second half of the evening was no better. Harry watched Sunderland's partner, a creaky brother with vacuous eyes, for indications of furtive signs. Other than a nervous tic that seemed to occur at random, he saw nothing.

He even took a long look at the decks, but the backs were all identical.

The community room was empty, save for the bridge players, a middle-aged priest reading a newspaper in front of a TV running a mindless interview show that no one seemed to be watching, and somebody bent over a jigsaw puzzle. "Everyone clear out for the weekend?" Harry asked idly.

Sunderland had just completed a small slam. "This is pretty much the entire community," he replied.

Wheeler looked up from the score sheet. "Harry, would you like to buy a nice place by the bay?"

"Is it really up for sale?"

Sunderland nodded.

"It can't be that bad."

"These aren't good times. We don't need this place anymore."

"You're serious."

"Oh, yes."

"What would happen to *you*, Rene?"

"Back to the mills, I guess. Unfortunately, most of us don't have Pete's education."

"Or his talent," said the brother.

"That, too. In any case, this time next year, I expect to be teaching in Philadelphia."

"They should send you to Las Vegas," observed Harry.

"Pete," said Sunderland, with sudden gravity, "what's going on at Greenbelt? Are you involved with these radio signals?"

"Pretty much," said Wheeler. "We're both with the Hercules Project. But there really isn't much to tell that hasn't been made public."

"There's actually somebody out there, though?"

"Yes." Harry picked up the deck on his left and began to distribute the cards.

"What do they look like?"

"We don't know."

"Do they look like us?"

"We don't know," said Wheeler. "I doubt it."

Toward the end of the evening, Harry and Wheeler rallied somewhat, but it never got respectable.

Afterward, they walked the clifftops, the priest and the bureaucrat, not talking much, listening to the sea and the wind. It was cold, and they hunched down into their coats. "It'll be a pity to lose all this," said Harry. "Isn't there any way the order can hold on to it?"

The moon was low on the water, and when Harry caught the proper angle, it vanished behind Wheeler's tall, spare figure, endowing him with a misty aura. "It's only real estate," he said.

Harry turned away from the bay, letting the wind push at his back. Looming over them, the two manor houses were gloomy and showed only an occasional square of yellow light. The dark trees beyond were in motion, whispering timelessly of other observers on other nights. It was a forest that might have stretched to the edge of the planet. "This," he said, "is exactly the sort of place where I'd expect to find the supernatural."

Wheeler laughed. "Rene does that to people." He pulled up his collar. "Well, whatever the spiritual characteristics of this place, we can't justify the expense." He shivered. "Want to start back?"

They walked silently a few minutes, along the flagstone pathway. At its far end, Harry could see the wooden stairs that led to the water's edge. "I wanted to thank you, by the way, for the invitation to bring Julie up here last weekend."

"It's okay," he said. "Anything we can do to help."

They reached the gravel walk, coming to it from a clutch of elms, and cut across a rear entrance where the warm air felt good. "We had our problems," he said. "We went walking along the cliff edge and got caught in a cloudburst." He grinned. "We got drenched."

"I'm glad to hear it."

"We spent half the night in an old boathouse."

"I know the place," said Wheeler.

Harry's mood lightened. "It's a *good* place. The boathouse. It doesn't look as if anyone's been in there for twenty years."

Wheeler didn't reply.

"We used to talk about how it would be to live on an island, away from everything. And there's a lot to recommend that. I think if we could somehow shut out the rest of the world—" Harry looked back over his shoulder, at the darkness. "Anyhow, for a few hours, I had my island."

MONITOR

You know, friends, yesterday afternoon I was starting home after spending a few hours with some of the good folks at our hospital. And I got down as far as the lobby, where I saw a young man I knew. His name doesn't matter. He's a fine boy; I've known him for many years and his family for many years. As it happens, he had heard I would be there, at the hospital, and something was pressing on him, something he wanted to ask me about.

Several of his friends were with him, but they hovered in the background, as boys will, pretending they were there for other reasons. I could see that the child was upset, that they were all upset. "Jimmy," I said to him, "what's wrong?"

He looked at his friends, and they all turned away. "Reverend Freeman," he said, "we've been watching the reports from Washington, you know, with the big telescopes they have there and the voices they're hearing from the skies. A lot of people say they shouldn't be doing that."

"Why not?" I asked him.

And he couldn't tell me. But I knew what he was trying to say. Some people are afraid of what they might find out there. Jimmy isn't the first to ask me that type of question since those scientists in Washington claimed, a couple of years ago, that they had seen the Creation. You don't hear much about that anymore.

But I will tell you this, brothers and sisters: I encourage their efforts. I applaud the attempt to listen in on this great universe of ours. I believe that any machine that can bring us closer to His handiwork can only fortify the faith that we've protected now for more than two thousand years. (Applause.)

The morning stars sang together, and all the sons and daughters of God shouted for joy. (More applause.)

I have been asked, "Reverend Freeman, why is the universe so very large?" It is big, you know, far bigger than the scientists who profess to know so much could even have guessed ninety or a hundred years ago. And why do you suppose that is? If, as the Gospel makes clear, man is the center of creation, why did the Lord construct a world so large that the scientists cannot even see its edge, however advanced their telescopes?

When I was a boy, I used to sit out by the barn on summer evenings and watch the stars. And I knew them for what they are: the shining footprints of the Almighty. And you ask why they are so far apart? I would say, because He recognized the arrogance of those who pretend to seize His secrets and reduce them to numbers and theorems. And I say to you that the size of the universe and the huge spaces between the stars and between the galaxies, which are great islands of stars, are a living symbol of His reality and a gentle reminder to us of the distance that exists between us and Him.

There are some now who have begun to say that the voices whispering out of the skies into those government telescopes are devils. I don't know about that. I haven't seen any evidence to support that notion. The skies, after all, belong to God; so I would rather suppose they're angels' voices. (Laughter.)

Probably, the creatures we hear will turn out to be very much like ourselves. There is nothing in the Gospel that limits God to a single creation. So I say to you, brothers and sisters, have no fears for what the scientists might learn in Washington; and do not be concerned with their theories. They are looking at the handiwork of the Almighty, but their vision is limited by their telescopes. We ourselves have in our faith a far better instrument.

—Excerpt from an address by the Reverend Bobby Freeman at his televised Sunday Morning Gospel Service. (Transcripts are available without charge from the American Christian Alliance.)

||| NINE |||

George Cardinal Jesperson had come to the archdiocese as a conservative in a time of troubles. He'd earned a reputation as a forceful, outspoken champion of the Vatican and the "old" Church. His stands on the nagging issues of priestly celibacy, contraception, and the role of women had been brilliantly argued, and had not gone unnoticed in Rome. His great chance had come in the clash with Peter Leesenbarger, the German reform theologian, on the question of the authority of the magisterium. Leesenbarger had argued for the preeminence of individual conscience over the accumulated wisdom of the Church. And his runaway bestseller, *Upon This Rock*, had for a time threatened a second revolution among the American faithful.

While orthodox churchmen argued that the book should be formally condemned, the Pope had wisely, in Cardinal Jesperson's view, satisfied himself by directing that its imprimatur be withheld. And the Cardinal, carefully avoiding any reference to *Upon This Rock*, had contributed to the defense of the papal decision with a brilliant series of closely reasoned essays that were picked up even by those elements of the Catholic press that were traditionally hostile to the Vatican. Leesenbarger had responded in the columns of the *National Catholic Reporter*, which became the arena for an extended series of broadsides by both combatants. In the end, Jesperson had emerged a clear victor to all but the most partisan observers. He was declared the heir apparent to John Henry Newman, with Leesenbarger cast in the role of the unfortunate Kingsley.

Unlike most other American cardinals, who were preoccupied with survival in an age of dwindling revenues and influence, Jesperson recognized early that the way to defend the faith in the United States had nothing to do with long-term loans, retrenchment, or conning the faithful with the guitars and spurious theology of Vatican II. He took the offensive. "We're about Christ," he told his priests' council. "We have the New Testament, we support strong family ties, we have God on our altars. The issues that divide us are not trivial, but they are a question of means rather than ends." He might have been a better psychologist than anyone in authority at the Vatican, which he unnerved by settling back to listen sympathetically to those who disagreed.

And in that way he had, to a remarkable extent, defused the liberal movement within the American Church. To many of its leaders he had seemed, and still seemed, their strongest ally.

But on this Friday evening, while the reports from Goddard continued to reverberate across the land, he faced a new kind of problem. So he gathered his staff, Dupre and Cox and Barnegat, and retired with them into the interior of the chancery. "Gentlemen," he said, sinking into a lush leather chair, "we need to think about what's coming. And we need to prepare our people so they don't get any rude shocks.

"Now, what is coming, I think, is a severe test of the faith. Certainly unlike any other in our time. We should consider, first, what the dangers are; second, how we may expect our people to react; and third, what approach we should take in order to limit the damage."

Philip Dupre was, by a considerable margin, the oldest man in the room. He was the Cardinal's touchstone, inevitably the composer of the provocative comment that changed the angle of light on a given problem. Generally lacking in creativity, he nevertheless had a good ear for nonsense, whether originating from the Cardinal or elsewhere. "There's no problem here," he might say, "unless our reaction creates one." On this occasion, he listened quietly while the issues were laid out, glanced at Cox, accepted his silent signal to proceed, and did so. "I think you're overstating the case, George," he said. "There's no real connection between the Goddard business and us."

Jack Cox struck a long wooden match and lit his pipe. He was the comptroller, a prudent investor, but a man who, in the Cardinal's view, tended to think of salvation as a series of puts and calls. "Phil's right," he said. "Still, depending on our stance, there could be awkward questions."

Dupre looked genuinely puzzled. "Like what?"

Lee Barnegat, a middle-aged man whose placid blue eyes concealed administrative and negotiating skills of the first order, removed his collar and placed it on the arm of his chair. "Do aliens have souls?"

Dupre's dour features broke into a slow smile. "Do we care?"

"If we still accept Aquinas," said Cox, "the ability to abstract from matter, to *think*, irrefutably defines an immortal soul."

"What," asked the Cardinal, "is the applicability of Christ's teachings to beings who are not born of Adam?"

"Come on, George," protested Dupre. "We're not tied to Eden anymore. Let the Bible thumpers worry about that."

"I wish we could," said Jesperson. "But I think we may have a few loose ends of our own." Despite his half century, the Cardinal still had the youthful good looks of his seminary days. "Did you see the pictures they got from the transmission? One of them is quite different from all the others."

Barnegat nodded. "You mean the one that looked like something out of Dali."

The Cardinal's usual serenity had become quite thin. He was clearly worried. "Yes," he said. "The speculation is that it is a self-portrait. Anyway, I'm glad to see that none of you is shocked by the claims. I hope the good people who show up at the cathedral Sunday share your equanimity."

"Why should they not?" asked Dupre.

"Man is made in the image of God. There is cause to doubt that simple truth, perhaps, when one sees what inhabits the streets these days. But it is doctrine, unassailable and eternal. What are we to say about these creatures, who, as Jack reminds us, themselves must possess immortal souls?" The Cardinal drew the last five words out, stressing their significance.

Dupre squirmed uncomfortably. He wore much the same expression he'd adopted at the last meeting, when the Cardinal had proposed granting still more latitude to the priests' council. "I hope," he said, "we're not really going to take any of this seriously. I'm certainly not prepared to believe that that odd little stick figure is a picture of a creature with a soul."

"Perhaps not," conceded Jesperson. "But I don't think it matters because if we can believe our experts, if we have indeed encountered aliens, whatever they look like, it will not be like us."

"But surely," objected Barnegat, "the resemblance referred to in doctrine is of the spirit, not of the body. Strictly speaking, God has no resemblance to any physical creature."

"Of course. But even so, we may find many among the laity who will be sorely tested by the notion of sharing salvation with, say, overgrown insects." The Cardinal's eyes moved among them, resting briefly on each. "What would we say if their transmissions revealed them to be, by our standards, by the standards of the New Testament, utterly godless and amoral—?"

"I see no problem with that," said Barnegat. "The human race fell from grace. There's no reason a variant of ourselves, if we might call them that, might not have done likewise. It's simply another failed creation."

"So," said Dupre, smiling, "God has a losing streak."

The Cardinal sighed. "What is our position should we be confronted by beings of compassion and apparent wisdom who, after a million years of examining the problem, have concluded that there is no God? Beings, perhaps, who have rejected His existence long before Jesus walked the Earth? Before Abraham, for that matter?"

Dupre grew thoughtful. "George, I think it might be our own faith that is failing here. Surely, we'll not have any revelations that will call into question what we know to be true. After all, we've never worried what they think in India."

"That sounds eminently reasonable," said Barnegat. "If these things are as unlike us physically as the stick figure implies, I doubt anyone is going to care much about their theology. If they recognize the authority of the universal Deity, fine. There's no problem. If they don't, I'm sure Phil's right. They can simply be shrugged off."

"Let me play devil's advocate for a moment," said Cox, "and ask a few questions that may occur to people after they've had a chance to think about things. Would every intelligent species in the universe be subject to a test, as Adam was?"

"We don't take Adam that seriously," said Dupre.

"The human race, then. We're agreed on that at least, aren't we? We were tested in some way, and we failed. I mean, that's the whole point of the Incarnation."

The Cardinal nodded, encouraging him to continue.

"Some failed the test," said Cox, "and, presumably, some must have passed."

"Maybe some weren't tested," suggested Barnegat.

Dupre's eyes closed while he considered the proposition. "That seems unfair," he said.

"Un-American," suggested Cox.

"Okay," persisted Dupre. "Some pass and some fail. Go on."

"The price of failure was death."

"I see where you're headed," said the Cardinal. "If some did not fall, then today they would have immortal bodies."

Dupre coughed. "We need a line of logic that avoids an undying species. I doubt anyone would take that kind of argument very seriously. Nothing that is physical can be immortal."

"Death," persisted Cox, "was the price of sin. Either we have immortals among the stars, or everybody flunked the test. And I submit that, if the latter is the true state of affairs, then we have a spurious test."

They were briefly silent. "If," Barnegat said, "we dismiss the validity of the test—"

"—We have," continued the Cardinal, "dismissed the validity of the Redeemer. Gentlemen, this sort of issue is the reason I am concerned. These are questions that will surely come up as this business plays out."

Dupre looked uncomfortable. "It's hard to get hold of any of this, George. I think our best course for now is to say nothing, to simply ride it out. Or wait for guidance from the Vatican. Let *them* deal with it. Surely, if it becomes an issue, there'll be a pastoral statement."

"You think," asked Cox, "they'll have better answers than we do?"

"That's not the point," said Dupre.

"It most certainly *is* the point," said the Cardinal. "We're not here to shift responsibility. What we need is a response that will safeguard the faith of the people in this archdiocese, who will be looking to us for answers. If we say the wrong thing, at the wrong time, we may find ourselves up to our elbows in alligators."

Elsewhere in the chancery, they heard the thump of the heating system kicking in. Dupre had been drawing figures in a notebook on a side table. Now he laid his pen down. "Does everybody," he asked, "remember Father Balkonsky? I think we're in danger of emulating his example."

"Who," asked Barnegat, "was Father Balkonsky?"

Jesperson's eyes crinkled with amusement. "He taught apologetics at Saint Michael's. His method was to set up one of the classic objections to the faith, the problem of evil, free will, God's foreknowledge, whatever. He then proceeded to rebut the arguments, relying more or less on Saint Thomas. The problem was that he seemed much more persuasive with the objections than with the rebuttals. A few seminarians complained. Others suffered through premature doubts about their faith, and a few left Saint Michael's altogether. And, for all I know, the Church."

"If," said Cox, "we don't have a coherent and persuasive position, we may raise the very doubts we hope to head off."

"There's something else we need to be careful about," said the Cardinal. "We don't want to take a theological position that might later become demonstrably false."

"Or worse," added Dupre, "ridiculous."

"I agree with Phil," said Barnegat. "Let's restrict ourselves to a general reassurance that nothing can come out of Goddard that is not provided for within the corpus of Church teaching. And let it go at that. Just a brief statement at the Masses."

The Cardinal's eyes had closed. The silver cross in his lapel glittered in the soft yellow light from a table lamp. "Jack?"

"That's probably prudent."

"I'm not so sure," said Dupre. "I can't imagine a better way to unnerve people than to tell them there's no cause for alarm."

They were silent for a minute. "Maybe," said Barnegat, "we should make no statement until we really know what we're dealing with. Inform the parishes we see no reason for alarm. Anyone raises a question, at least for now, we can simply suggest they have faith until things sort themselves out."

The Cardinal nodded. "I don't like it much, but I guess it's our safest course for the moment. Anyone strongly opposed?"

"It's our best approach," said Dupre. "People will keep the

faith no matter what." He smiled at Cox. "All we need do is emulate their example."

"All right, then. We'll draft a letter to the pastors, to be kept in strictest confidence. Jack, you write it. Express our concerns. Instruct them, if questioned, to take the position that the revealed faith is God's message to man and has nothing whatever to do with external agencies. Priests are not to bring the subject up."

For a long time after the others had left, the Cardinal sat silently, sunk in his chair. Until recently, the only other worlds he'd ever thought much about had not been of a physical nature. But since the government had begun listening to the stars, he'd taken time to think out the implications. And when, two years earlier, the survey of nearby solar systems had suggested that men were alone in God's creation, he'd been relieved.

But now, this.

When I behold your heavens, the work of your hands, the moon and the stars which you set in place—What is man that you should be mindful of him, or the son of man that you should care for him?

Dr. Arleigh Packard adjusted his bifocals and spread his prepared address on the lectern. This was his third appearance before the Carolingians. He'd marked previous occasions by revealing the existence of a journal maintained by a servant of Justinian I, covering in detail the emperor's reaction to the Hippodrome revolt; and a document in the hand of Gregory the Great excoriating the Turks and recommending that the crossbow be used against them. He'd let it be known that he had yet another juicy surprise for the society this year.

Consequently, his audience was in a state of considerable anticipation. He was happy to see that Perrault was present, from Temple; DuBay and Commenes from Princeton; and Aubuchon from La Salle. And it would be understating the facts to fail to notice that Packard himself was excited. The rich Viennese curtains behind him concealed a glass case that held a holograph letter from John Wyclif to a previously unknown supporter, outlining his intention to produce an

English translation of the Bible. The letter had been discovered in a London trunk only months before, the property of a dying garment manufacturer who'd never known he owned it.

At the lectern, Packard paused briefly, allowing Townsend Harris to step down after his introductory words, using the time to study his text and to allow suspense to build. He was surprised when he raised his eyes to find Allen DuBay on his feet. "Before we begin, Arleigh," he said in an apologetic tone, "I wonder if we might briefly address another matter of some urgency."

Informality had always been a hallmark of the Carolingians, but they were not inclined to tolerate outright boorishness. Olson, in front, grumbled loudly of Philistines, and a few others turned with obvious irritation toward DuBay. Packard, maintaining his equanimity despite a barely noticeable tensing of the jaws, bowed slightly and stepped to one side of the lectern.

DuBay's complexion was curiously tinted, perhaps by the sunlight filtered through the stained-glass window on his right, which depicted Beatrix of Falkenburg. Or perhaps it was an internal production of a more common sort. In any case, he was clearly not himself. His thin hair was disheveled, his tie hung at an awkward angle, and his fists were shoved aggressively into the pockets of his tweed jacket. "I regret interrupting Dr. Packard, who knows I would not do so lightly," he said, moving from his seat near the rear into the center aisle and proceeding briskly toward the front of the chamber.

"Sit down, DuBay!" roared a voice from the forward tier that everyone recognized as belonging to Harvey Blackman, a paleontologist from the University of Virginia whose interest in the Carolingians was more social than professional. He had developed a passion for another member, a nimble young antiquities collector from Temple.

Art Hassel, a specialist on Frederick Barbarossa, jumped to his feet. "This is no time for politics!" he shouted angrily, by which everyone understood that Hassel had already tried to dissuade DuBay from his demonstration.

"Ladies and gentlemen." DuBay reached the lectern and raised his hands, palms outward in a placating gesture. "I'd like first to thank Dr. Packard for relinquishing—"

"—More like you just took it over—" called a voice in back.

"—Relinquishing the microphone. I've spoken with many of you privately. And we share a common anguish at the events of the last few weeks. The Hercules Text belongs to us all, not to one government, or to a privileged few. Surely, if anyone recognizes the importance of this hour, it should be us—"

"That's quite enough, DuBay," cried Townsend Harris, rising from the speakers' table. "You're out of order."

But he plowed ahead. "I would like therefore to move that we issue a statement—"

"DuBay!"

"—Deploring the existing position of the government—"

Harris grabbed his sleeve and tried to pull him away from the lectern.

Everett Tartakower, on the right, rose majestically, a tall, graying archaeologist from Ohio State. "Just a minute." He crooked one long finger at Harris. "I don't particularly approve of Dr. DuBay's methods, Harris. But he has a point."

"Then let him make it with the steering committee!" shot back Harris, still struggling with DuBay.

"To be discussed when? Next year?"

Grace McAvoy, curator of the University Museum, wondered aloud whether it would not be wise to get some sense of the content of the Hercules transmission before continuing the discussion. "Next month," she said, "we could convene an electronic meeting—"

A chorus of hoots erupted on the left. Radakai Melis, from Bangkok, leaped onto the proscenium and pleaded for order. When he got it, or a semblance of it, he decried the economic policies of the United States and their role in ensuring the continued exploitation of the downtrodden peoples of Asia. Harris, having dragged DuBay off to one side, now went after Melis. Packard took advantage of the distraction to return to the microphone.

A woman whom Packard had never seen before stood up on a chair in back. "If matters are left to the goodwill and humanity of *this* government," she bawled, "we can be sure we'll *never* get the whole truth. It's probably already too late! We're going to go on forever asking questions and wondering whether critical pieces of information haven't been squirreled away somewhere because some bureaucrat in high office thinks they might be dangerous to the national security. I'll tell you what's dangerous: Hiding the truth, that's what's dangerous!"

Everyone was out of his chair now, and the shouting became general. A fight boiled out of the seats about eight rows back, spilled across the proscenium, engulfed the speakers' table, and swallowed DuBay.

The only journalist present, a reporter from the *Epistemological Review*, got the story of his life.

Packard, who knew a lost cause when he saw one, watched forlornly for a few seconds, took an elbow in the eye, walked behind the curtain, unlocked the display case, extracted the Wyclif letter, and left the building by a rear entrance.

H = .000321y/1t/98733533y

Well, thought Rimford, the old son of a bitch is still in the ball game.

It was almost 6:00 A.M. He'd appropriated an office for himself at the west end of the spaces serving the Hercules Project. He sat in it now, tired, irritated, his feet propped on his desk, staring at the ceiling. The days since they'd received the second signal had been an embarrassment. Despite his reputation, his contribution to the translation effort had been overshadowed by Majeski's single-minded brilliance and remarkable facility with computers. They'd made a reasonable start by noting that the transmission was divided into 417 sections. Data sets, divided by a repeating set of characters.

Four hundred seventeen subject areas? Four hundred seventeen chapters in a history? Four hundred seventeen segments in an architectural how-to manual? Who knew?

The 46.6 million characters broke out to approximately 7 million words. Give or take. The equivalent of, what, the *Encyclopedia Brittanica*? Did they have an encyclopedia here?

The next analytical step had been somewhat more difficult: isolating a few dozen syntactical constructions, thereby demonstrating that they were indeed looking at a language. They'd established some syntactical functions and even begun to put together a provisional vocabulary. The terms so far were all mathematical, but it was a start. Through all of this, Rimford had been little more than a bystander.

Everyone knew that mathematics was a young man's pastime, but to have it illustrated so convincingly, and by an arrogant individual who seemed unaware of Rimford's reputation, had been painful. The numbers no longer came together for him. He sensed no lessening of his ability, yet the intuition of earlier days, when equations rose from a different level of perception than he could now reach, was gone.

But maybe not entirely. Who else would have recognized the significance of the equation in data set 41, and consequently the importance of the entire segment?

The Hercules Project, if he could get his act together, would constitute a sublime climax to his career. When it was done, the essence of the transmission solved and its secrets extracted, when the details could be safely turned over to technicians, he would withdraw gladly to a contemplative existence. And to history.

$$H = .00032ly/1t/98733533y$$

Where y equals the distance light travels while Beta completes one orbit of Alpha, and t equals sixty-eight hours, forty-three minutes, thirty-four seconds, the period of Beta's orbit, the resulting figure is suspiciously close to our own best guess as to Hubble's Constant: the rate of expansion of the universe.

Magnificent! It was one of the more satisfying hours in a life resplendent with victories large and small. Rimford had settled in to look for other mathematical relationships, the Compton effect, possibly, or Mach's principle. Hurley had said it for them all: Who knew what might be buried in these electronic pulses?

But despite his exhilaration, he was tired. And he was violating his lifelong credo: to work at his own pace, to take time out to refuel, and to refuse to recognize pressure. Yet there was much in the numbers and symbols that lay before him that would not allow sleep: suggestions and relationships tantalizingly familiar, their significance just beyond reach.

He had begun to feel a reluctance about breaking into a

transmission from a culture that could manhandle stars. What knowledge might such a culture possess? Would they not have measured the length and width of the observable universe, counted all its planks, analyzed its cogs and sprockets? Might they even understand the manner of its creation? And perhaps have worked out a rationale for its existence?

His eyelids slid shut.

He needed rest. Moreover, the operations center and its offices were not conducive to thought. He didn't like working back at his quarters. Even though he had a copy of the complete transmission, he didn't have access to the project software or to the developing data banks, which were needed to attack the transmission efficiently.

Nevertheless, he was just too weary to hang on at his office. So he shut down, slipped on his jacket, and said good night to a couple of the technicians who looked up as he started for the door. He wandered out and checked through the security gate, which was now installed at the front of the lab.

The villa provided by the center was spare but practical. It had a glass-enclosed, heated porch, where Rimford enjoyed spending time, and which he'd converted into a workspace. The furniture in the compact living room was comfortable, and Harry had equipped it with a supply of books on Rimford's second love, the theater.

He showered and tried to slow himself down by making bacon and eggs even though he was not hungry. But he hurried through the meal nonetheless, leaving the toast half-eaten. He'd closed down his porch workspace after the new security procedures had gone into effect, moving everything back inside so he could work without being seen. Notes were not permitted outside the lab, and discussions of Hercules data were prohibited altogether. It was, of course, an absurdity to expect investigators to say nothing about a discovery of this nature, but nevertheless there were signs now conspicuously posted setting out monumental fines and jail terms for violators.

He'd hidden the Hercules disks in his collection of *The Essential Bach*. He sighed at the exigencies imposed by a retrograde world and retrieved the first disk in the series, which contained DS 41, and loaded it into his computer. But concentration was becoming difficult. He stared at the screen for a minute. It was covered with lines of numbers and letters representing Althean characters, and they were running together. He sighed, closed everything down, put the disk back into the Bach container, and lowered himself onto a sofa.

———

"We've got a lot of people down here, Harry," said Parkinson. The public-information officer was calling from the visitor center, just inside the east gate.

"I'm not surprised," Harry said. "We'll probably have big crowds until the story dies down a bit. Can we handle them?"

"Harry, the gift shop can't get enough of this. But they do tend to overflow the demonstration areas."

"Anybody hostile?"

"A few. Not many. Mostly, they're just like the people we always get here, except now there are so many of them. We got some carrying signs."

"Like what?"

"'We don't need aliens.' Stuff like that. There's a banner out there that demands we stop keeping secrets. And there are some Jesus signs. I think they want us to convert the Altheans."

"Okay," said Harry. "Just do business as usual. Try to speed things along so we can move as many as possible through the center and out. I'll notify Security and get some extra units to you."

Harry notified Schenken. Moments later, Sam Fleischer, his administrative assistant, came in. Sam was middle-aged, balding, with a ridge of red hair ringing his scalp. "We're having an interesting morning, Harry," he said.

"I think we're in for an interesting *year*. What's the problem, Sam?"

"The phones are swamped. I brought Donna and Betty in again to help out. Plus I've drafted a couple other people. By the way, most of the calls are complimentary. People think we're doing a nice job here. They're excited about Hercules."

"Good."

"We're getting a few cranks. One lady down in Greenbelt, for God's sake, claims she has a flying saucer in her garage. Somebody else told us that a bunch of terrorists in pickup trucks were on their way to seize the place." His smile faded. "But some of what we're hearing is eerie. There are rumors around that we're tied in with the devil. Some people are saying we're doing Satan's work and looking into stuff that God doesn't want known and, well, you know. It's kind of unnerving to sit there and listen to that."

"We ought to put Pete on TV," said Harry. "Get him to do his best Dracula imitation. That would really bring them out."

"Listen, there's something else, and I suspect it's tied in with the devil syndrome. That funny-looking picture of the thing with all the arms and legs: It scared a lot of people. They want to know what it is, and it's hard to explain to them how far away the Altheans are."

"What are we telling them?"

"Ted Parkinson told somebody that he thought it might be a battery cable or something. We've been responding along those lines."

"Okay. That's good. Do that until events catch up with us."

"Uh, Harry?" Fleischer's voice suddenly changed.

"Yes?"

"You think that's what the little bastards really look like?"

"Probably. Got anything else?"

"Yeah, we're taking more heat for not releasing everything. I understand they're having trouble at the White House, too. A lot of it over there is apparently coming from Democratic congressmen, who are trying to use the issue as a stick to beat the President."

It figured. Harry took a deep breath, wished devoutly he had followed through on an early ambition to become a dentist, and decided he needed to get outside for a bit. He told Edna he was going over to the visitor center, pulled on his jacket, and went out to the car.

Politicians always seemed to be willing to sacrifice the general welfare to win votes. And the fact that there would be a presidential election next November magnified every decision concerning the Hercules Text. It was curious to think that events that had occurred more than a million years ago could have an impact on a twenty-first-century presidential campaign.

One of Dave Schenken's first acts had been to construct a cyclone fence around the visitor center, sealing it off from the rest of the facility. Harry parked in the lot outside Building 17 and used an auxiliary gate to get in. Parkinson had not exaggerated: A holiday crowd overflowed the approach road and parking area. They carried balloons and banners, lunch bags and coolers. Greenbelt police had arrived outside, on Conservation Road, and were trying to keep traffic moving on the normally sedate two-lane blacktop.

Visitors had spread out over the grounds and, on the north side, they pressed against Schenken's fence. Many showed no interest in trying to get into the center. Rather, they wandered around in idle conversation, devouring sandwiches and Cokes. It looked like a good-natured crowd. The few signs evident among them bobbed up and down from strategic positions on hilltops, but no one seemed to be taking it all that seriously. He got the sense that most simply felt the impact of history and wanted to be nearby.

This, he thought, was the way it should be: a quiet, friendly celebration of an achievement that in a sense belonged to them all. He'd intended to enter the visitor center through the rear door, avoiding the crowd. Instead, he went around to the front and walked among them.

They were all ages and races. Some looked suspiciously like government executives who'd taken the day off. A special day, perhaps. Not a day to be passed in the confines of an office, in the manner of a thousand others. They sang and held kids on their shoulders and took pictures. But mostly, they just sat in the warm sunlight and looked at the dish antennas.

The Reverend Robert Freeman, D.D., finished the draft of a fund-raising letter that would go out with the hospital appeal at the end of the week. He read it over, satisfied that it would enlist the sympathies, and money, of his two million followers, and dropped it into the out-box.

Freeman was not unlike most of his colleagues, in that he heartily disapproved of other television preachers, but his annoyance was not based on doctrinal differences, or on the natural irritation with a rival who also has his hand in the pot. The simple truth was that Freeman didn't like fakes. He objected in strenuous terms to the flimflam practiced so brazenly on Sunday TV. "It makes us *all* suspect!" he'd roared at the Reverend Bill Pritchard during the celebrated confrontation between the two leading media preachers at Pritchard's annual revival, which until then had been held in Freeman's home state of Arkansas.

Backwoods Bobby was a rarity on the Fundamentalist circuit. He tried never to say anything he didn't truly believe, a policy that was difficult to pursue since he could see there were a few problems with Fundamentalist interpretations. Nevertheless, if there was an inconsistency or a contradiction buried here and there in Scripture, he knew it was nothing more than a translator's blunder or a transcriber's oversight. A divine typo, he'd said once. Not to be allowed to invalidate the Gospel simply because we're not sure where the problem might lie. Scripture should be seen as a river. The banks and currents change over the centuries, but the flow is surely toward the Promised Land.

He pushed a button on his intercom. "Send Bill in, please, Barbara," he said.

Bill Lum was his public-relations specialist, and Freeman's brother-in-law. Many of his subordinates believed the latter fact to be Bill's sole qualification for his job. But Lum was dedicated to his family and his God. He was handsome, good-humored, undaunted by personal calamity. His wife, the preacher's sister, had contracted Hodgkin's, and they had a retarded daughter. Lum projected, in fact, precisely the sort of image that Freeman wished to believe typical of his adherents. He was God-fearing, long-suffering, happy in spite of everything. The kind of person you wanted to have living next door.

"Bill," said Freeman, after Lum had made himself comfortable with a chocolate mint and a Coca-Cola, "I have an idea."

Lum always dressed in knit, open-collar sport shirts. He still looked muscular at an age when most men had begun an unsightly expansion. "What's that, Bobby?" he asked. His enthusiasm was never far from the surface.

"Folks are paying a lot of attention to what's coming out of Goddard these days," the preacher said. "But the real significance of what's happening over there is getting lost in all the scientific jargon. Someone needs to point out that we've found another branch of the family of God."

Lum took a long pull at the Coke. "You going to do another sermon on it next Sunday, Bob?"

"Don't know if that's the way to go or not," said Freeman. "I'd like to get an outing together with some of our people in the Washington area. We should go to Goddard. Hold a rally."

Lum looked uncertain. "I'm not sure I wouldn't feel uncomfortable at a place like that. Why bother? I mean, we covered it last week on the show. And I thought you did a fine job, Bobby."

The preacher blinked. "Bill, the story of the age is happening at Goddard. Someone needs to put it into perspective for the nation. For the world."

"You could do it from the studio."

"There'd be no impact. The ones we need to reach don't watch the *Old Bible Chapel*. No, we need a wider pulpit. And I think the place to find it is on the front steps of the space center."

"Okay," Lum said. "But I think it's a mistake. You got no control over the crowd there, Bob. You remember that mob in Indianapolis last year? There was no talking to them at all."

The preacher looked at his calendar. "The Christmas season would be a good time. Set it up just before the holidays. Four to six buses for the local folks." He closed his eyes, picturing the visitor center. "Better make it eight. I think we'll get a pretty good turnout. Try to arrange things so we get there about midafternoon, okay? I'll lead it myself."

"Bob, did you want to get a release out on this? If we notify the White House, they'll clear the way."

Freeman considered it. "No," he said. "If we alert Hurley, he'll try to argue me into forgetting it. Or show up himself and grab the cameras."

When Lum was gone, the preacher conjured up an image of himself carrying the ages-long battle between godless science and the faith directly into the camp of the enemy. This would be his opportunity to take his place among the prophets.

Russian Foreign Minister Alexander Taimanov had been at the United Nations when Ted Parkinson announced the reception of the second signal. He'd immediately requested a meeting with the President, to which the State Department acceded. It was set for 10:00 A.M. Tuesday.

Taimanov was a severe, uncompromising man in public, an inveterate skeptic regarding Western intentions. He came of peasant stock, had risen to power during the latter days of the last century, and had survived the turmoil of the following years. In private, however, he was a different man altogether. "Ah, my remarks last evening," he might say, following a blistering attack on some U.S. policy or other, "those are for public consumption. Part of the show. We have to keep up appearances, or people would get confused." He was viewed by U.S. diplomats as predictable and a force for stability in a nation that still showed dangerous stress lines.

It couldn't be said that Hurley enjoyed dealing with Taimanov, whose statements to the media all too often drove him to distraction. But he'd developed a reluctant affection for the man, whom the press had dubbed the Little Bear. Hurley's secretary of state, Matthew Janowicz, and the foreign minister had cooperated on at least two occasions to defuse potentially explosive situations in the Balkans.

Janowicz arrived a few minutes before Taimanov. A former backcountry lawyer and a onetime power in Arkansas politics, Janowicz was tall, bearded, rough-hewn, with a rumbling voice and a tendency to tell tall stories. Hurley suspected the resemblance to Lincoln was more than coincidental. But he was a talented diplomat, a hard bargainer, and a shrewd analyst. He confessed that Taimanov had told him only that he wished to speak with the President about the Hercules transmission. "They'll want access," he added.

Of course they would.

"They're telling me," Hurley said, "that it's just one long information dump. They haven't begun to sort it out."

"We can't turn it loose," said Janowicz. "Not until we know what's there."

"I know," said Hurley.

They showed Taimanov in at precisely ten o'clock.

The foreign minister had aged visibly during the last year. The CIA had been unable to confirm rumors that he'd contracted cancer. But Hurley could see that something was wrong. The cold, intelligent eyes peered out from deep wells of despair. His flesh had loosened, and the sense of humor with which he'd parried thrusts by Western diplomats and newsmen appeared to have deserted him. "Mr. President," he said, after several minutes of small talk, "I'm sure you understand we have a problem." Hurley had learned early not to talk to Russians from behind his desk. For reasons he did not entirely understand, they interpreted the act as defensive and became suspicious.

Taimanov unbuttoned his suede jacket and sat down opposite Janowicz. Hurley had the foreign minister's favorite brand of vodka brought in. He settled for a dark wine himself. Janowicz, a recovering alcoholic, stayed with coffee.

The President eased onto a sofa. "What sort of problem, Alex?" he asked. "How can I help?"

"Sir, your action in withholding the Hercules transmissions from the general public is quite correct."

"Thank you," Hurley said. "I wish everyone agreed."

"One must expect dissent from the media, whatever course of action one chooses." He glanced at Janowicz. "Back in the old days"—he smiled—"we had *that* problem under control. Now—" He shrugged. "With the blessings of Western-style liberty, editors are free to attack honest men and make governing quite difficult."

"That seems to be so," said Hurley, waiting patiently for his guest to come to the point.

Taimanov continued in the same vein for another minute or so, then turned so that he faced the President squarely. "You're aware, Mr. President, that although we understand why you've responded as you have in this matter, nevertheless, the current state of affairs creates severe difficulties for both of us."

"How so?"

"President Roskosky has been placed in an untenable position. The scientific establishment at home wields a substantial degree of influence."

"We know," said Janowicz, "that it is extensive."

"Yes. Our scientists lack direct political power, but they have access to the media, and they have the sympathy of the people. Gentlemen, as you know, these are difficult times for my country. The economy remains weak, the government is not as stable as we would wish, and the people are very close to losing confidence in the administration's ability to correct matters." He leaned forward, and his eyes grew intense. "It would not take much to push us into chaos. Perhaps even civil war. The President's enemies would not hesitate to turn the tide of popular opinion against him if opportunity offered." He tasted the vodka, nodded, tasted it again. "The scientific community is outraged that a discovery of such importance to us all has been withheld. As I said, *I* know why you've acted as you have. And President Roskosky knows. But it *does* create a serious danger."

"I understand," said Hurley.

"I knew you would. What is necessary to keep in mind is the sensitivity of his situation and the potential for mischief in this business of the radio signals. I do not personally believe you will find anything worth concealing, that is, anything of military value. But then, we do not really know, do we? And therein lies the difficulty." He angled a shrewd look at Janowicz, and Hurley knew he was trying to read their expressions. "Do you play chess, Mr. President?"

"Moderately."

"That fact does not appear in your campaign biography."

"It would not have won any votes. Maybe even cost a few."

Taimanov smiled. "I will never understand the United States. It seems to be a land that extols mediocrity yet produces engineers of exceptional quality."

"Why did you want to know?" asked Hurley.

"Ah, yes, the point. The point, Mr. President, as any good chess player knows, is that the threat is of considerably more use than the execution. As in diplomacy. The government's enemies will not deliberately provoke a reaction to the situation because they recognize that matters could very easily move beyond their control also. Bring down the administration, and no one knows what would follow. Rather, they will try to use the uncertainty surrounding the Hercules message to undermine confidence in the government. They know that the road to power, for them, requires them to espouse the old policies. A return to more nationalist times."

He was talking about the last of the old-line expansionists, the *NeoConservatives*, who were quite willing to sacrifice Russia's modest progress and the present chance at creating a stable international order to their own ambitions.

Taimanov tilted his glass, examined it in the light, and sipped it again. The President picked up the bottle and leaned forward to offer more, but Taimanov demurred. "It is all they allow me," he said. "John—" The formality dropped from his tone, and Hurley glimpsed real concern in his eyes. "I cannot believe that there is any threat contained in the transmission to match the one my country now faces. We need your assistance in this matter. I urge you to release the transmission and take this weapon at least out of their hands."

The President nodded. "Alex, I'll consider what you've said."

Taimanov got up and pulled on his coat. "Thank you for your time. I will not be returning to Moscow until Wednesday should you wish to speak further."

"He wants an answer to take back," Janowicz said after he had left.

A few minutes later, the President walked out to the Rose Garden for his next appointment, which was a photo session with some union people. His guests found him distracted. His usual ability to push problems aside to concentrate on the matter at hand had deserted him.

MONITOR

ANACONDA HAS BEEN MARRIED
2 YEARS

POPULAR ROCK STAR
IS INSURANCE AGENT'S SPOUSE

. . .

ISRAELIS, PALESTINIANS
JOIN IN NEW ACCORD

JANOWICZ: "WE ARE IN A NEW ERA"

HOPE LAND SWAP WILL BRING
PROSPERITY TO BOTH SIDES

. . .

BRITAIN IS BROKE

CLEARY APPEALS FOR AID
TO MEET DEBTS

BANKERS SEEK FORMULA

FRANCE MAY BE NEXT, WARNS GOULET

. . .

MARYANNE FOUND WEDGED IN WELL

RESCUE WORKERS DIGGING
SECOND SHAFT; RAIN CONTINUES

. . .

MAN IN LEWISTON, MAINE, CHARGED WITH 81 KILLINGS

NEW RECORD FOR MASS MURDERER

QUIET CARPENTER "ATTENDED CHURCH EVERY SUNDAY"

. . .

CONROY WILL NOT QUIT

TRACK STAR WILL TRY TO QUALIFY DESPITE LEUKEMIA

HOMETOWN STARTS BRAD CONROY FUND

. . .

SAMARITAN KILLED ON BUS

CAME TO WOMAN'S AID DURING ATTACK

. . .

"INDIA TEAM" STORMS LAKEHURST PLANT

3 TERRORISTS, 1 HOSTAGE KILLED

TIDAL WAVE OF CRITICISM

"IT COULD HAVE BLOWN," SAYS PHILLY MAYOR

HURLEY ACCEPTS RESPONSIBILITY

. . .

DEATH PENALTY SOUGHT
FOR NUCLEAR TERRORISM

. . .

LASER REPORTED USED
AGAINST TWA FLIGHT OVER O'HARE

FAA INVESTIGATING; 166 ON PLANE

. . .

MERCHANTS EXPECT
BANNER CHRISTMAS SEASON

MAJOR RETAILERS
LEAD DOW JONES SURGE

||| TEN |||

Ed Gambini was absorbed by events and clearly resented having to take time out to deal with a politician. Even a president. Though he made a few of the daily reports to the White House, the chore rapidly became Harry's responsibility. The project manager assigned Majeski to put together a summary each evening, which Harry found on his desk in the morning. He duly phoned it in to the private number provided by the President and submitted an eyes-only hard copy the same day by special messenger.

Harry didn't resist the procedure even though he was uncomfortable bypassing the chain of command. He informed Rosenbloom of the requirement, and the director shrugged and told him to proceed. "See that I get a copy," he said. "And if you come up with anything out of the ordinary, I want to know about it."

Not that Harry developed a working relationship with Hurley. At first the calls had gone to a designated assistant, and as the weeks passed and Christmas approached, the assistant was replaced by another designee. The reports were, of course, couched in general terms. When, occasionally, a matter arose that Harry thought might be considered sensitive, he took Gambini's memorandum personally to the White House, where the document was passed in a secure envelope to the designated assistant and signed for.

Harry quickly came to enjoy showing up outside the Oval Office, being recognized by members of the presidential staff, and even on a couple of occasions catching glimpses of Hurley himself. On one visit, he was introduced to the National Security Advisor who, a few days later, shocked him by remembering and using his first name. It was a heady experience for a minor federal employee. If things went well, if he could avoid blunders and pinpoint the type of information that Hurley needed, he could foresee reaping an agency directorship. Consequently, he invested a disproportionate amount of his time in the Hercules Project. To his credit, Gambini never grew impatient with his questions. The idealist in Gambini, Harry realized, would never have looked for an ulterior motive. Ultimately, he found himself swept up in the excitement of the hunt for the elusive nature of the Altheans.

The work of penetrating the "language" of the transmissions was proceeding slowly but with moderate success. That it was proceeding at all, Rimford told Harry, considering the enormous complexity of the problems involved, was a tribute to Cord Majeski and his team of mathematicians.

Harry brought his son out to Goddard on his visiting day. There'd been a delay at home because the insulin supply had run low, and Harry had to take the boy to the People's drugstore. That was always a depressing experience, rendered even more so by Tommy's good-natured resignation about his disease.

The boy loved to ride around at the space center, looking at dish antennas and communications equipment and satellite models. But in the end, he'd been most interested in the duck pond. There were still seven or eight mallards floating around on the cold water. Harry wondered when they would leave.

Tommy was tall for his age, with his mother's elegant features and Harry's oversized feet. ("That'll change as he gets older," Julie had reassured him.) The ducks knew about kids, and they crowded around him before he had a chance to get his bag of popcorn open. They were quite tame, of course, and when Tommy proved a little too slow, they tried to snatch the food from his hand. The boy giggled and retreated.

Harry, watching from a distance, recalled the evenings he'd worked late, the weekends given to one project or another. The government had recognized his efforts with scrolls and cash awards, and last year he'd been inducted into the Senior Executive Service. Not bad, on the whole. But a tally of some sort was mounting, with his scrolls and cash on one side. And on the other?

Tommy among the ducks.

And Julie in the boathouse.

Later, they had dinner and went to a movie. It was a bland science-fiction film with a group of astronaut-archaeologists trapped in an ancient ruin on another world by a killer alien. The effects were good, but the dialogue was wooden and the characters unbelievable. Nobody, thought Harry, could be *that* casually brave. During the film, Harry realized he was near the end of his tolerance with aliens.

Julie had moved into a condo in Silver Spring. When Harry returned Tommy Sunday evening, she took a few minutes to show him through the unit. It looked expensive, with hardwood appointments and central vacuuming and a scattering of antiques.

But she seemed dispirited, and his tour was, at best, a mechanical display of rooms and knickknacks.

"What's wrong?" he asked, when they stood finally alone on her patio, looking north on Georgia Avenue from the fourth floor. It was cold.

"They've increased Tommy's dosage," she said. "His circulation hasn't been so good. That's why he needed more this morning."

"He didn't say anything to me," said Harry.

"He doesn't like to talk about it. It scares him."

"I'm sorry."

"Oh, Harry, we're all sorry." She closed her eyes, but tears ran down her cheeks. "He's taking two shots now." She'd thrown a white woolen sweater over her shoulders. Below, a police car approached Spring Street, its siren loud and insistent. They watched it angle through a jammed intersection and pick up speed until it turned into Buckley. They could hear it a long time after that.

Gambini's morning memorandum was strange: "We have the Witch of Agnesi."

Harry put it aside, went through the rest of the IN basket, and disposed of the more pressing business. He was looking at a new set of management-analysis guidelines when his buzzer sounded. "Dr. Kmoch would like to see you, Mr. Carmichael."

Harry frowned. He had no idea what that could be about.

Adrian Kmoch was a high-energy German physicist who'd received a Hercules Project exemption. He was working with the Core advisory group that functioned as technical consultants for the High Energy Astronomy Observatory elements of Skynet.

He did not look happy.

Harry pointed him to a chair but made no attempt at diplomatic niceties. "What's wrong, Adrian?"

"Harry, we wish to hold a meeting." His German accent was barely noticeable, but he used the precise diction that invariably marked the educated European speaker. "I've reserved the Giacconi Room for one o'clock this afternoon. And I thought you might want to attend."

"What's it about?"

"It is becoming very difficult to continue working here. There are serious ethical problems."

"I see. I assume we're talking about Hercules?"

"Of course," he said. "We cannot, in conscience, support a policy that withholds scientific information of this nature."

"Who is *we*?"

"A substantial portion of the investigators currently working at Goddard. Mr. Carmichael, please understand that this has nothing to do with you personally. But what the government is doing here is quite wrong. In addition, its actions are putting extreme pressure on those of us who seem to our colleagues to acquiesce in this behavior. Carroll, for example, has been informed by his university that if he fails to speak out against the government's position on Hercules, his tenure will be reviewed."

"I'm sorry to hear that. I don't think his university is thinking things through." The area behind the bridge of his nose was beginning to hurt. "What's the purpose of the meeting, Adrian?"

"I think you can guess." Kmoch's eyes fastened on Harry. His limbs were long, and he walked with a peculiarly stiff gait that, in Harry's view, was rather like the way his mind worked. Kmoch was a subscriber to ideals and ethical systems, a man who took principles very seriously, no matter who got hurt. In all, there was much of the wooden plank in Kmoch's thinking. "I'm going to urge that we walk out."

"Strike? You can't strike. It would be a violation of your

contract." Harry got out of his chair and came around the desk.

"I'm aware of the contract, Harry." His tone grew more threatening with the use of the first name. "And please don't try to intimidate me. Many of us have careers at stake. What will the government do for us when we cannot continue to earn our livelihood? Will you guarantee me employment within my specialty?"

Harry looked back helplessly. "You know I can't do that. But you have a commitment here."

"And *you* have an obligation to *us*. Please keep it in mind." Kmoch turned and stalked out of the room. Harry stared after him, considering his options. He could deny the use of meeting space, he could warn of sanctions, or he could attend the meeting himself and use it as an opportunity to present the government's point of view.

Harry knew there'd been some friction. Several of Gambini's people had spoken of a growing coolness among their colleagues. He wondered whether he should alert Security. It was SOP that they were to be notified of any gathering of a political nature. But the unit was no longer his to direct, and he didn't trust Schenken. The presence of uniforms or of the hard-eyed young men in snap-brim hats could well provoke trouble.

Hell with it.

He turned to the dictionary, looked up "Witch of Agnesi," and smiled. It was a geometrical term, describing a plane curve that is visualized as symmetrical about the y-axis and asymptotic to the x-axis. Harry wasn't sure what "asymptotic" meant, and after he consulted *Webster's* again, he was still not sure. He understood that it was somehow tied to infinity.

Harry added the Witch to the other principles the aliens were known to possess: Faraday's Law of Electromagnetic Induction, the Cauchy Theorem, assorted variations of the Gauss hypergeometric equation, assorted Bessel functions, and so on. None of these rang any bells for Harry. But they caused him to wonder when the Altheans were going to tell us something we didn't already know?

It was obvious also that the White House was getting impatient. The reaction against administration reluctance to release the transmission was becoming more intense. At home, only a few right-wing newspapers supported the President's position; and the television networks were on the attack nightly. Callers complained each morning on C-SPAN, and scientific groups across the country issued anti-Hurley statements.

Some American embassies were being stoned. The State Department established a special task force to field official protests, which were coming from virtually everywhere, even the nation's closest allies. Only Britain and Germany refrained, although British astrophysicist Evan Holcrum appeared on the BBC personally to denounce the President's policy, an action that Harry thought carried more weight than any official pronunciamento would have. The government was pilloried daily at the United Nations. And for all this, the President had little to show: The analysts at Greenbelt had recovered only a few well-known mathematical exercises, now augmented by the Witch of Agnesi.

Harry came gradually to resent the daily report. Everyone seemed to know it was being submitted, and somehow a degree of culpability and collusion had come to be associated with it. No one attacked him by name because he was simply not a big enough fish. Unlike Gambini, who was regularly assaulted in scientific and academic journals, Harry was simply a flunky, beneath the notice of everyone who understood his role.

It crossed Harry's mind that Hurley had allowed himself to be placed at Gambini's mercy. If the project manager reached the end of his patience and went public, the administration would have its hands full containing the damage. But the President obviously trusted him, as did Harry. Still, Gambini would understand that a discovery of military significance, or one that might affect the security of the United States, would necessarily increase the chance of the project's being taken from him. And it would certainly eliminate any lingering possibility that the government would give him what he wanted: a release of the transcripts. Consequently, if any such discovery were made, Gambini would be tempted to withhold it.

Harry knew, and the President should have guessed, that Gambini remained under terrible pressure from his colleagues, most of whom would not welcome him back when his assignment at Greenbelt had ended. A week never passed when some major figure did not use the press to assail the project manager and urge him to refuse to cooperate with the current "paranoid" policies of his employer. Ed never defended himself and never, in public, criticized the President.

But when this was over, he would be a pariah.

Edna buzzed. "Ted Parkinson on the line," she said.

He punched the call in. "Yes, Ted?"

"Harry, I think we ought to close the visitor center for a while. Maybe clear the area."

"Why?"

"Some of the people out here are turning ugly. There are more demonstrators now and college kids carrying signs. We've had a couple of incidents today."

"Anybody hurt?"

"Not yet. But it's just a matter of time. A lot of the kids are bringing alcohol in with them. There's no easy way to stop it. The security people have been tossing them out whenever they see it, but that just tends to make things worse. An hour ago, we had a guy waving a gun around."

"No shots fired?"

"No. Fortunately. But it's getting scary out there."

"I'd like to avoid shutting it down, Ted. That would look as if we're going into a state of siege, and it'd probably just produce more demonstrators."

"Things may be about to get worse, Harry. I got a call a few minutes ago from Cass Woodbury. She said that Backwoods Bobby and several busloads of his supporters are going to be here this afternoon."

"You're kidding."

"You ready for the kicker?"

"Go ahead."

"He's on *our* side this time."

"Yeah," Harry said. "He would be. There's no way he'd want the Chinese to get their hands on anything we have. Anyhow, he's supported this President all along. They think alike. Hurley's just a bit more sophisticated is all."

"I've let Security know."

"They may have their hands full out there today. What time is he due?"

"About three."

"That gets the top evening news spots. Freeman's no dummy. He loves to see the investigators at one another's throats. This gives him a chance to get in on the fun and grab some national publicity. I think we can count on him to do what he can to keep things stirred up." Harry looked at his watch. "Okay, Ted. Alert Security, but don't do anything else for the moment. I'll be over shortly. Freeman's not likely to be interested in talking to us, but if he is, be careful what you say. He has a talent for twisting things."

"By the way," said Parkinson, "I heard there's trouble at Fermi. They're meeting even as we speak to decide what they want to do. The word I'm getting is that a formal protest is a foregone conclusion and that the only thing in doubt is how tough they'll get with the government."

"Hell, they're cutting off their own noses," said Harry. "Who cares whether an accelerator lab in Illinois closes down? Certainly not the public. And consequently not the President."

It was almost nine o'clock. Harry had just time to go over and talk to Gambini. Maybe, at least, he could come up with something to break the long streak of negative reports to the White House.

———

Cord Majeski could not have said just when he realized the strings of numbers constituted a schematic. He recognized the basic design of a set of solenoids and a transducer. There appeared to be heating and cooling elements and a timer. "And the rest of the stuff," he told Gambini, "I can't make out at all." He'd drawn a rough diagram, but it didn't look like anything either of them was familiar with.

"Can we build a working model?"

Majeski blinked and pinched the bridge of his nose. "Maybe," he said.

"What's wrong?"

"I can't find any power specifications, Ed. What do you figure it will take to make it work?"

Gambini grinned. "Start with house current. See if you can put it together, Cord. But give it a low priority. I'd like to get deeper into the translations."

Majeski's disappointment was plain. "How deep?"

"*Deep*. That's what we really want to know: What do we have here?"

"You could be talking *years*, Ed. We've got a lot of material."

"I think we can do better than that. But just put the thing aside for now. Get to it when you can."

Harry found Leslie at the facility cafeteria nibbling thoughtfully at a tuna sandwich. She didn't see him until he slid into a seat beside her. "Harry," she said. "How are you doing?"

"Okay. I didn't know you were back in town."

"I got in last night. Just in time, apparently. I hear Bobby Freeman will be paying a visit today."

"The word's out, huh?"

"On every channel."

"They're expecting him at the visitor center this afternoon." He couldn't make out whether she was serious or not. "You sound interested in Freeman."

"Harry," she said, "he is a one-man study in mob psychology. He never says a word that makes sense, yet two million Americans think he walks on water."

"Backwoods Bobby is living proof that you don't have to have a brain to acquire power in this country. You can't be ugly, but it sure as hell doesn't matter if you're stupid."

"That's a little harsh," she said, amused. "By what standard is he stupid? If you can get him off religion, he seems to be reasonable enough. In fact, given the parameters within which he works, he's remarkably consistent. If the Bible *were* to turn out to be divinely inspired, I think he'd have a leg up on the rest of us."

"You're talking nonsense," said Harry.

"Of course I am." She smiled slyly. "I guess you know they had a breakthrough of sorts yesterday."

"We're not supposed to talk about any of that stuff in here," Harry said. "Secrecy is the order of the day. What happened?"

"Something about quantum mechanics. I have no idea, but Majeski was happy." She took a deep breath. "No way to know whether there's a military aspect. I really don't know what I'd do if I were in Hurley's place. Although I'm not so sure we need to worry about weapons designs. I was thinking how I'd feel if we got the impression that these creatures were all geniuses. If, contrasted to them, Baines was a dummy."

Harry excused himself and chased down a cup of coffee. "Baines a dummy, huh?" he said when he came back. "He'd like that."

"Or maybe the stick figure's a misinterpretation. Maybe they all look like angels. Maybe they're just going to be a lot better designed than we are."

"What are you driving at, Leslie?"

"I don't know. I think the transmission is dangerous, but for a different set of reasons than everybody else. What happens to us if we find out we're hopelessly inferior in some way?"

"Won't happen. *Never* would to some of us."

"Like Bobby?"

"Good example."

"What about Ed?" asked Leslie. "How would he react? Say, to finding a supreme genius at the other end?"

"I don't think he frightens easily. He'd like very much to find a congenial mind. Somebody to talk to. I can't imagine his being intimidated no matter what. Baines, maybe, wouldn't like it much."

"You could be right," she said. "I think what Baines wants most is to discover whether the Rimford Model will survive. And what about you, Harry? What would you like to see happen?"

"I'd like to see an end to it. Too much hard feeling. We're getting attacked from all sides. I'm tired of all the animosity."

"I suppose."

"You *suppose*? You want to sit in there and answer my calls for a day?"

She shook her head. "No. Still, it's exciting. We're on the ultimate adventure, Harry. Enjoy it. Years from now, you'll look back on this and be able to say, *Yeah, biggest thing that ever happened, and I was right in the middle of it.*"

"Right now," said Harry, "it just feels like a lot of bitching. The latest is a meeting this afternoon called by some of the contract investigators. They're threatening to walk out."

"Well," she said, as though the possibility of a strike were of no consequence, "we're beginning to get some sense of the structure of the language. But there's something very odd about it."

"Hell, Les, there's going to be a lot of odd stuff before we get finished."

"No, I don't mean *unusual* odd; I mean irrational odd. The language is clumsy, Harry. It's so clumsy that I hesitate to call it a language."

"Clumsy?"

"Awkward. Comparative degrees, for example, are expressed by numerical values, both positive and negative. It's as if you talked about *good* on a scale of one to ten, without ever introducing *better* or *best*."

"That seems reasonably precise."

"Oh, it's precise. My God, yes, it's precision incorporated. Adjectives are the same way. Nothing, for example, is ever dark. They establish a quantification standard for illumination, then give you a benchmark on the standard. It's maddening. But what really fascinates me is that if you translate it into English, freely substituting general terms, you get some very striking poetry. Except that it isn't poetry, I don't think, but I don't know what else to call it." She shook her head in bewilderment. "One thing I'll tell you, Harry: In this form, the way they transmit it, it is *not* a natural language. It's too mathematical."

"You think it's something they devised purely for the transmission?"

"Probably. And if that's true, we'll lose a major source of information about them. There's a direct link between language and the character of its speakers. Harry, we really need to be able to send this stuff out. I know all sorts of people who should be getting a look at it. There are too many areas where I just don't have expertise. Or even a decent working knowledge. Sitting here bottled up with it, it's frustrating."

"I know. Maybe things'll change now. Some clearances have come through, and we can start bringing in a few more people."

"It's a code, Harry. That's all it is: a code. And you know what's strangest of all about it? *We* could have done better. In any case, what counts is that we're starting to read it. It's slow going because there's still a lot to do." She discovered her sandwich, almost untouched, and took a bite. "I think Hurley's going to be disappointed."

"Why?"

"The bulk of the material that we've been able to break into so far reads like philosophy. I think the technological jump start he thinks we might be getting—"

"—Is that what he thinks—?"

"Sure. Read between the lines, Harry. There's a lot of speculation in the media and in the journals about what *might* be in the transmission. You think his mouth isn't watering over the possibilities?"

"But it's *philosophy*?"

"Well, we can't be sure because we don't understand most of the terms, and maybe we never will. I'm not even sure we aren't being subjected to some sort of interstellar gospel."

Images drifted through his mind of the President and Bobby Freeman reacting to that. He grinned. "Maybe it's the best thing that could happen to us."

"Harry," she replied, "I'm glad you think it's funny, because there's an awful lot of it."

"Is there any history? Do they tell us anything about themselves?"

"Not that we've been able to find. We're getting commentaries, but they're abstract, and we can't really make out what they relate to. There are long mathematical sections as well. We think we found a description of their solar system. If we're reading it correctly, they have six planets, and the home world *does* have rings. They *are* circling the yellow sun, by the way."

"Gamma."

"Right. Gamma." She paused and made a face. "But this other stuff. They paint with broad strokes, Harry. From what I've seen, they're not much interested in the sorts of things you build weapons from. You know what I really think the transmission is? Basically?"

Harry had no idea.

"A series of expanded essays on the good, the true, and the beautiful."

"You're kidding."

"We know they're interested in cosmology. They have

enough knowledge of physics to baffle Ed. They've supplied mathematical descriptions for all sorts of processes, including a lot of stuff we haven't begun to identify. We're probably going to learn what really holds atoms together and why water freezes at thirty-two degrees and how galaxies form. But there's a sense in the text that all that is"—she searched for a word—"incidental. Trivial. The way they establish their credentials, maybe. What they really seem interested in, where it seems to me their focus is, is in their speculative sections."

"It almost figures," said Harry. "What else would we expect from an advanced race?"

"I'll tell you. You remember we talked about an encyclopedia? That's more and more what it looks like. Their whole store of knowledge. Everything they consider significant."

———

Harry was coming to realize how much he enjoyed spending time with Leslie. Her laughter cheered him, and when he needed to talk, she listened. Her willingness to leave her Philadelphia practice at the slightest whim to travel to Greenbelt suggested not only professional flexibility but also that she had no strong emotional attachment back home. He did not, of course, ask her point-blank, since that would have conveyed the wrong impression. Leslie was far too prosaic a woman to engage any romantic interest. Still, unaccountably, he felt comfortable with his conclusion that there was probably no man in her life.

They walked together toward the lab, Harry carefully keeping a proper distance, but warmly aware, perhaps for the first time, of her physical presence. She needed almost two strides to each of his. But she stayed with him while they continued the conversation. She'd concluded the Altheans *did* have an aesthetic sense, and now wondered aloud whether that quality would necessarily be part of the equipage of any intelligent creature.

They walked across a bleak landscape under a gray-white December sky, threatening snow. When they arrived at the lab, Leslie hurried into the rear office that she'd taken over, and Harry wandered over to talk to Pete Wheeler.

The priest was seated at a computer, painstakingly entering

characters from a set of notes. He looked relieved to have a chance to get away from it. "Hi, Harry," he said. "Are you going to Kmoch's meeting this afternoon?"

"I haven't decided yet."

"It should be a live audience. There's a lot of hostility right now. Did you know that even Baines is beginning to get some pressure? There was a delegation in to see him last night. Jackson and Chang and Gropner, among others. They want him to refuse to cooperate further with the project. And to join them in taking a public stand."

"How the hell can *anyone* pressure Baines?"

"Directly, they can't. But you know how he is. He hates to have anyone think ill of him. Especially all those people he's worked with for a lifetime. To make matters worse, of course, he sympathizes with both sides."

"How about you?"

"I gather some people have complained to the abbot. He says there's been some pressure from the archbishop, but he's encouraged me to hang in and use my best judgment. They're caught in the middle, don't want to be seen as cooperating with a cover-up, but on the other hand, they don't want to become a roadblock to progress."

"Galileo," suggested Harry.

"Sure."

"You look worried."

"I keep thinking how all this must look to Hurley. He's in a no-win situation, and he'll be heavily criticized no matter which way things go. You really want my opinion, Harry?" He rubbed the back of his neck. "Historically, governments are not good at keeping secrets. Especially about technology. The only nation I can even think of that retained control of an advanced weapon for a long time was Constantinople."

"Greek fire?" asked Harry.

"Greek fire. And that's probably it for the whole course of human history. Whatever we learn here, Harry, whatever's in the Text, will sooner or later become common property." His dark eyes were troubled. "If Hurley's right, and we discover the makings of a new bomb or a new bug, it'll be only a matter of time before the Chinese have it, or some Middle Eastern terrorists, or some of the other assorted loonies on the planet.

"I don't think that's the real danger, though, at least not in the short term. Harry, we're possibly about to be inundated by a culture from another world. This time *we* are the South Sea islanders." He shut off his monitor. "Do you remember a couple of years ago when Ed and Baines and Breakers used to get into those long arguments about the number of advanced civilizations in the Milky Way? And Breakers always said that if there were others, we'd be able to hear some of them. They'd be transmitting to us." Wheeler removed the disk he'd been working with and gazed at it. "So now we've got the greeting card, and I'm not sure there's anything it might say that won't turn out to be bad news."

"How about if it contains a cure for cancer?" asked Harry.

"That would be nice," he said. "But it's unlikely." Wheeler put the disk away and got up. "I need some fresh air. Care to join me?"

"I just came in," said Harry. But he followed the priest outside anyway, thinking about Breakers. He'd been a cynical old son of a bitch from Harvard who'd died two weeks before the Hercules contact had been made. Hadn't quite made it.

"Baines published an article recently," continued Wheeler, "titled 'The Captain Cook Syndrome,' in which he says a wise culture might recognize that contact with a more primitive society, however well-intentioned, could do nothing but create problems for the weaker group."

"*Star Trek*'s prime directive."

"Sure. It might be that even the knowledge of their existence could cause trouble. Upset religious views, that sort of thing. So Baines thought maybe there was some sort of generally-agreed-to ethical code requiring everyone to avoid the use of radio. That communications between advanced societies, if it were happening at all, was using a more sophisticated technology.

"But our aliens chatter. Not only that, they do it on the radio. And they tell us everything. Why would they *do* that? Ed thinks they're not too bright. Maybe being stranded out in intergalactic space has affected them in some way. Remember? We talked about skies with no stars. It also means that no matter how good your technology, there's nowhere to go.

Absolutely nowhere. So maybe the Altheans are deranged. Been out there for millions of years, completely isolated."

"It's a possibility," said Harry.

"Ed's also convinced they bungled the transmission code, made it more difficult than necessary. That suggests they might be slow-witted. Incompetent."

"How could that be? After they manipulated that pulsar?"

"Maybe the engineering was done by their ancestors. Maybe all the transmitting generation does is make bureaucratic decisions and punch buttons."

"No," Harry said, "I can't believe they're nitwits. That's too much of a stretch."

"Whatever the reality, Harry, we are about to be invaded as surely as if the little critters arrived in saucers and began rumbling around the terrain in tripods. We are just now beginning to read the transmission, and I can guarantee you that, whatever's in it, it is going to change us beyond recognition. Not just what we know, but how we think. It's a prospect I can't say I relish."

"Pete, if you feel that way, why are you helping?"

"For the same reason everybody else is. I want to find out who they are. What they've got to say. And maybe have a hand in moderating the effects although I'm not optimistic about that. It's all I care about anymore, Harry. And it's the same with everyone. Everything else in my life right now seems trivial. And that brings us back to Kmoch's meeting. And why so many people are so upset. If I were standing outside looking in, I'd be upset, too. So everybody who's *inside* is getting leaned on by everybody who *isn't.*"

"Kmoch's talking about a strike."

"He's not the only one. But if you go in there today, you'll be lucky if you don't get assaulted. I mean, tempers are running high."

A stiff cold wind had begun blowing out of the northwest. Harry noticed a few flakes. Just beyond the perimeter fence, three men crouched on the roof of a two-story frame house, repairing shingles. In the adjoining backyard, two teenagers were unloading firewood from a pickup.

Wheeler wore an ugly, oversized green cap. "It belonged to

a student I had a few years ago at Princeton in a cosmology class. I admired it pretty openly, I guess, and at the end of the semester, he gave it to me." It jutted far out over his eyes.

"It looks like something you took from a mugger," Harry said.

They stopped at an intersection and waited for a mail truck to pass. "I've got something to tell you," said the priest.

Harry turned his back to the wind.

"I found some equations in the Text that describe planetary magnetic fields: why they develop, how they work. Some of it we know already, some of it we don't. They go into a lot of detail, and it isn't really my specialty. But I think I can see a way to tap the earth's magnetic field for energy. Lots of energy."

"Would it be practical?" asked Harry. "Can we get at the magnetic field to use it?"

"Oh, yes," replied Wheeler. "Easily. All that's necessary is to put a few satellites up, convert the energy to, say, a laser, and beam it to a series of receivers on the ground. If it actually works, it'd probably solve our energy needs for the indefinite future. And it would be *clean*."

"How certain are you?" Harry's heart was beginning to beat faster. *Here* was something to juice up the daily report.

"Reasonably. I'm going to tell Ed about it this afternoon."

"You sound hesitant."

"I am, Harry. And I don't really know why. Solving the power problem and getting away from fossil fuels and nuclear plants sounds like a pretty good idea. But I wish I had a better notion how something like this, sprung all at once, might shake things up. Maybe we need an economist out here, too."

"You worry too much," said Harry. "This is the kind of information we need. Something *useful*. The good, the true, and the beautiful may make for fascinating talk at lunch, but taxpayers would be more interested in doing something about their electric bills."

"Yeah. Still, I don't think it would be a good idea to make it public. Until we know for sure."

"Pete," he said, "you're absolutely right. But the President should be told."

Harry called his White House number. "Please tell the President we might have something," he said.

The voice on the other end belonged to one of the lower-level contacts. "You want to tell me what it is so I can alert him?"

"No," said Harry. "I need to see him. Tell him it'll be worth his while."

There was a long pause. Then a new voice came on the line, a young woman: "Mr. Carmichael? Come in this evening. Seven o'clock."

MONITOR

The stars are silent.

Voyager among dark harbors, I listen, but the midnight wind carries only the sound of trees and water lapping against the gunwale and the solitary cry of the night swallow.

There is no dawn. No searing sun rises either east or west. The rocks over Calumel do not silver, and the great round world slides through the void.

—Stanza 32 from DS 87
Freely translated by Leslie Davies
(Unclassified)

||| ELEVEN |||

A bubble universe drifted in a superspace ocean.

Rimford's features widened into a broad grin. He pushed the mound of paper off the coffee table onto the floor and, in a sudden surge of pure joy, lobbed his pen the length of the room and into the kitchen.

He went out to the refrigerator, came back with a beer in one hand, and dialed Gambini's office. While he waited for the physicist to answer, he pulled the tab and took a long swallow.

"Research projects," said a female voice.

"Dr. Gambini, please. This is Rimford."

"He's tied up at the moment, Professor," she said. "Can I have him call you?"

"How about Pete Wheeler? Is he there?"

"He went out a few minutes ago with Mr. Carmichael. I don't know when he'll be back. Dr. Majeski's here."

"Okay," said Rimford, disappointed. "Thanks. I'll try again later." He hung up, finished the beer, walked around the pile of notebooks and printouts on the floor, and sat down again.

One of the great moments of the twenty-first century was occurring, and there was no one with whom to share it.

A quantum universe. Strabonovich and the others might have been right all along.

He didn't understand all the mathematics of it yet, but he would; he was well on the way. By Christmas, he thought, he would have the mechanism of creation.

Much of it was clear already. The universe was a quantum event, a pinprick of space-time. It had been called into being in the same way that apparently causeless events continue to occur in the subatomic world. It had been more bubble than bang. And once launched, the bubble had expanded with exponential force. There'd been no light barrier during those early nanoseconds, because the governing principles had not yet formed. Consequently, its dimensions had, within that fraction of an instant, far exceeded those of the solar system, and indeed those of the Milky Way. There had been no matter at first, but only the slippery fabric of space-time and energy erupting in a cosmic explosion. The appearance of matter had swiftly imposed an ironclad stability, physical law, expansion dropped below light speed, and substantial portions of the energy of the first moments were frozen into hydrogen and helium.

Not for the first time in his life, Rimford wondered about the "cause" of causeless effects. Perhaps he would find also the secret of the unaccountable: the deSitter superspace from which the universal bubble had formed. Perhaps, somewhere in the transmission, the Altheans would address that question. But Rimford understood that, however advanced a civilization might be, it was necessarily tied to this universe. It was unlikely there would be any way to tunnel out, to look past the physical limits or beyond its earliest moments. One could only speculate, regardless of the capability of the telescope or the subtlety of the intellect.

There was nothing really new about the many-universe theory. But it had always seemed unlikely, a desperate effort to account for design without falling back on a creator. It had never risen above the level of sheer guesswork. Nevertheless, there was something comforting, exhilarating perhaps, in learning that the Altheans had come to much the same conclusion. And maybe they *would* be able to supply evidence of one kind or another. Who knew?

He paced the small living room, too excited to sit still. There were any number of people with whom he would have liked to talk, men and women who had dedicated their lives to this or that aspect of the puzzles to which he now held partial solutions, but security regulations stood in the way. Horner, for example, at Wisconsin, had invested twenty years working to solve the mysteries of universal expansion. Koestler at MIT had grown almost blind pursuing dark matter. Yale's Amorante had done valuable work on the flexibility limits of expanding space.

Now Rimford understood that the expansion rate varied, sometimes *increasing* to maintain equilibrium, that it could have been no other way. The latter effect was at least in part fueled by an unexpected factor: According to the Altheans, gravity was *not* a constant. The variation was slight, but it existed. It was local, and it was temporary, returning to the standard value within a few years, if Rimford was reading the equations correctly. All of this would explain, he was sure, recently found disparities between deep-space observations and relativity theory.

He wanted to be present when Horner saw what was in the transmission.

Unable to sit still, he left the cottage, drove out to Greenbelt Road, and turned east under slate skies.

He'd been on the highway about half an hour when rain began to fall, fat icy drops that splashed like wet clay against the windshield. Most of the traffic disappeared into a gray haze, headlights came on, the rain stopped, the sky cleared, and Rimford sailed happily down country highways until he came to an engaging inn on Good Luck Road. He stopped, went in, collected a scotch, and ordered a prime steak.

His old notion of the initial nanoseconds of the expansion, which had included the simultaneous creation of matter with space-time, brought about by the innate instability of the void, seemed to be wrong on all counts. He wondered whether some of his other ideas were also headed for extinction. In the mirror across the dining room, he looked like a prosperous businessman, self-assured, smug, even somewhat arrogant. But he represented the part of the universe that thinks. The point of it all. If so, there was justification for a bit of arrogance.

The scotch was smooth, and it accented his mood. He could not recall in his entire life ever having experienced a rush of emotions quite like those charging through him now: It was a glorious moment, exhilarating and elegant and probably beyond anything he could hope to experience again.

He ordered Zinfandel with his dinner.

It occurred to him that he had little reason to celebrate. His life's work had blown up, yet he felt no regrets. It would have been good to be right. But it was more important to *know*.

The steak was delicious. He sliced off long, juicy strips, chewed them with great deliberation, washed them down with the wine. Midway through the meal, he scribbled an equation on a cloth napkin and propped it up where he could see it. It was a description of the properties and structure of space. If any single mathematical formula could be said to constitute the secret of the universe, this was it.

Good God, now that he had it in his hands, it all seemed so logical. How could they not have seen it?

The Altheans did indeed manipulate stars, in Gambini's phrase, not only in Gambini's sense of adding or subtracting materials but in the wider meaning of the verb. In fact, they manipulated space, changed its texture, altered its degree of curvature. Flattened it altogether, if they wished.

And, provided with an appropriate energy source, so could he!

His hands trembled as, for the first time, he considered the practical applications.

A shadow passed through the room. It was only a waitress, bringing coffee. She was an attractive young lady, bright and smiling, as waitresses in country inns are inclined to be. But Rimford did not smile back, and she must have wondered about the mundane individual at the corner table who'd looked so unresponsive at her approach. She was probably not accustomed to men who looked directly through her.

He finished his coffee, wiped his lips with the expansion equation, dropped it on the table, left a generous tip, and strolled casually out into the night.

————

"I don't think I understand why you'd want me involved in this project." Cyrus Hakluyt folded his hands carefully in his lap and watched an old, battered station wagon pass the government car in a storm of slush and dirty water.

"We have in our possession," said Gambini, "a complete physiological description of an extraterrestrial life-form. Are you interested?"

"Are you serious?" Hakluyt asked in a fragile monotone. If there was a single characteristic one might use to describe the microbiologist, it would have been the contrast between his feathery voice and the conviction with which he customarily spoke. His smile was weak and perfunctory, and his long, spindly trunk rose into a set of narrow shoulders. He blinked behind heavy bifocals. Gambini knew that he'd once been a high-school baseball player, but that was hard to believe now. "Edward, is it really so?"

"Yes, it's really so. Some of the material in the Hercules Text appears to be an attempt to describe genetic structure and broader biological functions. We think they may have tried to give us a comprehensive account of the biosystem on their world." Gambini paused. "Unfortunately, we have no one here with the necessary qualifications to confirm that guess."

"Where are we going now?" Hakluyt asked.

"Goddard. We have a VIP villa set up for you. If you choose to stay."

The tip of Hakluyt's tongue touched his delicate lips. "The villa can wait. I want to see what you have first."

If we can get you past security.

––––––––––

Leslie and Harry were at the visitor center when Bobby Freeman arrived in a caravan of eight sleek, polished church buses. They'd been scrubbed down for the occasion, and black hand-painted letters on their sides proclaimed them the property of the Trinity Bible Church. A cheer went up from the crowd. The buses rolled past heavy automobile traffic into the parking lot, past demonstrators, some carrying banners demanding that Hurley be impeached for withholding the translations, and others calling for the Hercules Text to be burned. The drivers took directions from base police and swung into assigned parking areas, while television cameras followed their progress.

Freeman descended from the lead vehicle, smiling broadly to enthusiastic cheers. He was hatless, wrapped in a threadbare coat and a long, loose scarf. The crowd continued to press forward. Some offered prayers while others thanked the Lord for the great man's presence. Security people, Freeman's own as well as the center's, mixed with the crowd, restraining it, trying to maintain a semblance of order. The preacher embraced a group of children, the ends of his long scarf flying. His supporters were middle-class types, mostly white, kids and their mothers and older couples. They were thoroughly combed, and the kids had shining faces and wore colorful school jackets. Everyone carried a Bible. It was cold, but nobody seemed to notice.

He lifted a young boy in his arms and said something Harry couldn't hear. The crowd cheered again. People reached out to touch his sleeve. An old man climbed into a tree and almost fell when Freeman waved in his direction.

The wind played with his gray hair. His cheeks were full, his nose broad and flat, and he appeared irritatingly content. But his manner was not the vacuous sort of complacency one usually finds in the professional television preacher; rather, the impression was of a man who had come to grips with the great dilemmas of human existence and believed he had found a solution.

"He's sincere," Leslie said.

"He's a fake," said Harry, who was unsure, but who felt a reflexive duty to attack televangelists.

She adjusted her sunglasses. "They're all trying to get to him, Harry. Somebody's going to get hurt out there."

Freeman's team had formed a wedge for him. Harry picked up a couple of security people and pushed through the crowd to the preacher's side. "Reverend Freeman," he said, "we can take you in through a side door. Avoid the crowd." Harry indicated the general direction.

"Thank you." The preacher launched his words into the general noise. "I'll wait my turn and go in the main entrance. With my friends." He joined the long line, while the people in the immediate area who'd heard the exchange cheered.

Harry thought about insisting but decided against starting a melee in the middle of the crowd. When he returned to Leslie's side, she shook her head. "Should have known," she said. "He *loves* this. It's why he's here."

Harry punched Parkinson's button on his cell phone. "How are we doing, Ted?"

"We're moving them in as fast as we can, Harry."

"All right. Do whatever you can to speed things up. Set up a special demonstration in one of the conference rooms if you have to. I want to get at least a hundred more inside as quickly as possible."

Parkinson growled. "Why don't we just claim we're having a power failure and shut down for the day?"

"Not on national TV," Harry said.

The buses were still discharging passengers. Signs continued to wave, carrying opposing slogans, and somebody got hit with one. A scuffle began. Dave Schenken, who had appeared at Harry's side, spoke into a cell.

A bus carrying Young Republican banners had just arrived. Students poured off and joined a growing contingent of counterdemonstrators.

A young man in a coat and tie, obviously one of Freeman's people, leaped onto the hood of a bus. "Reverend Bobby!" he cried, above the noise of the crowd. "Reverend Bobby, are you out there?"

A few *amens* drifted upward.

"This is a setup," said Leslie.

"I'm over here," came the preacher's cheerful baritone.

"Reverend Bobby," said the man on the bus, "I can't see you."

Someone must have produced a portable pulpit or a wooden box. Freeman rose suddenly, head, shoulder, and waist out of the crowd. He raised his hands. "Can you see me now, Jim? Can you see me, friends?"

The crowd cheered. But when the noise subsided, Harry heard a few catcalls.

"Why are we here, Reverend?" asked the man on the bus.

"This is not a good situation, Harry," said Leslie.

"We're here to bear witness, friends," said Freeman in the deep, round tones that seemed so much bigger than he did. There was more applause, and this time some sustained booing broke out. "There must be some Philadelphia football fans here," joked the preacher, and the crowd laughed. "We are standing in a place where people have not always been friendly to the Word, but where they are being touched by the Word all the same."

The laughter stopped. The outer perimeter of the crowd stirred uneasily as it was infiltrated by people carrying signs that read *RELEASE THE HERCULES TEXT* and *TELL THE TRUTH* and *WE ALL HAVE A RIGHT TO KNOW* and *SATAN*

LOVES LIES. Someone in back threw something. It landed close to Harry with a sound like soft ice. "Jimmy wants to know," continued the preacher, "why we have come here today. I can tell you: We're here because God is using this place, this scientific installation"—he pronounced the words the way somebody else might have said "whorehouse"—"for His own purposes. God is at work here today, using the devices of these men of no faith to confound them."

Harry blinked. Who'd told him Freeman was on *our* side this time?

"But that is not important," he continued. "God can confound the unbelieving anytime He wishes." He pronounced "God" in a singsong manner and gave the name two syllables. "What *is* important is that the message from the skies, whatever it may be, has been delivered, like the message from Sinai, to a nation that has yet to learn to fear God." More cameras were moving in his direction, and a TV news team climbed atop a CNN van. "There are some among us who are afraid of what might be in the transmission. Even some of *you* are urging that the message be burned. Burn without reading, you say. But I would point out that the message can only come from one of two sources, and I assure you, my beloved brothers and sisters, we'll have no trouble sorting it out."

"Sit down, buddy," came an angry voice. "You're holding up the line." That got some cheers, too. In spite of himself, Harry smiled.

"I'm not sure why you're laughing," said Leslie. "You've got a dangerous situation here."

A substantial space had opened between Freeman and the visitor center.

"That man has a point," said Freeman good-humoredly. He climbed down and disappeared into the crowd, which surged forward, then he rose again, closer to the building. "Are you still there, Jim?"

The man on the bus waved. "I'm here, Reverend Bobby."

"Can you see the antennas?" He held both arms out toward the twin units mounted atop Building 23, visible over a patch of trees. "We've come a long way from Moses, friends. Or we like to *think* we have."

"Why don't you go home?" someone bellowed. "Nobody here wants to listen to that."

"And take your loonies with you," added another voice.

The crowd surged suddenly, and a few people fell forward onto the grass apron that surrounded the visitor center. There were screams of fear and anger, and Harry could see someone with a *Jesus* sign raise it high and bring it down on the head of an older man. The man went down, and the crowd scattered. The person with the sign, a middle-aged woman, got in a few more whacks with it before it disintegrated.

Several fights erupted back near the buses. The crowd began to churn. A wave of people broke loose and ran for their cars.

"That's it," Schenken told his cell phone. "Shut it down."

"It may be a little late," said Harry.

Uniformed officers moved in.

Freeman was still talking. The trouble had developed so quickly, it had caught him in midsentence, and he was not a man to leave any thought unexpressed. But he was lurching violently, and Harry suspected someone had hold of an ankle or a leg and was trying to pull him to the ground.

"Leslie," Harry shouted over the noise, "maybe you'd better wait inside."

She glanced at the crush of people now in the main doorway, some trying to get clear of the commotion, others moving toward it. "I can't get inside now, and I couldn't see if I did."

"You can watch it on the news," said Harry, looking around for an escape route.

"Friends," Freeman continued, raising his hands and his voice, "why are you so easily angered?"

Leslie cupped her mouth. "He needs to get out of there. He isn't used to this kind of crowd."

"A hit in the head might do him some good," said Harry.

Abruptly, the preacher vanished.

The area where Freeman had been standing was completely engulfed now, and a series of pushing matches deteriorated into a general scuffle. The fights in back spilled into one another, a few beer bottles flew, and the line into the visitor center surged and heaved like waves crashing into each other.

Then it broke apart. Most people scattered along the sides of the building, heading toward the rear. A few tried to rescue their cars, and others took to cheering combatants, threatening security people, and for the most part enjoying themselves.

The visitor center was constructed mostly of glass and steel. Harry watched a rock arc gracefully out of the parking lot, sail overhead, and crash into one of the doors.

The security forces hauled a few adolescents out of the struggling mob, and it appeared briefly as if they might get things under control. Then someone fired a shot.

Whatever holiday mood might have remained dissipated. A howling sound like a lost wind rose from the crowd. There was an uneasy hesitation, and a second wave began to run for cover. One or two here, a few there, and, rapidly, the retreat became general. People spilled across flagstones and out among the surrounding trees. One of Schenken's security guards appeared, holding her hands over her head, blood spurting between her fingers.

A group of screaming schoolchildren, shepherded by a couple of frightened teachers, was overtaken and run down. Harry looked around for help, saw none, told Leslie to get to the rear of the building, and charged into the mob. He immediately lost control of all forward motion and was simply carried along. A punch glanced off his shoulder, and somebody—a woman, he thought—got in a kick. He couldn't see Leslie anymore, and the one or two security people nearby were unable to do much other than watch.

He would have been pushed off his feet except that the crush prevented his going down. Someone screamed at him for no apparent reason, but he kept his eyes on the spot where the schoolkids had been, and kept moving. Some of them were down, others were crying, one or two writhed on the concrete off to the side. A few had got clear and huddled with sympathetic adults. One of the security people picked up two children while he watched and was trying to lead them to safety when more shots sounded. They were like firecrackers, not particularly loud, but they ignited a fresh panic. Harry watched people go down to their knees and get trampled. A small mound of injured children, off to one side, was suddenly in the path of the beast.

In perhaps the finest moment of his life, Harry pushed through the tumult and placed himself between the mob and the kids. People hammered into him, driving him back. Individual screams became general and merged into a deafening roar. He pushed a few people away, dug in, absorbed the surge, and was still standing when it passed.

Abruptly, the roar died, as if all energy had been expended. It was replaced by cries, tears, screams, car horns. Several people wandered in shock across the battleground. Off to one side, he could see Leslie, fragile in a torn jacket. She looked a bit bruised.

A news helicopter roared in and hovered over the scene. The space center's ambulance, which had been standing by, came through the utility gate on the west side and rode across the lawn, red lights flashing. Moments later, the Greenbelt medivan arrived.

One of the Trinity Bible Church buses was trying to get away from the melee with barely half a dozen people on board. Someone had thrown paint on it, and several of its windows were broken. One bloodied boy, a year or two younger than Tommy, lay still on the grass immediately behind Harry. Leslie ran to him and was joined almost immediately by a medic. He put a stethoscope to the child's chest and signaled for a stretcher.

Schenken came over to complain about the large numbers of people who were allowed into the visitor center. "You need some restrictions," he said. "You see what happens when you operate too free and easy. We'll put a checkpoint on the gate over there, just like the one at the main gate, and stop letting just anyone come in here."

"You mean keep the visitors out of the visitor center?"

"Look," said Schenken, "I got three people in the hospital as a result of this, and we have had a riot on the premises. None of this is going to do my career any good, so I'm already not very happy. Don't get smart with me, okay?" He started to walk off, but spun around and jabbed a finger at Harry. "If I had my way, there wouldn't *be* a goddam visitor center. What purpose does it serve, anyhow?"

"It's the reason we're here." Harry smoldered. "And by the way, if you wave that finger in my face again, you're going to have it for dinner." Schenken appraised him, decided he meant it, and backed off. It was the first time Harry could recall that he'd physically threatened another adult. After all the carnage, it felt good. "What was the shooting about?" he demanded.

Schenken was still glaring at him, but he must have decided there was no point in antagonizing Harry further. "One of the Reverend's security people, an off-duty cop, fired the first shot. He told us it was a warning shot. You believe that? In a crowd like this?" Schenken sighed loudly at the depths of human stupidity. "Waving a gun around in a mob. Goddam lunatic. We haven't accounted for the rest of the shooting, but apparently nobody got hit."

"What happened to Freeman?"

"We got him out of here first thing. He's over at the dispensary now. He's limping a little." Schenken smiled maliciously.

The grounds were covered with the rubble of battle: beer bottles, placards, sticks, paper, even a few articles of clothing. In the driveway immediately in front of the visitor center, the CNN van lay on its side. A few of the facility's employees, in blue coveralls, were beginning the cleanup. Approximately two dozen cars remained in the parking lot. Some had been damaged, and a couple had been smeared with paint. A young woman was recording plate numbers so they could begin the task of locating the owners, who might be in a hospital, or jail.

Harry excused himself and drove to the dispensary. As he arrived, he got a call from Schenken. "Harry." His voice was somber. "We lost one of the kids."

————

Freeman was sitting on a plastic couch. His right arm was in a sling; his jaw and the bridge of his nose were taped. "How do you feel?" Harry asked.

The preacher looked disoriented. "Dumb," he said. He was slow to focus on his visitor. "Wasn't it you," he asked, "who wanted me to use the side door?"

Harry nodded. "It was."

"Should have listened." He offered his hand. "I'm Reverend Freeman," he said.

"I know." Harry ignored the gesture.

"Yes. Of course you do."

"One of the kids died."

"What?" Freeman's face paled.

"Trampled." He paused and they stared at each other.

"Who was it? What's his name?"

"I don't know. They didn't have it yet." He fought down a growing rage. "My name's Carmichael. I work here. I wanted to be sure you were all right. And I was also curious why you did that."

"Did what?"

Son of a bitch. "Started the riot," rasped Harry.

Freeman nodded. "I guess I did. I'm sorry. I came here to help. I don't understand how it happened. I mean, there weren't that many people out there, other than mine. But I know why they didn't want to hear what I had to say. It's a hard thing to look truth square in the eyes."

"Reverend Freeman, you want the truth? It was cold out there today, and you were holding up the line."

The President looked grave. His features had taken on a hard, flinty appearance in the glow cast by the table lamp. "Harry, I was sorry to hear about the trouble today. It doesn't sound as if we thought things out very well."

They were alone in the Oval Office. "I'm not sure yet how it happened," Harry said. "But Freeman didn't help."

"So I heard. Why did you give him the opportunity to speak?" There was a tired bitterness in his voice. "Schenken, anyway, should have known better."

Harry was surprised that he knew Schenken's name.

Hurley peered at Harry, and his assessment was visibly unfavorable. "Never mind," he said. "It's not your fault. Did you know we had a fatality?"

"Yes." Harry wondered whether it was the child he'd seen carried away.

"A third grader from Macon." Hurley picked up a pack of cigarettes from his desktop, offered them to Harry, and lit one. Harry had never before seen Hurley smoke. "Judging by the tapes, I suspect we're lucky we only lost one. Pity it had to be a kid, though. I understand Freeman's planning a memorial service tomorrow. I'd ask him not to if I thought he'd pay any attention."

"Why's he doing it?" asked Harry. "He's already admitted culpability."

"Really. To whom?"

"To me."

"Not in a public venue, I don't suppose?"

"No. In the dispensary."

"Not much help." He looked at the cigarette, frowned, took a deep drag, expelled a cloud of smoke, and stubbed it out. "Goddam things'll kill me yet," he said. "I hate to be a cynic, but the bastard's doing the memorial because he knows the networks will cover it, and he just loves the exposure. He'll use it to berate the godless elements, whoever they are. But we're the ones who'll look negligent. And responsible. And we are." He shook his head in frustration. "I hope what you're bringing me tonight is worth the price we're paying."

Harry was seated under a portrait of Theodore Roosevelt. Teddy was in an armchair beside a fireplace, in contemplative mood. Leading the charge, on safari, hunting buffalo, Teddy had always seemed to him the most outrageous of presidents. Unlike, say, Jefferson or McKinley, who belonged to distant epochs, the Rough Rider seemed to embody a romantic age that had never quite existed. Who stood for reality today? John W. Hurley? Or Ed Gambini? "Mr. President," he said, "Pete Wheeler thinks he's found a way to extract energy from the Earth's magnetic belts."

"Oh?" Hurley's expression did not change, but an interested glow came into his eyes. "How *much* energy?" He leaned toward Harry. "How complicated a process?"

"Pete thinks in time it will provide global supplies. The source is damned near limitless. We don't have the practical details yet. That's going to take some time, but he says the mechanics won't be difficult."

"By God." Hurley grew radiant. "Harry, if it's true, *if* it's true—" His eyes stared off into the distance. "When will I have something on paper?"

"By the end of the week."

"Make it tomorrow. By noon. Give me what you have. I

don't care if it's written on the back of an envelope. I don't care about theory. I want to know how much power will be available and what it will take to get the system up and running. You got that, Harry?"

"Mr. President, I don't think we can put it together in so short a time."

"Sure you can, Harry."

"I don't think—"

The President rose and looked at his watch. Harry took the hint and also got up. "Your jaw's swollen. Is that from the riot? Or are the women getting too tough for you?" He grinned, lost in a celebratory mood now. "Be more careful," he said. "I need you. Ed and the others over there, they're good people, but they don't have any responsibilities, really, except to themselves. I understand that. They live in a world where people are reasonable and there are no enemies except ignorance.

"I need your good judgment, Harry." Hurley fixed him with a nod that told him quite clearly he was a necessary part of the President's team. "If I were to ask Ed what to do about the gun problem, he'd tell me to stop the manufacture of firearms. A beautifully logical response yet utterly wrongheaded, of course.

"Well, maybe we can solve some of our internal problems by putting a new energy source online. We'll see. Is there anything else you wanted to tell me?"

"No, sir," said Harry, heading for the door. He knew he'd been manhandled again. But Hurley's skill was at a sufficiently high level that he came out of the White House feeling good anyhow.

Baines Rimford did not drive back to his quarters after leaving the inn on Good Luck Road. Instead, he wandered for hours along bleak highways, between walls of dark forest. The rain that had cleared off in midafternoon had started again. It was beginning to freeze on his windshield.

God help him, he did not know what to do.

He soared over the crest of a hill, descended too swiftly down its far side, and entered a long curve that took him across a bridge. He could not see whether there was water below, or railroad tracks, or only a gully; but it was in a sense

a bridge across time. Oppenheimer waited on the other side.
And Fermi and Bohr. And the others who had unleashed the
cosmic fire.

There must have come a moment, he thought, at Los Ala-
mos, or Oak Ridge, or the University of Chicago, during
which they grasped, really understood, the consequences of
their work. Had they ever met and talked it over? Had there
been a conscious decision, after it became clear during the
winter of 1943–44 that the Nazis were *not* close to building a
bomb, to go ahead anyway? Or had they simply been caught
up in momentum? In the exhilaration of penetrating the
secrets of the sun?

Rimford had spoken once with Eric Christopher, the only
one of the Manhattan Project physicists he'd ever met. Christopher had been advanced in years when Baines had gone to
see him at a book signing. Christopher, who had gone off the
track by then, was trying to tie physics in with Far Eastern
mysticism. Rimford had bought a copy and been pleased to
see the reaction when he gave his name. And he had merci-
lessly put the question to the old man. It was the only occasion
he could recall on which he'd been deliberately cruel. And
Christopher had said, yes, it's easy enough for you, so many
years later, to know what we should have done. But there were
Nazis in our world. And a brutal Pacific war with projections
of a million American dead if we could not make the bomb
work.

But there must have been an hour, an instant, when they
doubted themselves, when they could have acted for the
future, when history might have been turned into a different
channel. The choice had existed, for however short a time.
They could have refused to let the genie out.

The Manhattan Option.

Rimford hurried through the night, pursued over the dark
country roads by something he could not name. And he wondered fiercely whether the world would not be safer if he died
out here tonight.

———

Leslie had a swollen eye. It was beginning to discolor. She'd
also acquired some other very visible bruises. And she winced

when she sat down. "Stay clear of revivals," Harry said. "You look like a boxer."

"And not a very competent one. What did Freeman have to say for himself?"

They were in the Napoli Restaurant on Massachusetts Avenue, just off Dupont Circle. "He accepted responsibility. I was surprised."

"It must have been difficult for him. I don't think he's seen much adversity in his life. At least not this kind. He knows a child died, and he knows it wouldn't have happened if he'd stayed away. Or even if he'd just kept his mouth shut and hadn't stirred everyone up. That'll be hard on him. No easy way to rationalize it."

"He couldn't resist playing to the cameras."

"That's true," she said. "But it doesn't go far enough. I don't think he does it for exclusively selfish reasons. Other than the inner satisfaction he gets from being the Lord's right-hand man, of course. Whatever else he may be, Freeman is no hypocrite. He's a believer. And when he talks about a world ringed by the Jordan, and directed by a deity who cares about His creatures, he means it. When Freeman quotes psalms that are so lovely one wonders whether they did indeed come from a divine source, it is very easy to want it all to be true. To want things to *be* that way. I mean, it's a better arrangement than the Darwinian world you and I live in. Ed tried to explain to me once why the universe has no edge, despite the fact that it began in an eruption, and I didn't have the vaguest idea what he was talking about. The world of the physicists is cold and dark and very big. Freeman's is, or was, a garden. The truth is, Harry, that I would rather have the garden. God, believe it or not, is more comprehensible than a fourth spatial dimension."

Her luminous eyes grew distant, as they had been on the first night he'd seen her. "Ed wouldn't want to live in a garden," he said.

"No, I don't suppose he would. Would telescopes work in Eden? What would he be able to see? Still, all these years, he's been a driven man. And what is it that's driving him? He wants the answers to the big questions. I think, in his own way, Ed's a kind of twenty-first-century Augustine. It's probably no coincidence that there's a priest among his closest collaborators."

She touched a handkerchief gently to the injured eye and winced. "I won't be able to see out of it tomorrow," she said. "How do *you* feel?"

Everything ached. "Not real good," he confessed.

Their dinners came, spaghetti and meatballs for Harry and linguine for Leslie. "You miss them quite a lot, don't you?" she asked suddenly.

Harry tried the garlic bread. "Good," he said.

She waited.

"Julie and Tommy have been a big chunk of my life. Julie said in effect that I didn't really care whether they lived or died. And I know she meant it, believed it. But it isn't true. It was never true. But I guess it tells me how poor a husband I was. And father. I'm going through the most interesting period of my career now. God knows where all this will lead. But the truth is that I get no pleasure out of it. I'd trade it all to have them back." Harry pushed his food around on the plate. "I'm sorry. This is what you do for a living, isn't it? Listen to people talk about how they've made a mess of their lives."

She reached across the table and took his hand. "I'm not your therapist, Harry. I'm a friend. I know this is a difficult time for you. And I know it must seem as if you'll never really come out of it. You're at bottom right now. But you're not alone, and things will get better."

"Thanks," he said. And, after a moment: "She's impossible to replace." He smiled at her. "For a moment, I thought you were going to say you'd been through something like this yourself."

The flickering candlelight etched shadows across her throat and in her eyes. She grew thoughtful. It struck Harry quite suddenly that she was achingly lovely. How had that simple fact eluded him until tonight? "You're right," she said, "in recognizing she's unique. You won't find another to the same set of specifications. But that doesn't mean you won't find an equally desirable set of specifications." She did not smile. "And no," she continued, "I was not going to tell you I've been through a similar experience. I'm one of the lucky ones who've never been touched by the Grand Passion. I can say, perhaps to my shame, that I've never known a man who wasn't easy to give up."

"You don't sound as if you think very highly of us." Harry tried to sound aloof, but he knew it didn't come off.

"I *love* men," she said, squeezing his hand. "They just— Well, why don't we let it go at that?"

They went to the Red Limit for a nightcap. It was late, and they listened to the music for a while. Leslie sat stirring a drink, gazing down into it, until Harry asked if she were still playing the riot over in her mind.

"No," she said, "nothing like that." Their eyes met, and she shrugged. "I've been spending most of my time translating. And I've been getting an impression from the Text that's, well, shaken me a bit."

"What do you mean?"

Her breathing changed. She opened her purse, searched through it until she found a wrinkled envelope bearing the logo of a Philadelphia bank. She smoothed it out, produced a pen, and began to write. Upside down, it looked to Harry like verse. "This is a liberal translation," she said. "But I think it captures the spirit of the thing." She finished and slid it across to him.

> *I speak with the generations*
> *Of those whose bones are in the barrow.*
> *We are restless, they and I.*

Harry read it several times. "It doesn't mean anything to me," he said. "What's it about?"

She wrote again on the envelope:

> *Having passed through the force that drives*
> *The world flower,*
> *I know the pulse of the galaxies.*

"I'm sorry," said Harry, frowning. "But I'm lost."

"It's out of context," she said. "And God knows how accurate the translation is. But the 'world flower' is, I believe, the evolutionary process. And the force that drives it is death."

Harry ordered another round of drinks.

She brushed back a lock of hair. "The data set I've been working on is filled with things like that, suggesting a very casual acquaintance with mortality. There are also references to a designer."

"A designer?"

"God, perhaps."

"We got a world full of Presbyterians?"

"Funny." She closed her eyes. "From the Hercules Text . . ."

I have touched the living chain,
Have known the dance within the proton.
I speak with the dead.
Almost, I know the designer.

"They're only poems," said Harry.

"Yes," she said. "I know. But I don't understand any of it. Harry, the composers of these verses tell us time and again, in a variety of ways, that they have died, that theirs is a community of the living and the dead."

"You could argue that Christian societies are also communities of the living and dead. And some religions hold that ancestors are still alive within the individual."

"I suppose it could be the same sort of thing." She crumpled the envelope and dropped it on the table. "I just don't know. And it's not simply a few odd quatrains. There's a sense throughout the material of a race that transcends mortality."

"I'd like to read some more of it," Harry said.

"Okay." She brightened. "Sure. I'd like another perspective."

After Carmichael had gone, John Hurley stood a long time near the curtains, watching the traffic on Executive Avenue. He'd come to the White House three years before, convinced that he could navigate through this difficult period in which so many nations had weapons of mass destruction, in which rebellion and genocide flourished in so many places, in which the West was under pressure from assorted terrorist groups.

Other presidents on other nights had stood brooding beside these windows: Kennedy, Nixon, and Reagan in the shadow of the nuclear hammer. And then, after the collapse of the Soviet Union, the first President Bush and his successors had struggled with different challenges: the creation of a new world order in which nation-states would live at peace, an effort to eradicate famine and disease around the world, and, after 9-11, the ongoing confrontation with religious extremists.

It was a noble mission, but one that seemed beyond the efforts of any group of nations. Population growth had leveled off somewhat, but it nevertheless continued to increase, outrunning the best efforts to provide at least a chance at a decent existence for everyone.

The terrible truth was that the planet bled constantly. But if Harry Carmichael was correct, if an inexhaustible power supply lay close at hand, then it might really be possible to take a constructive step toward acquiring a thriving human future.

It occurred to the President that Carmichael might have brought him immortality.

MONITOR

HOUSING BIAS CHARGED IN SEATTLE

CITY, EIGHT SUBURBS PROBED BY U.S.

. . .

CHINESE SUB REPORTED
TRAPPED IN CHESAPEAKE

(Associated Press)—Informed sources revealed today that U.S. Coast Guard and Navy vessels had tracked a Chinese Y-Class submarine into the mouth of Chesapeake Bay—

. . .

BEAR KILLS CAMPER
AT YELLOWSTONE

BOY TRIED TO SAVE LUNCH,
SAYS GIRLFRIEND

. . .

CONGRESS APPROVES
GENERAL FUNDING FOR CITIES

POLICE, EDUCATION, JOBS PROGRAMS
TO GET HELP

. . .

BOLIVIAN GUERRILLAS OVERRUN
POLICE POSTS OUTSIDE PERU

ARMY ROUTS REBELS
IN HEAVY FIGHTING NEAR TITICACA

. . .

LAKEHURST TERRORIST
SUES FOR DAMAGES

SKULL FRACTURED
DURING ASSAULT BY SWAT TEAMS

FAMILY OF DEAD GUNMAN
ALSO CONTEMPLATING ACTION

. . .

NORTH DAKOTA
CURBS MEDICAL COSTS

UNDER NEW BILL, STATE TO SET FEES

AMA WARNS
QUALITY OF MEDICINE WILL DECLINE

. . .

PAKISTAN REQUESTS $6 BILLION LOAN
FROM WORLD BANK

. . .

PRAGUE DEFIES ARMY ULTIMATUM

WORKERS RIOT; ARMY CORPS REBELS

. . .

NUCLEAR WEAPONS IN TERRORIST
HANDS "PROBABLE" IN THIS DECADE

TWENTY-SIX NATIONS
TO POOL INTELLIGENCE, RESOURCES

||| TWELVE |||

At approximately 3:00 A.M., Harry's phone began to ring.

He rolled over, stared into the dark, reached for it, and knocked the receiver onto the floor.

"Carmichael," he finally growled into the instrument.

"Harry?"

What the hell? It was Rimford. What could possibly have him stirred up at this hour? "Yes, Baines? What's wrong?"

"Nothing's wrong. But I need to talk to you."

"Now?"

"Yeah. There's an all-night waffle house on Greenbelt Road. Arlo's."

"I know where it is."

"Meet me there in forty minutes."

He clicked off and left Harry lying on his back, gazing into the dark.

What could Rimford possibly want with him? He thought briefly about calling Gambini but decided that Rimford wanted Harry alone or he'd have made *that* call himself. He threw his legs over the side of the bed, shook the last of the sleep out of his eyes, and headed for the shower.

Rimford was there reading the *Post* when Harry arrived. Otherwise, save for two washed-out middle-aged waitresses, the place was deserted. It had just stopped raining, and the big plate-glass windows were still wet. The lights were hard bright, but the coffee smelled good.

Rimford looked up from his table and greeted Harry without a smile.

Harry sat down, and they brought him coffee. "Did you want to order?" asked the waitress cheerfully.

"Might as well," said Harry. "Bacon and eggs. And toast."

When she was gone, he turned to Rimford. "So what's going on?" he asked, keeping his voice down.

Rimford looked crumpled and tired. He reached into his pocket and pulled out a plastic-wrapped package and held it up for Harry's inspection.

"It's the transmission?" said Harry.

"Complete."

"How'd you get it?"

"Walked out with it. I made it before they put the restrictions on. I'm giving it to you because I wanted to remind you that there might be others out there. I doubt I'm the only one who thought it would be more convenient to work at home."

"Thanks," said Harry, not sure he even wanted to touch it. "Best way is just to destroy it and forget it. Otherwise, we'll be into a security breach, and you and I will both be filling out reports into next year."

Rimford nodded and drank from his cup. "Whatever you think."

"What's that supposed to mean, Baines?"

His gaze screwed into Harry. "You want some advice?"

"Okay." Harry slid the package cautiously into a pocket.

"When you've got rid of *that*—" He looked at the pocket. "Use *this* and get rid of the rest of it." He produced a disk and passed it across the table.

The disk was labeled *Valse Triste*. "What is it, Baines?"

"It's a virus. Take it into the lab, load it into the system, and it'll erase everything."

Harry stared at him. "You're not serious."

"Call it the Manhattan Option. It's what Oppy should have done."

"Baines—"

"Don't forget," he continued, rumbling ahead as if Harry'd said nothing, "there are a few sets, I'm not sure how many, five or six, on disks. So you'll have to get those, too. Go in at night." He looked at his watch. "This would be a good time. You could take out the hard drives and probably get all the sets without any problem."

Harry wondered if Rimford was having a breakdown.

"Why?" he asked. "Why would we want to do this?" He could see that the cosmologist was upset, so he softened his voice, prepared to be reassuring. And with it came a curious satisfaction at becoming a father figure to Baines Rimford. *It's all right, Baines. Whatever's bothering you, it's okay.*

The blue eyes blazed. "What's the last thing you'd want to find in the transmission, Harry?"

"I don't know," Harry said, weary of it all. Goddam problems never stopped. "Plague. A bigger bomb. A planet-buster." He slipped the virus into the same pocket. "What did you find?"

"I got up this morning intending to go into the lab and do it myself. Can you believe that?"

The waffle shop felt cold. "Why didn't you do it? Why call me?"

"It's not my decision to make. Not my responsibility. It should be erased, all of it, disks, notes, drawings, whatever else they've got down there. But—" The waitress arrived with two plates, waffles for Rimford, bacon and eggs for Harry.

"I'm glad," Harry said, "that the problem hasn't affected your appetite."

Rimford laughed, scooped butter onto the waffles, and added powdered sugar. "Harry, this is *not* my problem, and if I go in there and take down the Hercules Text, my career is over, and I will probably end as the most despised professional on the globe. I didn't ask for this, and it's not up to me. I have no intention of sacrificing myself for it."

"What's *in* it?" asked Harry.

Rimford bit into the waffle. "A cheap way to end the world," he said. "It could be done with the resources of virtually any Middle Eastern nation. Or even with a reasonably well-financed terrorist group. The procedure is not all that difficult once one is put on the right track. By any measure you can think of," he concluded, "I am now the most dangerous man in the world."

"I was under the impression," said Harry, "that you were limiting yourself to the cosmological stuff they'd found."

"That's correct."

"What on earth could you possibly find in a cosmology treatise?"

"A way to bend space, Harry."

"Explain."

"Thanks to the Altheans, we now know the specifics of spatial curvature. Or at least we know what they maintain. Apparently, there are, under normal circumstances, in the area of fifty-seven million light-years to a degree of arc. That number would vary, depending on local conditions. And if that seems too small a number, it's because the universe is not the hyperbolic sphere I predicted, and we all assumed."

Harry was trying to follow, but he'd already fallen helplessly behind. "I thought," he said, "that it was supposed to be *flat.*"

"At the end of the nineteenth century, we thought that. It's been back and forth, Harry. But if the Altheans are right, and there's no reason to think they aren't, it's a twisted cylinder. There's much of the four-dimensional Möbius in it. Look, if you headed straight out *that* way"—he pointed toward the eastern sky, dark and starless—"and kept going, eventually you'd come back from over *there.*" He indicated the opposite direction. "But a little lower, of course. You'd be below the horizon."

"Okay," said Harry.

"I see you're right-handed."

Harry was buttering his toast. But he paused at the observation. "And—?"

"When you got back," Rimford said, "you'd be left-handed."

Harry let it go. "So why do we want to get rid of the transmission?" He was uncomfortable carrying on this conversation in a public restaurant.

"Do you have any physics, Harry? We're talking about bending space here. Within a finite area, the degree of curvature can be increased, eliminated, or inverted. It doesn't require much power. What it *does* require is technique. We're talking about gravity! Antigravity. Artificial gravity. It's all in our hands now."

"That sounds like good news, Baines."

"If that were as far as it went, I suppose it would be. No more problems lifting heavy loads into orbit. Housewives could slap a couple of antigravity disks on a refrigerator and move it into the basement. But what would you say if I told you I could arrange to have New York City fall into the sky? Or turn the state of Maryland into a black hole?" Rimford got wearily to his feet. "God knows what else is in those disks, Harry. But I think you, or your boss, or somebody better see to getting rid of them. They're just too much for us."

A cold paralysis was seeping through Harry's muscles. "It's already classified," he said.

"Don't be a fool, Harry. You know it would be just a matter of time before the secret was leaked. Or stolen. Or *used*. The only way to be safe is to shut it down now, while the thing's still contained. If it *is* contained."

"You're talking about other copies."

"Of course. It may already be too late."

"Baines, you know we can't just destroy the thing. Gambini wouldn't hear of it. Rosenbloom would have a heart attack. And they'd be right. The Hercules disks are a source of knowledge beyond anything we'd dreamed. We can't just throw them away!"

"Why not? What can we possibly learn from it that exceeds, in any substantive way, what we already know? Hurley, for God's sake, understands that. They've shown us we're not alone, he said, before we really knew they'd speak again. That's what matters. It's *all* that matters. The rest of it is detail." He finished the waffles, drank the last of his coffee, and signaled for the bill.

"I've got a morning flight, Harry," he said. "If you do erase the damned *thing*, and you get caught, or if you do it openly and get criticized, you can tell them I advised it. I'll go that far. I'll back you and tell them you did the right thing."

He put the disk with the copy of the transmission in the bottom left-hand drawer of his desk and threw a newspaper on top of it as if it would somehow help protect it from anyone who broke in. Then he locked the desk, stared at it for several minutes, got up, and, with the virus in his pocket, walked over to the lab.

It was not yet six o'clock. The only people there when Harry walked in were Majeski and two technicians. Cord looked up at him, nodded, and went back to working on a schematic.

Harry would never have seriously considered taking it upon himself to erase the Hercules records. But he couldn't resist wandering through the spaces analyzing how it could be done.

There were six numbered copies. Plus what was on the hard drives.

———————

"No matter how dangerous it might turn out to be," Harry said, "it's just not our decision."

"I agree with that," said Gambini. "I think we need to avoid overreacting." He'd found a second message, from Rimford, when he'd come in that morning: *"Ed, I can't stay with the project. Sorry. Good luck."*

Pete Wheeler and Gambini were both in Harry's office. Harry had described his conversation of the previous night, omitting the information that Rimford had handed over an extra copy. Gambini sat nodding throughout as if he should have seen Rimford's reaction coming. Wheeler's emotions were masked.

"What scares me," Gambini said when he'd finished, "is how easy it would be to walk in and destroy everything. It never occurred to me it was something we had to worry about. First thing we have to do is make another copy and put it under lock and key." He looked at Harry. "Where's the virus?"

Harry produced the disk and held it out as if it were a piece of evidence. Gambini took it, examined it by lamplight, and broke it.

Harry's heart sank.

"He's been worried," said Wheeler. "In hindsight, I can see it. Should have known something like this was coming."

Gambini shook his head. "Poor bastard. Pity he didn't talk to somebody."

"He talked to *me*," said Harry.

"I meant one of the specialists. Well, no matter. Listen, I'll call him. Try to reassure him."

"What are you going to tell him?" asked Wheeler. "Judging by what Harry says, the only thing that'll reassure him is hearing that we've deep-sixed this thing."

Gambini frowned. "You sound as if you agree with him."

"Maybe we should talk about that," said Harry. "I don't think that, until last night, I understood how dangerous this thing is." He was staring at the broken disk.

Wheeler's lips formed a thin smile. "Harry, how could you have missed it? Why did you think they put in all the security precautions?"

"Of course there are hazards involved," said Gambini. "We all know that. But they can be managed."

"You really think so, Ed?" asked Wheeler. "We're talking about technology that can juggle stars. If that's all in there, are we really ready to handle *that* kind of power? We're still trying to deal with gunpowder."

"You've been fairly quiet about this until now, Pete," rasped Gambini. "If you've been all that worried, why haven't you said so before?"

"I'm a priest." Wheeler took a deep breath. "Any action I take tends to reflect on the Church. And it's especially difficult in a matter like this. It's only been a few years since we admitted that evolution really happens. We're still trying to explain ourselves about Galileo. I've sat passively by; I certainly could not have acted as Baines did. But I can tell you that, whatever their motives might have been, the Altheans have done us no favor. I'm sorry they didn't settle for saying hello."

"Why?" demanded Gambini. "Because Rimford could see a way to misuse some of the information? Hell, there are always risks. Whenever we move forward, there are risks. But think about what we've got here. A message from another world. A chance to compare what we know and what we think we know with a fresh perspective. A chance to get some sense of whether man has a real purpose in his existence. *You*, *Padre*, should be interested in that if anyone is.

"We need to just take it easy and not panic. I suggest we simply alert the investigators to our concerns and have them report anything that could create a problem. Then, if something develops, we'll deal with it in a rational manner."

"I'm not so sure we're talking about things that can be identified all that easily," said Wheeler.

"Goddammit, Pete, there's no way I can argue against that

kind of logic. But I think we have to be reasonable about this. Has it occurred to you that our best hope for survival as a species might depend on what we can learn from the Altheans? If we get technological breakthroughs, maybe we can get a handle on some of our problems." A plea for understanding had crept into his voice. "With the gifts we're getting from this, everything's opening up to us. There's no limit to what we can do after we've eliminated gravity and harnessed the kind of power this thing is going to give us." He looked up at Harry. "Would *you* want to take the responsibility for destroying a source of knowledge like this? Even Baines, despite what he believed, couldn't bring himself to do it."

"That's what makes it so dangerous," said Wheeler. "It's a tar baby. Whatever the potential for damage, we can't get rid of it."

"We need a political solution," said Harry. "Which is to say, we should temporize. Stall. We won't know the real nature of the problem until we know more about what we have."

"I agree," said Gambini. "That's very sensible. But I think we need to know a couple of other things right now. Pete, are you going to stay with the project?"

"Yes," said the priest, his voice hardly a whisper.

"Do I need to worry about the safety of the Text?"

"No. Not from me."

"All right. Good. I'm glad we got that settled. Now—" He looked pointedly at Harry. "Is anyone else having morality problems about this?"

"I'm not going to take it into *my* hands," said Harry. "But I don't know about anybody else. We'd better get the extra copy made and locked away."

"First thing when I get back to my office."

Harry felt himself relax. "We've got something else to talk about. Good news for a change."

"I'm delighted to hear it."

"The White House is still getting a lot of pressure to release the Text. So Hurley's going to set up an office to review what we're getting. They say they'll release whatever they can."

"Well, that's good to hear," said Gambini. But after he'd had a moment to think about it, he asked quietly, "Who's going to decide what's safe?"

Harry kept a straight face. "Oscar deSandre," he said. "Who?"

Even Wheeler grinned.

"Oscar deSandre," Harry repeated. "They tell me he's a top man in military high tech. And I guess he's getting a staff of experts in related fields, and they can always talk to us if they're in doubt about something."

"A lot we know," murmured Wheeler.

Gambini glanced at him with obvious irritation. "Okay," he said.

"I think we'd be wise to police ourselves," said Wheeler, "and not automatically ship everything out."

"I agree," said Harry. "Ed, I'll get you deSandre's phone number. I'd like you to call him today, bring him in, and try to give him some ideas of the sorts of things he should be looking for. We won't mention Baines, okay?"

"Of course not," he growled. "That gets out, it'll scare the pants off the general public. By the way, he didn't say anything about talking to the media about this, did he?"

Harry reran the conversation in his head. "No," he said finally. "He made it pretty clear he was leaving it up to me. To *us*. I'm pretty sure he won't say anything."

"Okay. I'll try to get a commitment when I talk to him."

Harry frowned. "Ed, I'd leave it alone if I were you. Now, what else? We need to set up a mechanism to make sure that somebody we trust reads everything we break out. And we need to get Cord, Leslie, and Hakluyt involved. Tell them what's at stake and ask them to red-flag anything that might create a problem."

"It seems to me," said Wheeler, "we've got three categories of information: material for DeSandre, stuff that can go only to Hurley, and stuff that shouldn't get out of here at all."

Gambini got up and circled the office a couple of times. "I'm not sure," he said, "but I think we're talking treason. Harry, what the hell kind of bureaucrat are you?"

"Probably not a very good one," he said.

Wheeler nodded. "What do you think Rimford's legal status would be if somebody had used his virus?"

Harry smiled. "Most they'd get him for is conspiracy to destroy government property."

Though Oscar deSandre thought of himself as a White House staffer, he was physically based in the Executive Office Building. He was not happy. Despite the personnel requests he had filled out, and the promises that had been made, he had only one assistant and a part-time aide available to help with the Hercules Project. And the aide was of limited value because she had not yet received her clearance.

The first package from Gambini arrived just moments after he walked in the door. DeSandre's responsibility was to read through the transcript, assure himself that it contained nothing that would adversely affect the national interest, and pass it along to the National Security Advisor, who would comment, or not. If it came back to his desk stamped RELEASE APPROVED, he would forward it for distribution at the daily White House press conference. That seemed simple enough, but he realized there were terrible bear traps hidden in this type of job. It was a position with negative potential; he could do well only by staying out of trouble. If he missed something, his whole career would dissolve. So he could look bad, but there was no way to excel. His superiors would notice him only if he screwed up.

Moreover, his time was constricted just now. Riding herd on Greenbelt wasn't his only responsibility. He was involved in a flap over lie-detector tests routinely used in some high-level security-clearance procedures. And he had responsibilities at Fort Meade as well. So DeSandre leafed quickly through the ninety-five-page document that Goddard had sent over, to get the flavor of it. Then he called in his assistant. The one with the clearance.

She brought several telephone memos with her and a list of e-mail queries for him to look at. He glanced quickly at them, put them aside, and handed her the Greenbelt report. "Look for technical stuff," he said. "Most of it reads like chunks of a philosophical tract. There's no problem with any of that. But we don't want anything going out that could conceivably have military implications. Okay?"

The assistant nodded.

And that was how the existence of a series of alien

philosophical precepts came to make the news the next evening. It did so in a relatively modest way, taking second billing
to a congressional vote that had defeated an administration-
backed attempt to remove price supports from the electronics
industry.

The precepts did not have the sort of effect they might have
had because the version released to DeSandre was literal and
bore little resemblance to Leslie's more poetic translations.
Furthermore, ethical and aesthetic similarities with generally
accepted values were apparent, and the media concerned
themselves with that facet of the story. It was a full two days
later that NBC produced a set of energetic translations and
thereby created a mild sensation. Cass Woodbury, in her studied, resonant voice, gave some of the lines pointed meaning:

> *I am alone.*
> *I make life, handle the atom, and speak with the dead.*
> *But God does not know me.*

There was a great deal more, along similar lines. At home,
watching the telecast, Harry shivered.

So did the Cardinal.

His phone began ringing shortly after nine o'clock, and he
called in his staff first thing next morning. Barnegat couldn't
be reached; he was in Chicago. Cox and Dupre arrived within
a few minutes of each other and were already in a heated argument when Jesperson arrived with Joe March, who was arch-
diocesan head of the Society for the Propagation of the Faith.
March was not part of the Cardinal's inner circle, but Jesperson had no reluctance about bringing in people who could
make a contribution. Dupre, who had seen the TV reports, was
indignant. "Communication with the dead! It's absurd. I keep
hoping that the media will eventually develop a sense of
responsibility. They've put the most sensational reading on all
this that they can. But the transcripts released by Goddard
don't justify any such interpretation."

"There wouldn't be a problem if the media would leave it
alone," Cox said. "These things happened a million years ago.

But if they're playing it up, then people can be misled. So we have a responsibility to act."

Dupre's heavy brows came together. "Nobody's going to take any of this seriously if *we* don't." He looked at the Cardinal. "Will the Vatican issue a statement?"

"In due time. They don't want it to appear that they're being stampeded." Jesperson allowed himself a smile. "They must have got His Holiness up in the middle of the night. There was a meeting of some sort. I talked with Acciari this morning. He thinks the whole thing is a plot by the Western powers in retaliation for the See's refusal to cooperate with their Middle East initiative."

Cox looked bored. "Do you have any idea what the official line is going to be?"

"They haven't decided yet. But Acciari believes His Holiness will maintain there's really nothing in the translation except a piece of poetry. He expects they'll dismiss the whole business as an absurdity and throw in a few choice remarks about the wanton direction modern society is taking."

"In other words," said Cox, "they're just going to tell everyone to ignore it."

"A sensible position," said Dupre. "We should do the same."

"Come on, Phil," objected Cox. "What better way could you find to call attention to the fact that we're a little jittery about it all?" He squinted at Dupre as if he were examining a balance sheet. "They can probably get away with that in Italy. But not here. The media will be asking questions, and we aren't going to get away with just shrugging it off."

"Jack," Dupre said with rising heat, "I'm not suggesting we tell people to look the other way. But I think we need to be very careful about getting everyone stirred up. The Vatican's right: It's a piece of poetry. Totally without context. If it weren't part of this ridiculous transmission, nobody would pay any attention to it. I think we'll do fine if we don't create problems for ourselves. Just ignore it. It's of no consequence. That's the way we should treat it."

Cox shook his head. "People are going to demand answers. And I don't think we have any because there're really no questions."

"The whole thing is crazy," said March, a short, stout man,

well into his sixties. But he retained a head of thick black hair. March had come out of south Chicago, a hard worker, tenacious, deliberate, efficient. Not brilliant, the Cardinal knew, but he got the job done. A blue-collar priest, the kind Jesperson liked best. "People talking to the dead. The good Lord wouldn't allow any such thing. Phil's absolutely right. We shouldn't dignify the proposition by paying any attention to it."

Dupre was drawing small circles on a notepad. "Absolutely correct. Although I suspect we'd be wise," he said without looking up, "to avoid declaring what God will or will not allow."

"Phil." In times of stress, the Cardinal's eyes seemed to take on a scarlet glow that matched the color of his office. He radiated that vaguely infernal light now. "What is the theological status of communication with the dead? Is it prohibited?"

"No," said Dupre, drawing the word out while he considered how to continue. "Many of the miracles are, after all, no more than such events. Fatima and Lourdes would be, I suppose, if we were prepared to consider Mary deceased. If not, certainly postmortem appearances by the saints have been officially accepted into the record. As you know. And Jesus himself talked with Moses and Elias in the presence of witnesses. What, after all, is prayer but an attempt to communicate with the next world?"

"Except in this case," Cox said, "the next world is answering."

"Yes." Dupre touched his lips with his index finger. "As uncomfortable as that may be, such notions are not new, and I think our best course is to suggest that we're not surprised and not particularly interested. Assuming we want to suggest anything at all. I'd still say we're safest just riding it out and smiling politely if anyone brings it up."

"Absolutely," March said with a chuckle. "It smells of fortune tellers and spiritualism to me. The Vatican's right. We should sidestep the whole business. Or denounce it. God only knows what they'll be claiming to hear next."

"It occurs to me," said Cox, "that the ability to communicate with the Church Triumphant might have been one of the preternatural gifts lost by Adam's sin. We talked about this before, but I wonder whether we aren't seeing a culture whose founder was wiser than ours. Whose first representative was smart enough to stay away from apples. Or whatever the nature of the initial offense might have been." The remark was followed by an uncomfortable scraping of chairs.

The Cardinal gazed steadily at him. "Jack, do you consider that a possibility?"

Cox seemed surprised at the effect his remark had produced. "Of course not. But it *is* theologically tenable."

March sat straighter in his chair but said nothing. Though the Cardinal seldom looked directly at him, he nevertheless observed the elderly priest carefully, as though gauging his reactions. March remained skeptical and unblinking throughout. God and Adam. There was no room in Joe March's theology for a second creation. Anyone who had been watching the Cardinal closely might have noted that he seemed visibly relieved by what he saw.

"All we have," continued Cox, "is somebody's interpretation of a phrase in a language no one's ever seen before. And that probably no one can really read. I agree with Phil that we don't want to get caught looking foolish. On the other hand, I think we need to recognize that some of our people may have trouble with these events. Consequently, we should be reassuring. Surely we'll be safe in pointing out that whatever might have happened on Mars, or wherever this place is, it is of no concern for us. We've seen nothing that should disturb any good Catholic."

The Cardinal listened until the arguments began to repeat themselves. Then he intervened. "I'd be less than honest with you," he said, "if I did not confess a certain amount of anxiety over this business. We may be entering a new age. And new ages are inevitably uncomfortable for those doing the steering. It strikes me as an odd paradox that the princes of the Church have traditionally resisted scientific advance."

Dupre and March frowned, but the Cardinal signaled that he wasn't interested in facetious protests. "It's really not open to refutation," he continued. "We, who should always have been in the forefront of the search for truth, have a sorry history in these matters. Let's not get caught at it again. At least not in *this* archdiocese. We'll take Jack's position that we've nothing to fear from the truth, that we have our assurances from our Redeemer, and that we are as interested as anyone else in new revelations of the majesty of God's work."

"I didn't say that," objected Cox.

"Odd," said the Cardinal. "I thought you had." He gazed serenely at the others. "We will not suggest, verbally or by our actions, that the people at Goddard have it wrong, that they are twisting the facts, or that they are misinformed. We will allow this thing to play itself out. And perhaps if we put ourselves in the hands of the Lord, we might even enjoy the experience. Meanwhile, any comment on the subject will come from the chancery office and from nowhere else."

"George," said Dupre, "the Vatican could change all that if they put out a statement—"

"Have faith," said the Cardinal, smiling. "No one listens to the Vatican anymore. Why should they start now?"

————————

Harry, who might not have been as interested in Althean philosophy as he'd allowed Leslie to believe, settled in for the evening with the bulky binder she'd given him. He read for three hours, but it was difficult going. Some terms were not yet understood; syntactical relationships were not always clear, and Harry sensed that even a perfect translation in simple English would have been baffling. The Text reminded him of a cross between Plato and haiku; but there was no escaping the overall sense of gloomy intelligence or, paradoxically, the suggestion of a wry wit whose meaning lay just beyond his grasp.

The Altheans were concerned with many of the problems that obsessed his own species, but there were subtle differences. For example, a discussion of morality explicated in considerable detail the responsibilities an intelligent being has toward other life-forms and even inanimate objects; but its obligations to others of its own species were ignored. Then, too, a philosophical treatise on the nature of evil examined only the catastrophes caused by natural forces, overlooking those that result from the malice of intelligent beings. Harry concluded that Leslie had confused evil with misfortune.

The world of the Altheans must have resembled Earth. Again and again, there appeared the metaphor of the seas, of the wandering ship, of the questing mariner. But the waters are calm. Nowhere do squalls rise, nor does one feel the surge of heavy tides. There are neither rocks nor shoals, and the coasts glide peacefully by.

Too peacefully, perhaps.

The great islands in the gulf are uniformly cold.

And the shores are dark.

MONITOR

Sec. 102(a) The Congress hereby declares that it is the policy of the United States that activities in space should be devoted to peaceful purposes for the benefit of all mankind.

(b) . . . Such activities shall be the responsibility of, and shall be directed by, a civilian agency . . . except that activities peculiar to or primarily associated with the development of weapons systems, military operations, or the defense of the United States . . . shall be the responsibility of, and shall be directed by, the Department of Defense . . .

(c) The aeronautical and space activities of the United States shall be conducted so as to contribute materially to . . . (1) the expansion of human knowledge of phenomena in the atmosphere and space . . .

—National Aeronautics and Space Act of 1958

||| THIRTEEN |||

Whatever it was about Cyrus Hakluyt that irritated people was difficult to put a finger on. Yet colleagues, associates, casual acquaintances, even family members, all were inevitably uncomfortable in his presence. It might have been his eyes, which were unnaturally close together; it was easy to imagine them focusing on one through the barrel of a microscope. His speech was guarded, and he showed no real interest in the people around him. He never gave direct evidence of an inflated ego, yet those in his presence always received the impression that they had not quite made it to Cyrus's level. Harry suspected that he was somehow limited by the dimensions of his specialty. He was a biologist, and it would have been easy to conclude that he perceived other human beings as colonies rather than individuals. Nevertheless, in his first report, given at Gambini's daily staff meeting on Christmas Eve, he displayed an unexpected sense of the dramatic. "I can tell you," he said, "more or less what they look like."

That got everyone's attention. Gambini laid aside his glasses, which he had been polishing; Wheeler stiffened slightly; Majeski's dreamy eyes focused. And Leslie glanced sharply at Harry.

"I isolated their DNA several days ago," Hakluyt continued. "There's still a great deal to be done, but I have a preliminary report. There's a fair amount of guesswork involved because I can't be certain of the construction materials. To begin with, the Altheans are most certainly not human. I'm not quite sure how to categorize them, and it would probably be best if I didn't try. I *can* tell you that these creatures could live quite comfortably in Greenbelt." The thin smile drifted across his lips. "Nevertheless, they are unlike anything in terrestrial biology. The Althean appears to combine both plant and animal characteristics. For example, it is able to photosynthesize." He looked directly at Leslie.

"Then they were never a hunting society," she said. "That might mean no wars, or even a concept of war."

"And consequently," added Majeski, "no thought given to weapons potential."

"Very good," said Hakluyt approvingly. "My thoughts exactly. The Althean also appears to have no vascular system, no lungs, no stomach, and no heart. It has teeth, however. Big ones."

"Wait a minute," said Wheeler. "How can that be? They have no stomach, you say? What would they do with teeth?"

"Defense, Father Wheeler. I would guess they had some predators to deal with at one time. They *do* have nervous systems and controlling organs that are brains. Their reproductive systems are asexual. And, although I can't be sure, I believe the creatures would be slightly larger than we are. Certainly on Earth they would be. They have exoskeletons, probably constructed from chitinous material, and they seem to have similar sense organs. I don't think they hear quite as well as we do." He leaned back smugly in his chair. "The eyes are especially curious: There are four of them, and two do not seem to be receptive to light."

Hakluyt's brow creased, and his voice was less pedantic when he continued. "There's no lens, so I can't see how it could function as a receptor for any kind of radiation. Moreover, the nerve that connects it to the brain doesn't appear to be capable of an optic function. No, I think the organ collects something, or maybe projects something, for all I know, but not any kind of radiation I'm familiar with."

"I'm not sure what that leaves," said Majeski.

"Nor am I." Hakluyt examined the tabletop. "I would estimate their life span at approximately a hundred fifty years."

"*Solar* years?" asked Majeski.

"Of course," snapped Hakluyt. "On a side note, I would add that we can be sure they're capable of genetic manipulation."

"How?" asked Harry.

"Because we can do it ourselves on a modest scale." His

tone implied that any idiot could see that. "I'm learning a lot from them, Carmichael. I don't know what their limits are, but I have a good idea about their minimum capabilities. And that's another curious thing. Their life span, by any reasonable measure, is exceedingly short."

"Short?" said Gambini. "You said it's a hundred and fifty years!"

"That's not much for a species that can dictate the architecture of its DNA."

"Maybe they tack on the extra years," said Harry, "*after* birth rather than before."

"No," said Majeski. "That would be the hard way to do things."

"Correct." Hakluyt smiled. "Why perform adjustments for millions of individuals when you can do it once? I don't understand it. They seem to have consciously chosen to wear out early."

"I have a thought," said Leslie. "Maybe we have a species that voluntarily accepts an unnecessarily early death. If we read them right, *they talk to their dead*. That can't be a coincidence. Cyrus, is there anything peculiar in their physical makeup that suggests a life cycle incorporating a second existence of some kind? A chrysalis effect?"

Hakluyt shook his head. "Not that I can see. But at this stage, I'm not sure how much that means. Unless there's an unknown factor, and there easily could be, the creature that would develop from the DNA plan they sent us would meet an organic death in the same way that any terrestrial life-form would. It would be dead. Period. No revival. No encore."

Wheeler nodded and scratched out something he'd written on his notepad. "I'm surprised," he said, "that they and we both use DNA to control genetic characteristics. Aren't there other possibilities?"

"Yes." Hakluyt bit off the word and let it hang in the still air. "Diacetylenes might work. Or crystals. But these alternatives aren't as flexible or as effective as the nucleic acid group. Actually, the options open to nature in this matter are surprisingly limited."

"Dr. Hakluyt," said Harry, "you say they have the means to prolong life. Do you now grasp some of these means?"

"Carmichael, you look to be about, uh, fifty?"

"A little younger," Harry said. "I've had a hard life."

Hakluyt's smile did not change. "You can expect maybe forty more years. By then you will have whitened, your blood will be sluggish, and I suspect the memory of youth will be quite painful." His eyes fell on Leslie. "And what will *you* be in forty years, Dr. Davies?" he asked cruelly. "And why do you suppose that is? Why does the mechanism you inhabit fall apart in so short a time? Gambini, how long a period is eighty years?"

Gambini's gaze never left his notepad.

"Ask a cosmologist," said Hakluyt, "and you're asking someone who really understands about time. Well, I'll tell you why you break down so quickly: Because your DNA *shuts you down.*"

"Please explain," said Wheeler.

"It's simple." Harry felt as if Hakluyt would at any moment announce a quiz. "We used to think that aging was really just an accumulation of wear and tear, diseases, damage, and misuse, until the body's ability to repair itself was simply overwhelmed. But that's not what happens. The DNA we carry controls evolution. Some people are inclined to think of it as a kind of external entity that seeks its own development and uses other living creatures as"—he looked around the walls, seeking a term—"bottles. Containers. In any case, one of its functions is to ensure that we are safely out of the way of our progeny. So it kills us.

"It shuts off the repair mechanisms. I would guess that's happening in you, Cord, right about now." Hakluyt adjusted himself more comfortably, straightened his glasses, and rearranged his expression, which now faded to a more somber glow, like coal in a dying fire. "If you want to avoid aging, all that's necessary is to tinker with the instructions your DNA puts out. All the equipment you need to stay young indefinitely is in place. We need only get it working. The Altheans seem to know quite a lot about the technique for doing just that."

"How much," asked Wheeler, "do *you* know about it?"

"You mean how much have I learned from the Text? Some. Not a lot, but some. There hasn't been time yet, and there's still too much material we can't read. But I'll tell you this: It's in there. And so is a lot more."

Near the end of the meeting, the door opened, and Rosenbloom put his head in. "Gentlemen," he said, "and Dr. Davies. I know you're busy, but I wonder if we could have a few minutes outside."

The people in the operations center had been gathered together, and Patrick Maloney stood at their head. A gold clasp anchored a gray-black tie, and his pointed black shoes were polished to a mirror shine. He was, Harry thought, a man of glossy qualities.

"Ladies and gentlemen," said Rosenbloom, "I think most of you know Pat Maloney, from the White House. Pat, this is the Hercules team." Harry caught the pride in Rosenbloom's voice. It was a good moment.

Maloney, however, had possibly presided at too many similar occasions. Despite the nature of his responsibilities, he projected the image of a public man, a failed politician, possibly, a man too honest for the calling and not subtle enough to hide his handicap. "I think I've met most of you at one point or another," he said, "and I know how busy you are. So I won't take much of your time." He rose slightly on his toes and sank again. "You've been under a lot of pressure, and we know it hasn't been easy for you. But we wanted you to be aware how important your contribution is.

"Let me begin by telling you that Hercules has already paid an enormous dividend. We may now have the means to defend ourselves against any aggressor by launching a satellite-based particle-beam attack against ground or air targets. Against any enemy anywhere in the world. It now appears that we will never again have to risk pilots in bombing runs over enemy territory." He looked around, caught something of the developing mood, and added, "Should the need ever arise, which, of course, we hope it does not."

Maloney paused for effect. He received polite applause, hardly what the occasion seemed to demand. It was a sober reflection of the scientists' resentment of the government's policies, of which he'd become a symbol. Toward the rear of the room, a mathematician from American University walked out.

"Over the last few weeks," Maloney continued, choosing not to notice, "the President has been under considerable pressure because he would not release the Hercules Text to the general public. We know that has made your job more difficult and created personal problems for many of you. But we can now see the wisdom of that decision.

"We owe the breakthrough to the work of Dr. Peter Wheeler. Dr. Wheeler, would you come forward, please?"

The priest was standing uncertainly near the rear. His associates parted for him, and he approached Maloney with the enthusiasm of a man getting on close terms with a scaffold.

Maloney rose again on his toes and settled slowly. "The new defense system will be known as Project Orion. A formal announcement will be made from the White House later today." He extended an arm to the reluctant Wheeler and drew him into an open circle. "To show his appreciation, the President has directed that the Hercules unit be granted the Jefferson Medal for Distinguished Achievement in the Arts and Sciences." He unsnapped a black case, revealing a gold medallion on a striped green-and-white ribbon. "Unfortunately," he added, "as is customary in awards of this nature, the fact that Orion is connected with the Hercules Project will remain classified. Consequently, the granting of the award is itself classified. There will be no mention of it outside these spaces. Usually, information of this sort is distributed on a strict need-to-know basis, but the President felt that the people responsible for such a significant contribution to the national defense should be aware of the importance of their work.

"The medal itself will be displayed in an appropriate location here in the operations center.

"In addition, President Hurley has expressed his wish that Dr. Wheeler become a recipient of the Oppenheimer Certificate for Outstanding Service." The two dozen or so people present applauded, and Maloney held up a framed, beribboned parchment for their inspection, then handed it gracefully to Wheeler. A flashbulb popped. The photographer was Rosenbloom.

"You have every reason to be proud, Dr. Wheeler," continued Maloney. "You may well have made a decisive contribution to the safety of your nation." Wheeler mumbled his thanks and smiled weakly at his colleagues. "The certificate," Maloney added, "will be placed alongside the Jefferson Medal."

After the ceremony, Wheeler lingered a moment with Harry.

"I thought," said Harry, "you were working on generating power from planetary magnetic fields?"

"So did I. I guess we've just seen the application." Wheeler inhaled. "Well," he continued, "the award is aptly named."

"How do you mean?"

"I keep thinking about Baines's comment: Oppenheimer is the guy who should have said no."

————

Harry had a long afternoon among the late shoppers. He wandered the downtown streets of the capital, hoping to lose himself in the crowds, loading up on game programs and books for Tommy and wondering about the etiquette of Christmas presents for a wife who'd walked away from him. Eventually, he bought a plant, a gift that seemed sufficiently neutral.

He arrived outside Julie's condo at seven. Lights were blinking across the porch and around a pair of azalea bushes. She greeted him at the door with a friendly but decidedly chaste embrace.

A bright, jeweled tree dominated the living room, wreaths were hung in all the windows, and colored lights were stretched in a bright sprinkle across the balcony. The scent of evergreen was everywhere, and she herself seemed sufficiently happy to see him. In the spirit of the season, she would have been reminiscing over past holidays. But Harry looked in vain for any real sign of regret.

She was properly grateful for the plant. After setting it near a window, she kissed him lightly and gave him his present. It was a gold pen. "Every rising executive should have one," she said.

He couldn't be certain whether he detected a note of irony.

Tommy's Lionel train was on a platform in the living room. Julie had tried to add a set of switches to the familiar figure-eight layout, but she hadn't tied the track down securely enough to allow them to work. Harry finished the job and sat for an hour with his son, while the little freight train looped endlessly through a mountain tunnel, past a couple of farms, and down the main street of a peaceful, snow-covered town with glowing streetlamps.

She poured sherry for Harry and herself, and they drank a silent toast: Harry, to what might have been; Julie, to the future. Then they embraced again, less formally. It was, they both knew, the last time they would meet as other than casual acquaintances.

———

President Hurley strode into the pressroom, took his place at the lectern, and welcomed the journalists. "We don't usually do formal business on Christmas Eve, and I want to apologize for keeping you away from your families and loved ones tonight. Consequently, I'll try to make this brief.

"I'm pleased to announce that the United States will soon launch an orbiting system employing particle beams that will be capable of striking targets in the air *or* on the ground. This system, code-named *Orion*, will obviate the need for warplane pilots should the United States find itself in combat. Ladies and gentlemen, we are a step closer to providing a devastating defense against any would-be aggressor while simultaneously protecting the lives of our men and women in uniform.

"We will be better able to keep the peace—"

He continued for eleven and a half minutes, spelling out the benefits for both the nation and the world, took a handful of questions, wished everyone a merry Christmas and a happy Hanukkah, and departed. It was, he thought as he headed for his private dining room to have dinner with his family, the closest he'd ever come to sensing that a group of journalists wanted to cheer.

———

Gambini, Pete Wheeler, and Leslie, the project's loners, met at the Red Limit for dinner. Candles, wreaths, and mistletoe had been placed lavishly throughout the establishment. The bar was almost empty, and only a few tables were occupied. "Close at nine tonight, folks," the hostess told them.

Leslie had considered making the run back to Philadelphia for Christmas, but she'd be just as alone there.

Ed, she knew, planned to stay at Greenbelt. He'd be at work tomorrow, bright and early, Christmas or no. Sad, she thought, that he had nothing else in his life. Pretty much like herself, except that she at least knew what was missing. Ed seemed not to be aware that he was leading a truncated existence.

They ordered a carafe of white wine and looked at the menu while she considered the judgment she'd just passed. He seemed happy enough. If Ed had a family, who was to say he wouldn't have found himself in the same desperate straits as Harry, trying to live simultaneously in two worlds.

If you find somebody to marry, she told herself, it would be best if he were a taxi driver. Or a welcoming guy at the Walmart. Somebody who'd be glad to get home. That was the ticket.

Pete poured the wine and toasted her, "the loveliest woman in Greenbelt, Maryland." It was a sweet gesture, and she gazed appreciatively at his sharp features in the flickering candle-light.

"You're a good man, Pete," she said. "If you ever decide to become available, let me know." She delivered a semiserious leer, and they all laughed.

Laughter at such times hides things. She knew what *she* was hiding, and she wondered about Pete, who seemed far more complicated than Ed, who never had a thought that didn't flash across his features. Pete, on the other hand, seemed always to be looking at her from behind a mask. She was never quite sure what he was thinking.

She settled for a pork chop, while the others indulged in steaks. They talked amiably, of people they should have got in touch with this Christmas but had somehow neglected; of what they hoped to be doing next Christmas; of how the holi-days this year seemed to have lost much of their old magic. They all agreed on that, giving different reasons, Pete because he usually spent the holidays with old friends at St. Norbert's Abbey in DePere, Wisconsin, where the order had its head-quarters; Ed because there just wasn't time to think about it; Leslie because she was away from home. But she understood the real reasons had to do with the fact they were alone here tonight. Alone with friends, but alone all the same. What was the line? *It is not good for man to be alone.* No, it was written in the software, that life's sweetest moments will be passed in the company of children and lovers.

There'd been a lover long ago for Leslie, despite her remark to Harry that she'd never been touched by the grand passion. That had been ten years back. He'd been the first one, really, the one she couldn't forget. The one she'd always thought would somehow return to her life.

Stop it.

Gambini left early, explaining he wanted to think about some aspects of the transmission and that he'd see them both after the holiday. "Merry Christmas, Pete," he said, shaking the priest's hand. And he repeated the wish for her, brushing her cheek with his lips.

She laughed and pointed at the ceiling. "Mistletoe," she said. "Surely we can do better than that."

Gambini grinned, pretended reluctance, and kissed her. A long one, braced with real affection. "That's better, Ed," she said. "Merry Christmas yourself."

And he was gone, out into the dark.

"So where will *you* be in the morning?" she asked Wheeler.

Pete was the only one of the three who'd ordered dessert. He was now in the middle of a slice of key lime pie. "I have friends in Georgetown. They'll put me up for the night."

"Priests?"

"One is. The other's a law professor. They share a house on Wisconsin Avenue."

"Good. This isn't a night to be alone."

"How about you, Leslie?"

She shrugged. "There are some people in College Park. They invited me over, but they have kids, and I didn't want to get underfoot. Not tonight."

"So you *will* be alone."

She shrugged. "I'm not alone *now.*"

He smiled. "You're one of the real benefits to come out of this business, Leslie."

"Thanks, Pete," she said. "You're not very optimistic about the project, are you?"

"No," he said. "I have a very bad feeling about this."

"You're a scientist," she said. "You're not supposed to believe in bad feelings."

"I've also been around awhile. I have a lot of respect for instincts."

———————

If Jack Peoples had expected any visible change in church attendance as a result of the Goddard revelations, he was disappointed. The number of the faithful neither lessened nor increased.

He took his usual station just outside the doors before the end of the nine o'clock Mass, which was being celebrated by a young priest from the District who helped out on Sundays. It was cold, and Peoples had wrapped himself in his black overcoat. Across the street from the church, two teenage girls were comparing jackets.

The Offertory bell rang, its bright, silvery cadence floating in the still, morning air. He thought of Pete Wheeler and his hopeless quest. Indeed, he thought, if man has a response at all to the gulfs beyond the Earth, it is in the fragile sound of that bell on Sunday morning.

Then they were singing, and he could hear people moving toward the altar rail for Communion. A few of his parishioners emerged, their formal obligation completed even though the Mass was not finished. They came down the stone steps and hurried past Peoples in embarrassed silence. The pastor was always sorely tried not to judge these persons, the same ones each week, who lived so close to the edge of their faith.

The second wave rolled out after the distribution of the Holy Sacrament, then came the general exodus, to the energetic accompaniment of Sister Anne's choir singing "O Little Town of Bethlehem." Peoples smiled and shook hands and exchanged idle talk. His parishioners seemed unchanged, untouched by the grotesque stories that now seemed to be proliferating on TV. With one exception, there was no sense that anything extraordinary had happened.

The exception came in the form of a child, Harriet Daniel, the nine-year-old daughter of a lawyer who frequently volunteered her time to the church. Harriet was intelligent, well mannered, a credit to her family and her faith. And she wanted to know about the Altheans and their dead.

Phil Dupre's prescribed response might have worked with a committed adult: "It has nothing to do with us."

But the child, what could he tell her? "I think there's a misunderstanding somewhere, Harriet."

She looked at him closely, smiled, and her lips formed a quizzical *oh*.

What, indeed?

Of such are the kingdom.

SUBLIMINAL ALIENS

Blue Delta, Inc., a distributor of electronic novelties, announced today that it will begin next month to market a subliminal CD composed of selections from the Hercules Text. According to a press release, "Much of what the Altheans have to say about nature and courage is remarkably like the best in ourselves. However, they have a mode of expression that, once one gets beyond the difficulties of translation . . ."

. . .

COLLIE DOVER
JOINS CONCERT GAMMA

Westend Productions, Inc., announced today that internationally acclaimed film and TV star Collie Dover will join an all-star cast set to open in Hollywood with Concert Gamma, a tribute to the Altheans. Ticket sales have been brisk . . .

. . .

STARSONG EXHIBIT
TOMORROW AT NATIONAL

Everett Lansing's collection of astronomical photographs, more than a hundred of which have been produced by the optical capabilities of Skynet, will be on display tomorrow at the National Art Gallery, and, for those who can't make it in person, on the Web. The collection includes *Views of Centaurus*, a series of stunning color photos of the sun's closest neighbor, which won the Kastner Award last year in the field of scientific photography.

. . .

LONGSTREET'S
ANNOUNCES ALIEN CUISINE

. . . Diners with more exotic tastes might wish to visit Avery Longstreet's Inn at either of its two locations, in the Loop or in Schaumburg. Instead of simply embellishing old favorites with new sauces, Longstreet's has actually produced a few dishes, mostly (but not exclusively) meat-based, which do indeed seem to be completely novel. We particularly recommend . . .

. . .

WHITE LINES SCHEDULES
INTERGALACTIC CRUISE

The Hercules group is particularly lovely when seen from the deck of an ocean liner, according to White Lines Tours, which expects overflow booking for its Sea Star cruises. In addition to the view from the deck, passengers on the four-day voyage will be able to look through the giant reflector at Hobson Observatory in Arizona by TV hookup. Cast off for the stars by contacting your travel agent or White Lines . . .

. . .

CASS COUNTY TOYS WILL MARKET
ALTHEAN ACTION FIGURES

Cass County, a small Nebraska toy and game manufacturer, will be first on the market with a wide range of movable Althean figures. Lydia Klaussen, announcing the coup to the company's shareholders, said that the aliens will "somewhat" resemble the image thought to be a self-portrait. She did not elaborate.

||| FOURTEEN |||

Cord Majeski got out of the oversized bed, padded across the wooden floor, and stood for a time looking out at the mountains beyond the Blue Ridge Parkway. They were lovely in the approaching dawn. Behind him, Lisa stirred. Her black hair was spread across the pillow, framing her face and a shoulder.

The cabin was his favorite getaway spot. And this time he needed it. Lately, Ed had become exasperating to work with. The political pressure never let up, and Gambini always took a beating no matter what he did. His health had never been good. Now it was deteriorating visibly and his self-possession with it. He'd been suffering from migraines and chest pains, which he refused to see anybody about. Majeski had begun to wonder whether he shouldn't alert Harry.

If Majeski were in Gambini's shoes, he'd tell Carmichael and the White House to go to hell. And then he'd walk out.

He looked across the room, at the Rensselaer portable generator set on a rubber mat on his coffee table. And at the rickety chest of drawers he'd bought at a garage sale years ago. He stared at it a long time. It was an unremarkable piece of furniture, scratched and chewed and discolored. And its bottom drawer stuck.

Who would have believed that it held, among his socks and underwear in that same bottom drawer, an alien device, a machine conceived on a world unimaginably far away?

Except that the alien device didn't do anything.

He turned on a lamp, tilting the shade to keep the light off Lisa, and opened the drawer. The thing looked like a carburetor with coils, loops, and a circuit board. It had taken him almost two months to assemble and he didn't know yet whether he had it right. Or whether he could ever get it right.

He removed it, carried it over to the coffee table, and tied it in to the Rensselaer. The portable allowed him to control the flow of power in a crude sort of way. But he could manipulate all he wanted, and it didn't seem to help much.

He sat down in front of it, opened a case of instruments, and made some changes in the circuit board. He proceeded in a methodical fashion so that he always knew where he'd been, what had yet to be tried. When he was ready, he switched it on.

He was still trying to get a response an hour later when he felt a prickling along his right arm, which was closer to the device than any other part of his anatomy. At about the same time, before he had a chance to think about the unusual sensation, Lisa gasped, threw off a quilt, cried out, and leaped from the bed, all in a single, panicked motion. She tumbled into a corner of the room, where she pressed herself against the wall and sat staring at the mattress and the rumpled blankets. Then her eyes found Majeski. They were full of terror.

"What happened?" he asked, glancing nervously behind him at the window. "What's the matter?" And in that moment he noticed that, whether from shock or from some less obvious cause, the hairs on his right arm were erect.

It was a few moments before she found her voice. "I don't know," she said at last. "Something cold touched me."

In another age, Corwin Stiles would have been picketing restaurants along Route 40 or lobbing bags of blood at draft offices. He thought of himself as an idealist, but Wheeler suspected that he rode the white horse because he enjoyed exposing other people's defects rather than actually righting wrongs. During the second Obama administration, he had taken a master's in communications from Yale and, after five uneventful years in commercial television, had won a post with Sentry Electronics, which supplied technical personnel for NASA operations. When Pete Wheeler began unraveling the possibilities inherent in planetary magnetic fields, Stiles had been with him. And if the priest was shaken by the fact that his discovery was being applied to military use, Stiles was incensed.

"Why couldn't he have announced the power breakthrough rather than the goddam death ray?" he asked Wheeler, knowing the answer full well. The particle-beam weapon needed enormous amounts of power, and that had always been the problem. You couldn't haul enough fuel into orbit, nuclear generators were prohibited by treaty and too easy to trace, and solar mirrors were too inefficient.

Therefore, to give away Wheeler's secret was to give away the monopoly on the particle beam.

During the first two months of the year, Stiles urged Wheeler, and anyone else who would listen, to mount a formal protest. "We should all show up outside the main gate," he told Gambini one morning, "and shake our fists in the general direction of the Oval Office. Let the press know we're going to be there and tell them everything."

Gambini never took the young technician seriously. He was accustomed to hearing preposterous proposals from the Hercules personnel. But Stiles learned to resent also the mindless inertia of his fellow workers. Even Wheeler, who understood perhaps more than anyone the enormity of what was happening, refused to act.

Stiles gradually recognized that, if the truth was to get out at all, he would have to be the conduit. But he was restrained by the habits of a lifetime, which sadly had thrown up few opportunities to break rules for good causes. Now he would have to risk jail.

The catalyst came during the last week of February. An elderly husband and wife were found frozen in their farmhouse outside Altoona, Pennsylvania, after a local utility turned off their electricity for nonpayment of bills. The utility explained that it mistakenly believed the farmhouse to be abandoned because its occupants did not respond to correspondence and couldn't be reached by telephone. An investigation was promised. But Stiles wondered how many more elderly couples were huddled in cold buildings against the bleak winter while John Hurley played politics with an unlimited power supply.

Where, he demanded of Wheeler, was there any sign that the administration was interested in tapping the colossal reserves of energy that had been made available to it? On the following Sunday, Corwin Stiles met one of Cass Woodbury's associates in a small restaurant in a remote town on the edge of the Blue Ridge.

———

A person is entitled to only one great passion in a lifetime. Whether it's music or a profession or a lover, everything else pales in its afterglow. The searing shock so changes one's chemistry that if the object is lost, the experience can never be repeated. Only anticlimax remains.

Cyrus Hakluyt, molecular surgeon, articulate observer of the natural order, and former third baseman for the Westminster Wildcats, had during adolescence pursued a seventeen-year-old cheerleader named Pat Whitney. Her lack of interest in him, and her departure from his life had, for many years, been the central reality of Hakluyt's existence. Now, a decade and a half later, he was pleased to think that she, too, was advancing in age, that her DNA had shut down her repair mechanisms, and that no level of beauty was forever.

It was a degree of consolation. Hakluyt had grown up in Westminster, Maryland, a leafy college town west of Baltimore. Although in later years he'd remained relatively nearby, he had not returned to it since his father's death, during his first semester at Johns Hopkins. Pat Whitney, he knew, had married and moved on. His old friends were gone, too, and the town seemed desperately empty. On the same Sunday that Corwin Stiles was having lunch in the shadow of the Blue Ridge, Hakluyt put aside his work and drove home to western Maryland. He could not have said why except that his research into Althean genetics had made him acutely conscious of the passage of time.

Hakluyt, in fact, had always been sensitive to the fleeing years. His thirtieth birthday had been traumatic, and he'd watched the premature retreat of his hairline with alarm. He could not enter a room with a ticking clock without being reminded of his mortality. Now, however, he'd begun to speculate on the possibilities suggested by the Hercules Text. And somehow, the rolling green hills around Westminster seemed, consequently, less threatening, and the lost days of his youth were no longer quite so remote.

Westminster had increased in size since his departure. Population had grown. Several office buildings had been erected on the outskirts, and a shopping mall had sprung into existence. Western Maryland College had expanded, too, and he passed several new housing developments on the south side as he drove into town.

The house in which he'd grown up was gone, swept away to make room for a parking lot. Most of the rest of his neighborhood had disappeared along with it. Gunderson's Pharmacy had survived, and C&I Lumber. But not much else.

They'd added a new wing to the high school, a glass-and-plastic monstrosity that threatened to overwhelm the old brick building. Bells sounded inside as he passed. They took him back to the old days. It was good to know there was still some stability in the world.

The athletic field had a new backstop. Despite poor vision, Hakluyt had been a fair infielder once, at a time when they'd all expected to play forever. But after leaving Westminster, he'd never put on a uniform again.

The hamburger spot where he used to take Pat Whitney was still there, occupied now by strangers. He smiled as he drove by, surprised that after all these years, he could still feel the familiar pulse in his throat that only she had ever induced. Where was she now? For the first time perhaps since the terrible night when she'd sent him into the dark, he could think of her without anger.

Ruley Milosky arrived at his executive suite in the state of disarray with which he customarily greeted Monday morning. But this had been an extraordinary weekend. He'd attended a Saturday evening dinner with the head of the City Council, planting the seeds for solving licensing problems on some commercial real estate held by his sister. And on Sunday he'd finally succeeded in bedding the black bitch who'd been running him all over Kansas City.

Two of his account executives, Abel Walker and Carolyn

Donatelli, tried unsuccessfully to intercept him on his way in. Both were wearing anxious frowns, but Walker fretted about everything, and Donatelli, of course, was a woman. An attractive one, but still only a woman. He'd fondled her with his eyes any number of times, but he prudently kept his hands off. Never fool with the office staff. It was Ruley's most basic moral principle.

His head hurt, and, of course, he hadn't had enough sleep. He got some orange juice out of his office refrigerator, decided against adding vodka, and slid down onto the leather sofa.

The intercom buzzed. When he didn't answer, his secretary pushed the door ajar. "Mr. Milosky," she said. "Al and Carol would both like to speak with you." While he considered his response, she added, "The market opened down eight hundred."

Ruley grunted, climbed to his feet, and swung around to his computer screen. "It's more than eleven hundred now," said Walker, pushing past the secretary.

Donatelli filed in behind him. "Pennsylvania Gas and Electric is off sixteen," she said.

My God. The geezers would have heart attacks. PG&E was still on the firm's buy list for conservative investors who wanted good income with security. "What the hell happened?" asked Ruley.

Donatelli raised her eyebrows. "Didn't you have your television on this morning?"

Ruley shook his head.

"There's a rumor that the people at Greenbelt, the ones who've been working on that message from outer space, have found a way to produce cheap power. A lot of it."

"Goddammit, Carol, nobody's going to believe that."

"Maybe," said Donatelli, "but some of the money managers must have expected the news to drive the market down. And they sure as hell didn't want to stand around and take a beating. They've sold everything, and they're probably looking to pick the stuff back up this afternoon or tomorrow at a substantial discount."

"Son of a bitch," said Ruley.

"Vermont Gas is down fifty-two," said Walker. His voice was squeaking. "The utilities are getting hit all over the board.

Everything's going south. Absolutely everything. It's free fall, Ruley."

Miloski brought up the stats. The major oil companies were already off more than 20 percent. Heavy-equipment firms, especially those that served the utilities, had crashed. Banks were in the basement. So were a number of service companies.

Goddam. Even the retailers, after what had been reported as record-high Christmas sales, were down sharply. Only the automobile manufacturers were bucking the general trend. GM, Ford, and Chrysler had all spurted. Naturally, if the rumor turned out to be true, oil prices would collapse, gasoline would become even cheaper, and more people would return to big cars.

"Have we begun calling our clients?" asked Ruley.

"They've been calling *us*," said Walker. "And they're upset. Especially the smaller accounts. Ruley, a couple of these people talked to me today about suicide. They're getting wiped out. Lifetime savings going up in smoke. Okay? These aren't people trying to make a killing in the market. These are our electric-company accounts!"

"Keep calm," said Ruley. "This kind of thing happens. What do we tell everybody who opens an account with us? Don't invest anything in the market that you can't afford to lose. It's in the brochure. But you're right, of course. We don't want it happening under our auspices. Make sure when you talk to these people that you blame it on the government. But tell them we expect to see a rally. The unfortunate thing is that utilities tend to be slow to recover from things like this. What about our major customers?"

"They've been on the line, too," said Walker.

"Of course they have. What are we telling them?"

"We don't know what to tell them," said Donatelli. "I called Adam at the Exchange, and he says the sell orders aren't coming in as fast now but that they're still heavily back-logged."

"Which means we'll lose another thousand points by noon. Okay, let's not join the panic." He stared at his desktop. "Let's just ride it out. We'll probably get a bounce this afternoon and recover maybe thirty percent of the initial losses. What happens after that will depend on what the government has to say." He shut his eyes tight. "Goddam, sometimes I hate this business.

"All right, start calling the list. Reassure them. Tell them we're watching developments. Personally, I think this might be a good time to buy. And you can tell them that." When he was alone, Ruley got on the phone to Washington.

———

Charlie McCollumb was a railroad man. He was retired now, but that didn't change his essential nature. Charlie had ridden the old steam-driven 2-8-2 Mikados across the prairies, hauling lumber to Grand Forks and potash to Kansas City. He'd started in the dispatch office in Noyes, Minnesota, in the 1960s. He'd tried to join the Marines in 1964, but he'd had asthma and they'd told him he'd be more valuable on the home front.

He had no love for things that didn't move, so he applied for every brakeman's job that came open until they gave him a freight that ran down to the Twin Cities. Later, he became an engineer on the Denver-Minneapolis route, and eventually he moved up to conductor with the Great Central. He rode the south arrow specials in that capacity for forty years and could have been stationmaster in Boulder once, but that didn't suit him, so Charlie kept riding until his hair turned white and, at last, the wind cracked his lips and carved his features to resemble the scored slabs along the tracks in the Rockies.

In the end, they gave him a few thousand dollars and a watch. He settled in Boulder, in a small apartment off the main line. He added the money to his savings, which were substantial because he'd never married, had never found a woman willing to live with a man who was always away. He invested his money in the Great Central, every penny of it. For years, he collected generous dividends, and the value of the stock went up a few points.

But the railroad's primary source of revenue was coal. The endless strings of hoppers carried it from the Western mines to the Eastern power companies; and when the Big Board crashed on Monday, March 4, the Great Central and Charlie's money went with it.

He was ninety-eight years old.

On Tuesday evening, after a daylong drinking bout in the Prairie Depot, a bar across the street from the Boulder yards, he drove downtown, walked up to the front door of Harmon & McKissick, Inc., Brokers, and threw a brick into the plate-glass window.

It was the first time in his life that he'd consciously broken the law.

———

Marian Courtney knew immediately something was wrong. The blue Plymouth was straddling two lanes as it approached from the west on Greenbelt Road. It slowed near Goddard's main gate and made a sudden left directly into oncoming traffic. Horns blared. It sideswiped a Toyota and spun it sideways against the center strip. The Plymouth's front was hammered in, and one wheel went wobbly, but it kept coming.

She stepped out of the inspection booth onto the small hook of paving that divided the roadway. Reflexively, her right hand brushed the .38 on her hip, but she did not unclip the safety strap that held the weapon in its holster. The car slowed. Marian had a glimpse of the driver as he struggled to maintain control. He looked, she realized with a chill, like the lunatic who'd been captured in the Appalachians a week earlier by police after killing three officers in an ambush. He was smiling at her when she saw the .45.

Behind her, a window exploded. And something hit her in the belly and drove her off her feet.

She collapsed inside the booth and lay on the floor, trying to hold herself together while he methodically blew out the rest of the glass. Then he drove past her station and poured automatic gunfire into a group of visitors coming out of the parking lot. Several went down, and the others scattered, screaming.

Security forces were slow to respond. The Plymouth turned onto Road 2 and was almost out of sight before a pursuit vehicle left the main gate. Marian's radio came alive. She brushed the glass shakily out of her hair. Her supervisor was sprinting toward her from the gatehouse, his eyes wide, his hands held out to her.

It was the last thing she saw.

The driver of the Plymouth killed three more in a wild chase across lawns and through parking areas before they cornered him behind the house that Baines Rimford had occupied and blew him in half. Altogether, seven were dead at the scene. Of the critically injured, three more, including Marian, died that night.

The assailant turned out to be a welfare father from Baltimore, who was under a peace bond for threatening employees of Eastern Maryland Power & Gas.

———————

Senator Parkman Randall, Republican from Nebraska, had no idea what the Oval Office meeting would be about other than that it concerned the Senate Armed Services Committee. He hoped they'd be able to talk about something other than weapons procurement. It would be nice if the President provided something Randall could take home to his constituents for a change. Farm policies during this administration had been a disaster. The senator had played the loyal soldier, supporting what he could and opposing what he had to, knowing always that the President understood. The near collapse of the stock market, now in its fifth day, wasn't helping matters. And there were other problems: abortion, the gun issue, prayer in the schools. The same dreary stuff that never went away, that allowed little or no room for compromise, that made life hell for any public servant and sometimes made Randall wish he'd chosen another line of work. He knew, as every good politician knows, that votes on sensitive issues seldom win friends and invariably lose voters.

He was up for reelection this year.

The members of the Senate Armed Services Committee gathered in their caucus room and rode the underground jitney to the White House. Chilton was waiting for them when they debarked, and he escorted them to the Oval Office.

The President stood as they entered and advanced to shake their hands. He was smiling, and Randall knew his man well enough to understand immediately that the news, whatever it was, would be good. He was grateful for that, at least. "Ladies and gentlemen," he said, after everyone had settled into place,

"I have an announcement of some importance." He paused, enjoying the moment. "We've successfully tested a ground-based particle-beam weapon which will constitute the heart and soul of this nation's defenses well into this century."

The men and women who sat around the perimeter of the office had, collectively, spent almost two centuries in politics. They were not easily impressed by talk. They'd known tests were under way, and they were aware that favorable results had been reported. But they sensed something different this evening. The eloquence was gone. Instead of the measured rhythmic tones and the sparkling phrases, they heard only his elation.

"The United States will, early this spring, activate Orion."

Through the window, Randall watched the inevitable demonstrators, protesting South American policy today, environmental issues tomorrow. They walked in tireless circles outside the gate. Like abortion and gun control, they never went away, they criticized everything, and they had no solutions.

The people in the office began to applaud, and Randall joined them.

"The important news is that we've moved beyond the concept of limiting ourselves to an orbital system. The United States has made solid progress, and it now appears that we will shortly be able to deploy particle-beam weapons on drones. Early indications are that the weapons will be quite accurate and quite deadly."

He gazed steadily at Randall, almost confidentially, implying that he and Randall were in this together, that Randall was out front and had already grasped the implications. Randall knew that everyone else in the room was getting the same impression. "I believe," Hurley continued, "we've succeeded in rendering missiles and bombs utterly obsolete. We are now able to erect a thoroughly intimidating national defense without the enormous costs of standard weaponry. If we have to go to war again, we won't be springing hundreds of millions for cruise missiles and munitions. Next time out, the taxpayers will barely notice."

An attendant was passing among them with a tray on which rested thirteen glasses. Each of the seven men and five women took one. The President took the last. He retrieved an ice bucket from behind his desk, lifted a bottle of champagne from it, and removed the cork. When Ed Wrenside of New Hampshire hurried forward to help, the President waved him back with a smile and filled their glasses one by one. "Ladies and gentlemen," he said, "I give you the United States."

MONITOR

WHITE HOUSE DENIES
NEW ENERGY SOURCE

"I WISH IT WERE TRUE," SAYS PRESIDENT

DJIA OFF 4040 POINTS IN WEEK

. . .

ALTHEAN RUNAWAY BESTSELLER

Michael Pappadopoulis's *Translations from the Althean* surged to the top of the *New York Times* bestseller list during the first week of its release. Despite criticism that the volume contains more of Pappadopoulis than the Altheans, bookstores reported mounting sales.

. . .

AYADI DENIES HAVING BOMB

"I have no use for one," the Ayadi Itana Arubi told a crowded gathering of Iraqis and Jordanians in Baghdad yesterday. "The Almighty does not need my help to destroy Israel." Later, he attended a soccer game.

. . .

MARKET SLIDE BLAMED
ON SPECULATORS

Short sales by insiders probably triggered the market collapse this week, according to several prominent Wall Street analysts. "The averages were too high, and we were ripe for a major correction," said Val Koestler, electronics specialist for Killebrew & Denkle. "There were other factors that contributed, of course: The steady climb in interest rates over recent months, increased tension in the Middle East, the latest unemployment figures. People were jittery . . ."

. . .

BAPTISTS SPLIT
OVER CLONING ISSUES

"NOT GOD'S WILL,"
SAY CONSERVATIVE LEADERS

. . .

MAN WIELDING PICKAX
KILLS SIX IN PEORIA BAR

CLAIMS EXTRATERRESTRIALS
TALK TO HIM ON CHANNEL 9

. . .

CHINESE REINSTATE
POPULATION CONTROL RESTRICTIONS

HUMAN RIGHTS GROUPS
DENOUNCE ACTION

STEIGLITZ DEMANDS U.S. BOYCOTT

. . .

TALIOFSKI WINS CHESS TITLE

RUSSIAN IS YOUNGEST CHAMP EVER
AT SIXTEEN

||| FIFTEEN |||

Harry was working late in his office when the fire engines went by, headed north toward Venture Park, the VIP housing area. His angle of vision was bad, but he could make out a fiery glare in the sky.

It was a quarter to eleven.

He pulled on his coat, walked swiftly to the north end of the building, and hurried out onto the lawn. Flames and moving lights were visible through a screen of trees. They seemed to be centered on Cord Majeski's villa.

From the direction of the main gate, he heard more sirens. Harry broke into a run, knowing somehow, with the fatalism that recent weeks had induced, that the fire would be connected with the Hercules Project. Always now, things were connected. There was no rest.

It *was* Majeski's villa. It had been a two-story frame, painted light and dark brown, with a narrow deck on the west side and a storm door and a single concrete step at the front entrance. Two fire engines had pulled onto the lawn on either side and were directing streams of water at the rear of the structure. A rescue vehicle, lights blinking, was just pulling away. People stood in small, puzzled groups, staring at what remained. It was the damnedest thing Harry'd ever seen.

The kitchen, the rear bedrooms, and part of the dining room were gutted. A few blackened timbers hung precariously together, hissing and sputtering. The air reeked of charred wood. A pall of brown smoke lingered over the wreckage.

The front of the house stood untouched, glowing frostily in the bright night, a lovely portico of blue crystal and cold fire. The revolving lights of the emergency vehicles and the steady glow of the streetlamps glittered against its polished surface.

A silver arc centered on the house spread out across the lawn almost to the sidewalk. Two elms and some azaleas, caught within the arc, were laced with hoarfrost.

"What is it?" someone asked, as Harry walked up. "What happened?"

Leslie stood off to one side. She'd thrown a coat over her nightclothes and, holding it tightly around her, stared disconsolately at the wreckage. She did not see him as he approached.

"Where's Cord?" he asked gently, placing his hand on her shoulder.

She filled the space between them and pressed against him. It was her only answer.

Harry heard an order to cut the water, and the hoses went limp. Some of the firefighters started poking at the rubble. More sparks flew up.

"Why is it so cold?" she asked.

Harry's face was already numb. "There's a wave of it coming from somewhere. I think it's the front of the house." He held his palms out in that direction. "My God," he said, "it *is*. What the hell's going on?"

Medical technicians and security officers were still arriving. Pete Wheeler's car bounced across some fields, dropped into the street, and stopped half a block away. He got out and hurried toward them.

The security people were cordoning off the area. "The front of the place looks as if it's encased in a sheet of ice," Harry said.

There was a momentary stir among the firefighters. They'd gathered in the rubble, where the kitchen had been, and they were looking down at the debris. Then they signaled, and someone came forward with a stretcher. They lifted a blackened human form, placed it on the stretcher, and drew a blanket over it. Leslie trembled in his arms.

Wheeler arrived; his eyes had gone wide at the sight of the house. It was the first time Harry had seen Pete Wheeler lose his equanimity. Harry murmured a greeting, but the priest's attention was fastened on the front of the dwelling.

They carried the stretcher toward one of the emergency vehicles. "If it's Cord," said Harry, "he's a Catholic."

Wheeler shook his head impatiently. "Later. Why is everything frozen up there?"

"Damned if I know." Harry trailed after the stretcher. "Who is it?" he asked one of the EMTs. "Can you tell?"

"Don't know, Mr. Carmichael," he said. "It's a *man*. That's about all we can be sure of right now."

Harry reached for the blanket, but the EMT intervened. "You don't want to do that, sir. Take my word. You wouldn't be able to recognize him anyway."

Harry let it go. The security people had been holding back the few bystanders who'd appeared, but now they themselves were looking curiously at the glazed siding and concrete and shingles. "Even the ground," remarked Wheeler. He stamped his foot, and the earth crackled. His breath hung in the air.

Harry had no feeling in his nose and ears. It was *cold*. The rocks and pebbles and concrete close to the front of the villa glittered. Windows were broken and frosted over, icicles hung from telephone lines, and the clapboard wall looked like dark ice.

Wheeler took his elbow and drew him back, then turned to one of the firefighters and showed an ID. "Keep everybody away from the house," he said. "Don't let anybody touch it or go near it."

The firefighter nodded and passed the word. A uniformed woman, who identified herself as the security duty officer, asked why. What was the danger?

"Anybody who touches the frozen part of the building," Wheeler explained, "and maybe the ground up close, for all I know, might not get his hand back." Harry's feet had been getting cold even through his heavy shoes. "Whatever happened here, it looks as if it's supercold. If that's true, it'll probably need a few days to thaw out. Meantime, we'll want to keep everybody at a safe distance." He walked toward the rear of the house.

The fire chief was a tall woman, middle-aged, with dark hair and dark eyes. Her brows were drawn together as she gazed around her.

Wheeler asked if he could look around, and she assented. He inspected the border between the section that had burned and the area that had apparently frozen, walking back and forth, kicking at timbers and brick dust and charred wood.

"What are you looking for, Pete?" asked Leslie.

"I don't know," he said. "But there'll be something here somewhere. In the middle." And with that, he gave a cry of satisfaction and pointed at a blackened beam. Harry helped two of the firefighters move it.

In the debris, they saw a blob of melted metal.

"This is where we found the body," said the fire chief.

"Pete," asked Harry, "what could cause something like this? You have any ideas?"

"Inferno at one end," said Wheeler. "Supercold at the other. I'll tell you what it reminds me of: Maxwell's Demon."

———

Leslie Davies was angry. Harry could see it in her eyes, and he wondered how she managed to conceal her emotions from her patients. She stood at her front door, with her hand on the knob, under bitter late-winter stars. Her mind was elsewhere. "We need some controls," she said finally, pushing the door open but still not moving from the concrete step. "Baines was out working on his own, too. You or Ed or somebody is going to have to set up some procedures to stop the freelancing. Did you see that hunk of slag that Pete pulled out of the debris? How's anybody going to make sense of that? It just means someone else gets to blow himself up later." Her eyes had fastened on him. They were round and weary and wet. "You think there's any chance that was somebody else?"

"Not Cord? Unlikely."

"When will we hear?"

"They'll call as soon as they have identification. With the records we have here, it should be pretty quick." Harry had never liked Majeski, and he suspected Leslie hadn't, either. But that didn't seem to matter now. "I'm sorry," he said.

They went inside. "Harry," she said, "Cord's not the only victim. Everyone associated with the Hercules Project, Ed, Pete, Baines, you, maybe even me, we should be at the peak of our professional careers, but somehow the project is starting to generate disasters."

Harry didn't know what to say; everything he could think of sounded frivolous, so he only watched her. Her voice shook, her nostrils had widened, and her breathing was uneven. The

long stem of her throat disappeared into the bulky folds of a
bland, shapeless garment that completely concealed the body
beneath. She started out of the room.

"Maybe Pete's right," he said. "Maybe we *should* destroy
the disks."

That stopped her. She turned and looked at him. "No," she
said softly, "that's no solution."

"Baines called it the Manhattan Option. Get rid of it while
there's still time."

"I'll make coffee," she said. "Pete doesn't have an open
mind." She disappeared into the kitchen. The refrigerator door
opened and closed, water ran into a pot, then she was back at
the doorway.

"Sometimes I think," Harry said, "Pete's primary concern
is that there might be a threat to the Church."

She came into the living room and sat down in an armchair. "No. It's more complicated than that. Pete's a strange
man."

"In what way?"

"I don't understand how he could have become a priest. Or
maybe it would be more accurate to say that I wonder how he
could have remained one. He doesn't believe, you know. Not
in the Church. Certainly not in God. Although I suspect he'd
like to."

"That's absurd. I've known Wheeler for years. He wouldn't
stay with the order if he didn't believe."

"Maybe," she said. "But he may not be aware of his true
feelings. We all keep secrets from ourselves. I've known people, for example, who don't know they hate their jobs. Or their
spouses. Or even their kids."

"How about *you*?" asked Harry impulsively. "What secrets
are *you* hiding?"

She nodded thoughtfully. "Coffee's ready."

"Pete is the sort of man," she said later, "who never stops
changing. He couldn't hold a credo for a lifetime. And anyhow, his training is all in the other direction. He's a skeptic by
profession. He makes his living by dismantling other people's
theories." The fire engines were beginning to pull away. "Does

that make sense? Compared to what he is today, he was a child when he took orders. The Norbertines saw to his education, and he remains with them out of a sense of loyalty."

"I don't believe it," said Harry. "I know him too well." She'd been standing by the window. Now she seated herself beside him on the sofa. It was a standard GSA issue, with sliding square vinyl cushions. She'd thrown an afghan over it, but it didn't help much; it was still lumpy and treacherous. "Why," he asked, "would he feel threatened if he has no faith to lose?"

"Oh, he has a faith to lose. Harry, he has probably, almost certainly, not admitted to himself that he no longer believes in the Christian God. But he's nevertheless convinced that the orthodox position is a sham: Pete Wheeler no more seriously thinks that he'll one day walk with the saints than you and I believe in ghosts." She kicked off her slippers, pulled her knees up under her, and sipped her coffee. "He's denied God in his heart, Harry. For him, that's the final sin. But there can be no sin where there is no God. And *that* is the faith that the Altheans threaten with their talk of a designer."

Harry found it difficult to imagine Pete's faith being shaken by *anything*. "And you?" he asked. "What threatens *you*?"

Her eyes dimmed. Shadows moved across her jaw and throat. "I'm not sure. I'm beginning to feel that I know the Altheans pretty well. At least the one who sent the transmission. And what I get is a terrible sense of solitude. We've assumed that the communication is from one species to another. But it *feels* as if there's only one of them, sitting in a tower somewhere. Utterly alone." There was something in her eyes that Harry had never seen before. "You know what it makes me think of, with all this talk of religion? An isolated God, lost and adrift in the gulfs."

Harry put his hand over both of hers.

"The transmission," she continued, "is full of vitality, passion, that odd business that people call a sense of wonder. There's something almost childlike about it. And it's hard to believe that the senders are a million years dead." She wiped at her eyes. "I'm not sure anymore what I'm trying to say."

He was conscious of her breast rising and falling. She turned her face toward his. The softly curving lip and high cheekbone warmed him.

"I'm never going to be the same, Harry. You know what? You talk about mistakes handling the transmission, *I* think it was a mistake to bring the translations back here and read them alone at night."

"You were doing that, too?" Harry sighed. "Does *anybody* around here obey the directions?"

"It's only a few notes. But in this case I should have. Obeyed the regulations. I'm beginning to see things at night, and hear voices in the dark." Her head fell back, and a sound like laughter rose in her throat. He caught her eyes and became aware of his own heartbeat.

He put an arm around her, and she folded herself into him. Their eyes joined, and Harry was acutely conscious of the body under the robe. It had been a long time since any female had signaled interest in this way, without reservation. He savored it, realized that it was probably a reaction to losing Cord, and that meant he would be taking advantage of a moment of vulnerability. But it was so hard to say *no*.

He traced the line of her throat with his fingertips. Her cheek was warm and damp. She was still a bit teary. But she whispered his name, and turned herself, turned him, so she could reach his mouth. She fitted her lips gently to it.

They were full of desire, and her breath was sweet. He explored her teeth and her tongue, and sensed the long well of her throat.

Slowly, he loosened the robe and drew it down over her shoulders. Beneath the filmy texture of the nightgown, her nipples were erect.

The confirmation call came in on Harry's cell phone at a quarter to four. The victim *was* Cord Majeski.

"More than burned," said the voice on the phone. "It was as if he was put through a blast furnace. Not much left."

Harry passed the news to Leslie, got out of her bed, and dressed.

"Where are you going?" she asked.

"To my office. I have to notify next of kin."

"My God," she said. "Isn't that Gambini's job? Or Rosenbloom's?"

He shrugged. "Quint would just hand it back to me. And I hate to dump it on Ed."

"Why don't you at least let it go until morning?"

He was pulling his shirt on over his head. "Because I don't want them seeing it first on CNN."

———————

Senator Randall knew why they were there before either said a word, had known since they called the day before to announce they'd be flying in. Teresa Burgess carried the same heavy black bag she'd carried through half a dozen campaigns in Nebraska. Like its owner, it was somber and inflexible, constructed of stiff leather and frayed around all the moving parts.

In her, as in most people with a fiercely competitive nature, competence and ruthlessness had erased the gentler qualities from her expression, if not from her character. She represented the banking interests in Kansas City and Wichita, where she'd supported Randall for twenty years as faithfully as her father had supported the first Senator Randall.

Her associate was Roger Whitlock, the ex-officio party boss in the state. Whitlock had been an auto salesman at Rolley Chrysler-Plymouth ("Deal with Your Friends") when Randall was trying to win a place on the Kansas City School Board. Later, he sold dealerships, and eventually, he sold influence.

Randall broke out the Jack Daniel's, and they laughed and talked about old times. But his visitors were restrained and not entirely at ease. "I guess you don't think we can make it in November," he said finally, looking from one to the other.

Whitlock put up a hand as though he was going to protest that no such consideration was abroad. But the gesture dissolved. "These haven't been good times, Randy," he admitted. "It's not your fault, God knows it isn't, but you know how people are. The goddam combines control the markets, interest rates are high, and your constituents aren't doing well. They got to blame somebody. So they're going to take it out on the President, and on you."

"I've done what I could," protested Randall. "Some of the votes that upset people, the second farm bill, the milling regulations, the rest of it, that was compromise stuff. If I hadn't gone along, Lincoln wouldn't have got the school appropriation, the defense contracts that went to Random and McKittridge in North Platte, out in your country, Teresa, would have gone to those bastards in Massachusetts."

"Randy," said Burgess, "you don't have to tell us any of that. *We* know. But that isn't the point."

"What *is* the point?" Randall asked angrily. These goddam people owed him a ton. Burgess's Wheat Exchange would still be a tin-pot operation in Broken Bow if it hadn't been for him. And Whitlock owed his first decent job with the party to the senator's intervention. He wondered what had happened to loyalty.

"The point," said Burgess, "is that there's a lot of money at stake here. The people who've backed you stand to lose their asses if they do it again, and you don't win."

"Hell, Teresa, I'll win. You know that."

"I don't know it. The party is going for a ride. Hurley is going to lose, no matter who the Democrats run, and the people associated with him are going to take the pipe. People may like him personally, but they're not going to stand for his policies anymore. And nobody is more closely linked to him than you are. Randy, the truth is, you probably won't even be able to get the nomination. Perlmutter is popular downstate. He's got the religious right in his pocket. And he looks strong in Omaha and Lincoln.

"Perlmutter's a kid. What could he do for the state?"

"Randy." Whitlock didn't sound so soothing now. He'd grown a mustache since Randall had last seen him. It was hard to understand why. He looked devious enough without it. "This isn't like before. There isn't a farmer in the state who'll vote for you. My God, more than half of those people out there are calling themselves Democrats now. You ever hear of Democrat farmers before?"

"Farmers always bitch," said Randall. "They forget their gripes when they get in the voting booth, and they're looking at a choice between one of their own and some goddam liberal who wants to give their money away."

Burgess's chin rose. "Randy, the farmers have no money. Not anymore. And so you don't get the wrong idea, they're not alone in this. Now, I'm not saying that my people would leave the party, hell no, but I *am* saying that, for the sake of the party, they're going to be pushing for a fresh candidate. And they like Perlmutter."

"You two," Randall said accusingly, "could change all that."

"We could keep most of the money in line," Whitlock admitted. "We could probably even cut Perlmutter out. But he'd take his people with him, which would split us at a time when we need everybody." He took a deep breath. "Randy, if you step down now, the governor will find a decent situation for you. They're talking about Commerce. And you get spared the embarrassment of November."

"Whit." Randall sought his eyes, but they were, as always, elusive. "Hurley isn't going to lose."

"I wish that were true." Whitlock stared straight ahead, not looking at him.

Burgess, who had heard something in Randall's voice, leaned forward. "Why not?" she asked.

"It's a defense matter." He hesitated. "I'm not free to discuss it."

The banker shrugged. "I'm not free to commit anyone on idle rumor, Randy."

No one moved.

"We're about to get a sea change in the military," Randy said. "Cost is going down. And efficiency is going *up*. *Way* up. Folks, the good old U.S. of A. is about to show the world what the term *superpower* really means."

————

On the night that Cord Majeski died, Cyrus Hakluyt was at home in Catonsville. Unlike most of his colleagues, he had no inclination to allow the project to swallow his personal life. He did not put in the overtime that Gambini seemed to expect of everyone, working seven days a week into the early-morning hours, then retreating to the bland frame villas that Harry Carmichael had provided in Venture Park. Hakluyt had spent the evening with friends, some of whom might have noticed in the usually somber microbiologist an uncharacteristic exuberance. Cy was in a good mood. No one present, even Oscar

Kazmaier, who'd known him from Westminster days, could recall the last time he'd seen him wearing a party hat.

Actually, it hadn't happened since the afternoon that Houghton Mifflin had bought his collection of scientific ruminations, *World Without Roads*. Even his Nobel, which had been awarded for his work with nucleic acids, had prompted no such eruption.

He was a little late getting up next morning, and somewhat under the weather when he arrived at the lab, where, of course, everyone was talking about Cord Majeski's death. A memo was tacked to the bulletin board, giving the name and address of Majeski's father and sister.

At a few minutes after nine, Gambini assembled the staff in the briefing room. "He was building a device he'd found in the Text," he said. "We don't know what it was supposed to be. But Pete thinks it had something to do with statistical manipulation of gases inside magnetic bottles. But it must have got away from him.

"Part of the blame's mine. He showed me a schematic, and told me he wanted to try putting it together. I should have known better, should have discouraged him. But I didn't. It's a mistake that he paid a terrible price for."

There were about twenty people in the room. "I want to take this opportunity," he continued after a moment, "to discourage *all* of you. We'll do no more experimenting on the side. Any more devices we find in the transmission, any more techniques, any more procedures, will be submitted in writing in detail to *me* before any experimental work goes forward. I hope that is clear. Any violation will be considered cause for dismissal."

Later, Hakluyt took him aside and asked about the nature of Majeski's device and whether Gambini knew yet why it had blown up.

"Cy," he replied, "I think he was trying to achieve statistical control of the first law of thermodynamics."

Hakluyt didn't laugh, but it took all his restraint. "That's impossible, Ed. Unless I'm not following you."

"The first law isn't absolute, Cy," said Gambini. "It doesn't *have* to be that heat passes from a warm gas to a cool one. It's only highly probable because of the molecular exchange. But some of the molecules in the warm gas move more slowly than some of the more active molecules in the cool gas. And vice versa. I think Cord's device was intended to manipulate the exchange."

Hakluyt was trying to visualize the process.

"Maxwell's Demon," said Gambini.

"Yeah. I guess."

James Maxwell was a nineteenth-century physicist who proposed that, if a demon could sit between two compartments, one filled with a hot gas and the other with a cool gas, he could create an interesting effect by allowing only the fastest molecules from the cool side to enter the hot chamber and letting only the slowest molecules from the hot side pass into the cool chamber.

"What we'd see," said Hakluyt, "is that the hot gas would get hotter, and the cold gas would become colder. And you think something like that happened to Majeski? It's absurd."

"Have you seen the house? Go down and take a look. Then come back, and we'll talk about absurdities."

Hakluyt stared into Gambini's eyes. His spectacles had slid forward on the bridge of his nose, and he persisted throughout the conversation in peering over them. "Okay," he said. "Maybe it's time we asked ourselves what we're dealing with on the other end of this transmission. Has it occurred to anyone that the bastards are vindictive? I mean, why else would they send us directions for something that would blow up in our faces?"

"I can't agree with that," snapped Gambini. "We're just not being careful enough. Nobody's going to all the trouble they did to play a goddam joke. Part of the problem here might have been that we simply didn't understand the specifications. Maybe we're not as bright as they expected us to be. We couldn't even work out the power specs. And that's probably what went wrong."

"Maybe they don't use electricity."

"Well, then, magnetism. Or gasoline. Or somebody turning a crank. Goddammit, I don't know. Whatever it is, there should be some indication of how much to use."

"Unless it's something you *don't* measure."

"You want to give me an example?"

Hakluyt thought about it and shook his head. "It's just talking before I get in gear, I guess." He still felt queasy from the alcohol. "How about some good news?" he said.

"I could use it."

They retired into Gambini's office, and the project manager wearily sank into a chair. "I don't ever want to go through anything like this again," he said.

"I don't guess," said Hakluyt.

"So what's your good news?"

Hakluyt removed his glasses and put them on Gambini's desk. The lenses were thick, mounted in steel frames. Hakluyt was physically so slight that he seemed somehow less substantial without them. "I've worn them all my life," he said. "I'm nearsighted, and I had an astigmatism. My family has a long history of eye problems." He smiled delicately and looked around until he spotted a *Webster's*. "They were all myopic." He picked up the dictionary and held it over the glasses. "I got my first pair when I was eight." He dropped the book. It smashed the spectacles flat.

Gambini watched, mystified. "Cy," he said, "what the hell are you doing?"

Hakluyt swept the pieces casually into a wastebasket. Then he opened the dictionary. "Got a word you'd like me to look up?"

"Xenophobia. Cyrus—"

He flipped pages. "Fear of strangers," he said. "Or of the strange. You want derivations?"

Gambini was staring at him now, eyes wide.

Hakluyt held out his hands. "I don't need them anymore." He gazed around the office. He could read all the book titles along all the shelves. He could read the script on all the awards. He could make out the individual buttons on Gambini's shirt, and the numbers on the radio dial on the side table over near the door. He could make out clearly the weave on the window curtains and the imprint on Gambini's coffee cup. *Stanford University.* "You know why we had all those vision problems?" he asked.

"Genetic," said Gambini.

"Of course," snapped Hakluyt. "But why? The repair mechanisms weren't properly directed, that's why. The equipment to maintain my eyes in decent order was always there. But the coding was screwed up. Ed, rewrite the coding, and you get twenty-twenty."

"Son of a bitch," said Gambini, beginning to glow. "You've been able to do that?"

"Some of it. I can do it for *you*, Ed, if you want. I can make your eyes twenty-one years old." He took a deep breath. "You know, my whole life, I've never known what it was to see well. I was always looking at the world through a sheet of milky glass. Now— This morning, from my car, I watched a cardinal sitting on a branch out near the main gate. A few weeks ago, I'd have had trouble seeing the tree."

"And you can do the same for anyone?"

"Yes," he said. "For you. For anybody. All it takes is a little chemistry. And I'd need a blood sample."

Gambini sat down. "We're talking about the transmission."

"Sure."

"You got this out of the transmission."

"Yes. I got it out of the transmission."

"My God, Cy. Who'd've believed it? I mean, these are *aliens*. How can this kind of stuff apply to *us*?"

"DNA. Same system. Same coding. Nature always goes the easiest way. It's all applicable." He hesitated. "Well, I don't really know that yet. But *some* of it's going to be."

"So we're going to have a revolution in eye care. But there's more here than that."

"Of course there is. Ed, I don't know enough yet. But this is only the beginning. We can jiggle the coding. Change it. Make it right. *Improve it.* I'm not sure there's anything we won't be able to do— Stop cancer, strengthen the heart, you name it."

"Are we talking about stopping deterioration generally?"

"Yes!" Hakluyt's voice literally rang. It was the first time Gambini had seen him actually appear happy. "Ed, I'm not sure yet where all this will lead. But we're going to come away with the means to cure epilepsy, Hodgkin's, cataracts, you name it. It's all there."

Gambini removed his glasses. He only used them for reading. He needed new ones, had for years, but he suspected that stronger lenses would weaken his eyes still more, and consequently

he'd avoided going back to his optometrist. It would be good to
be rid of them. To be rid of the back that ached on damp mornings and the loose flesh around his waist and under his jaw. To
be rid of the dark fear that came occasionally in the night when
he woke, suddenly aware of the beating of his heart. My God,
what would such a thing not be worth? To be young again. "Does
anyone else know?"

"Not yet."

"Cy, you're suggesting we'll even be able to control the
aging process."

"That seems to be what we're talking about. Yes." He considered it. "I'm not sure what the psychological effects would
be. But as far as physical welfare goes, if you don't get
betrayed by your DNA, and if you stay off the wrong airplane,
it's hard to see why anyone's going to die."

Gambini picked up a large paper clip and turned it over and
over in his fingers. "Probably we should say nothing about this
for a while."

"Why?" asked Hakluyt, immediately suspicious.

"Because we would have a few problems if people stopped
dying."

"Well, of course we'd need to establish controls and eventually make some adjustments."

"How do you think the White House will react when they
hear about this?"

"I'd think the President would be delighted."

"Really. You've seen the problems we've had because we
released some Althean philosophical tracts. And the goddam
energy story caused a stock-market crash. What would *this* do?"

"Who *cares*, Ed? Think *big*. Let somebody else worry
about the details. Our responsibility is to turn it over to the
National Council for the Advancement of Science. Or the
NSF."

"Or the Boy Scouts of America." Gambini laughed. "It's
too dangerous. If people find out that something like this is
around, God knows what would happen. I'll tell you this
much: If we give this to Hurley, we'll wind up with a bunch of
immortal politicians, and nobody'll ever hear of the technique
again."

"That's why we have to release it ourselves."

"Cy, I don't think we're communicating. Baines thought he'd found something so dangerous in the transmission that he advised us to destroy the Hercules Text."

"What did he find?"

"A way to manufacture black holes." Gambini let that sink in. "These things all seem to be potential disasters. My God, Cy, imagine a world in which people stopped dying. Even for a little while. If they don't die from natural causes, they'll start dying from something else. Famine, probably. Or bullet holes."

"But the NCAS—"

"No one can handle something like this. We've got to deal with it the same way we dealt with Rimford's problem."

"No!" It was almost a cry of pain. "You can't bury this. Who the hell do you think you are to take that kind of decision on your own shoulders?"

Gambini's forehead was damp. "I'm the only person in a position to do it. If it goes beyond this office, we'll never contain it." He stared for long moments at the wall. "We'll talk about it," he promised. "But in the meantime, no one's to know." He took a ledger out of his desk and consulted it. "You've been working with DS 101."

"Yes."

"Bring it here. Along with your notes and any other records you have on this."

Hakluyt's eyes went very wide, and the blood drained from his face. He looked near tears. "You can't do this," he said.

"I'm not doing anything right now except ensuring that nothing happens until I want it to."

Waves of pain and rage rolled through Hakluyt's eyes. "You're a madman," he said. "You know, all I have to do is tell Rosenbloom or Carmichael what you're doing, and you'll find yourself in a jail somewhere."

"Maybe," said Gambini. "But I wish you'd stop a moment to consider the consequences." He held out his hand. "I'll also need your library ID."

Hakluyt produced the plastic card, dropped it on the desk, and started out the door. "If anything happens to those disks," he said, "I'll kill you."

Gambini waited a few minutes, then went out to Hakluyt's station, retrieved the laser disk, gathered the microbiologist's papers, and locked them in his filing cabinet. An hour later, he let himself into the storeroom at the library and signed out the duplicate DS 101. With an armed guard at his side, he brought it back to the Hercules spaces and put it, too, in the cabinet. Then he resisted the temptation to destroy both and be done with it.

MONITOR

HUNDREDS DEAD IN LIBYAN FIGHTING

BOTH SIDES CHARGE ATROCITIES

. . .

MASSACHUSETTS FIRM HITS BIG-TIME
WITH ALTHEAN T-SHIRTS

. . .

BASEBALL SEASON DELAYED
BY STRIKE

FIRST TEST OF NOBF

FANS' ORGANIZATION
THREATENS BOYCOTT

. . .

PROGRESS IN WAR ON CANCER

EARLY DETECTION REMAINS KEY

. . .

SIGNALS OPENS IN WASHINGTON

NEW MUSICAL SALUTES ALTHEANS

. . .

SCIENTIST KILLED AT GODDARD

GAS LINE EXPLOSION IGNITES FIRE

. . .

WHITE HOUSE PREDICTS
MARKET RECOVERY BY END OF YEAR

PRESIDENT POINTS TO STRONG
HOUSING STARTS, EMPLOYMENT FIGURES

. . .

KANSAS CITY STAR REPORTS WIDER
ROLE FOR PARTICLE-BEAM WEAPONS

PENTAGON DENIES REPORTS

. . .

AYADI ATTACKS HERCULES PROGRAM

"TRAFFICKING WITH SATAN"

Baghdad (AP)—In a statement issued today from his headquarters at Government House, the Ayadi Itana Arubi branded the U.S. Hercules Project as either "a pack of lies" or a communication with Satan. In either case, he said, "it should be stopped and a just God will surely reward the avengers." This was widely seen as a call for action by terrorist groups known to be operating in Western Europe and the United States.

. . .

BAINES RIMFORD
ANNOUNCES RETIREMENT

||| SIXTEEN |||

Harry's allergies were getting worse every day. He went to the dispensary to see if he could talk Doc McGill into a stronger prescription, and a strange thing happened. While he waited, Emma Watkins, the attractive young receptionist who brightened the otherwise sterile sitting room, mentioned casually that she'd mailed off the copy of his medical record just an hour before. "To whom?" asked Harry, feeling as if he'd come in during the middle of a conversation.

She hesitated, trying to remember, and pulled his file. "Dr. Wallis," she said.

"Who?"

"Dr. Adam Wallis." She showed him a formal request, with Harry's signature on an accompanying release. But it wasn't his handwriting. Not quite.

"Who's Adam Wallis?" he asked.

"Don't *you* know, Mr. Carmichael?" Her manner suggested that Harry was one of those high-ranking people who have a hard time keeping their minds on practical matters. "His stationery says he's a G.P." She disappeared into a back room and returned with the *Physicians' Directory*. "That's odd," she said, after a few moments of page-turning. "He isn't listed."

"Does that mean he doesn't exist?"

She looked at the cover. It was the current edition. "No," she said. "It probably means he just started his practice. Just graduated." She was getting somewhat concerned. "Is there a problem, Mr. Carmichael?"

Why would anyone be interested in his medical history? He knew nobody named Wallis, physician or anyone else. He wondered whether it might be somehow connected with Julie.

The address on the stationery was in Langley Park. He

drove over in the evening and found a two-story frame house in a new subdivision. Lights were on, and children were visible through the windows. The name on the mailbox was Shoemaker. There was no indication of a doctor's office.

"I never heard of him," said the man who answered the door. He told Harry he'd been living there for eight years. "I don't know of any doctors *in* the subdivision. The local ones are over at the Medical Building."

Harry stood on the doorstep, puzzled. "You'll probably get a package for him tomorrow, from Goddard." Harry took out a copy of Wallis's letter and compared the addresses again. He was at the right place. "I'd appreciate it if you'd just turn it around and send it back."

"Sure," he said.

Two days later, Harry's medical record was back, marked "Return to Sender."

Leslie routinely went to Philadelphia three days each week. But work with patients who were having problems with kids or suffering from sexual dysfunction—those two complaints constituted about 90 percent of her practice—had become tiresome. Her attitude toward that aspect of her life's work had, in fact, been deteriorating for two years. She'd been preparing to dissolve her practice and devote herself exclusively to research and consulting before the call had come from Goddard last September. She knew now that she would close the office down shortly, and that once she did, she would never go back to it.

But life would seem a trifle dull after Hercules. She'd been thinking about accepting an offer from the House Media Committee to conduct a study on Web-based pornography and to come up with some suggestions on how to control it. That such data would be helpful she had no doubt. But how tiresome gathering it would be. How tiresome the rest of her life would be after Hercules!

One of her patients for some years had been Carl Wieczaki, a former Phillies infielder who had made the All-Star team at twenty-two in his second season. He'd suffered a series of injuries, his skills diminished accordingly, and he was out of baseball at twenty-six. When he came to Leslie, he was a pot-bellied bartender, and she'd seen how terrible it can be to achieve too much too early.

The Wieczaki Syndrome. National fame and big money at the very beginning of adulthood. And downhill the rest of the way.

No, not downhill. More like over the precipice.

She wondered if she was headed in the same direction.

When the last appointment for the day canceled, she decided to walk home. The weather had turned summery, and since she didn't plan to go out that evening, she could leave her car in the lot with no inconvenience.

She cut across the Villanova University campus, stopped at the bookstore to pick up a novel, and enjoyed an early dinner on City Line Avenue.

There was a ball game most evenings at Mulhern Park. Tonight was no exception, and she lingered to watch the last few innings.

A couple of hundred people had turned out for the contest between two high-school teams. It was, she learned, opening day, and the crowd was being treated to good pitching and defense on both sides. Leslie was particularly struck by the visitors' center fielder, a tall, lean boy of exquisite grace. Although Leslie had played basketball in college, she'd never taken much interest in watching organized sports. They seemed to her a scandalous waste of valuable time. But on that warm evening, hobbled by the uncertainties in her life, she was happy for the opportunity to lose herself in something harmless.

It was hard to take her eyes off the center fielder. He pulled down several long drives, cut off an extra-base hit that should have rolled all the way to the cyclone fence bordering the field, and threw out a runner who tried to stretch a single into a double. She watched, after each inning, as he came in from his position. His eyes were blue and intelligent; he had a good smile; and once, when he looked up and saw her, he grinned and, just perceptibly, nodded.

He was a lovely child, and she wished him a good life.

He came to bat late in the game with two out, the bases empty, and the score tied and lined the first pitch into the alley in left center. The spectators leaped to their feet, forcing Leslie to stand so she could see.

The boy was off like a young leopard. With two outfielders in pursuit, the ball hit the base of the fence on the fly, and caromed irrationally toward the left-field corner. The shortstop hurried out to take the throw, while the runner rounded second and sprinted toward third. Everyone realized he had a chance to go all the way. The left fielder finally caught up with the ball and fired a bullet toward the relay man. The third-base coach was frantically waving the runner home.

He cut the corner at the bag and raced down the final ninety feet.

"Go, Jack!" the fans screamed.

The shortstop stepped aside and allowed the throw to go through. It bounced once and arrived, Leslie thought, simultaneously with the runner. But the catcher blocked off the plate and swept the tag across a leg as both players sprawled into the clay. The umpire's right fist went up!

In the bottom half of the inning, the home team scored on a pair of hits wrapped around an infield out, and the game was over.

The center fielder helped his team collect bats and gloves. But when they headed for their bus, he lingered near the bench. At first Leslie thought he'd misunderstood her interest in him, but he never looked up at her. Rather, he stood quietly in the shadows, and she knew that the final sprint around the infield was replaying itself in his mind.

She could see how desperately he'd wanted to win. She wished there were something in her own life that she wanted as much.

———

The Russian Reconnaissance Satellite XK4415L, of the Chernev series, floated in geosynchronous orbit above the Mojave Desert, where it could observe two U.S. Air Force bases and a missile-tracking range.

On the thirtieth of April, during the late morning, its

infrared cameras picked up a series of six plumes, long streaks of white mist soaring toward the summit of the eastern sky. The satellite's instruments identified them as MXs and tracked them out of the atmosphere. An array of electronic scopes and sensors collected data and fed it into onboard computers, which compared performance against known capabilities. But well before the missiles arrived at their apexes, they began to go awry. All six wobbled off in unexpected directions, lost power, and began to fall back toward the surface.

Several hours later, a second series of eight ICBMs staggered across the sensitive registers of the satellite. At a few minutes before midnight Moscow time, Colonel Mikos Zubarov entered one of the numerous briefing rooms on the west side of the Kremlin, threw his bulging briefcase onto a flat wooden lectern, handed a computer disk to an aide, and removed eight copies of the reconnaissance analysis from the briefcase. Each was in a red folder stamped with a supersensitive classification. Marshall Konig arrived moments later. He walked quickly to the front of the room and scrutinized Zubarov. "It is true?" he asked.

"Yes."

"They destroyed all fourteen?"

"Yes."

He was silent. One by one, the others entered, Yemelenko and Ivanovsky and Arkiemenov and the rest, grim men who understood the nature of the threat and who were tonight, perhaps for the first time in their military careers, pessimistic about the nation's future.

Zubarov waited until they were all seated around the green baize-covered table, then he briefly recounted what the Chernev had observed. His aide projected images taken a few seconds apart, which chillingly revealed the simultaneous loss of power and control in both flights of missiles.

"Do we have any additional information on the technology?"

"No," said Zubarov. "We know only what they have chosen to release."

They heard Taimanov's voice in the hall. A moment later, the foreign minister entered and took his place at the far end of the table. "But," persisted Konig, "it might be an elaborate hoax. The missiles could have self-destructed."

"That is possible," said Zubarov. "But the Chernev detected microwaves from a higher orbit. We suspect that it is peripheral radiation of some sort."

"And the device emitting the radiation—?"

"—Is not in my field of expertise. Rudnetsky believes their claims. That they *do* have a particle-beam weapon."

"If *they* have it," said Taimanov, "it will not be long before others have it." He looked grimly at his military colleagues. "Technology moves more quickly than good sense," he said. "Soon no one will be safe."

———————

Harry was suffering. The new prescription was making him sleepy, but it didn't seem to be doing much else. His eyes swelled, his throat still hurt, and he couldn't stop sneezing. It was so bad when he woke up that he quit in the middle of getting dressed, called in, and told them he was taking the day off.

Actually, he took two. When he got back, still feeling terrible, Gambini told him he should get away for a few days. Find a drier climate. He then reported some progress in translating Althean descriptions of electromagnetic phenomena. In addition, he invited Harry to sit in at the staff meeting while Majeski's former associate Carol Hedge did a presentation supporting Wheeler's thesis ascribing the accident to Maxwell's Demon.

Hedge was an attractive African-American from Harvard-Smithsonian. Harry watched her appreciatively and once caught Leslie noting his reaction. When she'd finished, Gambini asked for comments, noted one or two expressions of concern for safety in future experiments, and declared the formal meeting over. "But I'd appreciate it," he added, "if Harry, Leslie, Pete, and Cyrus would stay a minute."

After everyone else had filed out, Gambini closed the door and nodded to Wheeler.

"I think I've got another bomb," said the priest. "We're finding detailed and exceedingly fundamental descriptions of electromagnetic radiation, harmonics, particle theory, you name it. At the moment, I have answers to all kinds of classic questions. For example, I think I know why the velocity of light is set where it is. And how a photon is constructed although that may be the wrong verb. And I have a few insights to offer into the nature of time." But Wheeler's comments, which should have elicited a celebratory mood, were delivered in a somber voice.

"You're not going to tell us," Leslie asked, "that we can build a time machine, I hope?"

Wheeler laughed. "No, I don't think we need to worry about Wells popping in. Fortunately, time machines appear to be prohibited. The nature of the universe won't permit their construction. But I wonder whether you'd care to settle for an exceedingly efficient death ray?"

"Thanks anyhow," said Harry, "but I think we already have one of those."

Wheeler shook his head. "Depending on what you're trying to accomplish, this might be better than the particle beam. It's articulated light, concentrated radiation that can be focused exclusively to kill. The particle beam disassembles everything. *This* thing would leave real estate intact. That could be a significant advantage. It can be tuned to penetrate most forms of matter, which means you can't hide from it. And it might even be possible to tune it to take out one specific person. I'm not sure about that, not my field, but Cy thinks if you had some physical details, you could go right in and kill the target without harming anyone else in the vicinity."

"No more problems with dictators," said Leslie.

Gambini took a deep breath. "I guess not," he agreed. "I think we have another segment to bury."

"There's more," continued Wheeler. "Unfortunately, a good deal more. Harmonic manipulation, for example."

"What can you do with harmonics?" asked Harry.

Wheeler folded his arms. "At a guess, we could probably disrupt climate, induce earthquakes, bring down skyscrapers. Who knows? I don't think I want to find out. Harry, what's so funny?"

"Nothing, really, I guess. But it occurred to me that Hurley is planning the new defense budget around a weapons system that just became obsolete."

It was an uncomfortable moment.

"I don't suppose," said Wheeler, "there's any way that a detailed description of physical reality could avoid having this sort of effect. I'm putting it all into a report, which you'll have before you go home this evening. I think we've reached a Rubicon, and we're going to have to decide what we want to do."

Gambini slumped back in his chair. "There's something else you might as well know," he said. "Cy, tell them about the DNA."

Hakluyt's appearance was different, and Harry needed a moment to realize he wasn't wearing his glasses. Probably switched to contacts. But it was more than that. He appeared healthier somehow. Harry had trouble, at first, understanding why his impression of the man had changed.

"I've discovered," he began, "some techniques for restoring the repair functions of the body. We're learning how to rewire our DNA so as to do away with most genetic disorders and also with those normally associated with aging."

"Wait a minute," said Leslie. "What precisely do you have, Cy?"

"At the moment, not very much. Ed found it necessary to lock up the data with which I was working."

Gambini colored slightly but said nothing.

"What were you working on?" pursued Leslie.

"A way to stop cancer. To prevent physical deterioration. To ensure there are no more crib deaths and to clear out the hospitals! We're getting information that, in time, can help us eliminate birth defects and mental retardation and damned near everything else. We can change the entire flow of human existence.

"We talk about weapons and war. Maybe, if we showed a little courage, we could remove some of the causes of war. Give everyone a decent life! With the things we're learning here, we can create prosperity around the globe. There'd be no point in maintaining standing armies."

"My God," said Leslie, "Ed, you can't sit on that."

"Think about it," said Gambini. "This isn't something we can parcel out. You either give it to the world, or you don't. People stop dying. What do you think's going to happen next?"

"I know it's not an easy question," said Hakluyt. "But with the other things we're learning here, we can create prosperity around the globe. That should mean education. We're looking at a golden age."

"You really believe that?" asked Wheeler.

"I think we need to try. But we have to get the information out. Make it available."

"What you are going to make available," said Gambini wearily, "is more misery. When there are too many people, you get famine."

"God knows," said Wheeler, "the Church has been saddled with that reality for a long time now, and they don't want to look at it, either. But I'm not so sure we'd be correct in withholding something like this."

Good for you, Pete, thought Harry, noting Hakluyt's relieved expression. He'd expected no help from that corner.

"Famine won't be the issue," said Hakluyt. "The birth rate will be. That makes it a political question. Offer people education, prosperity, and extended health, and you won't have to worry about millions of new babies because it won't happen."

"It's obvious," said Leslie, "that we need to make a very basic decision. We've talked about withholding things from the White House, but until now we haven't had to do it. We have to think about that, and we have to think about what's going to happen down the road. What are we going to do with the material we *can't* release to anyone?"

"If we start holding stuff back," said Harry, "and we get caught at it, everything will unravel. The project will be taken away from us and given to people the government can trust."

"No." Gambini's index finger was pressed against his lips. "They'd have done that already if they could. Their problem is that there's no one they can trust who'd be any real help to them. They've got codebreakers and engineers, but for this stuff they need physicists. That's why they've been so patient with us."

"Cy," asked Wheeler, "I take it you'd vote to turn everything over to NCAS?"

"Yes. It's not a move I'm comfortable with, but it's the best of several bad alternatives."

"How about you, Harry?" asked Gambini. "What would you recommend?"

It was a bad moment, and Harry hadn't yet sorted everything out. If they withheld information and got caught at it (and you could not rely on these guys to be discreet), his career would go, his pension, everything he'd worked for all his life. Worse, it might even open them up to charges of treason.

But what alternative was there? If they released this stuff to the White House, advanced weapons and DNA reprogramming and whatever the hell else was in the package, what would the world be like in five years?

"I don't know," he said. "I really don't know. I guess we have to sit on some of this. Even Cy's material. I keep thinking about what would happen if people stop dying."

Gambini's eyebrows rose in surprise, and Harry thought he detected, after that, a new respect in the project manager's bearing toward him.

"Pete?"

"The DNA material should be released. We have no right to withhold it. As for the rest of it, we really have no choice but to keep it to ourselves. *I* certainly won't be party to turning it over to the government. *Any* government."

"Okay," said Gambini.

"I haven't finished yet," said Wheeler. "There's no way we can retain control over this information indefinitely. Leslie's right when she says we need to think about the long term. Eventually, if we continue to collect it, it'll get out. We have in this building knowledge that would provide almost anyone with the means to obliterate an enemy so quickly and completely that retaliation need not be taken into account. *That*, so we're all clear, is what we're talking about. And when the disaster comes, it is we who will be responsible. The Text is a Pandora's box. For the time being, the information is contained. Some of it's out, but most of it is unknown, even to us. I suggest we shut the lid on everything except the DNA. Forever."

"No!" Leslie was on her feet. "Pete, we can't just destroy the disks. Do that and we lose too much. I know there's a terrible risk here, but the potential for gain is enormous. Hercules may eventually prove to be our salvation. God knows we're not doing all that well on our own."

"Okay." Gambini shook his head. "We seem to have some disagreement here. I think Pete's right, except for his suggestion that we release the DNA material. I'm sorry about that, Cyrus, but I don't like the options. I don't know how long we can simply bide our time. The longer we hang on, the more difficult letting go is going to be."

"Pete," said Leslie, "you're a dealer in ultimate causes and final purposes. What practical reason have we for existence other than to learn things? To know what lies beyond our senses? If we destroy the Hercules recordings, we do a terrible disservice not only to ourselves but to the people who conquered a pulsar to let us know they were there."

"It's a pity," said Wheeler, "they didn't just wave a hand and say hi."

Gambini looked at them, holding their eyes momentarily. "Sometimes it's hard to tell the weaponry from the blessings. But I want you all to understand that, whatever rumors you might be hearing, I am trying to act in the best interests, God help me, of everyone.

"All right. We can lose what we don't like. We can turn part or all of what we have over to higher authority. Or we can even bite the bullet and release some of this ourselves. Like Pete's breakthrough on magnetic power. I want you to think some more about it and send me your views. In writing. Keep it short and to the point. And no yelling. I'm tired of getting yelled at. We're going to have to work together. If we get some of this wrong, the price is going to be high. For example, if Cy's technology gets out before we're ready for it, we could have a serious problem with resources very quickly."

"I don't think this is our decision to make," said Leslie. "The country has elected leaders—"

"Put it in writing." Gambini was holding his forehead. "Convince me. Keep in mind that the first thing the elected leadership did when we gave them something was to convert it into a weapons system. So far, after several weeks, there's still no talk of any other advantage to be had."

All of Harry's training told him they should simply pass it on to the Oval Office. And he would probably, in the end, argue for that position. He might even see it as his duty to inform Ed that he would blow the whistle if the Hercules team seemed to be taking too much into its own hands.

And yet—part of him wished that Gambini, or somebody,

would just turn the damned thing over to the media. Or destroy the disks. Damn it. He couldn't make up his mind.

"Maybe we could use a new perspective," said Leslie. "The Arena sent us some tickets for *Signals*. Tomorrow night's show. Anybody interested?"

"Isn't that the show about us?" asked Gambini.

"Yes. Or at least it's about an interstellar radio contact. It's a musical."

"That," said Wheeler, "seems appropriate."

When Harry arrived at his desk next morning, Gambini's summary of the team's reaction was already waiting. They would inform the White House about Cy's discovery and put everything else on hold for the time being. It was a decision Harry could live with.

He called the White House. They had a standing order, apparently, to make room for him whenever he requested an interview. "We can fit you in tomorrow afternoon, Mr. Carmichael. But you'd only have a few minutes."

"Okay," he said.

He and Leslie had announced their intention to go to dinner, then the show. To Harry's surprise, Gambini agreed to meet them at the theater, as, after some prompting, did Wheeler.

At the Arena, the million-light-year-long radio signal was represented by a coterie of glowing, winged dancers who floated across center stage beneath a Saturnian world and a slowly rotating galaxy. In this version, the Althean signal was picked up on an old Zenith console receiver in a gas station in Tennessee. At first, of course, no one believed the broadcast. The sender spoke English in a sultry female voice, replied to questions, and made witty asides to the audience.

"She has," observed Leslie, "a more lively personality than *our* aliens."

In the end, things turned out happily, as they tend to in musicals.

Harry was now reading regularly from the Althean binder, which Leslie kept supplied with fresh translations. Her writing was improving, but Harry still found most of it incomprehensible.

The night after they saw *Signals*, he came across a disquisition on the nature of aesthetics. But the only classes of objects considered were natural: sunsets and misted seas and flying beasts of undetermined type.

Yes, he thought, always the seas. These guys do like their coastlines.

There was never a hint that the Altheans found any beauty in their own kind, either in their appearance or in the works of the mind.

And if there was a single overriding image from the binder that he could not get around, it was that of the dark shores slipping silently past.

MONITOR

COAST GUARD SEIZES
CANADIAN TRAWLER OFF HATTERAS

FISHING WAR WITH CANADA HEATS UP

. . .

FELDMANN
SWEEPS THREE PRIMARIES

PARKER CONCEDES

HANCOCK SAYS SHE IS IN IT
FOR THE LONG HAUL

. . .

THEATER ROUNDTABLE

BY EVERETT GREENLY

The Signals are mixed. *Signals*, which opened last
week at the Arena, had a lot of good music, some
energetic dance routines, a fine cast, and solid
direction. Unfortunately, it's not enough to save a
script that gets mired almost immediately in
sacrificing substance for cheap laughs. We've come
to expect more from Adele Roberts, who, last
season . . .

. . .

CANCER CLAIMS
17-YEAR-OLD ATHLETE

Mesa (Tribune News Service)—Brad Conroy, the
young track star who, six months ago, seemed

headed for the Olympics, died this morning of a rare and virulent form of leukemia . . .

. . .

800 DEAD IN MISSILE ATTACK
ON PAKISTANI JET

TERRORISTS DEMAND
MASSIVE PRISONER RELEASE

. . .

WS&G MAY GO CHAPTER 11

The giant utility, whose stock lost 70 percent of its value during the March slide, is still in deep trouble. A projected new-issue offering, which was to have helped meet long-term obligations due this month, had to be canceled. WS&G is now seeking extensions from several worried creditors.

||| SEVENTEEN |||

Harry was surprised to find Cy Hakluyt waiting in his office when he returned from a morning seminar on motivation. "I need help," he said, after Harry'd hung up his jacket and dropped wearily into a chair. "What do you plan to say to Hurley?"

"About your work?"

"Yes. Of course."

"I can show you the report Ed's prepared."

"I've seen the report. It's too dry. And it's shaded to Ed's point of view. The President can't help agreeing that it should be put on the shelf."

Harry nodded. "What do you want me to do, Cy?"

"Talk to him. Explain how important this is. You might point out that eventually people will know about this. That he won't look good if it comes out he had, say, the cure for meningitis in his hands and didn't do anything with it."

"I'll try to make an honest presentation, Cy."

Hakluyt looked at him for a long minute. "Okay," he said. "If you do that, it should be enough."

Harry's throat tickled. He blew his nose, then put a eucalyptus lozenge in his mouth.

"What would you think of me, Carmichael, if I could cure your hay fever, and refused to do it?"

Harry blew his nose again and smiled weakly.

"And that's only a runny nose, Harry. For God's sake, suppose you had cancer!"

"I told you, Cy, I'll make sure he understands. He's no dummy. He can figure out the realities."

Deep in Harry's stomach, something ached. Was he getting an ulcer? My God, why was it always up to him? These people around him—Gambini, Hakluyt, Wheeler, Leslie, Rimford—they always seemed to know what to do. He'd seen no evidence of hesitation in any of them, save perhaps with Baines's reluctance to destroy the Text.

"I'd like to provide a demonstration, if I may," Hakluyt said. He extracted a black leather case from his pocket and opened it.

Harry looked suspiciously at him, then at the case. Inside, a vial, a bottle of alcohol, and a hypodermic syringe lay on a red felt lining. "What is it?" he asked.

"A young man's eyes. I'm not sure what more."

Harry took a deep breath. "My eyes are fine."

Hakluyt held one of the vials up and squinted into it at crystal-clear liquid. "They can be twenty-twenty again if you like."

Harry took his bifocals off, and Hakluyt went slightly out of focus. "You're not wearing glasses anymore," he said.

"That's correct, Harry. Don't need them."

"I'm okay," he said at last. It wasn't so much that he wanted to avoid compromising himself as that he didn't think he wanted to be a test case. "Find somebody who needs it."

"It won't work for anyone else. It's designed for *you*, Harry."

"How could that be?" Harry looked narrowly at the microbiologist. "*You're* Adam Wallis," he said. "The nonexistent doctor who requested my records."

"I needed a recent urinalysis, a DNA sample, a few other things."

"How'd you get the DNA?"

"Used Kleenex." He shrugged. "I apologize, but I wasn't sure how you'd react." He produced a cotton swab and saturated it with alcohol. "Roll up your sleeve, Harry," he said. "No charge."

On the other hand, Harry told himself, it apparently *had* worked for Cy, whose thick lenses were gone.

"Is there any risk?" he asked.

"Harry, I'm a doctor. Relax." He drew a small amount of the liquid into the syringe, measured it with his eye, squirted a little out of the needle. "You have a son, don't you?"

"Yes." Harry's defenses went up.

"His name's Thomas."

"That's right." Reluctantly, Harry bared his arm and felt the needle slide beneath the skin. "You'll need a booster in about a week. Since I'm not licensed for this sort of work, I can't arrange for anyone else to do it. I'll come by your office Thursday afternoon."

"And that's it?"

"That's it."

"Why did you bring Tommy into the conversation?" Harry, sensing what was coming, had begun to perspire.

"I understand the boy has diabetes."

"Yes."

"Harry, I can't make any promises. Not at this stage. I know a little, but not enough. If we are able to proceed with the research, I might be able to do something." The microbiologist rose from his chair like an avenging deity. "Tell the President what we have. For God's sake, *tell him*.

Roger Whitlock allowed a beatific smile to light up his cherubic features.

Hobson signaled for his secretary to draw the curtains against the harsh Wichita sunlight. "All right, Roger," he said, "tell us why Randall's a winner and why we should back him."

"It's basic arithmetic, Ron. He's going to win whether we're on board or not."

"Come on, Roj," objected Teri Keifer. "He's not going anywhere without our help." Keifer was a partner with Babcock & Anderson, one of the city's more prestigious law firms.

"Ladies and gentlemen, Randall's very tight with the administration. As you all know."

"The administration's shaky," said Horace Krim, owner of the CBS affiliate. "It's going down in November."

"Friends," said Whitlock soothingly, "I want you to think *particle beam*."

"What?" demanded Hobson. "Why? You really think a new weapon's going to have any effect on the vote? The world's at peace. Everybody's our friend now. Except the crazies in the Middle East."

Whitlock nodded sagely. "Think about the applications."

They fell silent, unable to make out what he was implying.

"Think about projectors mounted on planes and ships. Think about how missiles and bombs are now obsolete."

Krim leaned forward, frowned, took out a notebook, and jotted something down.

"Ask yourself who, ever again, will challenge this country. And then ask yourself what the campaign is going to look like when it really gets going."

Taimanov declined the offer of a drink. "Mr. President," he said, "I've been meeting with you and your predecessors for almost thirteen years. I must confess to a personal affinity for you. You're an honest man, insofar as persons in our profession are permitted to be honest. And I'd like to believe that there is a bond of friendship between us."

Hurley was alone with him. He'd granted the interview at a time when the secretary of state was engaged elsewhere, so he could pay Taimanov the compliment of a private discussion without offending Matt Janowicz.

"I must also confess," the Russian continued, "that, although many of these meetings have taken place under difficult circumstances, this is the first time I've spoken with a man in this office"—he paused and leveled a knife-edged gaze directly at the President—"under circumstances quite so serious."

The foreign minister came from a prominent St. Petersburg family with ties back to the Romanovs. They'd survived the Revolution more or less intact, maintained their influence and traditions, and continued to send their sons abroad to school. Taimanov was born during the autumn of 1955, when the Cold War was at its height.

"To what circumstances are you referring?" asked Hurley, allowing his concern to show but mixing it with a sense that the significance of the remark eluded him.

"Mr. President, have you considered the destabilizing effect of your Orion project? Assuming it really works."

"You know it works."

"Yes, we do."

"You also know it will not be used to threaten Russia."

"Not by you, I am sure. But can you speak for your successor? Can you assure me there will be no future round of anti-Russian paranoia, perhaps at a time when you are in no position to intervene? I say this to you here although I would never say it outside this office. But the truth is that you now possess a first-strike capability against which there is no defense. None. The attack comes, should it come, with the speed of light.

"Sir, you'll forgive my presumption, but the President of the United States is no longer simply the leader of a single nation, or even of an alliance. You have a responsibility now to the world community. And I put it to you that providing one nation, *any* nation, with an invincible weapon, invites terrible dangers for all.

"I have told you that I trust you. The Russian government trusts you. But your hold on this office is as tenuous as a heartbeat. And in any case, you will be gone in a few years. You know as well as I that a long line of imperfect men have sat behind that desk."

Hurley nodded. "Some more imperfect than others."

Taimanov nodded. "You are aware without my saying so that there are many in Russia, and undoubtedly in other parts of the world, who cannot tolerate such a position. Ask your British partners how *they* feel. Or the Israelis. Or the Canadians. And there is still *another* consideration."

"Security."

"Of course. How long will it take before someone *else* has acquired the technology?"

"We intend to hold it very close," said Hurley.

"Can you *guarantee* that nobody will *steal* it? You'll excuse my frankness, John, but your record for guarding secrets does not inspire confidence."

"No one knows that better than *you*, Alex."

Taimanov smiled. "My point exactly."

Hurley had given a great deal of thought to these issues. There would be a brief opportunity, a window, in which the U.S. would have exclusive use of the new weapon. But how best to exploit it?

The President saw himself increasingly as the man who would be remembered for bringing peace to this period, for setting the stage for an entry into the sunlit meadows of a new age. The Hurley Age.

Prosperity would follow, an era of good feeling, at first enforced by the total military domination of the world by a benevolent United States and its partners. But eventually there would develop a global order unlike anything the world had seen before. It could be done; it was within reach.

"You cannot make it happen," said Taimanov, as though he'd reached into the President's mind. "There are too many things that can go wrong. I'm sorry to say this because I know your intentions are good, but you have climbed on the back of a tiger."

Rain was falling. Hurley was suddenly aware of the cold gray day, of the weather beating at the windows. "What would you have me do, Alex?"

"We are once again close to being run down by our technology. And I do not know what advice to offer. A weapon that one cannot see coming is simply too dangerous. For everyone. It's unfortunate there is no way to put the genie back in the bottle. But if I have no solution, I can offer an option that might relieve the pressure. It's not particularly satisfactory. But it would be an improvement over the present situation."

"Yes?"

"You might consider sharing it with us."

Hurley smiled. "You know I can't do that, Alex. Couldn't if I wanted to. Agreements would have to be signed. The Congress would have to approve—They'd impeach me if I tried."

"Yes. Of course. Well, it seemed worth the effort. It is the nature of the tiger's back that one cannot climb down."

The Oval Office felt cold.

Harry was waiting in the outer office when Taimanov left. Burdened with his own problem, he took no particular note of the visitor who strode quickly past him and disappeared into the corridor.

He was uncertain how best to handle himself in the Oval Office. Indeed, he did not yet know his own mind on the DNA issue. He was still trying to sort it out when the secretary rose and showed him through the door.

Hurley came around the desk and greeted him by name, shook his hand, and sat down with him near a worktable set against a window. They were absolutely alone. No Secret Service agent was in sight, no science advisor. No witness to the conversation. "How are things going at Goddard?" he asked.

"Quite well, Mr. President."

An aide brought in a coffee server, set it on the table, poured two cups, and withdrew.

"What do you have for me, Harry?" he asked.

"Another breakthrough, Mr. President. Do you know who Cyrus Hakluyt is?"

"The name's familiar."

"Microbiologist. Geneticist. He says he's been learning how to manipulate genes."

"Meaning?"

"He used to wear glasses. Thick ones. Now he seems to have twenty-twenty vision."

"Are you telling me we've got a damned fool over there experimenting on himself?"

"Cyrus is anything but a fool, Mr. President."

"Doesn't matter. We've already had fatalities. I don't want any more." He sighed. "So what are you telling me? That we've got a cure for astigmatism now?"

"I think he feels he can tweak our DNA to get better performance. Not only eyesight."

"Really?" said Hurley. "Good. Is it applicable to the general population?"

"He says it is."

"Well, that's fine. We can give everybody decent vision." He took off his own glasses and stared at them. "Get me some sort of confirmation, Harry. I want to know for an absolute certainty. As soon as I do, we'll announce it." He stopped and his brow furrowed. "You say *not only* eyesight? What else are we talking about?"

"He thinks almost everything. Heart problems. He mentioned meningitis."

"Cancer?" asked the President.

"Yes. That's what he says. Maybe not cure it. I'm not clear on that. But stop it. Arrange things so nobody gets it anymore."

"Wonderful. That's extraordinarily good to hear, Harry. What else?"

"I guess, pretty much everything."

Hurley was glowing. "Birth defects?"

"Yes."

"Okay." He looked carefully at Harry over his raised cup. "You're not telling me something."

"Cyrus thinks people will stop breaking down physically, Mr. President. He says we can learn how to reverse old age."

Hurley's jaw dropped, and he repeated the phrase to himself. "*Reverse old age.* What does that mean?"

"The way he explains it to me, you get a couple of shots, and you not only get no older, but your body recovers. After a while, you're twenty-two again."

"My God. Then people are going to stop dying?" Hurley was rising slowly from his chair. His face reflected a range of emotions. He was simultaneously pleased, rattled, worried, delighted.

"Apparently. This is all still theory, of course. Nobody's going to be sure of anything until we do some more testing."

"I see."

"I'm supposed to tell you that no serious experiments have been performed because of security restrictions, and no outside help has been brought in. But Cyrus *does* have a reputation, and he says he can see no reason why it shouldn't work."

Thunder boomed overhead, and a gust of wind struck the windows, drove the rain against them.

"All right," he said. "Anything else, Harry?"

"No sir."

"I guess that's enough, isn't it?" he asked, smiling.

"I'd think so, Mr. President."

"What with one thing and another—" He left the statement unfinished, turned to his desk, activated a speaker. "Jane, get me Tillman."

Harry didn't recognize the name.

The President picked up the phone. "Jim, we need better security for Hercules. I want you to pack up the entire mission. Move it to NSA. Forthwith." He listened, nodded, and glanced out at the storm. "Tomorrow then. I don't want to waste any time on this."

He came back and shook Harry's hand. "Good job, Harry. You and your people have been outstanding. I won't forget."

Harry was thinking, my God, they're shutting us down. Tomorrow. It's over. He wanted to tell Hurley not to take the program away from Goddard. Not to turn it over to the code-breakers with orders to lose it. But it was all too intimidating. "Thank you, sir," he said.

"Incidentally, I think you could use a little more responsibility. You might start looking around. When this is over, maybe we can find you a deputy directorship at one of the major agencies."

————

Julie called him. "Good news."

"What?" he asked. "I could use some—"

"There's been some sort of breakthrough. Kilgore wants me to bring Tommy in tomorrow."

"Wonderful." Kilgore was cautious. If he was talking breakthrough, there *had* to be something to it. "Did he give you any details?"

"He said they were going to have to do some tests. But he's hopeful."

"*Hopeful.* What's that mean?"

"He thinks they'll be able to get some control over the diabetes. Cut back a bit on the shots."

MONITOR

WILLY'S WORLD ONLINE

At a meeting in Wichita today, I have it on good account that Roger Whitlock, the state Republican party boss, let slip that the administration plans to put Orion, its new particle-beam weapon, into mass production. The idea, as I understand it, is that it will function as a kind of death ray. Bombs are out, folks . . .

. . .

Partial transcript of interview with Andrew Feldmann, candidate for the Democratic nomination, appearing on CNN's The Defenders:

CNN: Congratulations, Senator. You're now assured of a majority of delegates. Is the nomination a lock?

Feldmann: Harold, you know better than that. Nothing's ever a lock in politics. But I think we've done about as well as we could have hoped.

CNN: Senator, in light of the stagnant economy, and the fact that there are no overriding problems abroad, would you agree that the big issues in the coming campaign will be fiscal policy and taxes?

Feldmann: That's the ground Jack Hurley would like to avoid if he can, but he's not going to be able to do that. There are too many people in this country who are still disenfranchised, Harold. We've been doing too much for too many people abroad for a lot of years now. It's time to come home. Take care of our own.

CNN: In your opinion, Senator, where is the President vulnerable?

Feldmann: It hurts me to say it, Harold, but the country doesn't have a lot of confidence in this President. We had a major stock-market crash not long ago, from which we haven't recovered. The economy remains flat. And a lot of people are worried. They're worried, I might add, because they don't trust Jack Hurley to make the right decisions.

CNN: The polls show you comfortably in the lead in a head-to-head matchup. You must be feeling pretty good, Senator.

Feldmann: I'm feeling good for the country, Harold. I think we have a chance to get moving again. And under our leadership, I see a bright future for us all.

||| EIGHTEEN |||

Harry took Leslie to his home, to the house on Bolingbrook Road and, by the light of the streetlamp, in the bedroom he'd shared with Julie, he undressed her. Revenge of a sort, he thought.

One by one, he dropped her clothes in the middle of the lush shag rug he and Julie had bought when they took possession of the house on their seventh anniversary. When he'd finished, she turned slightly, on some whim perhaps, or from reserve, and her navel and breasts passed into shadow. But her eyes stayed with him, and her hair was a pale radiance in the light that came through the curtains. "You're lovely," he said.

She opened her arms to him, and he felt the soft press of her through his shirt. Her lips were wet and warm, and he tangled one hand in her hair. They rocked gently, while the box elders rubbed the side of the house, and Harry's manual alarm clock ticked loudly on the bureau. The flesh at the nape of her neck, just below the hairline, was firm and almost muscular.

He lifted her. She burrowed into him, and he could feel her heartbeat. On the queen-size bed, she pulled at his shirt, laughed when one button stuck, and jerked it loose. "I'll fix it for you," she whispered, sliding the garment down off his shoulders. She flipped it casually into the dark and slipped one palm down inside his belt buckle.

Harry bent over her, fitted his mouth to hers, and in good time took her.

They talked, and slept, and made love, and talked again.

They talked about themselves mostly, and how they enjoyed each other. And they talked about the Altheans, from whom they expected to glean little more. "I wonder why," she said, while they lay lazily entangled with each other, "they

never tell us about their past. There was no history that I could
find. And no psychology. In fact, nothing of the social sciences. It's over now, and the illusion of the lone alien in the
tower is stronger than ever. I really don't understand *that*."

Harry propped himself up on an elbow. "What will *we* be
like in a million years?" And, without waiting for an answer,
he went on: "There's a priest in Pete's order who plays bridge
like nothing I've ever seen. You get the feeling when you play
with him that the cards are all faceup on the table. I mean, he
did things that were just not possible unless he could see all
the hands. And I wonder whether, in some sense, he could?"

"I'd be more inclined," said Leslie, "to suspect he just has
very good instincts for the game. Pros do the kind of thing
you're describing. Read the bridge columns once in a while."
She traced the line of his shoulder with a fingertip. "I'm not sure
I'd want to be around someone who was truly telepathic."

"Is it possible?"

"Mind reading? I don't think so."

"But you're not sure."

"No way to *be* sure. Nobody's ever shown a medium that
would make it possible. We're not quite sure what thoughts
are, and we've no idea how you'd go about transferring them
directly from one brain to another."

"So it *could* happen."

"I don't know."

"If it were possible, what's the end product after, say, a million years of evolution?"

She closed her eyes and lay back. Her head sank into the
pillow. "If ESP is possible, and if we developed it, I would
think that in time we'd lose our individual identities."

"And *language*?" asked Harry. "What use would a race of
telepaths have for language?" They looked at each other, and
both recalled Leslie's analysis of the transmitted language: *We
could have done better.*

"It would fit," she said. "For that kind of community, I suspect history, at least as we use the term, would cease to exist.
There'd be no more politics and probably no conflict. And I
have another thought for you: In a group being, if such a thing
is possible, there'd be no real death. The individual cells,
units, members would die, but not the central intelligence."

"Only the bodies would die," mused Harry. "Memories remain forever."

"More or less."

She stirred against him, and he stroked her cheek lightly, and her hair. For the time, the Altheans fled into the night.

––––––––

"I'm going to call a press conference," Hakluyt told Harry while Leslie and Pete Wheeler looked on.

"Check your contract, Cy. You talk out of turn, and they can put you away for twenty years or so."

"I don't care," he said. "People need to know what's going on here."

"What can you prove?" Harry asked.

Hakluyt turned toward him, his eyes shining. "I notice you're not wearing your glasses, Harry."

"I think it worked," he said.

"Of course it worked. If you're interested, and you can get these nitwits to give us access, I can probably do something for your allergies." That required a quick explanation to Wheeler. When the priest looked doubtful, Harry demonstrated his newfound capability by reading a copy of the *Wall Street Journal* from several feet away.

"Amazing," he said.

"I think it's too late to help my allergies," Harry said.

"Dammit." Hakluyt was furious. "I think we should call his bluff. Make everything public. Turn it all loose. That'll change the equation."

"We can't produce it," Wheeler said frostily. "Anyhow, you can't release that stuff no matter what. What about the new weapons?"

"We've already got doomsday weapons, Pete," said Hakluyt. "Don't you think a nuke can be transported by suitcase? There's nothing in the Text that can make things any more dangerous than they already are."

"That's a point," said Leslie. "The human race has shown a remarkable restraint since the end of World War Two. The transmission may be what's needed to force us, finally, to confront the issues and do what needs to be done."

"And if it doesn't?" asked Harry.

"Then," said Hakluyt, "we're no worse off. Listen, Baines was excited because he'd found the Grand Unified Theories in there somewhere. But he'd already been working on that. In fact, he predicted somewhere that we'd have it ourselves during his lifetime. The same thing is probably true of most of the technical material. It's certainly true of the genetic data. All we're doing is moving the timetable up a few years. Well, what the hell, let's do it! Let's tell the public what he's hiding. This is an election year. He'll be forced to make an accounting."

"I think," said Wheeler, "that we need to disengage our personal involvement with the project and stop being investigators for a few moments. We tend to assume that knowledge, in and of itself, is good. That the truth will somehow make us free. But that can be an illusion. It seems to me there's only one consideration before us, and that's the welfare of the species. What are we really talking about here? I'll tell you what *I* think it is: We're trying to balance our curiosity about the structure of the double helix with human survival."

"That's really unfounded," said Hakluyt, who was visibly hurt by the implication. "It doesn't have anything to do with my curiosity. This is a chance to help a lot of damaged people. You want to hold this thing back, go ahead. But the next time you see a kid with cerebral palsy, you might want to remember that we had a chance to help and threw it away."

The color went out of Wheeler's face, but he said nothing.

"I vote with Baines," Harry said, jumping in. "If Hurley wants to hide it in a vault, I say let him do it."

"No." Leslie was near tears. "You can't let that happen. God help me, I don't have an answer to this, but I know that just chucking everything and hiding under a rock isn't the way to go."

"I can't see," said Wheeler, "that this is our choice to make. Hurley seems fully cognizant of the risks, and I think he's taking a sensible course."

They covered the ground again and again. Harry, the bureaucrat, knew that Wheeler was right, that the Hercules Text was far too dangerous to release. And while the increasingly angry conversation swirled around him, he thought about the Altheans under their starless skies: a species with no traceable history (did time, somehow, stand still under Altheis

Gamma?), no art, with devices that seemingly lacked a power source. Their dead were somehow not really dead. They transmitted principles that could be used to make terrifying weapons. And they indulged in Platonic philosophy.

The man in the tower, Leslie had said. Not unlike Father Sunderland rattling around in the priory overlooking Chesapeake Bay, playing preternatural bridge.

What was her comment about the linguistic system employed in the transmission? Not a natural language. Awkward. *We* could have done better. How could that be?

Eventually, the meeting broke up, as all the others had, in indecision and rancor. And when they were filing out, while Harry was still thinking of Father Sunderland, Cyrus Hakluyt took him aside. "I don't know about *you*, Harry," he said, "but *I* don't expect to sleep very well anymore."

An hour later, Harry received a phone call from a friend in the General Services Administration. "NSA has ordered a fleet of vans sent to your place, Harry," she said. "Did you know about it?"

"More or less," said Harry. "When?"

"Tomorrow morning, nine o'clock. What's going on?"

"We're moving," said Harry.

He hung up and was sitting listlessly in his office, staring at a pile of financial reports, when Edna called. "Dr. Gambini on the line," she said.

He pressed the blinking light. "Hello, Ed."

"Harry." The project manager sounded excited. "They're here."

"Maloney?"

"Yes. They've kicked us out. Sealed off the Hercules spaces. Nobody's allowed in."

"Where're you calling from, Ed?"

"Outside. I'm in the street with my cell phone."

"Where's the rest of the staff?" asked Harry.

"Hell, I sent them home."

MONITOR

YEAST-MADE VACCINE SHOWS
POSITIVE RESULTS AGAINST LEUKEMIA

EARLY DETECTION STILL VITAL

. . .

SURVEY: ORGANIZATION HEADS,
CEOS, OFTEN EMOTIONALLY DISABLED

LEADERS SHOW TASTE
AND TALENT FOR POWER

. . .

ARE YOU A POTENTIAL MANIAC?

NEW STUDY LAYS OUT EARLY WARNINGS

LOOK OUT FOR THE MAN
WHO EATS ALONE

. . .

MOBS SMASH FOREIGN CARS
IN DETROIT

1 DEAD, 14 INJURED IN OUTBREAK

VICTIMS CLAIM COPS STOOD ASIDE

. . .

DAMASCUS RIOTING IN FOURTH DAY

SAUDIS URGE TRUCE

ALAM IN HIDING

. . .

RUSSIA WILL NO LONGER CARRY
U.S. ASTRONAUTS TO SPACE STATION

ROSKOSKY DENOUNCES ORION

DEMANDS U.S. SHARE HERCULES DATA

. . .

EARTHQUAKE KILLS SIX IN MONTANA

TREMORS CONTINUE;
MORE SHOCKS EXPECTED

. . .

SUPPORT GROWS
FOR FILM CENSORSHIP

LEVEL OF VIOLENCE INTOLERABLE,
SAYS MCDONALD

DRIVE TO KILL SECOND AMENDMENT
GAINS IN SENATE

. . .

ICELAND, BRITAIN ARGUE
OVER FISHING RIGHTS

BOTH SIDES THREATEN RENEWAL
OF POTATO WAR

||| NINETEEN |||

There was in fact nothing to be done about Hercules. Harry made a few calls, confirmed what he already knew to be true: The Greenbelt staff would not be allowed access until security checks had been processed. "Includes you," one of the voices told him.

No surprise there. He put it out of his mind as best he could and proceeded to other business. After lunch, he conducted the second meeting of a three-day management seminar on methods of encouraging creativity in subordinates. The attendees were from a wide range of government agencies, and after his experiences with the White House, they constituted a refreshingly amenable group. But while they talked earnestly of free-rein techniques and taking care not to concentrate on negatives, it occurred to Harry that the Hercules strategy had, from the beginning, been in the hands of the investigators. And therein, perhaps, lay the problem. Harry had been their one manager. He should have been thinking all along about the short- and long-range effects of the discoveries, of public relations within the government, of the potential for misunderstanding at all levels. But he'd done nothing except stand passively aside, allowing himself to be overawed by the team of geniuses Gambini had assembled. Now it was too late. The hour of the bureaucrat had come and gone. The Hercules unit had lost control of its own program. And in all probability, whatever remained of it would disappear altogether into the cavernous vaults, probably, of the GSA archives.

Still, he couldn't convince himself that was altogether a bad idea.

When he arrived to pick Tommy up for their trip to the Smithsonian, Julie took him aside. She looked gray. Frightened. "The tests are back," she said. "They were negative."

"Negative? How were they *negative*?"

"Tommy's the wrong type or something. They can't do anything for him. Not now, anyhow." She slid down into a chair. "Maybe later, Kilgore says."

That afternoon, Harry and his son wandered among the dinosaurs and spaceships in the bright galleries, but there was, as always now, a shadow between them. Tommy's manner, when with his father, was almost mournful. The sense of loss was palpable.

It felt almost like old times in the archaeological sections, where they walked among water-stained stone blocks from excavated temples whose towers had once gleamed in a Mexican sun.

In the Hall of Technology, beside a model of the proposed New Hampshire accelerator, Tommy asked, as he did whenever they went out together, whether things had changed, whether he might be coming home. Harry shook his head. Julie had continued to recede in recent weeks. The life they'd had together seemed remote now, like the Mexican temple, and its individual parts were artifacts, so many dried stones laid out in a row.

Only Tommy retained life.

Harry watched him tracking mesons through an electrical field, quick yellow streaks across a green screen, liberated by a process described in detail on a metal plate. The boy had gotten interested in subatomic physics after a conversation with Ed Gambini, during which the physicist had described particles so small that they had no mass whatever. "That's *small*!" Tommy had said, trying to visualize what such a condition meant.

And Harry had stood by, fingering the packet of sugar cubes he always carried as insurance against hypoglycemia. He'd been present when his son was learning to administer the insulin. The doctors had explained to Tommy, and to his parents, that it was important to rotate the injection site to prevent skin damage. They'd made a chart; and the shots had gone into the arms and the legs and the abdomen. The boy had accepted the situation more easily than his parents had. Probably because Harry and Julie understood the long-term effects of diabetes.

Harry stood now watching Tommy peer again at the devices he'd seen so often before. The Smithsonian was his favorite spot in the D.C. area. And he thought how Cyrus Hakluyt maybe had the cure.

Harry backed off several feet and read the tiny print on the plate on meson liberation.

By this time tomorrow, he expected that Hercules would be gone. Rosenbloom could be expected within the next few days to work out a deal for Gambini. There'd be something juicy for Wheeler and Hakluyt, too. They'd try to buy off the team, ensure their silence, guard against whatever resentment might linger.

Tommy and Harry stayed until closing time. Later, they walked through the warm evening along Constitution Avenue, talking about pterodactyls and computer games. Tommy announced that he had decided he was going to be an archaeologist. "In Egypt," he added.

It was a good moment.

————————

Next morning, a summons was waiting from Rosenbloom when he walked in the door. Harry sighed, had his coffee, and strolled over to the director's office. Gambini was already there.

"—Glad to be rid of it," Rosenbloom was saying.

The project manager looked beaten.

"Look at it this way, Ed," said Rosenbloom. "You've made your reputation with this thing. Even though it's been nothing but a headache from the start. You're better off. Now the goddam National Society for the Preservation of Science can get mad at somebody else for a change." He nodded toward Harry. "Harry'll tell you. Isn't that right, Harry?"

"Right," said Harry.

"Look." Rosenbloom rapped his knuckles on the desk. "There was no way it could work out. Not with all the national-security revelations coming out of that thing."

"They're on their way, Harry," Gambini said.

Rosenbloom nodded. "Vans'll be here within the hour."

"They need us to do anything?" asked Harry.

"They'll want everybody available to open lockers and filing cabinets and whatnot."

"Oh," said Gambini. "They're going to let us back in?"

Rosenbloom ignored the sarcasm. "I've been warned that anything they can't open, presumably including desks, they'll take."

"Okay. When can I get back into my office?"

"When Maloney gets here, they'll open up." He rubbed the back of his neck and made faces as if he were hurting. "After it's over, Harry, I want you to take Ed and his people out for lunch. Get them away from here. Use the government card. I'll approve it."

"And when you've done that, Harry," he continued, "I want you to take some time off. You've earned it."

———

Maloney was with them when they came. He rode in the front vehicle, a black Ford station wagon marked *General Services Administration*, gazing stolidly ahead, as de Gaulle must have done going into Paris. Two other men with expensive suits and granite expressions rode with him. Six GSA vans trailed behind.

They circled the lab and came at it from behind, backing the vehicles in close to the rear entrance. The doors of the vans popped open, and a dozen men in coveralls climbed down onto the asphalt. Each had his name and picture on a plastic badge. The driver of the station wagon talked briefly with Maloney, picked up a clipboard, and led them to the front of the building. Their bearing was a mix of military and Ivy League, drill-squad precision and casual talk of the Redskins and quantum mechanics. Harry realized that sprinkled among these people were a few investigators whose job it was to ensure that nothing got overlooked. Would they be used later to probe deeper into the transmission? He wondered. His gut feeling was that, whatever might happen in the immediate future, by the time John Hurley left office, the Hercules Text would no longer exist.

Harry and Gambini stood off to one side, watching. Leslie joined them. The front doors opened, and the GSA team were escorted inside.

Maloney came over. "Ed, can I have you and your people go in and open up?"

Harry followed the crowd. He was surprised that they admitted him. The first security breach was now on the record.

Maloney's people appeared to have been well briefed. They divided into several groups and spread through the building.

In the lab, they began with the computers, simply disconnecting them and carrying them outside. They brought in cardboard cartons and filled them with the copies of the Hercules Text. They went systematically through the operating spaces and seized all disks, all ledgers, notes, journals, and printouts. These were also placed in the boxes. They also took the trash cans, dumping the contents into white burn bags, sealing them, and hauling them outside.

Harry stood in a doorway near the operations center, where he could watch but be out of the way. His office had been outside the Hercules operational area; consequently no one ever looked in his desk.

The process moved quickly. Leslie and Gordie Hopkins and Linda Barrister and Carol Hedge and all the others who'd worked so hard on the project during the previous eight months stood in angry silence while the brown cartons bobbed along the corridor, past the water fountain, up one flight of stairs, and out into the sunlight.

Maloney led a search through all locked spaces, which produced a mountain of notes and formal documents. Harry was surprised that, even in the computer age, the project had generated so much paper. They labeled everything according to location: "Gambini's desk, second left-hand drawer," and so on. "It's the way archaeologists do a dig," said Pete Wheeler, who'd arrived just as they were ready to break into his desk. "I don't think Maloney expects us to be much help."

Hakluyt came over and watched while his records were removed from Gambini's filing cabinet. The security people placed them inside a large white envelope, labeled it, and took it away. Harry judged briefly by the microbiologist's expression that he was considering trying to seize the documents and run with them.

When they were finished with Gambini's office, Ed walked over to Maloney. "Anything else you need from me?" he asked.

Maloney thought about it. "I think that's about it, Ed."

Gambini nodded and turned away without a word. He picked up a sweater, retrieved a gold pen he'd left on his desk, and held both items out to Maloney for inspection.

"It's okay," Maloney said, refusing to get angry.

"Good-bye, Harry." Gambini offered his hand. "You've done a hell of a job." The operations center had grown quiet behind him. Leslie and Wheeler and Hakluyt, and the systems analysts and communicators and linguists had stopped everything they were doing and were watching him. Some eyes were wet. "You've *all* done a hell of a job," he said. "I'm proud to have worked with you on this. Some of you have been invited to continue with this project. I know how much it means to you, and I want to tell you that if they really mean it, it would be no disgrace to accept the offer. I'll understand. I think we'll all understand."

Then he was gone, and there was an awkward silence, filled finally by Maloney, who cleared his throat and asked for attention. "I wish I could extend to everyone," he said, "an opportunity to continue with the Hercules Project. Unfortunately, our requirements are limited. In any case, Mr. Carmichael informs me that Goddard has need of most of you. We've offered positions to a few. A list will be posted by the end of the day. We urge those whose names are on the list to stay with the project. Please inform Mr. Carmichael of your decision by the end of the week." He glanced at Harry, thanked him for helping, and moved on.

By one o'clock, everything was out of the building. Maloney presented Harry with a signed inventory of what they'd taken. It included the Oppenheimer Certificate and the Jefferson Medal. "The National Security Agency," he said curtly, "will inform you of their new location. I suspect, though, that you won't have clearance to get to them." He smiled. Turned it into a joke. Then, under a brilliant sun, the six-vehicle convoy set off toward the main gate.

Most of the Hercules team gathered that evening at the Red
Limit for a farewell dinner. They were not literally scattering:
the technicians would be staying on at Goddard in various
projects. Among the investigators, Carol Hedge and Pete
Wheeler had been asked to assist in ongoing operations. Harry
did not expect that Pete would stay.

Cyrus Hakluyt had checked out without a word to anyone.

Leslie would be going back to Philadelphia. "Then maybe
to an island in the South Seas," she said. "I've had enough for
a while." There were no speeches that night, but several got up
to express their feelings. "It was," said one of the systems analysts, "a little like being in combat together." Harry thanked
them for their loyalty and predicted that, when John W. Hurley
had long been forgotten, the Hercules team would be legend.
"They may not remember our names, but they'll know we
were here."

They applauded that, and for the few hours they remained
under the familiar beams and arches of the Red Limit, they
believed it. For Harry, the comment marked yet another mile-
stone: It was the first time he'd been disloyal in public to a man
for whom he worked.

Farewell parties always impose a kind of funereal atmosphere, he thought, occasioned by the symbolic close of an era.
Every handshake, every brief meeting of the eyes, takes on
special significance. But the relatively subdued affair staged by
the Hercules team was especially intense, perhaps because this
event was unique in human history, and the forty-some men
and women gathered in the modest restaurant off Greenbelt
Road represented everyone who had ever looked at a star and
wanted some answers. Well, they had by God found some
answers, and maybe no one could really ask for much more.

Harry stayed late, until they'd broken up into small groups
and begun to drift apart. They shook hands as though they
wouldn't see one another again, even though most of them
would be reporting for work at the same place tomorrow.

Toward the end of the evening, around one, he found himself alone with Leslie. "When will you be leaving?" he asked.

"Tomorrow."

"I'll miss you." He found himself suddenly staring into an empty space.

She squeezed his arm. "Philly's not that far, Harry."

He nodded. "I was hoping you'd say that."

Angela Dellasandro watched her opportunity, and told Harry that he was inordinately good-looking. She had, by then, put away several manhattans. She added that she was worried about Ed Gambini. Harry reassured her, and she drifted off.

"She's right," Leslie said. "He's safer away from the project, but there'll be a dangerous period until he makes an adjustment."

"No," said Harry. "He found his aliens. I think he's satisfied now. He'll be okay."

"I hope." She looked pensive. Almost, he thought, *lost.* "Do you believe in magic, Harry?"

He thought he knew the answer she wanted. Nevertheless, he shook his head and tried to lighten the moment. "No. The only real magic is public relations."

She grinned. It was that mischievous little-girl smile that transformed her entire being. Then it faded and was gone, replaced by something else, something rather stoic. "We had the king's touch in our hands," she said. "And we've let it get away."

Harry frowned. "The king's touch?" What did he remember about that? That monarchs were supposed to be able to cure illnesses by the mere laying on of hands. "I guess we did," he said.

She moved into his arms. "I'm sorry I didn't make copies the first day and mail them all over the world." She'd had too much to drink, or maybe she was angry. In any case, her voice got loud, and everyone was staring. "The next time we see somebody with multiple sclerosis or cerebral palsy," she told them, "or somebody who's blind or deaf, we can remember that we might have had the cure. And that we stood by while it got buried."

Harry's insides churned.

"Hey," he said, trying to lighten the moment. "We did what we could."

"It wasn't enough, lover." She wiped her eyes. "I wouldn't be surprised, though, if our politicians start living inordinately long lives."

"You don't really believe that?" he asked.

"Why not? It's the kind of temptation *I'd* be inclined to give in to. Wouldn't you?"

Harry felt a wave of guilt. She was watching him closely, and he wondered whether she knew about the injection he'd received.

But she broke the moment. "Harry," she said, "can I ask you to take me home? I'm too drunk to drive."

———

Gambini was lost in a dream, struggling up the side of a hill whose top kept receding so that he never got any closer. There was a bench on the crest, a place where he could rest and look out over whatever view lay on the other side. But the ground underfoot kept crumbling, and he was constantly losing his balance and sliding back downhill. His heart was pounding when the ridge suddenly blinked out, and he was lying twisted in sheets, looking up at the darkness gathered like an animal overhead. The sullen roar of the sea filled the bedroom.

His heart was still beating furiously, hammering against his ribs, threatening to explode. He lay quietly, trying to slow it down by a sheer act of will. He could literally *hear* it mingled with the beat of the ocean.

He'd had problems with his heart before, a touch of arrhythmia, nothing serious, if *anything* concerning the heart can be said to be *not serious*. But he felt it building and swelling, and he understood that he was suffering an attack. He fumbled with the phone, found the handset, punched nine-one-one.

"Heart attack," he told the male voice at the other end. "I think." He gave his name and address, and the voice assured him help was on the way.

"Don't hang up," the voice said.

"Okay."

"Are you in bed?"

"Yes."

"Do you have any aspirin handy?"

"Medicine cabinet. In the bathroom."

"Okay. Let it go. Can you sit up?"

"Don't know."

"Try."

The edges of his vision were getting dark. "Not good," he told the phone.

He didn't hear the response. He was thinking that he was going to die, and he wasn't really as afraid of it as he'd always thought he would be. If there was an accounting over there somewhere, he should be all right. He had never tried to hurt anybody. Had been kind to dogs and nitwits.

He smiled at that, almost his last conscious thought.

Maloney and Hurley actually believed they were doing the right thing.

He wondered what else might be in the transmission.

CYRUS HAKLUYT REPLIES TO A CRITIC

Dr. Idlemann's assertion that death is an integral part of nature's plan for the ongoing renewal of the species assumes that there is, in fact, a design of some sort. One is hard-pressed to find anything that could be described as conscious intent in the harsh system into which we are born and which, in the end, kills us and our children. One can only wonder at the sort of reasoning that regards blind evolution as benevolent and somehow wiser than we.

The truth is, we owe nothing to the future. We are alive now, and that is all that matters. To paraphrase Henry Thoreau, we stand on the dividing line between two vast infinities, the dead and the unconceived. Let us save ourselves, if we can. When we have done that, when we have ceased to hand to our children a legacy of cancer and aging and loss, then we can begin sensibly planning for the sort of existence that an intelligent species should have.

—Cyrus Hakluyt

Extract from *Harper's* letter column, June issue, author's response to a communication from Max Idlemann, M.D., an obstetrician in Fargo, North Dakota, who objected on numerous grounds to an article by Hakluyt in the May issue. Dr. Idlemann seemed particularly incensed that Hakluyt had failed to recognize the long-range damage that would occur from any major breakthrough in prolonging the human life span.

TWENTY

Harry tossed and turned during the early hours of the night. He dreamed about people he hadn't seen for years. Vivid dreams that made no sense. He was back in old jobs, even back in school. When he woke at about five, he buried his head in his pillow but stayed awake, and after a while, he gave up and made himself breakfast.

He was just finishing when the phone rang.

The nature of Harry's work was that it was extraordinarily mundane. Nothing at his office was ever going to prompt anyone to call at an unusual hour. Save, of course, when unexplained signals came from faraway places.

He picked it up just before the machine answered it. It was Wheeler.

"Harry!" he said. "I just got a call from one of our priests over at St. Luke's. They brought Ed in last night. He had a heart attack."

Harry sat down heavily. "How serious?"

"I don't know yet. He's still alive, but they tell me he's critical. I'm going over. I'll call you when I find out."

"Thanks," said Harry. "I'll meet you there."

"No point in it. They're not going to let anybody in to see him. I'll keep you informed."

Harry drew his legs up onto the sofa and wrapped his arms around them. He called Leslie. "Where are you?" he asked.

"On ninety-five. Twenty miles east of Baltimore." Her voice was detached.

"I didn't expect you to leave so early," he said. She'd looked wrecked the night before. He wondered how she did it.

"Running start. I wanted to get around Baltimore before the traffic kicked in."

He paused, heard something heavy rumble past her. "Pete just called me," he said. "Ed's in the hospital. Heart attack."

"Damn," she said. "What are they saying? Any idea how serious?"

"Critical."

"Do you know where he is? Which hospital?"

"St. Luke's."

Neither of them said anything for a long time. "All right," she said finally, "I have a couple of things to do in Philly tonight. I'll be back tomorrow."

"Okay."

"Thanks, Harry." Some of the detachment had gone out of her voice. "I'm sorry. He's a good guy."

"Yeah. I know."

"He'll probably be okay. Cardiac cases, if they get to them quickly enough, they aren't like they used to be."

———

They lost him about an hour later. Wheeler called and told him that the doctors said he'd never regained consciousness. "I'm sorry," Pete said.

"Does his family know?"

"That's being taken care of now. Did you want me to call Leslie?"

"No," said Harry. "I'll take care of it."

He decided not to hit her with the news while she was on the road. Instead, he called her home number and left a message asking her to get back to him.

"Never came out of it," Harry told her. Why did *that* detail seem important?

Her voice shook. "When's the memorial?"

"Thursday." Day after tomorrow. He gave her the details, when and where. She said she'd be there.

"You okay?" Harry asked.

"Yeah. I'm fine."

"You think the project killed him?"

"You mean, having it turn out the way it did?"

"Yes."

"I doubt it. People don't usually die of disappointment, despite what everyone thinks. He's had a problem all along. It's a safe bet that if it hadn't happened last night, it would have come down on him in a week or a month. Usually, it's just a matter of *when*."

They talked a few more minutes, about how much Gambini would be missed, then she said good-bye, have to go, call if there's anything I can do. "See you Thursday," she said. Then she was gone.

The lab was back to normal. Or it would be when the new hardware got installed. NSA would be keeping all the old computers, but the replacements were due in a few days. Much better stuff, Harry had been assured. State-of-the-art.

He was glad to hear it. Now, it seemed, it was time to get rid of the last copy.

He dug his keys out of his briefcase and unlocked the lower left-hand desk drawer. He opened it, took out the package, and assured himself that the disk was still there. When he had done so, he put it into his briefcase and closed it. Then he removed a plastic clothes wrapper from his closet, looked around, spotted an old Civil War paperweight, a bust of Robert E. Lee that someone at the office had once given him as a Christmas present, and dropped it into the wrapper. He carried everything into the outer office and told Edna he wasn't feeling well. "I'll be gone for the day," he said.

He drove casually out the front gate and turned toward the Beltway.

A few minutes later, he exited onto Route 50 east and followed it toward Annapolis. His pulse began to pick up. As a good bureaucrat, Harry hated doing anything irrevocable. All his instincts and his experience rose against him. Yet he knew that, whatever principle might be involved, *he* personally would be better off once the damned thing was gone.

The damned thing.

Odd way to think about the package of arcane knowledge that had fallen into his hands.

The morning traffic was light, and he moved swiftly past Bowie and crossed the Patuxent River. Julie reached him as he turned onto Aris Allan Boulevard.

"I need your advice," she said. "Ellen thinks we shouldn't give up so easily on Tommy. She thinks we ought to get a second opinion."

Harry hated the ups and downs of these things. Julie read all the science magazines, stayed up with the recurring predictions that a cure was imminent. There was something every other month, it seemed, about a breakthrough of one kind or another. But somehow nothing ever really changed.

"We could try it," he said.

"You don't sound hopeful."

"I just don't want him getting put through any more tests unless there's a reasonable chance, Julie."

"I know," she said. "But we have to try."

They agreed they'd find another specialist and get his opinion. Surely, that couldn't hurt.

Then she was gone, and he was traveling south on Aris Allan, past white picket fences and wide lawns and well-kept churches. Near a 7-Eleven, he swung moodily left toward the bay, stopped to let a woman push a baby carriage into traffic, and continued on into Port Annapolis. He parked on the waterfront and looked out across Chesapeake Bay, gleaming in midday sunlight.

The area was crowded with piers and boats and shops. A yacht under full sail was headed south down the channel. He rented a motorboat, wishing he could use an assumed name. But they required a driver's license, of course, and he only had one to show them. Still, what the hell. If anybody asked questions later, he could say he was just following Rosenbloom's advice and taking some time off.

The attendant was a bored, gangly teenager, too dull even to wonder why Harry was carrying a briefcase onto the launch. He brought the boat around, and Harry got in and headed out into the channel in a leisurely manner.

The boat had a depth gauge and he watched it as he moved east, steering toward the Love Point Lighthouse on the far side. A couple of other boats were out, one feeding popcorn to screeching gulls. The gulls swirled overhead in clouds, and some checked out Harry to see whether he had anything for them.

It was a pleasant, warm afternoon. The water was smooth and quiet, and there was no wind at all.

Another yacht passed. A man with a couple of kids. A boy

and a girl, both about four or five. They were wearing sailors' hats and life jackets made to order. The boy was playing with the gulls while the girl stared rapt at the lighthouse. She noticed Harry and waved. Harry waved back.

The lighthouse was a big, rusty canister sticking out of the water. It grew larger as he approached the eastern shore.

The water began to get deep. It went to sixty feet, then to ninety. At about a quarter mile off the lighthouse, it fell away to 210 feet. The Deep Hole. It was, as far as Harry knew, the deepest water in the bay.

The bottom was soft mud. An ideal place to lose something.

He cut the motor, and the boat drifted to a stop and began to rock gently in the current. He opened the briefcase and took out the package. A couple of gulls flapped in close, took a look, and lost interest.

Harry put the package inside the clothes wrapper and added Robert E. Lee. Thus be it ever to rebels. He tied the wrapper shut and punched a few holes in it to let the water in.

A light breeze blew his hair into his eyes. It was absolutely quiet save for the wind and the water lapping against the gunwale.

He went to the side of the boat and imagined he could peer down into the depths.

The boat rocked. Far to the south, he could see the lean gray shape of a warship, a destroyer probably, moving out to sea.

Put the thing in the bay and be done with it.

He scanned the eastern shoreline, picking out cars and houses and people. It was such a pleasure to have twenty-twenty again. He hadn't realized how much his vision had deteriorated. It had all been too gradual. The whole world now stood out in sharp detail, the battered sides of the lighthouse, the gulls, the retreating warship.

The briefcase was still open. And there among a stack of papers, pens, rubber bands, and business cards were both sets of his bifocals. One ordinary pair, one pair of sunglasses. Both were in plastic cases.

He removed both, took them out of their cases, and dropped them into the water. They sank quickly.

The sun was warm on the water.

The boat drifted gradually away from Deep Hole, past the lighthouse, and out into the channel. A blue-and-white sailboat skimmed past, about two hundred feet off at its closest approach. The crew appeared to consist of two young women.

They were both beautiful.

"Hell," said Harry. He put the disk back in his briefcase. Then he restarted the engine and headed for shore. Two hours later, he put the disk into his safe-deposit box at Greenbelt Federal.

———

Pete Wheeler was more than happy to see Harry and settle in for an evening of bridge at the Priory. They started promptly at eight and played until eleven. Father Sunderland was a bit off his game. But it didn't matter other than to permit Wheeler and Harry to lose by a respectable score.

"You both seem down tonight," Sunderland commented, near the end. "Anything wrong?"

Harry had been unaware of any change in Wheeler's normally reserved demeanor. But it was true he'd been buried in his own dark thoughts. "I just seem to need more aces," he replied.

Wheeler shrugged it off, but when they were outside, strolling across the unlit parking lot, Harry asked whether Pete was still trying to come to terms with the transmission.

"Sure," he said. "We've lost quite a lot."

The night sky was full of stars. A quarter moon drifted just off the treetops.

Harry slowed the pace slightly. "You've maintained all along that we're better off rid of it," he said.

"I did. I still feel that way."

"Then what—?"

"I don't know. It's like being shown a lot of good stuff but finding out you can't have any of it." He stopped and gazed at the sky.

"We'll get by it, Pete," he said.

"I know."

They reached the car. "We had it in our hands, Harry," he said.

"Have faith."

He nodded, not letting Harry see his eyes.

"You don't, do you?" Harry continued, knowing he was sailing into uncharted waters, where he should not go.

"Don't what?"

"Have a great deal. Of faith."

He buttoned his sweater against the cool night. "Not really," he said.

"What happened?"

He did not reply.

"I'm sorry," said Harry. "It's none of my business."

He shrugged. "Feynman comments somewhere that the universe is too big. It's hard to believe God needed all this space just for us."

Harry opened up the Chrysler, and they got inside.

"It makes a shambles of the biblical story," Wheeler continued. "It just doesn't seem that the Christian God fits with the type of universe we live in." He was sitting straight up, staring straight ahead into a dark line of trees. "I can't really put it in words that make sense. But my instincts tell me we've got it wrong."

"I'm sorry," Harry said.

"No reason to be. It's not your fault. Not anybody's fault."

He started the engine. "You've been an astronomer your whole life. If you don't mind my asking, when did this happen?"

"The crisis of faith?" Wheeler smiled. "It's been coming on gradually, I suppose."

They sat quietly for a long minute. "Pete," Harry said at last, "it's hard for me to believe anybody could lose his faith looking through a telescope. I'd think it would have the opposite effect. Remember those guys praying in orbit and on the moon? One of them came back and went looking for Noah's Ark."

Wheeler laughed. But the sound possessed a quality of loss.

"If Leslie were here, I think she'd tell you that the big stage is a cover story."

"You think so?"

"Yes. And she'd also say that it helps to talk."

They drove out of the parking lot and started back toward Greenbelt. There was almost no traffic, and the occasional houses along the roadway all seemed dark.

"I don't know," he said, breaking a silence of several minutes. "Right after I'd been ordained, my first assignment was in Philadelphia, teaching physics to seniors. We have a high school there. Neumann-Goretti. And there was another *Harry*. Harry Tockett.

"Harry was seventeen when he showed up in my class. He had recently been diagnosed with amyotrophic lateral sclerosis and was in the first stages. Lou Gehrig's Disease. Which we all knew would in a very short time leave him in a body that had all it could do to keep breathing." The highway lights swept past rhythmically, every twenty seconds or so. "About the third month, they put him in a wheelchair. Do you know how kids with serious handicaps are treated by their peers?"

Harry remembered a boy in his eighth grade who'd been subject to epileptic seizures. "I know," he said.

"The other kids try to be nice, but they're put off. They can't help it. They don't know how to handle it, so the child has no friends. Harry's doctors explained that he'd continue downhill. That he would probably not survive more than a few years. The Make-A-Wish Foundation heard about him and stepped in." His voice had developed a catch.

"What did they do for him?"

"He wanted to meet Jimmy Rollins, the Phillies' shortstop. They set it up. Rollins arranged box seats for Harry and his folks at one of the games, took them to dinner, gave him a baseball signed by the team. Invited him to come back anytime he could."

They slipped onto a narrow bridge. The steady hum of the tires changed tone on the metal roadway.

"I got to know the family pretty well. That was a mistake, I guess. We were all believers, and I found myself trying to explain why things like that happen. Not only to the parents. But to myself. And you know what? I *had* no explanation. I might have satisfied *them*. They were prepared to accept the idea that suffering is part of the deal. Part of some sort of incomprehensible arrangement with the Almighty. But the experience *hurt*. My God, Harry, it hurt. I used to see that kid every day. And in the face of it all, he hung in there, behaved as if he had a future. And somewhere in all that, I lost my way."

Harry, knowing that Wheeler wasn't looking at him, nodded.

"I used to believe that faith needed to be tested. That it took an ordeal before you could really think of yourself as a believer. I guess I got *that* right." He drew a deep breath. "Makes me feel like a hypocrite."

"Why?"

"*Why?* I'm a *priest*, Harry."

"That's okay. The world needs priests. And you must have a reason for staying."

He thought about it. "I'm not ready to make the break," he said. "To let go."

"Then don't."

They were approaching a traffic light. It turned red just before Harry got there, and he braked.

"If *I* were running things—" Wheeler said after they'd stopped.

Harry nodded. "—The universe would operate differently."

"Yes. It damned sure would. And I know how arrogant that sounds. But I'd step in. No young widows. No kids dead in bus accidents. No birth defects."

An empty flatbed tractor trailer made a left turn toward them. After it rumbled past, the light turned green again.

"I just wouldn't allow it. There's no reason. It's not that the universe is so *large*, Harry. It's that it's so *mechanical*. It operates exactly as you'd expect a machine to function. Things go wrong, people fall into the works, they pray, it doesn't matter—"

"Not ever?"

"Sometimes it gives people strength to get through whatever's happening to them. But one never sees direct intervention. *Ask in my name, and it will be given.* I knew Harry's parents could spend their lives begging for help, and he'd never get out of that chair." He made a noise deep in his throat. "If He is there, Harry, why does He permit such things? Why does He not step in?"

———

In the morning, Harry called Cy Hakluyt. It might have been that he was getting paranoid because he used a public phone.

"Cy," he said, "if you had access, could you extract the stuff you need?"

"What happened?" asked Hakluyt. "Hurley change his mind?"

"No. Just answer my question."

"Sure," he said. "It'd take a while. I'd need some help. But I could do it."

MONITOR

You want honest answers to hard questions? Vote for John Hurley.

—Hurley campaign battle cry

||| TWENTY-ONE |||

By early October, it was obvious the election was a lock. The economy had picked up, despite projected cutbacks in defense industries, the country was at peace, and the Democrats simply had no issues. John Hurley was spending his time looking presidential, inviting world leaders to the White House for highly visible conferences, visiting classrooms to read stories to children, visiting the scenes of the Tulsa tornado and the wild shooting spree in Columbus, Ohio, to commiserate with survivors and families. Middle East terrorism had subsided. In a few days, when the World Series ended, he'd have his picture taken out in the Rose Garden with the winners. Life looked very good.

It was therefore a trifle unsettling when his secretary informed him, on the second Tuesday of the month, four weeks before election day, that Mr. Carmichael wanted to see him. Mr. Carmichael, she reminded him, was still on the quick-access list. Was that still effective? Was the President available?

He hadn't heard from Harry for several months. Since Hercules had gone over to NSA, where he'd put it to sleep.

A few select people were still working on the project, but they were doing so under extreme security conditions. They had been complaining they couldn't get the experts they needed, but that was okay. The President couldn't quite bring himself to destroy all vestiges, but he'd made it known that he'd be just as happy if he never heard of Hercules again.

So what could Carmichael possibly want? It occurred to Hurley that he hadn't come through on his promise to get him an agency. Well, he'd see to that.

There was also a possibility of trouble, someone's wanting

to go public. Hurley was more or less aware of the tension and resentment the Hercules incident had generated among those working on the project at Goddard. And Harry had been a good early-warning source. Somebody he could rely on. "Yes, George," he said. "See if you can squeeze him in tomorrow. In any case, as soon as possible."

"Sir, we have a spot this afternoon. The Swedish photo op canceled."

"Okay," said Hurley. "Bring him in."

———————

They scheduled him at 4:40 for ten minutes. As he had done in the past, the President made it a point to clear the office for Carmichael's visit.

Hurley was a few minutes late getting back from a conversation with his campaign manager. But everything was going well, and he was in a particularly good mood when he arrived at the Oval Office, called George, and told him to send Carmichael in.

"Hello, Harry," he said, meeting him at the door with an extended hand. "How are you doing?"

"Fine, Mr. President." Harry took the hand, and the President drew him in and directed him toward the settee. Outside, George closed the door. They were alone.

"I've been meaning to talk to you, Harry. We're going to have an opening soon over at Homeland Security—" Hurley continued in that vein for a few moments but saw quickly that his visitor was under pressure. He stopped and sat down beside Carmichael. "What's wrong, Harry?"

"Sir, you're aware of the potential for acquiring genetic knowledge out of the Hercules disks?"

"Yes. Of course. It's one of the aspects of that thing that's most dangerous because it's so seductive."

"Mr. President, I would like very much to see us make the genetic segments of the transmission available to researchers."

Hurley shook his head. "Harry, I know how you feel. God knows, I feel the same way myself. Don't you think I'd like to help people with serious illnesses, but we have to look at the long-term consequences.

"Think where we'll be if we suddenly started living too long. Do you have any idea what would happen to the social-security system if life spans started expanding past one hundred—?"

"Mr. President," said Harry, "to hell with the social-security system."

Hurley's jaws stiffened. "I beg your pardon, Harry—"

Harry looked squarely into his eyes. "I'm sorry to take this out of your hands, Mr. President. But I can't stand by and watch people live with multiple sclerosis and leukemia and the rest of it because it's going to put pressure on social security."

"Harry, I think you've forgotten where you are."

"I know *exactly* where I am, Mr. President. And I'm sorry it's come to this, but I'm not going to live the rest of my life knowing I stood aside—" He lost momentary control of his voice. "There'll be a press conference tomorrow, making the material public. Either you can conduct it and take credit, or *I'll* conduct it, and people will draw their own conclusions."

Hurley stared at him. "Harry, Harry," he said, "you have to be reasonable here. I understand this thing has been preying on your mind. But you have to get hold of yourself."

Harry got up. "Do you want the credit? This is your chance."

"Harry, you're talking about releasing classified material. That's *treason*."

"You're right, Mr. President. I've been spending a lot of time lately thinking about treason. And I think sitting on the Hakluyt information is a betrayal of everyone in this country suffering from a birth defect. I can't walk away from this, and I won't let you do it, either."

Hurley shook his head. "Harry, I'm not going to allow it."

"You can't stop it."

"*That's* simple enough. I can have you detained here. Although I'd prefer not to do that."

"If you do, somebody else will take my place."

The President considered summoning assistance but then thought better of it.

"I've forwarded a fairly wide distribution of the information to a number of friends. If I don't touch base with them by this evening, I'm sure you can guess what they'll do with it."

"Put it on the Internet?"

"Exactly."

"Harry, I trusted you." Hurley took a deep breath. "I *will* prosecute, Harry."

"Do what you think is right. What I suggest is that you call a press conference." Carmichael produced a disk. "Have copies made of this and distribute it."

"Carmichael," Hurley said, "you're going to ruin the country. You understand that, I hope."

––––––––––

Rimford had gone out for some eggnog. But he drove onto the desert. Sirius and Procyon, the bright pair, lingered on the horizon. Guarding their secrets, he used to think when he looked on them a few years ago. They lay exposed now, open to the world's eyes through Skynet technology. The two suns possessed fourteen known worlds between them, indexed and cataloged by mass and composition. All were believed to be sterile.

The mesas moved ponderously against the desert sky.

The Altheans had done a remarkable thing. They'd examined a pair of quasars, widely separated in the viewing hemisphere, each approximately thirteen billion light-years distant, one a little more, the other a little less. *And they had determined they were the same object, seen from different perspectives! That could only mean that their telescopes had penetrated completely around the vault of the cosmos!* Moreover, since the quasars were not precisely on opposite sides of the sky, it was clear that the universe was not spherical.

The desert looked unfamiliar. Years before, when his sister had first come to live with him, they'd driven across this same stretch of wilderness on another Christmas Eve. He was on the staff at Kitt Peak then. It seemed a long time ago now. In those days, the sky was filled with mysteries. But tonight, he held the universe in his hands, understood much more about its architecture, understood perhaps everything that was important except the secrets of his own existence.

A few details remained unclear, but they were trivial: points about light and wave theory, that sort of thing.

He knew the size and shape, the essential geometry of the cosmos. And he understood why the cylinder was twisted, the only reason it could be twisted: It was wrapped around something else. And what could that something else be but a second universe? Or, possibly, the antimatter twin of this one. Beneath the desert stars, he tried to summon his old powers, to visualize the two systems locked in each other's embrace, a cosmic double helix.

For him, the great question had never been the shape of the universe but the subtle mysteries of its working parts. How had the laws that decreed where light speed should be set or how much energy should be packed into the atom or what the inner design of the proton should look like come to be? That the universe was habitable, indeed that it existed at all in a structured form, required a set of coincidences of incredible proportions. He recalled the old analogy of the monkeys with the typewriter. How long would it take the team of chimps to produce, by pure accident, the complete works of Shakespeare?

The odds on the monkeys were considerably better than the odds that *this* universe could happen by accident. Which was to say, it was essentially impossible for a Baines Rimford to drive a car across a desert on a December evening.

There were theories, of course. There were always theories. Some argued for an infinite number of bubble universes drifting through a superspace void. Others believed that the universe happened an infinite number of times until, *by accident*, nature got everything right.

The latter notion was out of favor now.

In time, the stars were going to exhaust their fuel and burn out. The galaxies would go dark and slide into endless night.

But the Altheans held out hope. They maintained that black holes beyond a given threshold produced baby universes, restarting the cycle. If he understood them correctly, they had also concluded that information could be processed down the throat of these singularities, leading to an infant that retained most of the characteristics of the parent. And maybe improved on a few.

Evolution.

It would explain a great deal. *This* works, and *that* does not. The mechanism remained unclear, to say the least. But his instincts liked the idea. Liked its elegance. It felt *right*.

Eventually, over incredible gulfs of time, you get an evolved cosmos.

You get starry skies over Pasadena.

But it was the next step that was unsettling.

If the universe was indeed evolving, what was it evolving *toward*?

One could argue that we were moving toward a refuge that was consistently more friendly to intelligence. And how could that be unless someone had written into the cosmic programming a directive that such an end be sought?

Rimford had no religious inclinations. The notion of a supreme being raised more questions in his mind than it answered. As did a suggestion offered some years ago that if indeed the bubble universe concept was correct, then the superspace in which it was adrift might be home to a race of designers.

But if so, where did *they* come from?

There was another possibility. He wondered whether the universe itself might not be holistic in some sense: a pattern that strove reflexively for order in its early incarnations. And having, after countless tries, learned how to make hydrogen, and consequently stars, it went on, seeking consciousness and, eventually, intelligence.

The red and white running lights of four jets lifted from the desert on his left, and he abruptly realized he'd gone all the way out to Edwards. He watched the planes climb into the jeweled dark. Immediately ahead of them, the moon lay partly hidden in a tangle of cumulus. Yes. However it had happened, it was a magnificent place.

He didn't carry a cell phone, so he continued up to the intersection with Route 58 and called Agnes from a restaurant. "I missed my stop," he said.

"Okay, Baines," she replied. This wasn't the first time he'd wandered off, but he could hear the relief in her voice. "Where are you?"

"Four Corners," he said. It was a pedestrian answer.

Hurley flashed his signature smile at the TV cameras and the reporters. "I'd like to make it clear that we don't know anything for certain yet. I don't want to raise anyone's hopes.

"But those who are close to the Hercules data say that at the very least we will derive substantial health benefits from this." He raised one of the disks so everyone could see it. "Maybe we are on the verge of effectively reducing birth defects. Maybe we will achieve some other major breakthroughs. Let us hope so.

"I'd like to assure the American people, and the people of the world to whom we are making this information available, that this administration will do everything in its power to achieve, during our lifetimes, a happy result. To use this information for the benefit of all. Especially the children."

———

Leslie looked particularly lovely in the late-afternoon light. "I think you're off the hook, Harry," she said. The Red Limit hadn't begun to fill up yet, and they were almost alone.

"He's got some problems to solve."

"He'll solve them. That's what politicians are for." She smiled at him. "Yep. It was pretty gutsy. Not many guys *I've* known who would have been willing to confront the President of the United States."

Harry tried to shrug. To say it was nothing. But his cheeks had grown warm, and, anyhow, it had been one of the finer moments in his life. No use saying it wasn't. "Yeah," he admitted. "I *was* pretty good, wasn't I?"

She laughed and fashioned a kiss with her eyes. "Of course, you won't have much of a career left in the federal service."

Harry shrugged. "I don't know. Presidents change. Everything changes."

They brought the wine. She filled both glasses and raised hers. "To you, Harry." She drank deep.

"How long do you think it'll take with the miracle cures?"

She shrugged. "A while. Probably not too long, though. I'll be surprised if Tommy's not off his shots sometime next year."

"Well," Harry said, "now maybe we can all relax for a bit."

"You've one other job to take care of, Harry."

"And what's that?"

"Track down Pete. He deserves to know the part he played in all this."

"I don't think he'll be happy to hear it."

Leslie drank up. "I don't think he was all that certain what he wanted to happen. Anyhow, he needs to hear that sometimes there *is* intervention."

MONITOR

There's a scene in Milton, in the eighth book of Paradise Lost, I believe, which may describe the situation. God and Adam are talking, and Adam is complaining about the landscaping and his economic status and one thing and another. And he complains about being alone. "All I have to talk to," he says, "are animals."

So God promises to look into it. And then I guess He must have thought about it some more. "Adam," He said, "who is more alone than I, that know nothing like myself in all the wide world?"

I hope, if there's any truth to Milton's insight, that God will take time, if He hasn't done so already, to introduce Himself to the Altheans who have provided us with such a gift. We have often pictured the being that sent us that remarkable e-mail as a creature alone in a tower. It strikes me that they would be good company for each other.

—Reverend Peter Wheeler, O. Praem.

Closing remarks on the nature of the Altheans at the annual gathering of the Eastern Division of the American Philosophical Association in Philadelphia in December.